Gemma's awareness of the world around her faded. She was alone within a totally alien world—a world of hard permanence and crystalline obstinacy, a world of ancient growth and unimaginably slow movement—a world of stone. At first, she thought it was cold and lifeless, but as her consciousness spread even further, beyond the confines of her warm fragile body, she found that it was not so. Within the rock, *something* stirred. . . .

Bantam Spectra books by Jonathan Wylie

Ask your bookseller for the ones you have missed

SERVANTS OF ARK TRILOGY

UNBALANCED EARTH TRILOGY

The Unbalanced
Earth Trilogy

DREAMS OF STONE

Jonathan Wylie

BANTAM BOOKS
TORONTO · NEW YORK · LONDON · SYDNEY · AUCKLAND

DREAMS OF STONE

A Bantam Spectra Book / March 1989

PRINTING HISTORY
Corgi edition published January 1989

ISBN 0-553-27974-2

Published simultaneously in the United States and Canada

Bantam Books are published by Bantam Books, a division of Bantam Doubleday Dell Publishing Group, Inc. Its trademark, consisting of the words "Bantam Books" and the portrayal of a rooster, is Registered in U.S. Patent and Trademark Office and in other countries. Marca Registrada. Bantam Books, 666 Fifth Avenue, New York, New York 10103.

PRINTED IN THE UNITED STATES OF AMERICA

O   0 9 8 7 6 5 4 3 2 1

For Annis and Jimmy,
Helen, Irrs and Brian

with much love

She walked, though the motion no longer had any meaning. The landscape about her stretched as far as the horizon, flat, unchanging. Nothing moved save the wind. Even her own progress seemed illusory.

She had run out of water three days ago. The strips of travel-meat and iron-bread still in her pouch were meaningless encumbrances now. She could no longer swallow.

By day, the sun shone from a merciless blue-white sky, turning the plain into a giant oven. At night, the crystal air turned as cold as starlight and the precious liquid lost in the day's perspiration turned to ice upon sleepless limbs. Until the sun rose again and the cycle was repeated.

There was nothing in the landscape to give her hope. The soil was a mixture of bare, broken rock and sand. Low, brown bushes that grew in every crack were the only vegetation. They bore no fruit or leaves, but the twisted, unbreakable branches were covered with needle-sharp thorns. The bushes offered neither shade nor sustenance, and any attempt to utilize them yielded only pain and frustration. They suited their environment perfectly.

Once—how many days ago?—she had seen a thick bank of fog in the distance, moving swiftly across her path, but had quickly realized that it was an illusion, a mirage. She had not even tried to follow, but trudged on, walking only because the alternative was to lie down and die.

The standing stone had attracted her attention because it was so obviously a break in the monotony of rock and thorn. It drew her like a magnet.

It will be as good a gravestone as any.

Having a marker by which to gauge her progress made her realize how slowly she moved. Stumbling now, she gained on it only by degrees. The gray monolith mocked her with its continued remoteness and she wondered if it too was a mirage, forever beyond her reach.

She was still short of her goal when night fell, and she spent the night huddled, shivering, in a bowl of sand.

She rose in the twilight before dawn and set off, irrationally determined to reach the stone that day.

It was only as she drew close that the size of the stone became apparent. It stood perhaps five times the height of a tall man and yet was only two paces in diameter, pointing at the sky like a monstrous finger. Its gray surface was irregular, showing no sign of having been worked, yet surely it could not have come to stand there by natural forces alone. It made no sense. Even its color was alien in that yellow-brown world.

A mystery.

She reached the stone at noon, when it cast no shadow, and found that its lower end was held in a pit. She peered in without hope; it was dry, of course. Reaching out, she placed a hand on the rock's surface, then stumbled. Reflexively, she arched her back, windmilling her arms as she tried to avoid falling forward into the widening gap at her feet. Steady now, her eyes confirmed what her loss of balance had told her. The monolith, huge as it was, had tipped away from her at the merest touch of her hand. Its massive bulk now rested at a quite different angle in the retaining hole, though it still pointed at the sky. It seemed stable once more, but its visitor was suddenly afraid.

She had been too surprised to notice much when the stone had fallen away from her, but now she remembered hearing a loud snapping sound and feeling the earth reverberate beneath her feet, as if her action had set off a subterranean chain of events.

A rocking stone?

She was intrigued as well as frightened, wondering curiously if anything so massive could indeed be so delicately balanced. Staring at the rock provided no immediate explanation. It remained still and silent, master of its own secrets. But then something moved upon the impassive gray surface: tiny blue lights, like the ghosts of flames, began to play along its grooves and ridges. They rapidly grew in size and brightness, and to the astonished onlooker the day grew suddenly cold, in spite of the desert sun.

She stepped back, retreating instinctively from the unknown power, but her weakened legs gave way beneath her as she stumbled on the rough terrain. She fell, and could only watch helplessly as the blue fire enveloped the monolith in a pulsing shield. Then, as if answering a force from within the earth itself, the stone began to move.

As it fell back toward her, its terrifying bulk blotting out the sun, she lost all curiosity, all fear, and descended into the blackest of nights.

———— • ————

Pain trickled into her darkness. She shied away from it, afraid of the life it implied. Cracked lips parted slightly and blood, cool and thin, dripped into her throat. She coughed feebly, choking, and her whole body trembled with fresh waves of agony. Awareness returned, unwelcome.

"No," she whispered hoarsely, clinging to the fading, painless void.

"Drink it, you silly bitch!"

The words fell harshly and echoed in her head, making no sense. More liquid filled her mouth and she swallowed involuntarily, wincing as her arid throat absorbed the moisture. *Not blood. Water.*

She struggled to open her eyes, expecting nothing, but curious now. One remained fast shut, the lashes gummed with sand and salt. The other saw a wash of color, a meaningless blur. Slowly the image cleared a little. Deep green eyes stared intently down at her.

Cold metal, a cup, was pressed against her lips and this time she drank gratefully, for her throat was on fire.

"That's better. I knew you couldn't resist my charm for too long." There was a smile in his voice. White teeth flashed.

"Cai?" she asked, her confused mind picking a name at random from her memory.

"What? Never mind," the stranger returned. "Don't try to talk." The cup was offered again and she drank. "Enough. Now lie back."

The hand that had, unknown to her, been supporting her head, tenderly lowered it back to the ground. She closed her eye, nausea and weariness fighting within her. Hands, rough-skinned yet gentle, moved over her face and arms, massaging the raw and flaking skin with a cool, odd-smelling cream. She found herself sinking back into darkness, but this time it was the warm embrace of sleep.

She surprised herself by finding that she looked forward to waking up.

———— • ————

Blue-green scales shimmered in the afternoon sun. The snake's head was bigger than her own. It had four red eyes but only two of them were watching her. She found that oddly comforting. Its mouth opened and a long black serpent's tongue flicked out, tickling her face. She giggled, then watched in fascination as several spiders emerged from the snake's mouth, pursued by flames that came from deep within. She felt no fear.

"Sweetness," she whispered, remembering.

There was a sudden stillness about the snake. All four eyes now focused on her.

"It won't last," said a mysterious voice. "Don't worry."

She smiled, feeling the comforting newness of her face, and sleep claimed her once more.

———•———

When she next awoke the stone was back in its original position, and the sun was low in the sky. She tried to push herself up on to her elbows, but she felt so dizzy that she lay back again. As she became aware, for the first time, that her head rested on a soft pillow, a man's face appeared in her field of vision and she saw her savior properly for the first time. Sunbleached hair surrounded a dark angular face, green eyes fixed upon her own.

"Are you the snake?" she asked, wincing at the shrillness of her voice.

"I preferred Sweetness," he replied, smiling. Then, seeing her confusion, he added, "You've been hallucinating. Sunbalm has that effect when you use a lot. Now drink."

He lifted her head and put a cup to her lips. Cool water flowed, wonderful and agonizing. New senses awoke in her body, pain and stiffness, yet she was alive, and her skin no longer felt as if it had been scraped off with blunt knives.

The cup was withdrawn and she tried to stretch after it, her thirst unsatisfied. A piece of soft fruit was put to her lips and she almost fainted at its overwhelming scent. She accepted the morsel and her mouth was instantly flooded with its sharp tang. She swallowed quickly, realizing that she was ravenous.

"Take it carefully. Your stomach won't be able to cope with much."

A few more slices followed and she tried, unsuccessfully for the most part, to eat them slowly.

Far too soon he said, "That's enough," and the tone of his voice brooked no argument.

"Now swallow this." He held out a small white tablet.

"What is it? Sunbalm?" Her voice sounded almost normal.

"Salt," he replied and held the cup for her to drink again.

"What *is* sunbalm?"

"A salve. It's made partly from dragonflower seeds, which is why you've been seeing things. I've been spreading it all over your skin."

Seeing the flicker of surprise on her face, he added, 'Wherever it's been exposed to the sun. There's nothing like it for healing sunburn or worse."

"Why does it make you see things?"

"Don't you know about dragonflower seeds?"

She shook her head carefully.

"They contain a drug which, apart from its regenerative powers, also causes vivid dreams and hallucinations. Some people use it just for that." The contempt was plain in his voice. "To escape from the meaningless nature of their lives, I suppose."

"But *you* use it."

"When I have to. It's done wonders for you already."

She thought about this for a few moments.

"That's true. I feel . . ." She paused, assessing. "Human. As if I could move again." Every bit of her body reported its unexpected suppleness. "Soft," she added in wonderment.

"Mmm," he responded. "Soft is right. In the head. How did you come to be in this godforsaken place?"

"God? Who's he?"

He grinned. "They've been trying to answer that one for centuries. Why don't you start with something simpler, like 'What's you name?' "

chapter 2

"What's your name?" she asked obediently.

"Arden. And yours?"

She hesitated for a moment, then replied. "Gemma."

"Is that your real name?"

"Yes."

"Why did you consider giving me a false one?" Arden regarded her curiously.

"Habit."

"Something tells me you have quite a tale to tell," he said, "but now is not the time. You need more sleep. Lie quiet."

Gemma did as she was told, enjoying the sensation of his hands moving gently but firmly over her skin as he masssaged her with more sunbalm. Soon she was in the land of dreams again.

When she next awoke awoke it was dark but there were no stars in the sky. This puzzled her until she realized that she was inside a tent. How it had come to be there was a mystery to her. An incredible sense of well-being bubbled within her, and she stretched luxuriously. As she did so, one of her hands encountered a soft, warm object wrapped in a blanket beside her. The object grunted and Gemma withdrew her hand quickly. Images flashed through her mind, but she was aware enough to recognize the influence of the dragonflower seeds. She felt as though nothing could dent her happiness at that moment, and was suddenly wide awake, needing to talk.

"Arden?" she whispered timidly.

"What?" he mumbled.

"Are you awake?"

"No."

"I'm thirsty."

He moved, and Gemma soon heard the enchanting sound of liquid being poured out. He loomed over her in the darkness.

"Can you hold the cup?" he asked.

"I think so."

Fingers met and fumbled as the cup was passed over. At this point, Gemma realized that she was completely naked beneath the blanket. She took a hurried gulp of water and tried to recover her composure. What had happened while she was in her drugged sleep?

"Sip it slowly," Arden advised. "You'll give yourself a cramp that way." After a moment he added, "Are you hungry? Wait a moment."

Gemma heard him scrabbling about near his side of the tent. There was a sharp click, then a spark, and a lamp glowed into life. Arden hung it from the tent pole then glanced over at his companion. Gemma, who had sat up to drink, quickly pulled her blanket up about her.

"There's not much point in false modesty," Arden pointed out.

"How do you know it's false?"

"Because people found wandering alone and near to death in the desert aren't usually bothered by such things."

They looked at each other, Arden's eyes twinkling with amusement. Once again he considered Gemma's red hair and dove-gray eyes and decided that she was someone special, someone worth saving—unless he was very much mistaken. Her skin had been fair and freckled; even after the ravages of sun and starvation had taken their toll, Arden could see that she had been lovely—and would be again.

"Where are my clothes?" Her tone was an odd mixture of timidity and imperiousness.

"You'll get them when you need them. They'll be much better for an airing." After a thoughtful pause, he added, "Besides, your body is nothing to be ashamed of. Quite the reverse, in fact, though you *have* been treating it rather badly of late."

Gemma knew that she was blushing furiously and hoped that Arden could not see too closely in the dim lamplight. His smile suggested otherwise. She was by now totally confused by the effects of sleep and medication on her reawakening body. This latest predicament left her thoroughly embarrassed, and it must have shown on her face because when Arden spoke again, it was clear that he was amused.

"You needn't worry. I only touched you when it was necessary—for *medicinal* purposes."

She relaxed at his words, but refused to meet his gaze. He began to feel irritated.

"Not that you'd be in any position to argue if I *had* wanted to," he said, a hint of malice in his voice. "You owe me something for saving your life, after all."

Gemma glanced up at him quickly. The shock in her eyes took him aback.

"Are you really such an innocent?" he asked, almost to himself.

"No," she replied quietly. "I'm just not used to people talking to me like that."

"Gods, who are you? A princess or something?"

Gemma's eyes flashed angrily.

"I won't discuss that!" she snapped. This second surprise left Arden doubly puzzled but he let it pass. After a few moments' silence, Gemma looked down again, apparently subdued.

"Well, you needn't worry," Arden repeated. "I don't force myself on anyone. Whatever the circumstances."

He waited for a reaction, fighting the urge to yawn.

Finally Gemma whispered, "Thank you," still not looking up.

"Besides," he went on, "in your weakened state it would probably kill you."

Gemma looked up at that, and grinned. "Are you *that* good?" she asked mischievously.

Her latest change of mood left Arden bewildered, but he managed to respond quickly enough.

"So they tell me, princess," he said, hoping to needle her into further revelations.

This time, however, Gemma only laughed, which for some reason annoyed Arden intensely.

"You certainly have a high opinion of yourself," she remarked.

"I have a healthy self-respect," he snapped back. "You wouldn't find *me* wandering about in the desert waiting to die of thirst."

At that, Gemma's expression became so solemn that Arden felt a pang of guilt. If only he could keep up with her changing moods! The salve explained some of it, of course, but . . .

"How are you feeling?" he asked as solicitously as he could.

"Much better, thanks to you," she replied softly. "I *am* hungry though." She sounded apologetic.

Arden produced more fruit, cutting small slices with his

knife before passing them to her. Gemma ate in silence, watching his hands at work as they stripped away the waxy outer skin of the green, star-shaped fruit to reveal the succulent flesh within. Small cubes of iron-bread followed. On Arden's instructions, she softened the bread in water before attempting to swallow it.

He yawned as he passed her the last piece.

"Am I keeping you up?" she asked, all innocence.

"No. I always like to spend the middle hours of the night feeding invalids."

"I'm sorry," she replied, sounding anything but. "Please, go back to sleep if you want. Shall I sing you a lullaby?"

"A few hours ago you couldn't even talk. Have some respect for your throat—and my ears."

They smiled at each other.

"That sunbalm is good stuff." Gemma remarked. "I'm hardly even sore."

"You will be. You're as high as a dragonflower now, but you'll have to come down sometime. Do you want some more? The back of your neck was especially bad."

Gemma explored her skin with cautious fingers, then nodded. "Just a little," she said. "I don't want to become an addict."

"I'll see to that."

"It's easy to see why people do, though. Some of my dreams . . ." Her voice trailed away. Arden smiled as he rubbed the salve into the nape of her neck.

"As we're quite obviously going to be awake all night," he said, "why don't you tell me how you came to be here?"

Gemma thought for some time.

"It all goes back to The Destruction," she said at last.

"The Destruction. Do you mean The Leveling?"

"Is that what you call it?"

"But that was years ago." Arden could make neither head nor tail of this latest turn of the conversation.

"Yes, but it all goes back to that," Gemma insisted. "Everything changed then."

"That's certainly true," Arden agreed.

"You know that the world as we perceive it is a dream of the Earth-mind, don't you?" she went on slowly, as if repeating a well-remembered lesson.

"I've heard the theory," he replied, "though the phrasing was different. I'm not sure I believe it."

"It's true!" Gemma exclaimed. "The dreams of the Earth-mind are so vivid that they become reality for us. We live in them. We're part of them."

"The Earth-mind's asleep then?" Arden asked, with an indulgent smile. "It must be, if it's dreaming."

"That's right!" Gemma was warming to her subject. "Except at The Destruction."

"What happened then?"

"We woke it up."

"We? Don't include me in that." Arden was becoming more and more mystified.

"I wasn't," Gemma replied, puzzled. "I meant Ferragamo and the others in the cave. Of course, I was only a little girl then."

Arden looked at her disbelievingly.

"Are you trying to tell me," he said slowly, "that you *personally* were responsible for The Leveling?"

"Yes. With the others."

Arden was about to speak again but the certainty in her voice stopped him.

"Don't you believe me?" she asked, twisting round to look at him. Long moments passed in silence. "Stop staring at me like that."

Eventually he said, "You are either completely mad or you have even more of a story to tell than I had supposed. And since I prefer not to be camped in the middle of nowhere with a lunatic, I'd better hear it."

Three hours later, as dawn broke over that dismal landscape, Gemma and Arden finally ran out of words, each silenced at the end by the other's obstinacy. Their only agreement had been over the timing and the scale of The Destruction, or The Leveling as Arden called it. That huge, world-shattering upheaval had begun fourteen years ago and its repercussions had lasted months, even years in places. The calamity had been of unbelievable proportions for both their worlds, combining as it had earthquakes, volcanic eruptions, hurricanes, and tidal waves. Thousands had died, many more had lost their homes, and the survivors had shivered for many days beneath a constantly darkened sky, as volcanic ash, smoke, and clouds had blotted out the sun.

Beyond that, the two travelers had little or no common ground.

Gemma *knew* that her story was true.

Arden *knew* that it wasn't.

And *both* had proof.

Gemma claimed to come from one of a group of islands far to the north, whose existence Arden regarded as improbable at best. It was there, according to her tale, that she had taken part in a bizarre magical ritual that had been the *cause* of The Destruction. As if this were not absurd enough, she had gone on to state that the great Southern Continent—as she called it—had not even existed until *after* The Destruction!

Arden had lost his patience at this point. He had listened calmly enough to her talk of wizards and magic, of good kings and evil sorcerers—though he believed none of it—because Gemma was a good storyteller. He suspected that at least half her words were the product of dragonflower seeds, but they passed the time agreeably. Now, however, she was trying to cast doubt on his own memories, his very existence.

"Wait!" he commanded. "You're telling me that until The Leveling, the land that I live on did not exist? That this nonsensical rite of yours *created* it?"

"Yes," Gemma replied, unmoved by his tone of outraged disbelief. "The people of the islands were great sailors and explorers. If it had already been there, we would have found it."

For a moment Arden was speechless. *She actually believes it!* he thought incredulously. As Gemma took a sip of water, with which she had frequently soothed her dry throat, he tried to gather his thoughts.

"How old am I, Gemma?" he asked.

She looked at him over the rim of her cup.

"Thirty summers?" she suggested.

"Twenty-seven, actually," he replied. Pushing aside the irritation of this minor blow to his self-esteem, he went on, "I've lived here all my life, Gemma. *All* my life. Do I look as though I spent my childhood under water?"

She didn't reply.

"And there are countless others *far* older than me who will tell you the same. Doesn't that seem a little odd? There are cities here that are centuries old. Mountains that have stood for ages."

"Mountains can fall or be created," she replied. "I've seen it happen."

"Shall I tell you what I think?" he said, ignoring the interruption. "There are elements of your story that I *can* accept. You probably do come from some far-flung island. Evidently my people are not such adventurous explorers as yours," he added with a touch of sarcasm. "And you've obviously had some pretty odd experiences in your travels. The gods know we have some strange religious cults even here—" He held up a hand to restrain Gemma's attempted interjection. "But as far as I'm concerned, there's no such thing as magic."

"You sound just like Cai," Gemma said, her face sullen.

"Who's he? Oh, yes. The *wizard.*" The apparent incongruity of finding himself in agreement with a wizard about the nonexistence of magic did not immediately strike Arden, and he went on, determined to make his point.

"This rite you talk about had nothing to do with The Leveling. That was a *natural* catastrophe. Some people find it hard to accept unpleasant truths and so they invent other explanations."

"I did not!" Gemma exclaimed angrily.

"I didn't say *you* did," he replied with infuriating calm. "But somebody did."

"You're wrong," she returned, tears of fury brimming in her eyes. "Even if I am as gullible as you obviously think, how could I have made up all that *detail?*"

"I'll admit that was impressive," he said. In fact, all Gemma's statements had the ring of truth about them, but some were just too farfetched to be believed, and that meant . . .

"You've been through a lot," he said gently. "Apart from anything else, you've been fried by the sun for a few days and then scrambled by sunbalm's aftereffects. We'd better talk about this later—when you've had a chance to recover."

His conciliatory tone did not have the desired effect.

"In other words," Gemma snapped, "you think I'm crazy! Well, I'm not! I may not be very strong just at the moment, but I'm not addle—" The diatribe came to an abrupt halt as her overused larynx finally broke down and she fell into a violent fit of coughing. Arden moved quickly to her side and helped her to drink. Once she was quiet again, Gemma lay down, exhausted.

"Truce?" Arden suggested quietly.

She nodded.

"Are you all right?"

"Throat hurts," she whispered hoarsely.

"Sleep. I'll leave you in peace. We're going to be here for a couple of days, so there are a few things I have to attend to." *And even more things I have to try to sort out in my head,* he added silently.

Gemma closed her eyes gratefully as Arden left the tent, securing the flap behind him.

———•———

She stood naked beneath the desert sun as the creatures danced in a circle around her. Their clear, high-pitched voices joined together in a hypnotic song of reverence. Squirrel-like, but with elongated bodies, and the prehensile tails of monkeys, the creatures swayed on their hind legs, stretching their necks as if trying to stand taller. Their intense gaze was both flattering and unnerving.

Then she was suddenly *outside* the circle, looking on as the creatures danced about the standing stone. Water began to flow from the rock, spilling down in rivulets of dazzling blue.

It's crying, she thought and felt a weight of sadness in her heart.

Then Arden appeared and she felt a jolt of excitement, yet when he spoke it was with Cai's voice.

"There is no magic."

"Only love," she replied, and began to cry.

The animals and Arden disappeared. The stone remained, defiantly erect.

———•———

When Gemma awoke, she was hot and confused, and lay unmoving for a few moments, trying to locate the source of her unease.

The material of the tent glowed above her. The sun had obviously risen since Arden had left her. Unwelcome doubts besieged her mind. *What if he isn't coming back?*

"Arden!" she called feebly.

The tent flap was pulled open, and he stooped to enter, bright sunlight rippling about him.

"You're here," Gemma whispered, feeling very foolish.

"You didn't think I'd abandon a valuable tent like this did you?" he replied, grinning. "How are you feeling?"

Gemma thought about it.

"Better."

"And hungry again, I'll wager."

She nodded and Arden attended to her needs, watching her closely as she ate. Eventually the constant scrutiny grew too much for Gemma.

"What are you staring at?" she asked, hoping to break the spell.

"My patient. As a doctor, I'm entitled to feel some concern."

"You're not a doctor!"

"I'm yours."

"Well, you needn't worry about me."

"No?"

Gemma stopped eating and looked at him.

"Are you still having strange dreams?" he asked solemnly.

"Yes. How did you know?" she exclaimed.

"You've been talking in your sleep."

Oh Stars! she thought. "What was I saying?"

Arden's demeanor changed. He looked upward and said lightly, "Oh, just that I was the most devastatingly attractive man you'd ever met, and that being rescued by me was a real honor. Things like that."

Gemma, who had been fearing the worst, realized that she was being teased.

"*You* said that. I'm sure *I* never did," she retorted.

"I'm crushed," Arden said with mock humility, and Gemma threw a piece of fruit at him. He caught it deftly and put it in his mouth, mumbling "Thank you," as he did so. Gemma laughed, wincing a little at the pain of the unaccustomed movement. Every muscle in her body felt stiff.

"Actually," Arden went on, "what you said made about as much sense as that stuff last night when you were awake. In other words, none at all."

"Can I help it if a man of your limited intelligence is incapable of understanding?" she countered.

"You *are* feeling better."

They grinned at each other then, knowing that they must still bridge the wide gulf between them, but content to leave the next attempt to the future.

"Can I come outside?" Gemma asked. "I need to stretch."

"The sun's too hot just now. You need to stay in the shade for a while, or all my good work will be undone. I'll put up the sides, though. I'll be less stuffy that way."

"Could I have my clothes?" Gemma asked.

"I'll get them—they should be dry now."

A few moments later Arden returned and tossed her things onto the blanket.

"You washed them?" Gemma exclaimed in astonishment. "Just how much water are you carrying?"

"Not much," he replied mysteriously. He left, and the tent flap closed again. "It's all around us. Let me know when you're ready to face the world."

Gemma struggled into her underclothes but then discarded the rest, feeling too hot and weary to bother. *Who is there to see me anyway? False modesty indeed!*

"Raise away!" she called, then suffered another coughing fit. By the time she had found the water and relieved her throat, Arden had made several adjustments to the tent's construction. Gemma was still shaded by a canopy but the "walls" had gone, leaving only four slim poles and several ropes between her and the surrounding desert.

Twenty paces away, the enigmatic monolith stood guard. Closer by were a neatly enclosed campfire with various cooking implements ranged about it and, to the other side, another, taller canopy had been erected. Two horses stood unmoving in its shade.

A light breeze ruffled Gemma's hair as she looked about, and despite the hot air, she felt better. Arden joined her in the shade.

"You're well organized," she remarked admiringly. "This tent is most ingenious."

"Yes, isn't it. I designed it myself," he added smugly.

"You don't suffer from my problem, do you."

Arden guessed her meaning.

"False modesty is not one of my traits," he said. "But then I have so much to be modest about." Seeing the expression on Gemma's face, he forestalled her response by adding, "I like your outfit by the way. Very becoming."

I will not blush, Gemma insisted to herself. *I will not.* It did her little good.

"Oh, don't you ever stop?" she laughed.

"Stop what?" he asked, feigning innocence. "Your undertunic is made of nice material, very soft. It must feel nice next to your . . . skin."

"You're hopeless . . ." Gemma began before a thought struck her. "It *does* feel nice," she said. "You *did* wash them."

"All part of the service."

"But the water . . ." Gemma said, looking round.

"Well, I wouldn't usually. It meant a little extra work, but I didn't think any of my clothes would have fitted you. At least not so snugly," he was unable to resist adding. "There's plenty of water here if you know how to get it."

"Where?"

For answer, Arden left the shade and picked up a strange tool. The metal blade looked like a cross between a spade and a sword, with a hooked crosspiece where it joined the long wooden handle. Arden inserted the blade into a crack in the earth at the base of a thornbush and then, with a series of practiced moves, loosened the soil and hooked the plant, pulling upward sharply. The root that emerged widened at one point into a bulbous growth half the size of Arden's forearm. He cut this part free and brought it over to Gemma, collecting another tool on the way. Squatting down, he placed the root inside the hardwood instrument, which looked like a cross between bellows and oversized nutcrackers, and squeezed the handles together.

"Put your hands under there," he instructed, indicating a small spout at the base. Gemma obeyed, cupping her palms as Arden twisted the handles sideways in opposite directions. To her astonishment, water gushed forth, filling her hands and overflowing onto the groundsheet.

"That's incredible," she breathed.

"I'm not usually so wasteful," Arden said, as he removed the root's husk and held it up. "The horses like this. You can eat it too, if you have to, but it tastes like . . . rather unpleasant."

"Where does it all come from?"

"It doesn't rain here often," Arden replied, "but when it does the thornbushes store up all the water they can. They wouldn't survive otherwise."

"And neither would we."

"All you need is the knowledge and the tools," Arden said, smiling.

"Don't tell me," Gemma replied. "You designed them yourself."

chapter 4

Later that day Gemma told Arden how she had come to be wandering alone in the desert. She had been reluctant to do this, because in retrospect the whole dreadful chain of events—and her part in them—appeared quite stupid. However, she knew that she would have to give Arden an explanation sooner or later. She found to her relief that, once she had begun, he was an attentive and sympathic listener, shedding his air of flippant cynicism. Somehow, her memories became easier with the telling. The greatest irony of all was that her journey had begun in such a buoyant, optimistic mood . . .

—————•—————

The decks and cabins of the *Dawn of Fire* resounded with laughter and high-spirited yells. The crew were mystified by their passengers' boisterous behavior, but were soon caught up in the festive atmosphere as they set the ship on its southerly course.

There were twelve passengers aboard, eight men and four women, who had come from all over the island, from all walks of life. Their backgrounds could not have been more diverse, yet on this day they were knit tighter than any family, sharing an understanding which went beyond mere words. Some of them knew who Gemma was but made no mention of it. The past was unimportant; the only thing that mattered was the future. On this adventure, all were equal.

They called themselves the Swallows, after the birds who migrated south each leaf-fall. The name was doubly apt, for they too were headed south, for the same unfathomable reason. They had been called.

None could explain their impulse to travel, yet each knew that *something* awaited them in the far south, perhaps in the fabled southern continent which had apparently sprung into existence little more than a decade ago. Each had felt its pull for some time, and each had had to fight his own personal battle with family and friends, and within his own mind, before admitting that his dream could not be denied. Their joy at finding that there were others like them, who shared this irrational and overpowering desire, was intense.

The group had formed slowly, but as soon as their number was complete, their plan had been set in motion. By pooling their resources—financial, mental, and physical—they were able to set sail. Gemma was the only member of the group who had ever left the shores of their home-isle before now—and she had reason enough to remain silent about her travels—yet the others showed no sign of nerves as the *Dawn of Fire* left harbor. Each was filled with a sense of destiny and an almost delirious anticipation.

In the days that followed, these feelings did not abate; even those prone to seasickness remained obstinately happy.

The Swallows learned all they could from the seamen. Apart from the technical details of the workings of the ship, a common fascination for all the passengers, they asked many questions about the southern lands. The *Dawn of Fire*'s destination was the large island, far to the south, of Haele. The name conjured up vague images for Gemma but she pushed these aside, knowing that since she had heard the island described, many years ago, the world had been born anew, and that much would have changed.

Instead, she absorbed the wealth of information imparted by the more voluble sailors, and in this way learned that the massive volcano at the island's center was still active, with flame and ash being thrown hundreds of paces skyward every few days. The lava flows had halted, however, and the islanders were able to take the minor eruptions in their stride. The rapidly expanding towns were described, sometimes in vivid detail, until they seemed as familiar as the Swallows' own homes.

The landscape too was described for their benefit. This apparently ranged from verdant jungle and swampland to the black, barren wastes of frozen lava, but there was also abundant farmland. Although the Swallows knew that Haele was not their final destination, they looked forward eagerly to their arrival. It was from there that they would begin the final stage of their journey southward. Or so they believed.

In contrast to the mass of detail about Haele, what the travelers were able to learn about the southern continent was sketchy at best. It soon became apparent that, for all their supposed knowledge, none of the seamen had actually visited that distant shore. As a consequence, their tales were a mixture of myth, thirdhand reports of dubious origin, wishful thinking, and, quite probably, downright untruths. There were stories of fearful monsters and giants with two heads, of rivers that ran uphill at certain phases of the moon, of jeweled cities that floated in the air, and singing sands that lured unwary travelers into the desert.

However, among all these and other fanciful tales—which the Swallows dismissed as nonsense—a few consistent details emerged. It was clear that the southern continent was huge. "Bigger than all the islands ten times over," was how one old salt put it. From Haele, the quickest approach was to sail due south, but as this led to a treacherous sea lane plagued by underwater reefs and unpredictable currents, the better route was to steer a southeasterly course for three or four days before turning south. The continental coast was reputedly well populated, with many towns and villages, so wherever landfall was made, the travelers hoped to find a welcome.

Long before Haele came into view, the island's presence was marked by a column of black volcanic smoke. Aboard the *Dawn of Fire* the level of excitement rose even higher until, after twenty days at sea, they docked at the island's main port, Bayard.

As most of the crew dispersed on shore leave, the Swallows decided to split up in order to seek out suitable temporary lodgings. Once settled, they would find a ship to take them further south. The longing was still with them and, however welcome firm ground was, they knew that any long delay would be unbearable.

Gemma went with Danil, a burly man with a gruff sense of humor, who had been a blacksmith and a well-respected man in his home village. As they walked through the dockside streets, they savored the noise and bustle of the town.

"That might do," Danil said, pointing to a tavern which looked more prosperous than most. The wooden walls were freshly painted and the windows were clean and bright. Above the door hung a sign with the words "Star of Adara" underneath the picture.

"Let's try it," Gemma agreed.

Once inside, the initial impression of cleanliness was reinforced.

"What can we do for you?" a smiling young man inquired.

"Do you have rooms enough for twelve travelers?" Gemma asked, knowing already that she wanted to stay here.

"I'll have to check with the boss. Sit down and I'll bring you a drink." With that, he disappeared into a back room. Gemma and Danil sat down, then looked at each other and nodded. Moments later the young man reappeared with three glasses of wine, which he set at their table.

"The innkeeper's on her way," he said.

"She's here," said a voice from behind him. "Thank you, Rob."

An attractive woman in her thirties sat down at the table.

"My name's Zana," she said, raising her wine glass. "Welcome to the Star." Her smile was warm and confident, and Gemma liked her immediately.

Their business was swiftly concluded. The rooms were clean and comfortable—as Gemma had known they would be—and the rates reasonable. Zana and her staff were friendly, eager to please, and competent. But more than that, it felt right. On this enterprise Gemma and her friends had learned to trust such things.

The Swallows were soon settled in, but most went out again almost immediately, eager to begin the search for their passage south. Gemma did not go with them but instead sought out Zana, finding her serving the few late-afternoon customers in the bar. They were soon sitting together at a quiet corner table.

"What brings you to Haele?" Zana asked.

"Curiosity."

"A long way to come just to satisfy curiosity. Are all northeners so eager for fresh scenes?"

"No," Gemma replied, weighing her words carefully. "Only a few."

Zana nodded. "You'll forgive me if I say that you seem an odd group. What brings you together?"

"A common longing. We're heading for the southern continent."

"I was afraid of that," Zana replied.

"Why afraid?" Gemma asked, her heart missing a beat.

Zana smiled but there was a bleak look in her eyes. "Let me tell you how you feel," she said. "It's as if something down there is calling you. You don't know what it is, just that it's important, more important than anything else in your lives. You only feel happy when you're getting closer to it—or making plans to do so. No arguments, no matter how strong, from family, friends, or lovers, have any effect in the end. You're compelled to go, yet you don't really know why."

Gemma could only stare at her.

"How do you know?" she asked eventually.

"I've heard it all before," Zana replied and this time her words held a touch of bitterness.

"From other travelers?" Gemma asked.

"No."

"Do *you* feel it?"

"No."

"Then why are you afraid?"

"Because I'm coming with you anyway," Zana stated.

chapter 5

The other travelers had met with little success in their search for a ship, and returned disheartened. They swapped accounts over the evening meal, and their depression deepened as it became obvious that their task would not be an easy one. Several captains of ocean-going vessels had been located, but all had given reasons as to why a voyage to the southern continent was impossible.

Some of these excuses had been contradictory. One sailor had told them that the late summer storms would begin in the southern seas any day now, whereas another said that he could not afford to sail past the southern pearl fields with only two months left before the storm season made diving impossible. Others were committed to voyages that were to take them north, east, or west but never south, though their ships showed no sign of being laden with cargo or even in ocean trim. No offers of financial inducement, however generous, were of any use. It became clear that something more than weather and business concerns was hindering their progress.

Throughout this discussion, Gemma sat quietly, wondering, when—and how—to tell them what she had learned. She knew that it would not be easy to put in a positive light, but trusted her own abilities. She just needed time to think.

She remembered her earlier conversation with Zana. After the innkeeper's surprising declaration, Gemma's mind caught the inference in the earlier exchange.

"Someone from here," she said.

Zana nodded.

"Your husband?"

"He would have been. If I'd let him. Better call him my lover."

"When did he go?"

"A year ago last month."

"No word?"

"There never is," Zana replied. "No ship ever returns from the southern continent."

That statement was to explain much of what Gemma heard later that evening but at the time she had found it hard to believe.

"Perhaps they sail back to other islands."

"No," Zana said emphatically. "Something happens to them, and I *have* to know what it is. It's been eating at me all this time and last month I made the decision that the next party to leave would include me. I knew there'd be one sooner or later." She paused. "It's either that or stay here and go quietly mad."

"What about your family?" Gemma asked quietly.

"My parents and sisters are dead."

"Children?"

"I can't have children," Zana said simply, with no trace of self-pity.

"And the Star?"

"Rob and the others can run it well enough. I trained them, after all," Zana replied with a smile. "Besides, I don't expect to see it again. I've more than enough ready money for my passage, and I'm fit. I won't be a burden to you."

"You're determined then?"

"Oh, yes. I'll even help you find a ship," the innkeeper said. "Not that it'll be easy," she added dourly.

How right you were! Gemma thought now as she listened to her companions' tales of woe. Choosing her moment, she said, "I have some news."

There was an expectant hush round the table as all eyes turned toward her. She related the facts that Zana had told her, and their expressions of dismay made it quite obvious that she held their attention.

"It's hopeless, then," one of her companions remarked. "No captain will agree to such a journey, or find a crew for it." There were murmurs of agreement.

"It's not *all* bad," Gemma said quickly. "Don't you see what this means?" She paused, looking from face to face. "We're not alone! There have been many others before us, and they'll be there—in the south—waiting to guide us. And we will guide those that follow."

"If we ever get there," one of the others put in.

"Don't be discouraged," Gemma went on. "Zana said that every person who felt the call—travelers like us from other islands, or on Haele—every one of them found a way to sail south. Even when the odds were stacked against them. We're *meant* to get there, you all know that. And we will!"

The others seemed hesitant, and Gemma pressed on.

"Zana will help us find a ship. She has contacts all over the island. What's more," she added, playing her highest card, "if it comes to it, we don't even need a crew. We learned enough on the *Dawn of Fire* to handle a small vessel ourselves. We can do it!"

Gemma believed it. And so did her audience. The seeds of new inspiration had been planted and grew quickly. The Swallows had rediscovered their purpose.

They were ready to fly.

———————•———————

Four days out of port, things began to go wrong.

The only vessel that had been available to them was an old, single-masted ship which had definitely seen better days. Nevertheless, it was declared seaworthy both by its captain—a clear-eyed, gray-bearded mariner called Barris—and by others whom Zana trusted. A crew had been impossible to find unless they had been willing to risk life and limb by employing criminals. Even had Barris allowed it, the voyagers were not prepared to do that. Buoyed up by their renewed sense of destiny, they volunteered themselves as crew and, after much talk and some practical demonstrations, convinced Barris that they were sufficiently adept.

At first, all went well. Their southeasterly route was favored by good winds and easy sailing, and the "crew" gained in confidence under Barris's expert direction. In the early hours of the fourth night, the captain set a southerly course and retired to his cabin, leaving instructions for him to be woken should any difficulty arise. It was the last intelligible thing any of the travelers heard him say.

As dawn broke, the wind shifted round to the southwest and dropped to a mere whisper. Danil, as acting captain, did his best, but the complicated maneuvering became too much for him, and they were almost becalmed. When they went to fetch Barris, he was found unconscious with two empty bottles beside his bunk. Nothing could wake him.

After that, the voyage was a nightmare. With their limited navigational ability, the Swallows were not even sure that they were making progress. Destiny began to seem like a very sick joke indeed.

When Barris came to, two days later, he raved like a

madman and grew violent when they refused him further alcohol, then relapsed into a stupor. When he next awoke he somehow managed to find another bottle, despite his "crew's" vigilance, and drank himself into a coma. He died the following day.

Their supplies began to cause concern, fresh water being the most obvious. They introduced rationing but this did little to allay their fears, and as their predicament grew worse, arguments broke out among the travelers for the first time, and grew increasingly bitter.

Both the ship and its passengers were in bad shape when land was finally sighted. Their first view of the promised land showed no obvious signs of life, and was not the joyous occasion it should have been. Their subsequent arrival was to all intents and purposes a shipwreck. None of their number was lost, but it was an unhappy, and dispirited band who came ashore with their few salvaged possessions. The southern continent—if indeed that was where they were—could have been uninhabited. They had very little food and only the clothes they stood up in.

Their spirit of adventure was wearing very thin.

"Why did he do it?" Gemma asked later, as they sat round a dismal campfire.

"I have no idea," Zana replied.

"So much for your *recommendations*," one of the others muttered.

Gemma was about to defend her new friend but Zana stopped her with a gesture. "Leave it," she said wearily.

Fortunately, the night was warm and dry and the morning brought with it a little renewed hope and vigor. Several of their number had had strange dreams.

"This *is* the place," one said, "I can feel it. We'll get there yet."

"If we live long enough," came the sour reply.

They scaled the small cliffs that hemmed in the shingle beach with little problem, and set off inland. Their progress was slow but their spirits soon rose when they came across a track running parallel to the coast.

"Which way?" Danil asked, voicing the question in everyone's mind. "East or west?"

They chose east, and walked into a trap.

chapter 6

The blue flames had been the first warning.

The Swallows had trudged along for most of the morning, all prey to conflicting emotions. The sand dunes or rocks on one side of the track and the gently rolling hills of scrubland on the other passed by unchanging and untouched by human hand. Only the road itself gave them any hope. After the first hour, they were so depressed by the lack of any sign of habitation that their conversation dried up. Then Danil spotted a change in the landscape ahead of them.

"Look!" he cried, pointing. "Beyond the flames. Farmland."

They looked. In the distance, fields were laid out, green and gold, but there were no other signs of life. Where the road passed into this country, there was a blue haze, and the keener-eyed among them saw that it was made up of sinuous flamelike beings who danced before their eyes.

"Are they alive?" Zana asked, voicing the unbidden thought of several of her companions.

"What *are* they?" another whispered.

"Well, we won't find out standing here," Danil stated, and set off. The others followed with varying degrees of reluctance.

As it turned out the flames melted away, spreading out over the surrounding area as the travelers approached. Suddenly, as they crossed the invisible border between wasteland and farm, the flames returned, swooping between the Swallows at dizzying speed before disappearing again. After their initial confusion, the group hurried on, anxious to be away from this haunted place. The scene about them changed, and they wondered how they could ever have mistaken it for farmland.

Only after a while did they realize that their numbers had increased.

They had been walking in silence for some time when from behind her Gemma heard Zana say: "That looks like a good place to rest." And another voice—which seemed oddly familiar—replied, "Yes, you're right. There's shelter there."

Gemma looked around to query the need for a rest so soon—and found herself staring into her own face. Beside her, Zana screamed, having experienced the same unnerving sight. Laughter sounded all about them and several of their number— the duplicates of Gemma and Zana among them—melted before their eyes, then swept away as blue flames, leaving the travelers bewildered and unnerved.

After the initial commotion, nobody spoke for a while, each of them busy counting their companions to ensure that all were real.

"Stars!" Danil breathed eventually. "What was all that about?"

Before anyone could answer, an arrow whistled out of nowhere and buried itself in the back of one of the men. As he fell, the others panicked, running in all directions, throwing themselves into what meager shelter they could find. Two more men were felled by the deadly missiles.

Gemma and Zana crouched behind a low boulder.

"Over there," Gemma whispered, pointing to the rock-strewn area which the Zana-flame had recommended earlier.

"I see them," her friend replied. "What do we do?"

Well camouflaged among the rocks, several gray-clad men were moving closer.

"Surrender?" Gemma suggested with grim humor.

One of their number broke cover and ran toward the sea. Before she had gone more than a dozen paces, an arrow smashed into her shoulder and she collapsed into the sand.

"Death to the demon-spawn!" an unknown voice yelled triumphantly.

"I don't think they're too interested in taking prisoners," Zana commented wryly.

"We can't just lie here."

"But—"

They were interrupted by a rising howl of frightening volume. As they covered their ears, they saw their assailants stand up and look around, then scramble away southward in a great hurry. A moment later the air was torn asunder as a huge metal bird flew overhead at staggering speed, making a noise like the roar of a volcano in full spate. Then, as quickly as it had arrived, it was gone.

It was a long time before the surviving travelers felt bold enough to go in search of one another, or even to break the eerie silence which had descended. Eventually, stunned and grief-stricken, they reassembled. Only eight were still alive.

"This is all wrong," Gemma said, wondering at her own words. "We have to go south. Now!"

"Yes," one of the others agreed.

"And leave the road?" Danil asked incredulously.

"That's madness!!" Zana put in. "Look at the terrain—nothing but barren rock. Further inland it'll be desert."

"*This* is madness," Gemma replied, indicating the track. "Look what's happened to us."

A heated argument developed in which Gemma and two of the men could not be dissuaded from their conviction that traveling directly south was their only hope. In the end, however, the majority view—that they should stick to their present path but proceed more cautiously—prevailed. They halted a league further west and prepared camp.

"We're bound to reach a village soon," Zana said as she and Gemma prepared to sleep.

"I don't think we ever will this way."

"We have to stick together."

"Maybe we're already dead," Gemma said dourly, "but no one's told us yet!"

"Don't talk like that."

"This place is madness. I don't understand *anything*."

Zana had no answer.

———————•———————

In the dead of night, one of the men who had also wanted to go south, shook Gemma out of a lovely dream of music and happiness. Even awake, the music continued.

"Do you hear it?" he asked urgently.

Gemma nodded.

The third of their conviction joined them, his eyes rapt. "The singing sands," he whispered, voicing the images of their common dream.

The music went on; its lilting melody and achingly beautiful harmony combining in a flawless siren-call.

United by an unspoken purpose, the three rose, silently gathered their few belongings, and slipped away into the night.

Only later did Gemma think to ask what had happened to the man who had been on night-watch—and by then it was too late.

chapter 7

"What happened to the others?" Arden asked, his face set.

"One didn't survive the night," Gemma answered. "The ground just gave way beneath him and he fell into a deep hole. Like a mine shaft. We heard his screams as he fell, but there was nothing we could do . . ." She swallowed, shuddering at the memory, then steeled herself to continue. "Eventually, Malin and I had to sleep. The music had stopped and we were completely lost. When I woke the next morning, he was dead. There were two little punctures in his ankle. The poison had worked so fast that he hadn't had time to cry out. I don't know why it didn't bite me too."

"You were lucky," Arden said.

"That's one way of putting it."

"I'm sorry. I didn't mean . . ." Arden looked unusually flustered.

"Don't apologize," Gemma said quickly. "I *was* lucky. The next thing I remember clearly is the stone. And then you." She smiled wearily. "You're the first good thing this land has had to offer."

"The best," he replied, recovering his normal composure. "But there are many other good things here. You've only seen the bad side."

"And that mostly because of my own stupidity," Gemma said disgustedly. "Can you explain any of it to me?"

Arden, who had been silent while Gemma told her sorry tale, shook his head slowly. "Only parts of it," he replied. Gemma waited expectantly but Arden seemed in no hurry to speak. *It's as if he's deciding how much to tell me,* Gemma thought.

"I don't know exactly where you came ashore," he said at last, "but I can guess. There are many long stretches of coastline that are uninhabited—in spite of the tales you heard—but there aren't many places where the elementals play."

"Elementals?"

"The blue flames."

"What *are* they?"

"Nobody knows. They tend to live in places where The Leveling had most effect, and especially where the coastline was altered. They seem to have a great deal of energy and can assume any shape they choose. Other than that, nothing much is known about them—except for their strange sense of humor."

"Sense of humor? They led us into a trap!"

"I don't think so. The men who attacked you just used the elementals to distract you."

"No," Gemma said firmly. "It was more than that."

"Elementals are notorious for playing tricks on travelers," Arden returned. "But so far they've never actually harmed anyone."

"All right. In that case, the men who attacked us were controlling them."

"That's impossible," Arden exclaimed. "No one can do that."

"Are you sure? Or is it something you'd just rather not think about?" Gemma stared at him fiercely, but he refused to be intimidated.

"It's impossible," he repeated flatly.

"Who *were* those men?"

"Thieves," he replied promptly.

"Then why kill us?" Gemma went on. "We were unarmed. And why were they shouting those things at us?"

"Living as they do is bound to make them vicious at times. You could hardly expect them to be polite." He grinned but there was as little conviction in his smile as in his words.

"What are you hiding from me?"

"Nothing!" A touch of anger crept into his voice. "I don't have to tell you *anything*." He made as if to rise, muttering, "I'm going to feed the horses."

"Don't go," Gemma said quickly, putting out a hand to stop him. "I'm sorry. It's just that there is so much that I don't understand."

"Me too," Arden replied ruefully. He remained seated, staring at his feet.

After a few moments, Gemma asked cautiously, "What about the metal bird?"

"We call them skyravens. They can kill you by just looking at you," he answered calmly. "They come from the South Lands, beyond the mountains."

Once again his voice betrayed that he knew more than he was willing to say, but this time Gemma did not press him. Another thought struck her.

"Are there elementals here?" she asked. "There were blue flames all over the stone."

Arden's face registered shock.

"You saw the pilgrim's fire?"

"Yes, if that's what you call it," she replied, wondering at his astonishment. "It was after I pushed it over," she added, but Arden did not hear. He had turned to gaze at the standing stone.

"No one's seen that in my lifetime," he whispered. "No one."

"Except the animals," Gemma said without thinking.

"What?" Arden was now totally nonplussed, and looked at Gemma as though she had suddenly grown a second head.

"I . . . I don't know why I said that," she stammered. "It was a dream, I think," she added quietly, then, as Arden remained silent, she went on to describe the creatures she had seen.

"Meyrkats," he said. "I wonder." After another pause, he asked, "What exactly did the pilgrim's fire look like?"

"Some of the flames made strange patterns," Gemma said. "There was one . . . I'll draw it for you."

Arden helped her move to the edge of the ground sheet. She picked up a stick and began to make an outline in the sand.

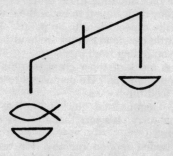

Before she could finish, Arden knocked the stick from her hand and hurriedly scuffed out the pattern, glancing about as he did so. It was as if he was afraid of them being overlooked. Gemma stared at him in disbelief and her amazement increased when he spoke.

"Gemma, do me a favor. *Never* draw that sign again." She nodded dumbly, his quiet vehemence overcoming her curiosity. "Later—when you know this land better—I'll explain," Arden went on. "For now, the *less* you know the better." He stood up. "Now I *do* have to feed the horses," he said and walked away.

Gemma suddenly felt very weary and crawled back into the shade. She watched Arden as he tended to the horses and noticed that he frequently glanced at the stone, as if expecting it to burst into flame again. Her last thought before she fell into an uneasy sleep was, *Perhaps, if I push it over again . . .*

When she awoke in the early evening Gemma found Arden watching her. The expression on his face was an odd mixture of tenderness and perplexity, but when he saw that her eyes were open, he smiled quickly.

"It's cooler now, and you could do with stretching a few muscles. Come and meet the horses." He helped her to her feet and guided her first few steps. "How do you feel?"

"Like a two-year-old—but with further to fall," she replied, tottering foward unaided. Arden stayed close by her side. The slanting rays of sunlight warmed her face and limbs, and made her skin tingle pleasantly.

"Well done," Arden said as they reached the other shelter. Feeling suddenly faint, Gemma took hold of one of the poles and found Arden supporting her other arm.

"How did I get myself into this state?" she moaned.

"You'll survive," Arden answered cheerfully. "You're tough. Not many people would have gotten this far alive."

She looked at him in surprise, gratified by his comment.

"You should be ready to ride in a day or so," he went on, "so you'd better introduce yourself to Mischa. She'll be carrying you, so it's a good idea for you to be on good terms."

"Hello, Mischa," Gemma said, gently rubbing the mare's nose. The horse lowered her head, shifted her stance, and stamped one forefoot.

"You're accepted," Arden said, a little surprised. "This is Lark," he added, indicating the other horse.

"They're fine-looking animals. And very patient," Gemma commented.

"They adapt to their environment," Arden said, pleased. "They're more intelligent than most humans that way."

"Point taken."

"I wasn't just thinking of you," he said, unabashed.

"That's a comfort."

"Besides, genius excuses a lack of common sense."

"So I'm a genius now, am I?" Gemma said, her eyebrows raised.

"Anyone who could come through all the things you have, ended up in the middle of the Diamond Desert, and still look as beautiful as you do *must* be a genius." Arden grinned, and before Gemma could think of a suitable response, he added, "I still like your outfit, by the way."

"That sums me up then," Gemma replied. "A pretty, stupid genius."

"There are worse combinations."

"Handsome and arrogant?" she suggested.

"Surely, my lady, you cannot be referring to me," he responded with mock humility.

"Perhaps handsome *was* stretching it a bit."

"Walk," Arden commanded. "It will do you good, wear off some of the stiffness." His expression was so severe that Gemma could only laugh and Arden soon joined in, unable to keep up his pretence of anger. They set off together, walking slowly in a circle about the standing stone. Gradually, movement became less painful for Gemma and their lighthearted mood was regained.

"Tell me about the meyrkats," she said. "Do they really exist?"

"Oh, yes, they exist, but you'll never see them," Arden replied. "I never have."

"Why?"

"They live in groups, and always act as a team. While some of them hunt or dig for water-roots, and others look after the group's young, there are always one or two on lookout duty. They'd see us before we got within four hundred paces."

"How do you know all this, if you've never seen them?"

"From old stories. I've seen their tracks and burrows too." Arden paused. "What I want to know is how *you* know about them."

"Dreams are funny things," Gemma replied thoughtfully.

"Especially yours," he returned.

"Do they sing?"

"Not that I'm aware of." He glanced at her curiously, but she was too intent on her uncertain progress to notice.

When they got back to the tent, Gemma said, "You haven't told me why *you* are here—in the middle of nowhere."

"That's easy. I'm on my way from one side to the other," he said flippantly.

"Couldn't you have gone round?" she replied in kind.

"Yes, but it would take longer, and besides, the desert is fine by me. I like the solitude."

"Sorry to have spoiled it for you." Gemma waited. "That's your cue to say something gallant," she pointed out. When Arden still didn't respond, she asked, "What are you thinking?"

"Not a lot," he replied, looking up. His green eyes held an uncharacteristically solemn expression. Seeing the question on Gemma's face, he added, "I'm going to Great Newport to plead for the valley." He paused, but seeing that this was hardly a sufficient explanation, went on. "Newport is the regional capital, the place where all the money and power is. The politicians." His voice rang with contempt. "The valley has had no water now for four years. If they don't get some soon they'll either have to leave, or stay there and die. I'm going to try and get something done."

"Is the valley your home?"

"No. I don't have a home."

Gemma let that pass. "Then why are you their ambassador?"

"Because they can't go themselves, and because they trust me. Traveling comes easy to me. but it's hateful to them, and *someone's* got to go. Besides, they're paying me."

"You let them *pay* you?"

"Of course. I have to live."

"So much for humanitarian motives."

Arden refused to let her words bother him.

"If I succeed, it'll be worth far more to them than any amount of money, and if I don't, then their money won't do them any good," he said firmly.

"But *you* will be able to spend it!"

"It has been known." He laughed. "Is that so awful?"

Grudgingly, Gemma recognized the common sense of his argument.

"What will you spend it on?" she asked.

"Dancing girls, Belavasian wine, and new earrings," he replied promptly.

"New earrings! For you?"

"No. For you. Those look terrible."

chapter 8

At dawn, two days later, Arden And Gemma dismantled their camp and set off for Great Newport, intent on making the most of the relative cool of early morning. Gemma was nervous, fearing a fall to the hard ground which seemed so far below her, but Lark and Mischa moved with the measured tread of experienced travelers, and before long she grew accustomed to the steady movement. Despite her weakness, she was soon able to relax. Arden rode alongside, obviously at home in the saddle.

"Tell me about the valley," Gemma said after a league had passed in silence.

"I can't," Arden replied. "You have to see it for yourself."

"Is it so special?"

"Yes."

After waiting for him to elaborate, Gemma tried again.

"So special that even *you* aren't capable of describing it?"

"Don't joke about it!" Arden snapped, glaring at the horizon ahead of them. His tone and expression were so grim that Gemma was shocked into silence, and for a while the only sound was the pad of the horses' hooves on the dry earth.

"I'm sorry . . ." they began simultaneously, then turned to look at each other. After an uncertain moment, Arden grinned and Gemma smiled back, sighing with relief.

"I didn't mean to pry," she said quietly. "You love the valley very much, don't you?"

"I suppose I do," her guide answered thoughtfully, then added, "I didn't mean to bite your head off." After another pause, he went on. "It *is* difficult to describe. It's not just that it's beautiful, though it is—or rather, *was*. It's the atmosphere there, the *feeling* of the place." He shook his head as if to clear it. "I don't usually ramble on like this."

Hearing the frustration in Arden's voice, Gemma could not resist teasing him a little. "Not even after a bottle or two of Belavasian wine?"

"Maybe after three," he replied with a grin. "And by

then my mind would be concentrating on more pressing matters."

"The dancing girls?"

"Quite possibly. Do I detect a note of disapproval here?" he asked, raising his eyebrows.

"I've never met one to disapprove *of*," Gemma returned. "Is dancing *all* they do?"

"No," he replied meaningfully. "Like all women, they ask too many questions."

Gemma responded by clapping a hand over her mouth with an exaggerated gesture. After a moment, she began to lose her balance and had to make a grab for support. She ended up clinging to the horse's mane.

"I'm sorry, Mischa," she whispered into the mare's ear, "but being female, I'm sure you'll understand." Her mount whinnied softly. "I knew you would."

Arden laughed as Gemma slowly righted herself.

"It's a good job *one* of you knows what you're doing," he remarked. "Are you sure *you* haven't been at the wine?"

"Your mere presence is enough to intoxicate me," she replied meekly, eyes demurely downcast. "I'm sure you have this effect on all girls."

"Usually," Arden agreed, straightfaced.

Some time later, Gemma tried again. "You still haven't told me about the valley," she said.

Arden gave her a measured, appraising look.

"I'll tell you a story," he said slowly. "About the first time I ever saw the valley. You might understand then . . ."

———•———

He had come down from the mountains, not really knowing where he was going, and not caring. He felt as though his whole life had been one long, pointless journey.

The pack he carried contained all his worldly possessions, but they were travelers' items, anonymous. Nothing betrayed his past or hinted at a trade, and there were no reminders of the home he had left behind. What memories he had were firmly locked behind the hard, green eyes that were far older than his sixteen summers.

Darkness was falling as he made his way through the trees into the valley below. The night would be warm, and he could sleep in the open if need be, but there were lights in the distance and the comfort of a barn would be a welcome luxury. The valley had appeared inviting from far above, lush and green, and Arden's spirit had lifted at the sight. He was mistrustful of his own feelings, however, and moved stealthily as he neared one of the outlyings farms.

The main house was two stories high, unusual in the post-Leveling years when few were willing to risk living above the ground floor.

It was built of wood, and even in the fading light, Arden could appreciate the craftsmanship which had gone into its construction. Golden lamplight shone from the lower windows and from them came the sounds of laughter and the chink of plates. The mild breeze carried further messages. Arden's sense of smell had been sharpened by years of living in the wild, and the delicious odors of the farm kitchen were almost painful. He had intended to find somewhere to sleep and then steal or beg for some food in the morning, but the noisy protests of his empty stomach and the sudden rush of saliva in his mouth were too much for him to bear. Ignoring the barn and other outbuildings, he crept toward the source of those enticing smells.

He had no clear idea of what he would do, but he went on, and soon ran out of cover. To get any closer he would have to step into the open space in front of the house, and all his vagabond instincts told him that this was foolishness. By now he could almost taste the food within. Glancing around in case the farm dogs were nearby, he crouched down and scuttled across the yard. As he knelt beneath the open window, trying to quieten his breathing, he heard the sound of a chair scraping backward and moments later the door a few paces away opened outward, spilling a fan of warm light across the yard. Arden froze.

A large, bearded man emerged and looked directly at the traveler.

"Come in, friend," he said in a slow deep voice. "Kris told us to expect you."

Arden found himself incapable of movement. The man's words were confusing, yet their welcoming nature was reinforced by his broad smile.

"There's food," the farmer added. "Come." He motioned Arden to enter.

The boy rose slowly, bewildered by this sudden kindness in a world that had usually treated him with pain and rejection or cruel indifference. He stepped forward, still fearing deceit, and turned into the doorway. He hesitated there, finding himself the focus of eight pairs of eyes. A gentle push from behind propelled him into the room.

There were three empty places around the huge wooden table. The farmer guided Arden to one of these, and a steaming bowl of vegetables, fragrant with herbs, was placed before him.

"Eat," his host commanded, pointing with his spoon.

Arden picked up his own spoon, feeling faint with hunger, then looked up at the farmer, now seated at the far end of the table.

"I . . ." he began hesitantly, his voice little more than a whisper. "I have no money . . . to repay you."

For some reason his statement provoked smiles and gentle laughter around the table.

"Eat," the big man repeated.

Arden needed no further urging and took his first mouthful. As his tastebuds rejoiced, the others resumed their meal, and the kitchen was once more filled with noise. Between swallows, Arden glanced at the people around him. They all seemed perfectly at ease with his presence.

His bowl was soon empty, and the girl who sat beside him refilled it without his having to say a word.

"Thank you," he murmured shyly.

"You're welcome," she replied with a smile. "My name's Mallory." She looked at him expectantly and he swallowed hurriedly.

"Arden," he said quietly.

"A fine name," she remarked. "That's appropriate."

Before he could ask what she meant, Mallory went on.

"That's my father, Elway," she said, nodding toward the bearded man who had ushered Arden in, and who was now laughing at some private joke with the woman who sat next to him. "And my mother, Teri. The old one is Fletcher, my great-grandfather."

Arden, who had not known his own grandparents, let alone any earlier generations, looked at Fletcher in astonishment. He didn't look very old; there were gray flecks in his hair, but his eyes were bright and his hands moved deftly.

"He'll be one hundred and ten next name-day," Mallory said.

Arden almost choked.

"And he's as good a tree-man as any in the valley," she added with a touch of pride.

Arden was so taken aback that he forgot to eat for a few moments, but Mallory had not noticed his surprise and was continuing her round of introductions.

"That's my eldest brother, Hunley, And his wife Dorcas. Her baby's due in two months."

Hunley was an almost exact replica of his father; dark head, broad shoulders, and strong sunburnt arms. Beside him, Dorcas looked small in spite of her expanded girth. She was no great beauty, but radiated health and contentment.

"On the other side are Annys—she's my sister—and Lang, who helps on the farm. I expect they'll be married soon."

"Stop gossiping, Mallory," the young man on Arden's other side put in. "Annys and Lang are perfectly capable of arranging their own affairs. They don't need any help from you."

"And this is Horan," the girl went on, unabashed. "My other brother. He's the one with no manners."

Horan grinned. He and Mallory shared their mother's coloring, light hair and deep-blue eyes.

"You'll have to excuse my sister. She's *very* young."

Mallory stuck out her tongue.

"You see?" Horan said, still smiling. "You'd never believe she was sixteen summers old, would you."

Arden, who had indeed assumed that she was his junior, shook his head. He was to find out eventually that everyone in the valley was much older than he had at first supposed.

"Have you come far?" Horan asked.

"Manesty," Arden replied, naming the last village he had stayed in.

"Is that your home?"

"No."

Teri saved him from having to elaborate by interrupting in a firm but kind voice.

"Let Arden eat, children. We can't have the berry cake until we're all ready."

Arden realized then just how delicious the food he had been gulping down was—and the thought of further delicacies renewed his appetite. Only much later did it occur to him to wonder how Teri had known his name. His own quiet announcement to Mallory could not have been heard at the other end of the table.

After the meal, now feeling pleasantly full, Arden noticed the remaining empty chair.

"Is there someone I haven't met?" he ventured, not sure why he was asking this.

"Oh, that's for Kris," Mallory answered. "We always lay a place for him just in case he chooses us."

"Kris? The one who told you I was coming?"

Mallory nodded. "Kris *knows* things," she said.

"You'll meet him soon enough," Horan added.

Teri appeared at Arden's shoulder.

"Let me show you your room," she said. "Where are your things?"

"My pack!" he exclaimed. "It's still outside."

"Well, go and fetch it then," she said, laughing.

He did so, then followed Teri upstairs and along a corridor to a small, neat room which contained a bed, some shelves, and a chest of drawers. The sheets were snowy white and already turned down to air.

"We rise early," Teri said. "Sleep well."

Arden sat on the bed, unable to believe his luck. He was so bemused by the kindness of these strangers that he could do no more than accept the unaccustomed luxury of a mattress and sheets.

He slept well.

chapter 9

Arden stayed with Elway and his family for three months. Though nothing was asked of him, he repaid their hospitality with work on the farm. His recent travels had made him physically strong, but even so, he could not match the power of the farmer or his sons. However, under the tuition of Mallory—who became his most constant companion—and Horan, he was soon able to make himself useful in spite of his lack of experience.

During his stay, he learned that, despite its far-flung nature, the valley community was a tight-knit one, held together by more than physical location or common interests. Something which Arden could not at first identify gave the people a sense of togetherness which he had never before encountered.

There were only two villages in the valley, known simply as Upper and Lower, with the rest of the population spread among the many farms, and it was in these villages that periodic meetings of the community took place. Arden attended one at the upper village, two leagues from Elway's farm. It had ostensibly been called to discuss a new system of crop rotation, the felling of certain trees in order to build a new farmhouse, and to attend the naming of three newborns. In fact, as Arden soon discovered, these matters had already been decided in all but the fine detail, and while it began with a good deal of spirited and humorous public speaking, it was clear that this was primarily a social gathering. The day ended with music and dancing in the open air, the drinking of a considerable amount of the amber-colored local wine, and much good-natured revelry.

Arden was introduced to a bewildering number of people, representatives from all parts of the valley, all of whom already knew his name. To his shame, he immediately forgot most of theirs and had to be rescued by Mallory on more than one occasion. He danced with her of course, a process which was as embarrassing for him as it was painful for her. Mallory suffered his inexperience and clumsiness patiently at first, then exasperation took over. Eventually, she dissolved into uncontrollable laughter, threatening to borrow her brother's boots if Arden didn't leave her toes alone. He was the butt of several jokes during their journey back to the farm, but such was his exhilaration with the rest of the day that he did not mind.

"Perhaps he just needed a better teacher," Horan suggested as the cart rumbled slowly along behind the two massive gray horses.

"And how would you know?" Mallory retorted. "Everyone can see you have two left feet. It's just that Arden has three! My bruises prove it!" With that she went off into another fit of giggles.

Elway spoke from the driver's position, where he sat with his wife.

"Perhaps your feet wouldn't be quite so tender if you hadn't monopolized the boy so much. There were plenty of other people who wanted to meet him."

"Why?" Arden asked.

"We don't get many strangers here," Teri replied. "The valley community tends to be self-contained."

"No offense, boy," Elway said, "but that's the way we like it."

"I never even knew any of this existed until I arrived," Arden said. "It's so beautiful."

"It is," Teri said, turning round to smile at him. "There's not many outsiders would see it, though."

Arden was about to protest when something stopped him. *Why had he never heard of this place?* Surely news of it would have reached surrounding areas.

"Not many come to us," Elway went on, "and we don't leave."

"Never?"

"That's the way of it, boy."

"Why?"

"Because we die if we do," Mallory stated flatly.

"But you're the healthiest people I've ever known!" Arden exclaimed. It was true. Even the oldest men and women were still full of life, and illness was almost unheard of.

"While we stay in the valley, yes," Elway replied solemnly. "But the world outside doesn't suit us."

"You'll understand when you've stayed with us for long

enough," Mallory added, looking at him with a strange, inde-cipherable expression.

"Are you sure your feet are up to my staying?" he asked, vaguely unhappy with the direction the conversation had taken and wanting to return to the earlier lighthearted atmosphere.

"Oh yes," she replied. "I'll wear clogs next time."

They smiled at each other, unaware that Horan watched them thoughtfully.

During his three month stay, Arden learned many things about the valley. He saw that, although there were animals on every farm—goats, horses, a few cows, sheep on the higher ground—the people ate no meat. Instead they ate the produce of the fertile soil, growing an extraordinary variety of vegetables, fruit, nuts, cereals, and herbs. At first, Arden could not understand how this system could provide such a varied and appetizing diet, but with Teri's patient help, he soon began to appreciate the subtleties of preparation and combinations. The fact that the valley also produced its own wine from the south-facing vineyard slopes, and the best beer Arden had ever tasted, made the food even more palat-able. When, out of curiosity, he asked Mallory about the lack of meat, her first reaction was one of shock and disgust. Then she thought about it for a few moments.

"They used to," she said finally. "Before I was born, that is. But it wasn't right. The valley belongs to the rabbits and birds and all the rest just as much as it does to us. Why slaughter them when we've no need to?"

Arden had never seen her so serious. He accepted her explanation as he accepted all the facts about her home. The valley's agriculture depended to a large extent on elaborate systems of irrigation. The climate was hot in summer and mild in winter, and the mountains to either side meant that there was very little rain at any time of the year. The central river was therefore all important. When Horan told Arden this, his immediate response had been to ask, "What river?" and he had been told about the most bizarre aspect of valley life that he had yet discovered.

"You must have seen the riverbed," Horan said, with a knowing smile. Arden thought about it.

"Yes," he replied at length, recalling the rock-strewn ra-vine which ran the length of the valley, crossed in places by sturdy wooden bridges. Both villages lay beside it. "But it's bone dry!"

"Full of dust," Horan agreed.

"It is like that *every* summer?" Arden did not understand how such a river, which looked as though it had been dry for years, could feed the impressive system of reservoirs, tunnels, and sluices that he had seen.

"No," Horan replied. "It only runs from the rain and melt-water from the southern mountains, from mid-winter to late summer."

"But . . ." Arden was even more confused.

"And it only runs every other year," Horan explained. "Since The Leveling."

Arden stopped to consider this.

"It flowed that year," Horan went on, "was dry the next, ran last year, and is dry now. Next year it will run again." He sounded so sure that it did not occur to Arden to ask how he knew.

"You mean this irrigation system was built in the last three years?" Arden's respect for the valley people rose another notch.

"It was here before that," Horan replied. "We just developed it more fully."

"That's incredible," Arden said, looking at the abundant greenery about them.

"We do have our moments," his friend replied.

"But *why* every other year? It doesn't make sense."

"The Leveling did many things, and it'll be a long time before we can explain them all."

Arden looked up at the huge mountains far to the south. *The source must be there somewhere,* he thought, a strange stirring in his heart. *That's where the riddle could be solved.*

Horan noticed the direction of his gaze but said nothing.

———•———

During that first visit to the valley, Arden learned much that amazed him and even more that pleased his spirit. He saw Fletcher climbing in the branches of an ancient apple tree and had to remind himself of the man's age. He was present at the naming-day of Dorcas's first child and shared in that communal celebration. He became familiar with much of their farming lore and skills, and with some of its backbreaking work. He even learned to dance after a fashion. Yet the most overwhelming experience in all that time occurred on his very first day in the valley.

He got up soon after sunrise to find the house already bustling. He took his place at the breakfast table and was included in the meal and conversation as if he had lived there all his life. Although he only spoke in response to the others, and had to have food pressed upon him, Arden could not help but feel accepted.

He was just finishing his third slice of bread and honey when Mallory burst in from the yard.

"Kris is here!" she exclaimed breathlessly, looking directly at Arden as if awaiting his response.

Feeling rather sticky, he rose to his feet and looked about uncertainly.

"Come *on!*" Mallory urged, waving him to the door. "It's *you* he's come to see."

"Don't rush the boy, Mallory," Elway said calmly. "He's new to our ways."

Arden went out into the yard, surreptitiously wiping his hands on his breeches. Not knowing what to expect, he glanced about and saw a child entering the yard. There was something odd about him. As Kris turned to face the house after fastening the gate, Arden had to stifle a gasp of horror. It was not a child after all, but a man, whose limbs and spine were so hideously deformed that he stood no higher than a ten-year-old. As he moved toward them his legs seemed uncoordinated and his crooked arms flew in all directions, yet he made steady progress. It was impossible to tell what he was looking at, for his head was bent forward as if studying the ground. He was barefoot and his clothes were black and shapeless, making him resemble an enormous wounded crow.

Arden instinctively took a step back, only to bump into Mallory, who pushed him forward again. Looking around, he saw the whole family ranged behind him. This meeting was obviously important to them. *What am I supposed to do?* he thought in panic. The cold fear of failure clutched at his stomach, but he was familiar with that and pushed it aside. He turned back to face the approaching stranger, and became absorbed by the top of Kris's head as it bobbed erratically toward him. The hair was thin and wispy, short but unkempt, and there was a curious bald lump in the middle of his crown. Arden found himself wavering between fascination and revulsion.

The newcomer's shuffling progress continued until he was only a pace—a normal pace—in front of Arden. There he stopped and slowly, painfully, leaned backward so that he could look up into Arden's face.

This time there was nothing Arden could do to prevent a sharp intake of breath. No amount of self-control or warning could have prepared him. Kris's eyes were yellow, variegated like an imperfect crystal—and the pupils were vertical slits. *Like a goat.* Arden began to tremble.

Kris held his gaze for a few moments then reached up with his right arm. The clawlike hand shook slightly, like dying leaves in the autumn wind.

Acting on instinct, Arden knelt down so that he could be studied more easily, and extended his left hand to grasp the one that was offered. As he did so, he felt his whole body stir into a new level of awareness, yet did not hear the murmur of approval from behind him. He stopped trembling.

Thoughts sprang unbidden into his mind. Foul memories rose to the surface of his consciousness but did not harm him. *He is protecting me.* Other processes, arcane and subtle, were taking place within him. Ideas beyond his understanding blossomed and died. *This is a test.* The fear returned, only to be banished gently, firmly.

Afterward, Arden did not know how long he had knelt in the dust. It seemed as if hours passed by, yet the time could have been encompassed by the blinking of an eye. When Kris withdrew his hand, it came as a shock, plunging him back into the normal world of noise and smells, and cool morning air. An indefinable sense of loss swept through his whole being, so sharp that he made a clumsy attempt at regaining the other's hand. Stunned, he remained kneeling while his eyes came back into focus.

Before him, Kris examined his own right hand, then licked a little honey from the fingers and smiled crookedly. Arden smiled back, but something inside him was crying. *Why was this very special person imprisoned in such a terrible, twisted frame?* Later, when he came to know just how healthy the valley was, Kris's fate seemed even more unjust. But by then he had also learned that Kris did not consider himself unlucky—for many good reasons.

Some of these became apparent that first morning. Arden slowly became aware of voices, full of welcome and delight. Kris still did not speak. In fact, as Arden realized almost immediately, he could not, but he responded with smiles and quick fluttering movements of his fingers. It was already clear that he was regarded with respect and affection by Elway and his family. Arden watched, still kneeling, as they came to meet their old friend, clasping his hands in a way that suggested more than a ritual greeting, and to usher him inside.

Arden jumped as he felt a hand on his shoulder.

"Come on," Mallory urged. "You can get up now." She was almost bursting with excitement.

Arden stood up slowly. The girl then surprised him a second time as she threw her arms about him and gave him a brief but fierce hug. As she withdrew, his eyes were full of questions.

"Why didn't you tell me?" he whispered hoarsely.

"Tell you what?" Mallory replied brightly, and skipped into the house to join the rest of her family.

Arden followed.

Inside, Kris was already installed at his place at the table, devouring honeycake with obvious relish. Around him all the others were busy telling him stories, asking questions, and laughing, until Arden wondered how Kris could make sense of any of it. He seemed quite accustomed to the uproar, however, replying with his birdlike sign language and spreading a warmth throughout the whole room. Arden stood in the doorway, watching, tears prickling at his eyes.

"Kris says you're the one he'd been expecting," Mallory yelled over the din. "That means you can stay with us!"

Arden did not understand it, but somehow that news was very important to him. He stepped into the room.

chapter 10

Arden was to meet Kris only rarely after that first traumatic encounter, but he saw his influence everywhere, and could tell that the disabled man was obviously held in great esteem by the valley community. Every household kept a place at table and a bed ready for him and considered it a privilege when, during the course of his travels, Kris took advantage of their hospitality.

His advice was keenly sought on all kinds of matters. Almost everyone knew a little of his mysterious sign language, and was thus able to communicate with him, and many of the older people were quite proficient, occasionally using it among themselves. When talking about him, they would often begin their sentences with "Kris says . . . ," unaware of the irony in quoting someone who had never spoken a word.

But more than this, it was the warmth that was part of Kris which ensured his popularity. Arden had felt it briefly when they had clasped hands and he had been drawn into a strange, peaceful world, but with the valley people it was a more lasting sensation, requiring only his proximity. The love and devotion Kris inspired was in marked contrast to the treatment of cripples in the outside world. Arden had seen them abused, feared, and driven into exile, and he knew that in many places, ill-formed babies were left to die of exposure rather than grow up to be a burden. Kris's strange eyes alone would have been enough to condemn him to death.

Arden had been full of questions that first day, but had to wait until the late afternoon before any were answered. Kris had left by then, in spite of his friends' protests, and Elway's family was free to give Arden their time, and reveal the truth of Kris's remarkable gifts.

As Arden watched Kris making his way along the track which led to the upper village, his ungainly movements emphasized by the flapping of his clothes, he wondered at such foolhardy independence.

"Will he be all right?" he asked of nobody in particular.

"Of course," Mallory exclaimed.

"There are several houses he'll pass before nightfall," Elway reassured Arden. "He'll not lack a welcome."

"Even if he did, the animals would look after him," Mallory added with conviction.

Elway laughed. "Aye," he said. "I've seen foxes eat from his hands and badgers run to greet him."

Arden took a deep breath.

"What . . . what happened . . . back there?"

The farmer turned to look at him.

"Walk with me, boy."

They set off down one of the hedge-side paths that criss-crossed the farm. Pollen rose in clouds about their boots as they walked, and a sneeze from behind them announced Mallory's presence. Elway beckoned for her to join them, and they went on, the farmer with one large arm around each pair of young shoulders.

"Was it a test?" Arden blurted out, unable to bear the silence any longer.

"Of course it was," Mallory said quickly. "He'd seen you coming, but he always makes sure of newcomers. He—"

"Slowly, daughter," Elway interrupted. "Give the boy a chance. You should consider your words occasionally. It would do you no harm," he added. Mallory grew quiet, but gave no sign of irritation.

"I need hardly tell you that Kris is a very special person," Elway began.

I know, Arden thought.

"The valley would not be the place it is without him. He has certain gifts . . ."

"He sees—" Mallory began, but was silenced by a look from her father.

"All of us here share them to a degree," the farmer went on, "but he is unique. I believe it's nature's way of compensating for what is denied him. Do you understand?"

Arden nodded. "I think so, but what *are* his gifts? What exactly did he do to me?"

"He did nothing *to* you, boy. That is just his way of saying hello, getting to know you. He can't ask questions like most of us can . . ." Elway glanced at his daughter and smiled. "So he uses his own way of finding out."

"You mean . . . he read my mind." Arden was aghast. *Then he knows!*

"In a manner of speaking." Elway seemed to find nothing strange in this idea.

"You needn't look so worried," Mallory put in, unable to remain silent any longer. "He likes you. Couldn't you tell?"

Arden was still struggling to make sense of it all. "So I passed the test?"

"If that's how you want to look at it," Elway said calmly. "Kris accepted you and so the valley will too. You are welcome to stay here as long as you wish."

"Kris believes you're going to help the valley one day," Mallory said eagerly. "He knew that you'd be coming."

"What do you mean? How *could* he know?"

"Kris can see certain events before they happen," his mentor said evenly, as if he were commenting on the size of a potato crop. "He told us several days ago that a boy . . . a boy would come who would be a friend to us in our need."

Arden looked at him in disbelief.

"He said a boy in—" Mallory began.

"Hush, child," Elway said quickly.

"What? What did he say?"

After a moment's consideration, the farmer gave in.

"He said, 'a boy in pain, whose hurts were hidden, who could heal others but not himself.' "

Conflicting emotions filled Arden's heart and mind. *What did it mean? Could Kris know* everything?

"I don't believe it," he claimed, but his eyes told a different story. "Nobody can see the future."

"There are many ways of knowing things, Arden."

"No one tells you about a call of nature," Mallory said. "But you *know* when you get one that you've got to take a piss."

Her father roared with laughter, a healthy, uncomplicated sound.

"Mallory's example is a little crude," he said, "but it is apt enough."

"That's something you learn through *experience*," Arden replied, fighting to keep himself from blushing.

"And we also know that the sun will set tonight and rise again tomorrow morning. You see, I can be a prophet too."

"That's different," Arden protested.

"Perhaps Kris has different experiences to draw upon,"

Elway said, serious now. "His world is certainly different from ours."

That evening, Arden spoke little, and his new friends were content to leave him to his own thoughts. He went to bed with Elway's words running endlessly through his brain. One phrase was repeated over and over again.

All of us here share them to a degree.

———•———

That conversation was among the earliest of Arden's lessons about the life of the valley and its inhabitants, and it was by no means the last. His curiosity was boundless and he worked hard, testing with his own endeavors what he had been told. He also found time—mainly at Mallory's insistence—to tell them something of his own life. He deliberately left out much of his history, but was happy to give details of his travels, of the sights he had seen, the landscapes, towns, and animals. He totally avoided the subject of his own family, merely saying that they had died in The Leveling.

His friendship with Mallory blossomed without his being really aware of it, and Teri and Horan also became especially dear to him. That first summer in the valley was the happiest time Arden had ever known, yet in the end, he knew he had to leave.

chapter 11

Horan found Arden sitting alone, staring out over the fields. It was late summer and the first leaves were beginning to turn. Arden was quite still, his chin resting in one palm. He jumped when Horan sat down beside him and, for a moment, stared at his friend as if he did not recognize him.

"You're going, aren't you?"

Arden looked at him without surprise.

"Do you know *everything*?" His voice was weary, resigned. "I've been expecting it for a while."

Arden turned back to the fields and the splendid mountains beyond.

"I don't belong here," he said eventually. "I don't *know* things the way you do. I can never be a part of the valley, I'll always be just an outsider, looking on." Arden paused, as if weighing some bitter truths. "I *can't* help the valley the way Kris says I will. I can only disrupt . . ." He turned to face Horan and the pain and regret were clear in his eyes. "I don't *want* to go. I *have* to."

"We'll miss you," Horan said, accepting the inevitable. "Mallory most of all," he added.

Arden looked surprised, then realization dawned. Somehow that knowledge only strengthened his resolve.

His departure was accepted without rancor or comment. Mallory was hurt but hid it well, and by unspoken understanding, they avoided being together except in company. They were both afraid that, once alone, Mallory might try to dissuade him—and that she might succeed. At times Arden felt that he would have preferred her to plead and rave—that way he could have tried to explain. Her sad acceptance was more difficult to bear.

For the most part though, the family, once informed of his decision, was more concerned with practical matters. Fletcher summed up their attitude best when he decided that, as the autumn mists were beginning to wreath the uplands, the boy would need a new set of waterproof clothing. This was duly provided, as were many other gifts. Eventually, Arden had to put a stop to their generosity—his pack was becoming too heavy to lift.

Arden half expected to see Kris on the morning when he left, but there was no sign of him. He did not know whether to be relieved or disappointed.

The whole family gathered in the farmyard to see him off, but their farewells were brief.

"You'll always be welcome here," Teri reminded him.

"Aye, remember that, lad," Elway said. "Any house in the valley will take you in."

"With a bit more practice we could even make a decent farmer of you," Horan said, smiling.

Mallory's face was white and set, and she did not speak. There was so much Arden wanted to say, but where was he to start? In the end his words were the simplest and most direct of all.

"Thank you," he said. "Goodbye." And with that, he turned on his heel and walked away. The chorus of farewells did not include the one voice he was listening for, and he had to steel himself not to look back.

At first he walked northward, down the valley, reluctant at the last to commit himself. Then he forced himself to turn west and began to trudge doggedly up into the mountains.

----------•----------

Gemma was silent for some time after Arden finished his story. She had the feeling that he had left a lot out—especially the parts referring to his earlier life—but now she understood why he felt so strongly about the valley. Intuition told her that his experiences there had been instrumental in turning him from an unhappy young wanderer into the confident, self-sufficient man who rode beside her. He too was quiet now, his eyes full of memories.

After a while, he glanced at his companion.

"That was eleven years ago."

Gemma took her chance.

"Have you been back since?" she asked.

"Several times."

"And Mallory?"

Arden grinned. *No need to exorcise* that *ghost,* Gemma thought.

"She's married now," he replied, "to a farmer in the lower

part of the valley. They have two sons who treat me as a sort of long-lost uncle every time I visit."

"So her feet are quite safe then?"

"Oh, yes. She's far too sensible to dance with me now," Arden laughed. "Besides, her husband's a lot bigger than me!"

"And the others?"

"Fletcher's dead," Arden said, his face clouding over. "He was one hundred and nineteen years old."

"I thought only wizards grew that old," Gemma said thoughtfully. "Ferragamo was two hundred and fifty."

Arden gave her a long-suffering look.

"It's true!" she protested. "But I've never known anyone else live that long."

"Fletcher would probably still be alive, but for the river," Arden replied. "It wasn't only the crop failure. He just couldn't believe that the river had let them down. The shock was too much for him."

"Did it *really* flow every other year?"

"Yes."

"What could have caused that?" Gemma was mystified.

"Nobody knows. That's just the way it was," Arden replied, his tone implying that the whys and wherefores did not matter.

"And now it's failed?"

"Twice," he said somberly. "The first time was two years ago. That was when Fletcher died. They couldn't really believe it, just kept waiting and waiting for the first tricklings. But they never came, and by the time they realized it wasn't going to run at all it was too late to preserve much water." Arden paused and swallowed as if his throat were dry. "They hoped it would happen last year, but that was always *supposed* to be a dry season. This spring was the crucial test."

"And it's failed again?"

Arden nodded. "It's well past the time for meltwater," he said. "The river should be in full flood now, but it's bone dry." He scowled, remembering the expressions on his friends' faces turning from desperate hope to despair. His last visit to the valley had not been a happy one.

"Four years without water," Gemma whispered, horror-struck.

"They've done what they can to hoard what little rain they get," Arden went on. "They've even trekked up into the mountains to see if there were any streams they could divert, but it's all produced very little. The vegetation is dying, crops have failed, even some of the trees are in a bad way. The soil is drying out and blowing away in places. Even if they got water now it would take a long, long time for them to recover." The sadness in his voice was mixed with anger. "Why is it that this world destroys anything that is really beautiful?" he demanded suddenly. "Why?"

Gemma could not find words to comfort him. She knew that he was speaking about more than the valley. When Arden spoke again, his voice was quiet, deliberately drained of emotion.

"They're not actually starving yet, though that will come soon, but everything else is falling apart. Many of the old ones have died, and the immunity to illness is crumbling. Food is so short that some have even left the valley. They won't last long." There was a strange undercurrent in his words.

He would have become like that if he'd stayed, Gemma guessed. *Trapped. Unable to leave.*

"They've had to slaughter some of the animals," Arden continued. "They can't afford to feed them. Some people even tried eating the meat, but it just made them sick. They tried it with wild animals too, but it was the same, and so they abandoned that idea." He shook his head sadly. "Even their special gifts are fading."

"What gifts?" Gemma asked, though she already had some idea.

"They used to *know* things," Arden responded. "One of them would see something, and before long everybody in the valley could describe it, even if the original witness had spoken of it to no one."

"Mind-talk?" Gemma queried.

Arden looked at her, puzzled.

"Silent conversations in your head," she explained. "Like wizards with their familiars."

"No," he replied angrily. "*Nothing* like that." His face became set in a grimace which said, as clearly as any words, *What nonsense you talk!*

Gemma was taken aback. *He expects me to accept Kris and his special talents, yet he won't countenance the idea of magic in* my *world*, she thought. Then something else occurred to her.

"Didn't Kris foresee this?" she asked.

"No. He's as bemused as any of them," Arden answered. "Some people even turned against him because he hadn't warned them." There was bitterness in his words.

"He was right about one thing, though," Gemma said.

Arden looked at her.

"What?"

"He said that one day you would be a friend to the valley. Help them when they needed it."

Arden's expression remained grim.

"I'm going to try," he said.

chapter 12

After two days of slow but steady traveling, the unforgiving landscape of the Diamond Desert gave way to gently rolling grassland which grew progressively greener as they rode onward. Even so, Arden still insisted that they rest during the hottest part of the day, and ride only in the morning and evening.

Late in the third day they came through some trees which stood upon the crest of a ridge, and looked down on the strangest and most beautiful building Gemma had ever seen. The great hall was enormously tall, its elegantly curved buttresses flanking pointed archways. At one end, a massive tower soared toward the sun, its topmost stones seeming to belong to the air and sky. About the hall stood other buildings, all built of the same light gray stone, and all in perfect proportion.

Gemma was so taken with its loveliness that it was some moments before she saw the missing roofs and empty windows, and knew that the only inhabitants were the rooks that circled the tower, crying raucously. The graceful building was obviously very old, and a cord of disquiet tightened within her. How could it be? This place had been constructed centuries before, and had been a ruin for more years than she could count. Yet the land on which it stood had not even existed until fifteen summers ago. She tore her eyes away and turned to Arden, finding him already looking at her.

"It's beautiful, isn't it?" he said.

"Yes."

"Men call it the Abbey. We can stay here tonight. The brothers run a small travelers' retreat in the old bath houses."

"The brothers?"

"Men dedicated to the gods. They live there because it makes them feel nearer to the eternal truths."

Gemma could not tell whether he was being sarcastic or not.

"Did they build it?" she asked quietly.

"Their ancient forerunners did," he replied, stressing his words. "It's hundreds of years old, Gemma."

"I can see that."

"Then you admit—"

"This whole land must have existed *somewhere else*," Gemma explained, interrupting him, "and The Destruction brought it here."

Arden stared at her.

"You really are from a different world," he said.

Gemma burst out laughing.

"I *was*," she stated. "But I'm not any more. Don't you see?"

"I can see you've been out in the sun too long again."

"I'm serious!" she exclaimed, her wide grin belying her claim. "Where does it say that the Earth-mind can only have *one* dream? You were in one and I was in another. The Destruction just brought them together."

Arden laughed at her eagerness. "It sounds as though the Earth-mind's as mad as you are," he said. "You make a good pair."

"Don't say that," she replied, shocked.

"I don't believe in gods, or your Earth-mind," he stated. "No being that powerful would have made such a mess of the world." He was serious now.

"It's not the Earth-mind that's made a mess of things," Gemma argued. "It's *man* that's done that."

"Don't leave women out of this," was Arden's sour response.

"Oh, we help—when you let us," Gemma replied, grinning.

"When have we ever been able to stop you?" Arden returned her smile. "Don't answer that!" he added quickly. "Come on. We could both do with a good night's rest and a roof over our heads."

He changes moods so fast, Gemma mused. *One moment he's angry, the next laughing, then sad. No wonder he's never settled down.* She nudged Mischa forward to follow Lark, then chuckled to herself. *Look who's talking!*

When they were halfway down the grassy slope, the music of the singing sands began. Gemma's ears rang with the melancholy beauty and she twisted round in the saddle to look back the way they had come. Mischa halted, not knowing what was required of her. A sharp longing awoke in Gemma's heart. *I should be going south. Why have I let this man drag me away to the north?* It was the first time she had questioned her course of action. Since Arden had saved her, they had both taken it for granted that she would travel with him. But now, as the seductive melody swelled and pulsed in her mind, Gemma knew that her destiny lay in the far south— and the sooner she got there the better.

She turned back and pulled on the mare's reins, only to find a restraining hand upon her own.

"It's just the wind," Arden said. Gemma did not hear the pleading note in his voice.

"I have to go," she said, gazing southward again.

"It comes from the caves beneath the desert," he went on desperately. "The wind gets into them and sets up all sorts of vibrations. I've heard it often, felt it sometimes."

"It's calling me."

"It's a *trick*, Gemma."

"No!" Her eyes snapped round to glare into his.

"If you follow that sound you'll die," he said calmly, anger boiling beneath the surface. "You're in no fit state—"

"You don't understand," she wailed.

"No, I don't!" he shouted, his eyes flashing. "You crazy bitch, why do you want to kill yourself?"

"It's not just the singing sands," Gemma tried to explain. "It's the south. Everything leads me there. This whole journey . . .

". . . has nearly been the end of you," Arden finished for her, "and I'm not going to let it happen again. You're coming with me if I have to tie you to the horse and *lead* you."

They glowered at each other, both quite still, as the music washed over them in waves, rising and falling, beckoning and repelling. It was Gemma who lowered her eyes first, exhausted by their argument.

"I'll come with you," she whispered. "For now."

Arden nodded, his face softening a little.

"But I still have to go south one day," she went on.

"If you must," he conceded, his tone implying that the future could take care of itself.

As they went on down the slope the music stopped abruptly, but the yearning it had awoken in Gemma's heart did not go away. Even the awe-inspiring grace of the Abbey failed to lift her spirits.

They dismounted, then entered the grounds, leading the horses between the buildings. The main hall was even more extraordinary when seen close to, and Gemma automatically

assumed that magic had been used in its construction. The
largest structures in her old home-isle—city walls, towers—
had been built by wizards long ago, using skills no longer
known to the world, and it seemed inconceivable that this
massive building could have been made by men alone. Windows towered over them, their arches pointing to the heavens, some forlorn pieces of colored glass still clinging to their
rims.

*It must have been like an enchanted palace when it was
whole,* Gemma thought in wonder.

They walked on in silence, the horses' hooves muffled by
the short, well-tended grass of the inner courtyards. They
passed other, smaller halls, some of them only broken walls,
yet all gave the impression of permanence, of tranquillity, as
if the peace of the Abbey had remained undisturbed by the
upheavals it had witnessed. In spite of her disquiet, Gemma
recognized the attraction of the place. It soothed her a little
and she understood why the brothers still lived among the
ruins.

She glimpsed vaulted cellars, thick-walled storage rooms,
the curved roof of an oast-house, long halls of severe design
with small high windows, and, finally, a rectangular building
whose roof was intact, and with glass in its windows. The
sound of chanting came from inside, solemn words she did
not understand to a tune that was simple and repetitive. It
was not without power, that sound, but it held none of the
mystery or magic of the singing sands. This was too human,
too tied to the earth, for all that it strained to rise upward.

Arden stopped outside the door.

"What is it?" Gemma whispered, gesturing inside.

"They're singing praises to the gods," he answered. "We'll
wait until they're finished."

"Do they welcome everyone? Even . . . nonbelievers?"

"They don't judge," Arden replied. He grinned. "And they
distill a remarkably fine liqueur."

When the chant ended, Arden knocked at the door. It was
opened by a man dressed in a long robe of the same gray as
the abbey stone.

"Rooms for the night," Arden requested. "If it is permitted."

The man nodded and beckoned them inside, into a small
hall furnished with trestle tables and wooden benches. Other
men appeared, similarly dressed, and two went out to take
care of the horses. Two others, one young, one old, led their

guests down passageways in opposite directions. All this was accomplished without a word being spoken by the gray-clad men.

"When the bell rings, come back to the hall," Arden told Gemma as they parted. "There'll be food."

Gemma followed the older brother, and was shown to a small cell. The stone walls were unadorned, and the window was too high to offer any view. Blankets were folded neatly upon the wooden bed and a table and a single chair provided the only other furniture.

"Thank you," Gemma said, putting down her small pack. The man nodded and made as if to leave.

"Is there anywhere I can wash?" she asked quickly, unnerved by the austere surroundings and wanting to prolong the human contact. She felt sure that once he left she would be quite alone in this wing of the building. For answer the brother showed her another room farther down the corridor. Inside was a huge stone bath, a few wisps of steam rising from the water. Then he turned to go and this time Gemma did not stop him.

She washed quickly in the tepid water, then returned to her room, arranged the blankets, and lay down, looking at the ceiling. *What am I supposed to do now?* she wondered. Was she allowed to go out? Explore as she pleased? Did any of the brothers talk? She did not want to rest in case she slept and missed the bell. Why had she and Arden been separated? She thought she knew the answer to that, but missed his presence.

And all the time something else, buried deep within her, protested at her confinement.

The bell saved her from further thought. Its languorous tolling was much louder than necessary. Gemma hurried to the hall and, finding it empty, sat down on one of the benches. Arden came in soon afterward, followed by several of the brothers. Bread, cheese, a sort of porridge, and raw, sliced vegetables were placed in front of the two guests, then the brothers took their places. I was noticeable that only elderly men sat near Gemma.

"All right?" Arden inquired.

Gemma nodded, daunted by the brothers' silence and not wanting to speak.

"Then eat."

After the meal, Arden excused himself and went over to

the brother who had opened the door to them. A short and whispered conversation followed, during which both men glanced at Gemma.

A suspicion grew in her mind. *He's arranging my guard!* she thought. *So I don't get away.*

Indignation welled up within her, but there was also a small part of her that was thinking differently. That small part was prey to another emotion entirely, one which left her shaken.

Relief.

chapter 13

Gemma surprised herself by sleeping quite soundly that night, allowing the serenity of her surroundings to affect her. She dreamt of her island home for the first time since she had left it, yet even that was comforting, not plagued by the restlessness and unhappiness that had marked her final months there. Cai spoke to her, his boyish face as handsome as ever, but on waking, Gemma could not remember what he had said. It felt almost as though he had been watching over her from afar and, once satisfied that she was all right, had withdrawn again. She woke smiling.

The sun was already up as she dressed hurriedly and peered around her doorway. *Do I have to wait for a bell?* she wondered. Her problem was solved by the appearance of Arden, who beckoned to her from the hall. There they ate a frugal breakfast alone—the brothers had been up and about for some time—before collecting their horses and setting out again. As they left the Abbey's cocoon of silence, Gemma asked, "Do they ever speak?"

"Only to the gods," Arden replied, "and the occasional trader, or visitors like myself. I believe the brothers who go into town to exchange their goods are given special dispensation."

"It was eerie," Gemma said, and shivered.

"It suits them," Arden commented dryly. He rummaged in one of Lark's saddlebags and fished out a small corked pottery bottle. "And there's nothing eerie about this. Try some." He removed the stopper and passed it over.

Gemma took a cautious sniff, wrinkling her nose at the smell, then tipped her head back to take a sip. She almost choked. The fiery liquid seemed to explode as it passed down her throat, and her eyes began to water. She quickly returned the bottle to Arden, who took a swig.

"Good, isn't it?" he remarked.

"I'll tell you when I can feel my throat again," Gemma replied hoarsely.

"Have some more. Your throat will still be numb but by then you won't care." Arden grinned, rolling his eyes wildly.

"No, thank you," Gemma laughed. "It's too early in the day for me."

"You might need it."

"Why?"

"We'll reach Newport by dusk. It takes a bit of getting used to." Arden took another swallow.

"Is that wise?" Gemma asked.

"Oh, yes," Arden said. "I might not be able to force myself to enter the place sober."

"Is it *so* bad?"

"Let's just say it's quite a contrast to the Abbey," Arden replied, bringing the bottle to his lips again. Then he hesitated, shook his head, restoppered the bottle, and put it away. "Gods," he said quietly. "You've only been around a few days and already you can make me feel guilty."

———————•———————

The city of Great Newport was indeed very different from anything Gemma had yet encountered on the Southern Continent. It owed its status as capital of the region of Cleve to history rather than to any economic or geographical advantages. Before The Leveling, it had been an important trading center, surrounded by fertile land on three sides. A deep river had flowed through the town and on into the great ocean to the north. Now all that had changed. The river was no more than a stream and only a small area to the south of the city walls could be considered good agricultural land. Food had to be imported from the larger, more prosperous cities to east and west, along the coastal road. Inland to either side was desert.

In fact, Arden claimed that the city's name was wholly inappropriate: only the most deluded citizen could call it great except in terms of squalor; it most certainly was not new—except in the endless variety of vice available—and, since The Leveling, it was no longer even a port, standing two leagues from the coast.

Many years of rule had accustomed the city to power, but since The Leveling there had been little to back up its claim to preeminence. As a consequence, Arden claimed, the people who wielded that power had grown cunning and vicious. The hierarchy of Great Newport were headed by the Overlord of the City, who was also, according to his official titles, the Master of Cleve Province, First Minister of Trade, and High Commander of the Army and Navy.

"I wouldn't be surprised if he was also claiming to be a direct descendant of the gods by now," Arden said contemptuously.

"What's he called?" Gemma asked, wondering what her companion would have thought of the royal houses of her home-isles.

"It was Hilger, last time I heard," Arden replied. "But that was a year ago. *Lord* Hilger may well have been replaced by now."

"Replaced? How?"

"Theoretically, the Overlord is elected every three years by the Merchants' Guild. In practice, this procedure is often too cumbersome, so they tend to take short cuts." Arden paused. "Since the river dried up, they've had no end of problems," he added cheerfully.

"Why?" Gemma asked, though she had already guessed the answer.

"Nowhere to dispose of the bodies," he replied. "It's hard to convince people that an overlord drowned in a stream no deeper than a puddle."

"You *are* joking, aren't you?"

"No. Overlords tend to come and go. What remains constant is the power of the Guild. You'll soon see for yourself."

Arden's prophecy was indeed accurate. The walls of Great Newport came into view in the late afternoon. They were built of the same gray stone as the Abbey, but Gemma would never have known it. The walls and towers were stained with all manner of residues, green, black, and brown. They were also partly obscured by the ramshackle town of hovels—from which smoke and steam rose constantly—which clustered about the city.

Arden and Gemma were met on the road by four soldiers on horseback, their armor and equipment shining in the sun. The leader eyed them narrowly.

"You are bound for the city?" he asked, his voice cold.

Gemma expected Arden to answer as flippantly as usual, but his response was sober and respectful.

"Yes, captain. With your permission."

"You wish for an escort?"

"Thank you. Yes."

The soldier motioned to his men and they arranged them-

selves on either side of the newcomers before setting off at a
stately pace.

"Is this really necessary?" Gemma whispered.

Arden nodded and put a finger to his lips.

The last part of their ride was unnerving. The flimsy wooden
huts by the road reeked of abject poverty and hopelessness.
Several of the dwellers in that shantytown watched the travelers pass by, resentment burning in their eyes. Naked children started forward, hands held up in supplication, before
their mothers dragged them back.

The soldiers rode in haughty silence, their immaculate
uniforms and sleek, well-groomed mounts contrasting with
the ragged humanity about them. Gemma looked around,
horrified by the squalid conditions in which the onlookers
lived, and by the sullen hostility in their stares. She was
angered and disgusted by the injustice and ugliness all around
her, but could not help but feel relieved when at last they
reached the city gate.

As they halted, the captain turned to Arden and held out
his hand, palm upward. Without a word the traveler took
four coins from his pouch and handed them over. The soldier
did not move but his gaze flicked briefly to Gemma, and a
thin, cruel smile touched his mouth. Arden gave him two
further coins, whereupon he rode away without a word, the
other soldiers following his lead.

"Prices have gone up," Arden muttered. Gemma heard the
barely controlled fury beneath his words, and thought, *He
hates doing this.* It was further proof—if she had needed
it—of just how much the valley meant to him.

"Stay on your horse," Arden commanded. "Let me to the
talking." He dismounted and hammered on the wooden gate.
A narrow shutter was thrown back and an anonymous pair of
eyes studied them from inside. The gate was opened and
Arden led the two horses inside, then helped Gemma dismount. As the gate closed behind them, another soldier
appeared. His uniform was less ornate than that of the cavalry
but his badge carried the same device, a pair of scales,
equally balanced. Gemma was bursting with questions, but
she remained silent.

"This way." It was an order. Gemma followed Arden out of
the gloom of the entranceway into a bare, lamplit room
within the city wall. The soldier sat behind a desk and mo-

tioned them to stand in front of it. Taking paper and pen in
his thick fingers, he spoke without looking up.

"Name?"

"Arden."

"Your home town?"

"Manesty."

"The purpose of your visit here?"

"A petition to the Overlord."

The soldier grunted. Looking up, his expression made his
opinion clear. *You'll be lucky*.

"Lord Lunkett is a very busy man. Your . . . *petition* had
better be important. It would be very foolish of you to bother
him with trifles."

"Life and death are not trifles," Arden replied evenly. "I
have heard that the Lord is a fair man. All I ask is justice."

"The Overlord is indeed the father of justice," the soldier
said portentously. "How do you propose to support yourself
while in the city?" he went on, glancing at Gemma.

"I have money," Arden said firmly.

"Manesty must be more prosperous than I realized," his
inquisitor remarked. "You do not propose to trade or work
then?"

"No."

The soldier looked at Gemma again, this time a lingering
appraising stare that swept her entire body.

"And this is?"

"My wife," Arden answered promptly. "Gemma."

"She does not look well."

"She is pregnant. The journey has tired her."

Gemma was burning with embarrassment and rage, but
forced herself to remain clam and say nothing.

"That's understandable." The soldier lost interest in Gemma
and looked back to the papers on his desk. He wrote a few
more words then said, "I must see proof that you have
sufficient money to pay for your visit here." He tapped the
desk top. "Accommodation and food are not cheap in the city,
especially when you are eating for three." He grinned.

Arden emptied his pouch onto the table. Stubby fingers
moved several coins to one side.

"This appears sufficient."

As Arden reclaimed what was left of his money, the soldier
stamped the forms he had filled out, and handed one to
Arden.

"A three-day permit. If you need to stay longer, you must return here." He waved them away.

Arden took Gemma's arm and hurried her outside. Another coin changed hands as they reclaimed their horses from a guard. Leading their mounts, they walked into the city of Great Newport, and entered a world of twilight bustle, of exotic smells, and a wild variety of sounds. The twisted maze of streets soon left Gemma completely bewildered, but Arden led the way confidently, motioning for her to remain silent.

When they were well out of earshot of the gatehouse, Arden suddenly threw his head back, raised his fists above his head, and roared at the sky.

"Aaarrrgh!" His face twisted horribly, then, just as quickly, he returned to normal and grinned at Gemma, who was regarding him with wide eyes.

"I needed that," he remarked pleasantly.

"No wonder you hate this place," she said. "Is everyone as corrupt as that?"

"Oh no," he answered. "Most of them are much worse."

"Did you show him *all* your money?" Gemma asked anxiously. "There doesn't seem much left."

"Of course not," Arden replied. "He was quite aware of it too, but we were following a certain ritual."

"Was claiming me as your wife part of the ritual?"

"If I hadn't, he would probably have made me an offer for you."

Gemma was speechless.

"I wouldn't be the first man to sell his wife here," Arden went on. "Being pregnant lowers your value and affords you a greater degree of safety."

"Thank you!" she sputtered.

"Think nothing of it," he replied, then grew serious again as he added, "For the time being, it would make things a lot easier if you *did* act the part of my wife. Can you cope with that? You handled it very well back there."

"You might have warned me," Gemma reproached him. "It's a good thing I have some experience at concealing my emotions."

"I thought you trusted me," he said artlessly, spreading his hands wide.

Gemma refused to be cajoled. "I have to," she said. "You know this place. I don't. Have you been here many times?"

"As few as possible. Maybe four or five."

"Who are those people outside?"

"The ones with too little money to enter the city or to survive once they're inside. The victims of the system, you might say."

"No wonder they looked at us that way." Gemma shuddered at the memory. "I'm beginning to agree with you about this place."

"I was right about Hilger too," Arden said. "He didn't last long."

"Do you know this Lord Lunkett?"

"Only by reputation."

"And?"

"Put it this way . . . if he was stranded unarmed in a swamp full of alligators, it would be the alligators I'd feel sorry for."

Gemma had no idea what alligators were but she understood Arden's point well enough.

"Is three days long enough to persuade him?"

Arden laughed. "No chance! It's unlikely that we *will* actually get to see the mighty Overlord. Should we by some miracle eventually thread our way through the maze of bureaucracy and soldiery that protects him, it wouldn't be for a month at least."

"Then how . . . ?"

"The three-day pass was just for form's sake. If the patrols catch us they'll throw us out, of course, but that's not likely. And no one expects us to go back to the guardhouse."

"But—"

"If—the gods forbid it—we *wanted* to stay, the city would tolerate us as long as we were useful. After that . . ."

"How do you cope with all this?" Gemma asked, feeling thoroughly despondent and bemused.

"By keeping in mind that *if* we succeed, the ends more than justify the means," he replied candidly. "We'll apply to the Guild Court for a hearing. With a bit of luck we might get something done." The hope in his words was not echoed in his eyes, but Arden was still able to smile. "Come on. Let's go and find somewhere to stay that won't cost us everything we own just for the first two nights."

"If you run out of money, you can always sell your wife," Gemma remarked.

Arden looked her up and down.

"I'd have to fatten you up a bit first," he said.

chapter 14

At first, Gemma was content to play the part Arden had assigned her, spending most of her time in their tavern room. As a sickly and pregnant wife, she was the recipient of much sympathy and care from the women of the establishment; and as a consequence she ate well, slept a lot—in one of the two single beds, her matrimonial duties not extending to sharing one with her "husband"—and began to recover her former excellent health.

Meanwhile, Arden went about the mysterious and daily business of furthering the claim of the valley. It was obvious that he found the whole process distasteful; he disliked talking about his progress even to Gemma. All that she could get out of him was that he was making contacts, persuading them to put him in touch with the next, and the next, and so on. It was slow, laborious work and Gemma's respect for her companion grew as she saw how he persevered.

For the most part, however, they spent what time they had together in lighthearted pursuits—talking, reading, playing table-games, and occasionally venturing out for a short walk or a drink in the tavern common room. Gemma knew that Arden who laughed and joked with her on these occasions was the real man, and realized that such times were essential to keep him sane and capable of carrying on. And in some obscure way she also knew that her presence was a help to him.

After a few days, however, Gemma found this passive assistance irksome; with the return of her bodily health came a restlessness that was familiar to her. The longing to be on the move once more and her continued confinement soon led to boredom. She pressed Arden to let her go with him, to help in his task, but he refused, saying that it would not be long now before his efforts would take on an unstoppable momentum. Then, he claimed, she would be able to witness everything for herself. This did not satisfy Gemma, but she was diverted by Arden's need for her to be in good humor, and so got no further.

Her lack of action eventually became intolerable and she began sneaking out alone during the day to explore the city. The tavern stood in the heart of a bustling trading district and there was always plenty to see. Carriages and carts moved ceaselessly along the cobbled streets, all manner of merchandise was on sale from shops or stalls, and the hot early autumn air was thick with vendors' cries and an extraordinary variety of smells. Spices, vegetables and fruit, fresh bread, human sweat, horse manure, perfume, rotting rubbish, and other, unidentifiable substances bequeathed their scents to the atmosphere. Gemma could only guess at the more nefarious trades that evidently flourished in the back alleys. One thing was abundantly clear, though. Here, money ruled supreme. With it, you could command almost anything, satisfy any desire. Without it, you were of less account than a sewer rat, and Gemma began to worry about the state of Arden's funds. Her presence must be a burden and she was sure that much had disappeared in bribes. What would happen if his money ran out before the valley's case could be heard?

Gemma gradually learned her way around and her boldness grew. She ventured further afield each day, and so saw a little of the different faces that Great Newport presented to the world. It was indeed a city of extremes. Some of the housing was so dirty and dilapidated that it made the hovels outside the walls seem almost desirable by comparison. Small children played naked amid the squalor and looked at Gemma with large eyes that haunted her dreams.

In one such area she came across what she at first took to be an unusual open space, but when she reached it she stood still, unable to believe her eyes. Before her was a vast pit hundreds of paces wide, in which was piled all manner of garbage, a seemingly endless vista of the city's rubbish. It was like a nightmare vision of another world. The stench which rose from it, wreathed in swirls of steam and smoke, was stomach-turning. But what made Gemma stare in horror was that there were *people* in the pit, moving over it slowly, clambering up and down the sides, picking over the detritus. Fires smouldered in places and, as she watched, one small mound in the distance exploded, sending flames and debris flying into the air. Several scavengers ran away from this eruption but after a few moments gradually moved back in.

"Better not stand too close, lassie," said a voice beside her. She looked round to see an old man, dressed in filthy rags, one eye permanently clouded over. He gave her a toothless grin and added, "It blows up quite often in the summer and autumn."

"What are they doing?" Gemma whispered.

"Looking for good stuff. Anything they can sell. Metal. Food."

"Food?" she exclaimed. "In there?"

"It's better than starving," the old man replied, but Gemma did not hear him. She turned and ran, trying not to be sick. The one good eye watched her go. "That's right!" he yelled. "You wouldn't want to get your nice clothes dirty!" He spat after her, then began coughing.

In marked contrast, another of her explorations had taken her into a district where wide avenues ran beside parks, and palatial mansions stood amid colorful gardens. Here the air was sweet but still left a nasty taste in Gemma's mouth. The affluence was an obscenity after what she had seen elsewhere, and it was obviously protected jealously. Armed guards eyed her suspiciously from several gatehouses, and at one they yelled, "Move on! We want none of your sort here!" She had run away, flustered and ashamed.

Gemma yearned to talk about her experiences with Arden but knew that he believed her to be staying in the tavern and would be angry if she told him otherwise.

Just when she thought that Newport could produce nothing else to surprise or disgust her, she came across another aspect of the city. This discovery almost cost her her life.

They had been in the city for ten days and Arden was growing more and more weary, yet there was an excitement bubbling within him that Gemma could feel when he left her that morning. *Perhaps today*, she thought as the door closed. And then, *I could follow him*. Adventure vied with common sense for a few moments, but once the idea had taken hold there was no shaking it off. She hurried down the stairs and out into the street, remembering childhood games in the castles that had been her home a lifetime ago.

Arden was just turning into another lane and she walked briskly after him, thankful that there were already crowds about. Peering round the corner, she saw him striding purposefully along and followed, keeping a good distance between them. Such was her concentration on her quarry that she bumped into several people, apologizing absentmindedly, and received many annoyed and puzzled glances.

All went well while Arden stuck to the main thoroughfares, but before long he turned into a district Gemma was not familiar with, a maze of tiny streets and alleys. She was not able to keep him in sight all the time as his route twisted and turned, so had to get closer and proceed with caution at each turn. Arden led her deeper and deeper into the labyrinth; several times she thought she had lost him altogether.

Eventually the inevitable happened. Gemma peeked into the alley she thought Arden had turned into, and found it empty, a dead end. A frantic search of the surrounding lanes failed to produce him, and it was only then that Gemma realized the extent of her predicament. Put simply, she was lost. That alone would have held few terrors for her, but with her awareness of her surroundings increased by Arden's disappearance, she began to notice other disquieting facts. There were no people about; indeed she had not seen anyone since she had lost sight of Arden. The unusual quiet was menacing. The alleys were incredibly narrow, some of them so confined that two people would have had to turn sideways in order to pass. The two-story buildings crowded in upon her, appearing to lean together, almost blotting out the sky. Many of them had no windows on the ground floor, which gave them a barren and inhuman aspect. And the lanes were amazingly clean, unlike any other area she had seen. Even the most prosperous district had not been so spotless. It was as if all inhabitants had vanished from this part of the city, leaving it pristine but dead.

Gemma's heart began to pound.

Don't be silly, she commanded herself. *Think rationally!*

She tried to retrace her footsteps, walking slowly and noting the features of every turn in case she had to double back. Before long, however, the impersonal alleyways all began to look the same and she despaired of making any real progress. Yet another lane ended in a blank wall and she turned, startled to find her way blocked by three silent men. The smallest man, in the center of the group, was dressed all in white, and Gemma could tell that the material of his garments was luxuriously soft. His hands and face were very pale, but his eyes were the most striking feature. They were covered with two circles of glass, held by metal frames, which made his pale blue eyes appear twice their normal size. He gazed, owllike, at Gemma, with obvious interest. The two large men flanking him appeared coarse and colorful by comparison. They stood with arms folded, legs slightly apart, as if awaiting instructions.

The pale man spoke, his voice oily.

"This is private property. May I ask your business here?"

"I'm sorry . . ." Gemma stammered. "I'm lost."

One of the big men whispered out of the side of his mouth.

"A redhead, boss."

"I can see that, thank you, Ziv." The quiet voice was contemptuous. Obviously coming to a decision, he said, "Bring her," and turned away as his guards stepped forward.

"Where are you taking me?" Gemma asked quickly, her voice shrill with sudden fear. "You can't do this."

The small man turned back.

"On the contrary," he said, with a cold smile. "Here I can do anything."

With that, he turned on his heels and walked away. Gemma gave up any idea of resistance as her arms were seized and held by the two burly men. They could have snapped her in half like a twig.

She was taken to one of the anonymous houses and led into an upstairs room. It was ornately decorated with silk drapes over wood paneling, and a deep red carpet. The room contained a large four-poster bed with a canopy and lace screens, a desk with a stool, and two large comfortable chairs. There were bars on the window.

Her abductors turned to leave.

"Wait!" she cried. "What do you want from me?" But the pale man had already gone and his servitors just grinned. The door closed and as Gemma heard the bolts being secured, she wished that this day had never dawned.

chapter 15

After an hour or so in the quiet house, Gemma stopped expecting her captors to reappear at any moment. She knew that hammering on the door or shouting for help from the window in this deserted area would do her no good, and instead she examined her surroundings. She had not seen such magnificent furnishings since her childhood, but there was something unhealthy about the predominantly red color scheme. It was obvious that no one actually *lived* here, yet it was designed for specific tastes. There were plenty of things that could be turned into weapons if need be—a vase, the stool—but to Gemma that only reinforced the apparent confidence of her jailers. Her examination complete, she did the only thing possible. She sat down, and waited.

———•———

When Arden returned to the tavern late that afternoon his mood was determined but tempered with a measure of jubilation. His efforts were bearing fruit at last! He ran up the stairs, taking them two at a time, and burst into the room to tell Gemma the good news.

When he realized that she was not there, his initial reaction was that she was somewhere in the tavern talking to her new friends. On investigation, however, his mood soon changed to anxiety and with it anger, as he was informed that Gemma often went out for walks alone. The maids had seen nothing harmful in that but pointed out that she had never been gone as long as this before. No one had any idea of where she was. Arden thought he knew.

———•———

"Put these on." A selection of flimsy clothes in varying shades of red was flung onto Gemma's lap. The heavily muscled man who had thrown them was the one called Ziv. "You better have them on by the time Mendle gets here," he added. "The boss don't like to be disobeyed." He withdrew, bolting the door again.

Gemma looked with distaste at the garments. They were

made of silk, and finer than anything she had ever seen, but the short skirt, skimpy blouse, and delicate underclothes would hardly cover her. She shivered, recalling Arden's tales of the city, her mind shying away from the implication of this latest turn of events.

Reluctantly she changed clothes, appreciating the touch of the silk on her skin and despising herself for it. She felt self-conscious and afraid. *Now what?* she wondered.

Gemma jumped at the sound of the bolts being drawn back once more. She stood, steeling herself for whatever was coming, ready to fight if necessary. Mendle entered, still dressed in white, and carrying a small black bag which he placed on the stool. Ziv stood guard just inside the door.

"I am glad you have decided to cooperate," Mendle said, his tone smooth. Magnified eyes looked at her approvingly.

"What do you want?" Gemma asked as aggressively as she could.

Mendle smiled, displaying perfect white teeth.

"You show spirit," he said. "Good. Your performance will be all the better for that."

"What performance?"

"My dear girl, I am sure you know that beauty such as yours has a certain *value*, especially here, where most of the women are of a darker complexion. Red hair also has a rarity value." His cold eyes continued their inspection as though he were cataloging an item of merchandise. With a shiver, Gemma realized that that was exactly what he was doing. "There are many gentlemen in this city who appreciate beautiful women," Mendle went on. "It is my professional duty—and pleasure—to maximize their appreciation."

Gemma's fingers twisted in the fabric of her blouse. *Please don't let this be happening to me!* she thought desperately.

"These gentlemen have considerable means at their disposal, of course," he continued, "and they are free to choose from among the many beautiful things that are offered to them. Hence the lovely clothes that you are wearing. I wish them to appreciate fully the value of choosing to bid for you."

"*Bid* for me?" Gemma fears made her voice strident. "You're going to *sell* me?"

"But of course . . ."

"You can't do this! You , . ." She took a step forward, her face contorted with fury. Ziv tensed and she stopped, frustrated.

"You are in luck, my dear," Mendle went on, totally unconcerned. "There is an auction this very night. With your looks, you will soon find a place in one of the most luxurious households in the city, where you will want for nothing."

"Except freedom. Except dignity," she spat.

"Meaningless trifles," he replied evenly. "What is freedom if you are in constant pain? Is dignity so important that you would rather starve?" The threat in his words was clear but Gemma was too angry to notice.

"You bastard!" she hissed.

Mendle laughed. "I do so love flattery," he remarked.

"Aren't you forgetting something?" she asked, calmer now. "You say my 'performance' at this perverted auction will be important. Well, after the performance I'm going to give, you'll be lucky to be able to *give* me away." Her words ran on, fueled by desperation, close to hysteria, but still within the bounds of rationality. "You need my cooperation. You can't force me. Your *gentlemen* won't pay for *damaged* goods— and you'd have to break every bone in my body before I agreed to be a slave."

"Tut-tut, my dear. Slave is such an *ugly* word." Mendle's gently reproving tone drove Gemma wild.

"Not as ugly as slave-*trader!*" she screamed. "I will have nothing to do with your disgusting schemes!"

Mendle's smile never faltered.

"Oh, I think you will," he said, opening his bag and taking out a small glass bottle. Gemma stared at it suspiciously as new fears leapt within her.

"I hope you're not going to be difficult about this," the pale man said earnestly. "It would be a shame not to proceed in a civilized fashion."

"Civilized?" Gemma exclaimed in disbelief.

"I do not wish to see you ill-treated in *any* way," he added, and this time the menace in his tone was chilling. He unstoppered the bottle and passed it to her. "Drink this," he said.

"What is it?"

"Something to make you relax, feel more at ease."

Gemma sniffed cautiously. The scent of the colorless liquid was instantly familiar, and she heard Arden's voice once again. *Dragonflower seeds cause vivid dreams and hallucinations. Some people use them just for that.* Reflexively, she flung the bottle from her. It shattered against the wall, filling the room with its pungent odor as the liquid ran down the paneling.

For a moment Mendle's face lost its civilized composure.

"That was foolish," he said, his voice tautly controlled. "And very expensive." He reached into the bag, taking out another bottle. "It was also quite pointless. It would be perfectly simple for Ziv and his colleagues to force you to swallow this. Even if you did not, there are other, more unpleasant methods. I had hoped you would be more sensible." Gemma glanced at Ziv, who grinned nastily.

"Well?" Mendle ordered.

Gemma extended her hand slowly and took the drug from him. *I can cope with it*, she lectured herself. *I have done so before. I can again.* She wasn't sure whether she believed herself or not, but, taking a deep breath, she tipped her head back and swallowed a little of the liquid.

"All of it," Mendle ordered.

Gemma complied. The pallid man's smile never reached his cold blue eyes. "Clear that mess up," he commanded Ziv, then turned back to Gemma.

"One last thing, my dear. Please do not attempt to escape. Ziv has been assigned to your protection and it would be unfortunate for *both* of you should you fail to appear at the auction."

Ziv was bent over, cloth in hand, and he looked up at Gemma, resentment and malice in his small eyes.

"We begin at midnight," Mendle added, "so you haven't long to wait. Should you desire any food or drink Ziv will arrange it for you. Goodbye, my dear. Until tonight."

Gemma watched him as he left the room. *What hold does he have over Ziv and the others?* she wondered. *That monster could smash him to a pulp in no time.* She looked at Ziv again and rejected the idea of appealing to his better nature. He stood up, slivers of broken glass cupped in one massive hand.

"You make any trouble for me and I *will* break every bone in your body," he promised. "And that won't be the half of it." He left without another word and Gemma heard the bolts being shot again.

Her most immediate concern was to monitor the effects of the drug on her body. So far nothing seemed to have changed. *How long do I have?* she wondered.

———•———

Arden could not understand it. The horses were still there. Gemma had no money to buy or hire another and she did not strike him as a typical horse-thief. But surely even her insane desire to go south would stop short of traveling on foot? *Damn the woman!* Arden cursed silently. *Why now? Just when I have so little time.*

He set off to contact acquaintances old and new, to see if they could help him once more.

———•———

Gemma watched the room through a haze; time had ceased to have any meaning. Her body was drained of all will and her eyes refused to focus properly. A man in white came in and gave her instructions, over and over again. Gemma could not understand anything but after a while he appeared satisfied and left. Just before he did, he clicked his fingers in front of her face. She was alert once more, and her sight was restored to normal but she could not remember anything of what he had told her.

Ziv returned, carrying a tray of food. He left it on the desk and glanced at Gemma, relieved to see that she was calm now. The drug was obviously taking effect.

"Eat if you want to," he said, his voice implying that he didn't care one way or the other. He left, securing the door once more.

Gemma had no stomach for the food, but picked up the glass of red wine which stood beside the plates. She sipped, then wondered whether this was wise on top of the dragonflower drug. Arguments broke out inside her head, but the advice she heeded was the simplest and most practical. *One glass of wine is hardly going to make much difference. It might even dilute the drug.* Besides, she had drunk nothing all day. She looked at the dark liquid. *You like red, don't you, Mendle,* she mused. *Or is it the favored color of one of your clients?* Amused in spite of her situation, she drank. The same practical reasoning made her consume the meal as well. She ate mechanically, tasting nothing.

All the while, she analyzed the changes taking place within her. Her brain was now functioning on several different levels, which should have been confusing, but she became adept at keeping each train of thought clear, separate, and direct. She was aware that her anger had gone, the thought of the night to come no longer filled her with dread, and she knew vaguely that this was not as it should be. However, it was too

comfortable a feeling to be abandoned. She was almost looking forward to her "performance," while at the same time a
small quiet voice told her things she didn't want to know. *My
movements are not affected,* she thought and proved it by
replacing her glass precisely in the circular stain it had left on
the tray. She stood up and turned a cartwheel, ending up
beside the bed. She fell back on it, laughing: she could put
on quite a show!

There is nowhere in these clothes to conceal a weapon, the
quiet voice insisted. A weapon? Why should she need a
weapon? *Remember the route to the auction,* her other self
instructed sternly.

Yet another part of her mind was daydreaming of the past,
the future, a mingling of times which seemed quite logical.
Smiling faces flashed before her: Arden, Zana, Keran, her
long-dead father, a soldier, an old man with one good eye,
Mendle, others she did not recognize, Cai. *Cai.*

Cai was not smiling. His green eyes were wide with fear,
or anger, she could not tell which.

Why aren't you happy? she pleaded, icy fingers clutching
at her heart. She resented his disruptive presence.

And then he was gone, replaced by others, and Gemma's
own smile returned. She lay on her back looking up at the
canopy over the bed, suddenly fascinated by its embroidered
design of two serpents, intertwined. What were they doing?
Fighting? Wrestling? Making love? Gemma giggled, and the
dragon-snakes began to move. Yellow eyes flashed, scales
glinted, nostrils spouted flame. She shut her eyes, suddenly
dizzy and nauseous. The pandemonium in her head subsided
slowly, and she carefully opened her eyes again: the serpents
were still, each stitch distinct but unmoving.

And beneath all this, unknown ideas stirred, began to
coalesce into something strange and mercurial, which she
could not grasp. She sensed its potential but not its power.
Waiting.

chapter 16

Gemma was waiting when they returned for her, some sixth sense having told her that midnight was approaching. She stood, bathed in soft lamplight, in the center of the room as the door opened. Mendle looked at her appreciatively.

"Like a rose," he said. "A red rose."

Gemma smiled. *Without his eyeglasses he would be quite helpless,* the small voice commented.

"Let me escort you," Mendle said. Gemma stepped forward and took his proffered arm, appreciating his courtesy. Another small, impotent part of her raged at the hypocrisy of the man who had locked her up, dressed her like a whore, and now was treating her like royalty. When the irony of this thought struck her she laughed, and Mendle glanced at her as they walked along the corridor, Ziv falling into step behind them.

"I am glad to see you are in a good mood," he said.

There were several Gemmas walking beside him, and they all considered his statement. Her reply was an amalgam of their conclusions.

"What choice do I have? I'm glad you chose to collect me yourself."

"It is a pleasure," he responded. "You are my star attraction, after all."

"Me?" Gemma was flattered, confused, and revolted all at the same time, but only surprise showed in her face. "I don't know what to do. You must show me."

"No one can teach you that," he said. "Least of all me. I have no beauty of my own. That is a natural thing. Those who have it—like yourself—have no need of teaching. Merely *be* yourself. All men with eyes to see will know and appreciate your true value."

And pay you for it, Gemma thought cynically. At the same time she said, "What a pretty speech." And meant it. *I can't even agree with myself!* She laughed and Mendle joined in, but behind the gaiety Gemma had made an important discov-

ery. Her anger was returning. What did this mean? The
effect of the dragonflower potion could not be wearing off so
soon. Was she at last able to control it? Or was something
else changing within her? Coils of thought spun inside her
head, sending her messages she could not understand. *It's all
nonsense*, she decided, pushing them aside. *Let me think!*

She forced herself to remain outwardly happy and calm as
they walked on, down seemingly endless corridors. There
was no hope of her ever remembering this route as it twisted
and turned, ran up and down, through buildings and under
ground. *This is his kingdom*, Gemma thought. *Here he can
do anything*. Fear was also making its return.

Eventually, they came to a plain, white-painted door.

"You will wait in here," Mendle said, making it sound like
a privilege. "Ziv will show you the way when you are called."

Gemma let the complaint part of her rise to the surface.
She nodded and smiled as Ziv ushered her inside. Five other
captives sat on wooden chairs, each with a guardian behind
them. The women turned to look at the newcomer, their
expressions pleasant but only mildly curious. They made
Gemma feel ill. The men, all the size of Ziv, looked at her
rather differently. Resentment, contempt, lust, and envy were
mixed in various proportions.

No help there, the quiet voice decided.

She took her place on the last remaining chair and Ziv
stood at her shoulder. No one spoke. A gong sounded in the
distance and one of the women stood up and left, followed by
her protector. Her smile betrayed no emotion. *Are they all
drugged?* Gemma wondered.

One by one the others were summoned until only one girl
was left with Gemma. She was small and dark, much younger
than the others. Her face was pretty, with clear, unblemished
skin and large brown eyes, but her smile was false and her
eyes had no life in them. The gong boomed once more and
she was led away.

"What happens now?" Gemma asked.

For an instant, Ziv looked surprised, then he grinned.

"You want to see?" he asked. "Come on then—you can
watch from the side."

As she stood, dark clouds of unreason swirled again inside
her head. Ziv regarded her closely.

"You all right?" he asked.

"Yes." *No. I don't know.* "I feel so far away."

He laughed, a cruel glint in his eyes. "You won't for long," he said. "Come the morning, you'll know *exactly* where you are." He opened the door. "Now move—or you'll miss all the fun."

They walked down yet another corridor, toward the hum of many voices, shouts, the clink of glasses. Ziv halted and Gemma found herself in the wings of a well-lit stage on which Mendle was standing at a podium. Beside him, the last young girl stood quietly. Mendle was exhorting the unseen audience to take note of her fine appearance, health, and grace, listing her accomplishments in the arts of the bedroom and in the skills of the kitchen. The former seemed to excite the most interest, judging by the rise in the level of noise. Gemma blushed for her sake but the girl seemed unconcerned and Gemma recalled with horror that it was her own turn next.

Mendle turned to the girl.

"Well, Elyse, what else can you tell these gentlemen about yourself? I am sure you will be more eloquent than I." He smiled encouragingly, his magnified eyes glinting in the stage lamps. Elyse blinked, then began to speak.

"I am young but not without experience." The words came out as if by rote, the overrehearsed speech of an untalented actress. *Surely they can tell it's false,* Gamma thought as Elyse droned on. *Maybe they don't want to.* Another idea occurred, even more sickening than the first. *Maybe they don't need to.* If she was drugged now, and cooperative . . .

Gemma's mind shied away from the images it had itself created, from the possibility that anyone could be kept in such a state permanently. She would do *anything* to avoid such a fate.

Anything?

She turned to look at Ziv. The movement brought unbalancing coils of black swirling back into her consciousness and she gasped, desperate to keep from sinking into it. Her guard was too intent on the proceedings on stage and did not notice. His eyes were rapt, his face covered with a film of sweat.

"This is where the *real* fun starts," he said quietly.

Gemma turned slowly back to face the stage. Elyse had stopped speaking, having exhausted the intimate details of her talents.

"Gentlemen," Mendle announced. "We will waste no more of your valuable time. The final bidding will now begin."

There were a few shouts of dissent from the audience but they were quickly hushed.

"He'll sometimes auction parts of their clothing first," Ziv explained in a whisper. He seemed disappointed.

"Shall we start at two hundred?" Mendle continued. "Thank you, sir."

The bidding went briskly at first, and each time it showed any signs of flagging, Mendle made further lubricious comments about Elyse's desirability. He was a slick and persuasive salesman. When he finally cried, "Sold!" and banged his palm down on the podium, the price had reached 655 marks, more than most men in Newport would earn in five years. Elyse's guard led her off the far side of the stage to make arrangements with her new owner. *Come morning you'll know* exactly *where you are*, Gemma thought, and shuddered. The gong boomed again, sounding far louder now. A fire started behind Gemma's eyes.

"At last we have come to the moment you've all been waiting for." Mendle glowed with pleasure. "This is a very special occasion, as I promised you, because tonight you have a unique opportunity, never before offered on this continent." He paused for effect. "The opportunity to purchase a white witch from the northern isles."

There was a moment's silence, followed by a low murmur of surprise; Mendle had their full attention now.

The fire grew, sending smoke and flame billowing in her mind. *He's talking about me?*

"She is beautiful," the auctioneer continued. "Pale complexion, hair of flame, her body . . ."

"Where is she then?" shouted an eager voice, thick with drink.

"Patience, gentlemen. As you will see—quite soon—she has all the physical attributes any man could desire, but that is but a tenth of her real worth. For she has secrets, forces which are beyond even *my* powers of description. The man who harnesses them will be truly blessed.

"Until now, it was only myth. The mysteries of the long-lost northern isles were introduced to us by the voyagers, but most of them were unreliable, madmen who died or fled from us before we could learn more than half-truths. Yet we know that their goddesses come to earth as radiant women, flame-haired witches who can take a man beyond the known peaks of experience by the subtle application of their erotic expertise."

Mendle was enjoying himself, as if the words themselves gave him pleasure. His pale face glowed with perspiration and his eyes shone brighter than the many lamps that lit him from above and below.

Gemma's mind surrendered to the blaze. *How can he expect me to live up to this billing?* she wondered, then thought no more.

"Gentlemen, I give you the northern rose!" Mendle spread his arms as if in welcome.

"Go!" Ziv urged. "Don't be surprised by anything." He gave her a push, but she had no need of it. Her body was moving of its own accord. There was nothing she could do to control it. She walked lightly, hips swaying, a smile upon her lips; within, she was in turmoil.

The blackness had taken hold of her like an animal, swallowing the fire and plunging her into swirling depths of madness. Yet her body remained a puppet, with Mendle holding the strings. One tiny part of her remained alert, observing all, yet could take no active part in the proceedings.

Her progress was marked by murmuring, gasps, and appreciative whistles from the audience. She saw a dimly-lit hall beyond the stage lamps, groups of men sitting round drink-filled tables, with others standing further back in the shadows. Smoke added to the gloom.

Gemma reached a white cross painted on the boards and stopped without thinking. She turned to face the audience and curtseyed formally. *Why am I doing this?* Straightening up again, she spread her arms wide in a dramatic gesture, flinging her head back. As she did so, flames, blue and green, billowed from the stage about her. *Don't be surprised by anything.*

There were shouts, even screams, of surprise. Then the flames disappeared and Gemma returned to a normal stance, facing the audience in the sudden stillness.

The dark coils were still moving within her head, interweaving, joining, dividing. Learning. Sparks of light invaded the blackness.

This is all fake! Gemma fumed. *Surely they can't be taken in by this trickery.*

She heard a voice and realized with horror that it was her own.

"You have seen!" she cried. "Who would wish to control

this power? The man who does so shall want for nothing." *I didn't say that! Where is this coming from?*

"The witch craves a master," Mendle announced dramatically. As the words were spoken, Gemma knelt down and bowed her head to the floor. She hated herself for the self-abasement of the act, but her body was dancing to another's tune.

She stood up again and the movement made the black eddies boil in her head with ever greater energy. Flashes of color invaded the dark.

"Speak, Rose," Mendle instructed. "Tell these honored guests of your talents." She hesitated. *He knows what I'm going to say!* Her lips began to open of their own volition, and rage leapt into the small part of her mind still capable of rational thought. *How?* But her traitorous tongue was stilled by a shout from the audience.

"No need for this. Let the bidding begin!"

There was a chorus of agreement. They were impatient. Mendle clicked his fingers and Gemma's need to speak subsided. He surveyed the crowd, the self-satisfied smile on his face telling its own story.

"Very well," he said slowly, rolling the words out. "Shall we began at—"

"One thousand!" called a voice from the hidden recesses at the rear.

For a moment, even Mendle looked shocked. Whispers of amazement and resentment ran round the hall, as those nearer the stage craned to see who had made the outrageous bid. Mendle, ever the professional, was the first to recover his poise.

"Thank you, sir," he called, "but surely for such a unique item that is hardly sufficient. Do I hear eleven hundred?" A few whispers followed, but there were no further bids. "Perhaps, Rose, you could demonstrate—" He was interrupted.

"Eleven hundred," a tentative voice called.

"Twelve hundred." Another, deeper voice.

"Twelve hundred and fifty," the first cried, more surely this time.

Mendle was in a state of glorified bliss, pointing to each of the bidders in turn. He was about to speak when the original bidder cut him short.

"Two thousand."

Again the hall was silenced. Greed battled with Mendle's innate business acumen. Good sense told him that this offer was too good to refuse. But perhaps the madness which had afflicted his patrons might be milked for even greater sums. Greed won.

"Speak, Rose," he said and once again Gemma felt the compulsion to talk . . . but this time, it was different.

As the auction had progressed, Gemma had fought her own battle. After resisting for so long, she had finally succumbed to the black coils, sinking into them with relief, not caring, abandoning her mind as her body had abandoned her. She had lost.

And won. On the far side of the darkness, deep within its labyrinthine pattern, there was light. Knowledge. Understanding. Something had awoken within her and now it was alive, ready to spring forth into the world. Gemma felt complete, more real than she ever had. She was no longer afraid. But she was *very* angry.

"Mendle is right!" she said, her voice quiet but ringing with conviction. "Two thousand is too poor a price for me." She smiled as she saw Mendle start, then beckon to the side of the stage. *That wasn't was I was supposed to say.* "I am *beyond* price," she added emphatically.

Ziv and two other lackeys were striding quickly toward her. As she turned to face them, they stopped in their tracks, eyes wide with terror. The witch they had created was real.

"This repulsive charade is *over!*" Gemma shouted, feeling the new strength within her. *How simple,* she thought. *Why couldn't I see it for myself?*

Mendle leapt at her from his podium, but she swept him aside with one hand. His eyeglasses spun away and smashed.

"Over!" she cried, and struck.

Every lamp on and above the stage exploded. Glass shattered, darkness fluttered, then the light returned as oil roared into flame. Real flame. Pandemonium broke out all around her. There was panic in the hall as everyone rushed for the exits. On stage the musclemen had fled, leaving Mendle stumbling around, half-blind, screaming obscenities. Gemma watched him for a moment then walked, untouched, through the flames and off the stage.

She soon found a way out into the clean, narrow streets and set off purposefully.

Cai was wrong! she thought jubilantly. *Magic still exists. And now I know how to find it!*

An hour later she was back in her room at the tavern.

chapter 17

Far to the north, in a very different bedroom, a man shifted restlessly in his sleep. Cai had often been troubled in recent years by strange dreams; he was haunted by the past and relived certain tragic events over and over again. By day he was the same outwardly happy man that all at court knew and loved. But by night he was a wizard again, no matter how strenuously he tried to deny it.

His dreams had gotten worse after Gemma had run away, although her disappearance had been less of a shock to him than it had to any of the others, even her brother Keran, who ruled their island home. She had at least revealed to Cai a little of her hopes and desires—perhaps because of this her desertion hurt him all the more. Although they had sometimes argued, he had been her friend, her best friend. Cai had never thought she would actually leave. The farewell note she had left had been addressed to Keran, not himself, but Cai still had every fateful word etched on his brain.

Gemma and Cai had spent much of their time together, and were often mistaken for lovers. Despite the fact that he was more than twice her age, Cai still had the handsome face and lithe body of a twenty-year-old. The wizard had not aged in two decades and despised himself all the more because of it. When Gemma left, he saw it as further proof of his failure and spent more and more time alone, unable to take comfort in the continued admiration of beautiful young women as he had done in earlier years.

Nothing in his life made sense any more. And still the nightmares plagued him.

But this dream was different . . .

There was a knock at the door. Cai sat up in bed.

"How long do I have?" he heard a faint voice ask from far away.

The door opened and Gemma walked in. Her pale limbs contrasted sharply with her short black tunic.

"You like black, don't you, Cai." Her hands moved deftly,

like a conjuror. "There is no room in these clothes to conceal a weapon," *she said, drawing forth a rose. A red rose.*

For a moment, he saw a vision of serpents coupling. The image seemed blasphemous after the sign of love she had just shown him.

"Why aren't you happy?" she asked.

He started to protest, then stopped. Gemma laughed but there was an alien glint of cruelty in her eyes.

"I am glad to see you," he said simply.

"I'm glad you chose to see me," she replied.

"You are . . . important to me," he said, cursing his inability to say "I love you."

"Me?" Gemma's eyes were wide. "I don't know what to do. You must teach me." Her appeal touched Cai's heart, but still he could not respond.

"No one can teach you that. Least of all me. I have no magic of my own." He felt weary—he had made this speech so many times before. "Be yourself."

Gemma appeared confused.

"This is your kingdom," she said. "Here you can do anything."

Dark swirls of night began to fill the room. Gemma glanced around. "No help here," she decided.

Cai started to tremble inside. He could not move.

"Are you all right?" he asked anxiously.

"Yes. No. I don't know. I feel so far away." Gemma's face mirrored her hopeless indecison.

The dream-scene shifted. Gemma now marched upon the spot, her limbs jerking, moving unnaturally.

"Why am I doing this?" she pleaded. Then her face changed, becoming blank, expressionless. "Who would wish to control this power?" she asked, her voice a monotone. "The man who does shall want for nothing."

Now Gemma was drowning in the darkness that filled the room. Then stars pierced the void.

"Speak, Gemma!" Cai cried.

Light flooded the room and he was suddenly, terribly, afraid. He had tried to protect her, to tell her the truth, but now she was too powerful. And free.

"I am beyond your help," she said. "It's over."

He felt her grasp the knowledge then, the knowledge he had denied and hidden for so long. He had no power to stop her; instead, his weakness became a gift to her, the only thing he had left to give.

"How simple!" she exclaimed delightedly. "Why couldn't I see it for myself?"

Suddenly, the room was plunged into utter blackness, but this time it was as still as the grave. Panic exploded within Cai.

He was blind, alone, helpless. She had abandoned him.

A fading voice said, "You were wrong. Magic still exists. And now . . ." It trailed away into silence.

Cai awoke with tears in his eyes. They were from the dream. The ones that followed were from his heart.

chapter 18

Arden reached the tavern in the gray hour just before dawn which Gemma had called the wolfing hour. She was asleep when he came in, still dressed in her brief red costume. No one at the tavern had known where Arden had gone, so she thought it best to stay where she was. After two hours she had dozed off, her ecstatic mood defeated by exhaustion.

She woke up when he entered their room and looked at him, bleary-eyed triumph in her smile. Arden stood, hands on hips, just inside the door. Relief, anger, and curiosity were reflected in quick succession on his face.

"Where have you *been*?" He shook his head. "And *where* did you get that outfit?"

"Don't you like it?" she teased.

"Gods," he replied. "You look like a . . . you look quite wonderful." He strode over to the bed, pulled her to her feet, and held her close. Gemma returned his embrace, touched and uplifted by his show of affection. They drew apart, both full of questions, and it was Arden who spoke first, breaking the spell.

"You have a lot of explaining to do," he said sternly.

"More than you could ever guess," she replied.

And so she told her story. Arden refrained from comment until near the end, when Gemma related her method of bringing the auction to an end.

"It was as though someone had been trying to tell me something all along, and I just hadn't heard him . . . no, that's not right." She paused, thinking. "In any case, I suddenly realized that I was capable of magic! Me! I smashed every one of those lamps with my mind."

"Oh, come on!" Arden exclaimed. "Not that old joke again."

"It's true. I swear it. They all exploded."

"Perhaps they did," Arden said. "The reports I've heard all say that it was quite a fire, but you can't expect me to believe . . ."

"It's true!" Gemma repeated. "I focused on them and *made*

it happen. There's so much in our minds we know nothing about, that we should be able to harness." She was in deadly earnest, but Arden remained sceptical. "Oh, I wish I could *show* you," she said in exasperation.

"Perhaps you can," he said quietly. "Make that lamp explode." He indicated the lantern hanging on their wall.

"I can't," she retorted. "It would set fire to the room."

"Do it!" he demanded.

"No."

"Then don't try to tell me—"

"All right!" she shot back. "Just don't blame me . . ."

She concentrated, trying hard to recapture the feeling of her earlier adventure, but it evaded her; the darkness revealed no secrets. Tears of frustration welled in her eyes. "I can't," she said eventually in a small voice.

Arden put an arm around her, and when he spoke his tone was gentle and reassuring.

"Gemma, you've been through an awful lot, and I'm proud of you. Your ability to survive even the most foolhardy escapades is nothing short of amazing. You've just been kidnapped by the most dangerous man in the city, drugged, hypnotized, and almost sold to a wealthy maniac, *and* you've walked away unscathed. Shouldn't that be enough for you? Not one person in a thousand could do what you have."

"Why don't you believe me?" she asked plaintively.

"The flames they rigged to make the clients think you were a witch probably went wrong," Arden replied. "With all that *stuff* in your blood, it's not surprising you imagined such crazy things."

"No—" she began.

"That's enough!" he snapped, his temper fraying. "I've been up all night looking for you and now I need some rest."

Gemma was quiet. *I'll show you,* she thought. *One day.* But now her mind had caught on something Arden had said. *The most dangerous man in the city?*

"Who *is* Mendle?" she asked.

"Let's hope it's who *was*," he replied. "Apparently, he was very badly burned—it's not certain whether he'll live or not. I sincerely hope he doesn't."

"Why?"

"Mendle is Great Newport's purveyor of niceties to the very rich," Arden said caustically. "Drugs, women, violence, all things unnatural—the decadent essentials of the high life.

The Guild may rule the city but Mendle rules the Guild, and there isn't a member of it who isn't in debt to him."

"Oh," Gemma said, the implications of this sinking in.

"Oh indeed," Arden said. "If he lives, you've made a very powerful enemy, Gemma. You'll have to stay right out of sight until we can get away."

Gemma considered this, then another thought struck her. "He hypnotized me?"

"It certainly sounds like it. Some of his words were triggers to make you do certain things. That's why you had no control."

"He could have made me do *anything*." She was aghast.

"Don't worry now," Arden said. "You're safe here, and we'll soon be leaving this accursed city."

Gemma looked at him questioningly.

"There's a preliminary hearing at a subsidiary court, and the valley's case is to be heard," he said, happy to be imparting his own news.

"When?"

"Tomorrow," he said, then looked at the lightening window. "Today," he amended. "I have to be in court very soon."

———•———

As it turned out, the court hearings were not held that day—nor the next. The fire in the White Quarter, as Mendle's district was called, had claimed several victims, among them men of influence in the city. As the Guild members also acted as Newport's judiciary, the whole legal system was in a state of some confusion. This was then compounded by the events of the next day.

At mid-morning, when Arden, in common with dozens of other frustrated plaintiffs, was trying to find out what was happening to their cases, the city came under attack from a number of skyravens. Reports varied from six to a hundred, and as the massive birds roared overhead, buildings beneath them exploded into piles of smoking rubble. Panic ensued, and it was some time before the Guild's militia could bring the situation under control. By then, rumors were flying thick and fast—with everything from witchcraft to volcanic eruptions being blamed for the fires. Most of these stories were patently absurd, but one tale which refused to go away told how several of the metal skyravens had landed on the level ground to the south of the city, where they had been met by a party from Newport. This group included an unknown person or persons in a carriage. The skyravens had then flown away again.

None of those who had supposedly met the ravens had been identified—it was believed that they had not returned to the city; some even thought that they had been carried off by the metal birds. Amid all this vivid speculation, one clear fact did emerge.

Whether he was dead or alive, Mendle was no longer in Newport.

————•————

Three days later, the Guild had come to terms with the new situation. Lunkett for one had used the turmoil to strengthen his hold on the reins of power, and was anxious to demonstrate his authority. In order to try and restore at least a semblance of normality, he ordered that court proceedings resume immediately. After cooling his heels for so long, Arden at last felt confident that he would get a chance to be heard. The open session was to begin tomorrow morning.

During all this time, Gemma had remained in her room. Arden had thought of moving, but decided against it—in the confused darkness it was unlikely that anyone had witnessed her return to the tavern, and she would be safer staying where she was. Frightened, and with much to think about, Gemma had accepted this, but now longed to be able to see the trial and tried to coax Arden into letting her attend.

"Where will it be held?" she asked.

"Colosseum Square."

"Outdoors? Is that why it's called an open session?"

"Not really," Arden replied. "It's so that as many people as possible can come to listen and pass their own judgment."

"That doesn't sound very practical."

"It's a tradition here. All the competitors get the chance to speak, not only to the judges but also to the crowd. That way, when the Guildmen make the trial-award to the winner, they can make sure it has popular approval."

"Just a moment," Gemma said. "Why are you called competitors? And what is a trial-award? Isn't this supposed to be a court of law?"

Arden smiled at her puzzled expression.

"Of course it is," he said. "But it's only a preliminary hearing to decide which case is taken to the Guild Court. *That's* where we'll get something done—but we have to be awarded the trial first."

"What a system!" she exclaimed.

"There are worse," he replied seriously.

"How many other contestants will there be?"

"Three."

"And what happens if we lose?" she asked quietly, careful to use the plural pronoun.

"We go home," Arden said flatly.

They looked at each other, then smiled.

"Where's that then?" Gemma asked.

"Anywhere but here," he replied, laughing. "But we won't lose. Have you no faith in me?"

"You know I have. Can I come and lend you moral support?" she asked quickly, taking advantage of his good humor. He shook his head, but before he had the chance to speak, Gemma went on in a rush. "I could disguise myself in men's clothes, cover my hair so no one could see it, even darken my skin. No one's going to be looking for me now that Mendle's gone."

Arden saw the eagerness in her eyes. *She's crazy, this woman*, he thought. It was almost a compliment. Still he said nothing.

"Please," she added.

"Show me what you'll look like," he said at last. "Then we'll decide." He paused and her sudden jubilation was stilled by his next words. "But, Gemma, whatever we decide, don't think you're safe. Mendle may be gone but someone will take his place. It's too good an opening to miss," he added cynically. "And too many people know about you now, and how valuable you are. Half of them think you *are* a witch."

This was still a sore point between them. Gemma was still convinced that magic had been responsible for her escape, but Arden would have none of it.

"And you don't, I know," she said.

"No," he replied lightly. "But you *are* a survivor. If your disguise is good enough, you can come to witness my performance."

Gemma winced at his use of the word, but pushed her memories aside with a determined effort.

"Give me an hour then," she said.

"All right. I'll come back when I've had a couple of drinks."

He left the room. Gemma listened to his footsteps going down the stairs, then set to work.

———————•———————

Arden bought himself a half measure of ale and sat at a corner table, thinking about what he was going to say at the hearing. The half-empty bar remained quiet and Arden was so deep in thought that he did not notice the stranger approach.

"You have the look of a traveling man, sir. May I join you and ask your opinion of some strange sights I have seen?"

Arden, still preoccupied, nodded absently.

"Thank you, sir. My name is Jordan." The stranger extended his hand and Arden shook it in greeting, looking at the newcomer properly for the first time. The man was tall and broad-shouldered, and dressed in traveler's garb. His skin was so dark that it was almost black and his short hair was tightly curled.

"Mine is Arden."

"Well met, Arden. Would you care for another drink?" Without waiting for an answer Jordan hailed the bartender and ordered ale for both of them. Turning back, he said, "What have you seen of the changes in the world?"

Arden did not know what to make of this question and began to wonder if he was keeping company with a madman. Jordan's eyes were intense but he did not look like a fanatic. Arden said nothing but this did not disconcert his companion.

"I've seen them ever since The Leveling," he went on, "but few have taken any notice. Nothing can be relied upon any more— not even the Earth itself! And it's getting worse!"

"What do you mean?" Arden asked reluctantly. He was already beginning to regret the encounter and wondered how soon he could make his excuses and leave.

"Take the weather," Jordan replied. "The seasons mean hardly anything now. Ask the farmers, they know. Why, I saw a thick bank of fog in the middle of the desert last month. My horses wouldn't even take me close.

"And then there are the boundaries, of course. Why is it that we see the land differently, depending on which side we stand?"

"The elementals—" Arden began.

"Yes," Jordan interrupted eagerly. "People say they're playing tricks on us. But why? What for? Their numbers are increasing too—I've seen places where it's almost like a solid blue wall."

Jordan continued in this fashion for some time, detailing peculiarities of landscape, light, and atmosphere, all of which he claimed to have witnessed. He posed many questions but gave his captive audience no chance to answer. Arden grew bored, only half listening to the monologue, and tried to turn his mind back to the morrow. Eventually, he realized that he was not the only one listening to Jordan. Looking up from his glass, he saw a slim young man whose swarthy complexion and rough clothing told of an outdoor life. Wisps of dark hair protruded from beneath his leather skullcap. When he spoke, his voice was thickly accented with the tones of the mountain village region.

"Your tales touch me, sir. Can I join you to 'ear more?"

Jordan looked round. "Of course, of course. Bartender!"

The young man, who introduced himself as Pazia, sat down and Arden was relieved. Now he would be able to slip away.

Pazia proved to be a more attentive audience and Jordan was soon addressing most of his remarks to him. The newcomer managed to interrupt the flow of words with a few questions of his own, and his curiosity seemed boundless, especially concerning the elementals and the increased activity of the skyravens. Jordan said they were yet another sign of the world's disintegration.

"They flew over the city a few days back," Pazia said. "Houses exploded."

"You see!" Jordan said. "The whole world is going insane."

"There are wilder tales too," Pazia put in.

"Yes," Jordan exclaimed. "I've heard . . ."

Arden's head was throbbing and he could take no more. He made to stand and said, "I must leave now. Thank you for the drink, Jordan."

"Don't go," Pazia said, a faint note of pleading in his voice. "This is interesting."

"I must. I'm . . . I'm meeting someone," Arden replied, realizing it was true. His hour must be up by now. "Goodbye."

The other two watched as he strode across to the stairs. He climbed them two at a time and burst into the room. It was empty.

"Oh no," he groaned. "Not again."

Turning on his heels, he was about to go downstairs again when a man blocked his path. Pazia placed a hand on his chest and shoved him back into the room, then followed and shut the door behind them. Before Arden could react, Pazia reached up and pulled off his headgear. Underneath were Gemma's fiery locks.

"I wanted to stay and listen!" she said.

chapter 19

When Gemma arrived, Colosseum Square was already crowded, a colorful arena in the bright morning sun. Arden had admitted, albeit with some reluctance, that her disguise as Pazia was effective, and he had been forced to agree to her attending the trial.

The buildings which surrounded the square were all built of a pale brown stone and gave off an air of importance—it was here that most of the Guild's business was undertaken. Although Arden had told Gemma what to expect, she was nonetheless impressed by the monumental Judges' Seat, which stood at the center of the northern side of the square; it was also built of the same light-colored stone and rose imposingly above the arena. At its midpoint was a single stone bench, with room enough for up to seven judges to sit. In front of the bench was a stone table and, to each side of it, the platforms from which petitioners could address both the adjudicators above and the crowd below.

After days of confinement, Gemma reveled in her freedom, threading her way through the crowd, drinking in the sights and sounds. All manner of street trading was taking place around her and the atmosphere was expectant, almost celebratory; the public trials were clearly festive events in Newport. This feeling was reinforced when she saw several professional gamblers laying odds on the result of the hearing and taking wagers from eager spectators. Gemma found their trade distasteful, especially when she learned that the odds favored two of the other contestants more heavily than Arden. As she watched the gamblers, she found herself the recipient of several suspicious looks, and hurried away to find a good vantage point. Having done so, she bought a fruit pie from a passing seller and waited, munching thoughtfully.

She wished that Arden had allowed her more time to talk to Jordan. By the time she had been able to return to the bar, the black man had left, presumably in search of a more appreciative audience. His tales had both intrigued and frightened Gemma; she felt that the strange events he described were somehow connected with her own quest to the far south. However, Arden would have none of her theory, and insisted that Jordan was just one of the many lunatics in this accursed city.

"You'll probably get more of that nonsense at the hearing," he had said. "There's usually at least one madman in any four." When Gemma pressed him, he refused to elaborate, saying only that he needed time to think in peace and to rest. Gemma had reluctantly granted his wish; she herself had not been able to sleep for some hours.

I'll find out now, she thought as the crowd hushed.

A herald, dressed in the livery of a Guild official, stepped onto the dais, followed by two servants carrying a large pair of metal scales. They placed this on the stone table, then withdrew. The herald called out in a voice which was clear and commanding, but his manner implied that the sooner this unimportant ritual was over, the better.

"Draw near all who would seek justice! By the grace of Lord Lunkett and by the power of the Guild of Great Newport, it is hereby decreed that the Justices Quillan, Medora, Warmond, Zared, and Mayer will preside. Draw near! The scales will render justice."

With that he drew back and five judges, dressed in ceremonial robes, filed up the steps to their seats. As they did so, the crowd applauded and whistled; two of the judges smiled and waved back, although the other three remained solemn. As each sat down they placed a curiously shaped stone on the table in front of them. Gemma could not see exactly what they were but soon forgot them as, at a signal from one of the judges, the first two competitors were shown on to the platforms. The noise in the square subsided and the first speaker was given the signal to begin.

From his clothes, Gemma took him to be a sailor and, to judge by his obvious apprehension, one who was little used to city ways. He began hesitantly, mumbling into his beard until requested by one of the judges to speak up. Turning to the bench, he started again.

"My lords, I am but a simple fisherman."

"We can see that!" someone shouted from the crowd, and there was a ripple of laughter. Gemma expected this interruption to further cow the fisherman but found that she had misjudged him. As he competed to be heard, his voice became firmer and his resolve stiffened. Looking alternately at the judges and the spectators, he spoke with genuine passion.

"Aye, a fisherman, and none the worse for that. All in my village are so."

"Our noses have already told us that!" a heckler cried. The contestant went on unabashed, almost shouting now to compete with the commotion all around him.

"But disaster has come to us. We cannot feed our young ones any more. The fish have deserted us!"

This brought a further outbreak of laughter, but Gemma saw that he would not be stopped.

"Why?" the man cried. "Because of the accursed island, that's why. One day it's there, then the next it's gone! It's unnatural and must be stopped!" he roared, then made an obvious effort to calm down. As he turned to the judges, the crowd hummed with interest. This was getting interesting. Quite a few people now had money resting on the fisherman's performance.

"My lords, there is an island a league off the coast at my village. We have spent many years charting the waterways and currents about it, and have always treated the islanders fair. Now they repay us with treachery."

"How so?" the nearest judge asked.

"There's mischief afoot. The gods be my witness—it is *sorcery!*" The noise level rose at his pronouncement and Gemma looked on with renewed interest. "What else *can* it be? The island disappears some days so that you can sail right through it in open water, and the next it is there again exactly as before."

"What proof have you of this?"

"The proof of my own eyes and those of all in my village. Boats and sailing are our life. We cannot be mistaken. And that's not all. Sometimes the island does not disappear entirely. Sometimes there are long shingle strands which reach up out of the sea, knife-sharp, for leagues on end, so that our boats are barred from going where they will. Some have been wrecked, some left to founder far out at sea, cut off from port and home. A few of our men refuse to go out any more. And the fish have deserted us."

"Can't really blame them!" a jester yelled.

"We're good people," the fisherman went on. "We've always paid our taxes, poor though we are. Our catch has graced many a table in this city. All we ask is justice!"

"What then is your petition?" another judge asked.

"That the Guild send forces to destroy the menace of the island and return our lives and our world to normality," the plaintiff replied. "We have tried talking to the islanders, but they will not see sense, and only laugh at us in our misery. They are in the thrall of sorcery and must be destroyed before they destroy us all."

As the fisherman's oration drew to a close, he was rewarded by shouts and whistles, stamping and clapping. The crowd approved. They were definitely getting their money's worth today. Gemma wondered if she was alone in feeling a coldness in her stomach at his words. *It's just a game to them*, she thought. *Can't they see the tragedy behind these charades?* She was not sure whether to believe the man's talk, but it was obvious that his distress was very real.

The crowd's attention now turned to the second contestant, who was dressed in baker's clothes and was already sweating in the sunlight. There was a wild look in his eyes.

He began well enough, introducing himself as the ritual demanded and then explaining his background. His business, he told them, had been destroyed by the skyravens' attack, leaving him destitute. As he went on, his voice became less sure and he began to jumble his words. The crowd became restless, taunting him, until the baker became increasingly desperate and made the mistake of advancing his own theories about the attack.

"The skyravens and the gray raiders are the same enemy!" he cried. This was greeted with howls of derision. Everyone knew that the skyravens often scared the gray outlaws away.

"It's true!" he screamed. "At first only outlanders were attacked . . ." More noisy ridicule was heaped on to him. "That was all right . . ."

Thanks, Gemma thought, beginning to feel some sympathy with the baker's persecutors.

". . . but now we are *all* in danger, as my fate proves."

"What then is your petition?" the judge asked formally.

"We must build a huge shelter," the baker replied eagerly. "An enormous dome to cover the whole city, so that the skyravens cannot see us or destroy our homes. See here, I have the plans already drawn up . . ." He fumbled in his pockets, oblivious to the uproarious laughter and outright scorn provoked by his suggestion.

The judge nearest to him waved the plans away. "That is

for the Guild Court to study," he said, "should you get so far." He smiled as the crowd reacted to his words.

The decision was obviously a foregone conclusion, but Gemma still found the process fascinating. One by one the judges stepped forward, picked up the carven stone objects from the table and placed them in one of the pans on the scales. Four went on the fisherman's side and the scales tipped decisively in his favor. He smiled and waved as he went down the steps.

She had no time for further speculation because the next competitors were already climbing the steps to their respective podiums. Gemma felt her stomach clench at the sight of Arden—he seemed so small in front of this multitude. Would they laugh him off as they had the mad baker? She glanced at Arden's opponent and was startled to see him dressed in flowing blue robes. Then Arden began speaking and she turned back to him.

"My name is Arden. I have no home." His voice was deep and resonant, and there was a murmur of appreciation from the throng. "My lords, friends, I come before you to plead for a valley in the mountains far to the southeast. No, do not turn away! Though it is remote, the valley holds significance for us all. It is a place of magic."

Gemma's eyes widened. Such was her consternation that her brain refused to form coherent thoughts. She could do no more than watch and listen. Arden continued, the conviction in his words ringing about the square.

"It is a place so wonderful that I feel myself unworthy of living there, and can only visit when the valley itself allows me to."

The crowd muttered. This was unlike anything they had heard before. No one chose to heckle.

"And yet this valley needs your help. For it is dying, and if it does, our world will be the poorer. I will tell you how." Arden swept the gathering with his gaze.

He's a master, Gemma thought in awe. *They're eating out of his hands. Is there no end to the ways this man can surprise me?* Then she too was swept away by Arden's words. He told of the beauty of the valley, of the health and longevity of its people, of their hardworking yet tranquil lives and, most of all, about their closeness, the way in which they shared all knowledge in a sense that transcended ordinary communication. He painted a picture so vivid that Gemma felt she had seen it for herself and longed to return to this wondrous place. She was obviously not alone in her sentiment, for the audience was unusually quiet, only a gasp or a whispered aside greeting each new aspect of Arden's tale.

He went on to explain about the biannual river, and how its failure had resulted in the sorry plight of the valley people. He described their suffering and desolation in such poignant terms that Gemma saw many people wipe away a tear.

When his words finally came to an end there was an expectant hush, so that when the judge asked the formal question everyone heard his words clearly. Arden, who had drooped a little, as if exhausted by his speech, roused himself to reply.

"My plea is that the resources of Great Newport be used to bring water back to the valley. There are many ways in which it can be done. And the people of the valley can offer us much in return." He paused. "The magic is fading. Save it for them. For me. For all of us."

At the last his voice was weary, as though his strength was completely gone. Silence descended on Colosseum Square.

Gemma felt a lump in her throat. *This is wrong,* she thought, as she felt the gathering teetering on the edge of the vocal response that Arden needed so badly. *What's holding them back? Do something!* she instructed herself. *Perhaps if I started the shouting* . . . But she could not. The same oppressive spell held her as it did the citizens of Newport.

Gemma saw the judges conferring uncertainly. *They don't know what's happening any more than I do.*

Then a distant mournful hooting broke the quiet. In common with many of those in the crowd, Gemma looked up and saw a number of geese flying far overhead. They flew in perfect formation, an arrowhead pointing to the north. She sensed their unity and purpose from afar. And then an idea struck her. *If only* . . .

The cry of the geese grew louder, and as more people looked up, the formation broke, the birds wheeling in confusion for a few moments. Then they came back into the familiar arrowhead and flew onward. To the southeast.

Directly toward the valley.

There were murmurs now in the throng, and several fingers pointed to the birds. Someone shouted "A sign!" and the refrain was taken up by others. Within moments the square was filled with yells of relieved laughter. Gemma, shaken to

the core by what she had witnessed, looked over to Arden
and found him gazing skyward and smiling.

After that the next stage of proceedings could only be a
formality. The blue-robed man made an impassioned de-
nouncement of the sun-stealers in the west, beyond the blue
flame wall.

"Each time it rises, our sun is smaller, weaker. The world
will soon be covered with ice." This was greeted with howls
of derision and much jeering, as was his further claim that
another world existed beyond the elemental wall. The insane
doctrines of the blue flame sect were well known in Newport,
and the crowd had heard all this before.

Gemma's mind still reeled in confusion and she only heard
a little of the fanatic's speech, but his last words caught her
attention.

"The whole world is becoming insane. We must heal it.
Destroy the usurpers before they destroy us."

A fresh round of heckling marked his conclusion, and the
crowd called for Arden to be granted the victory. The judges'
vote was a foregone conclusion—unanimously in Arden's favor. The blue-robed man descended and the fisherman returned, joining Arden to await the final decision. The central
judge rose, amid much noise, to give a brief résumé of the
two petitions. It was clear that the crowd's sympathies were
now less than unanimous. Perhaps some of them remembered the financial investments at stake. Competing chants
sprang up in sections of the throng while the five judges
conferred together. At last they were ready and an expectant
hush fell over the square.

The first judge rose to his feet. He picked up his stone
marker and faced the crowd. "The judgment of Mayer is
thus." With those words he placed the weight on the fisherman's side of the scales. Groans and shouts of glee filled the
air.

The next judge waited until the uproar subsided before
declaring his name and casting his vote for Arden. The scales
moved smoothly to the balanced position once more. Amid
mounting noise the next also sided with Arden, but the
fourth was for the fisherman, leaving the final decision to the
central judge.

I wonder who his *friends put their money on,* Gemma
wondered, then forgot her cynical thoughts as the man rose

to his feet. All that mattered was that Arden should win. *Please!*

The last judge surveyed the crowd, who assailed him with a noisy mixture of advice, encouragement, and threats. His face remained impassive. Finally the noise fell to a level at which he could make himself heard.

"The judgment of Quillan is thus." The deep voice rolled round the square as he placed his counter.

On Arden's side.

Gemma closed her eyes in relief as the cacophony of sound erupted again and there was a rush toward the gamblers' tables. Her heart was still beating fast when she opened her eyes several moments later. Arden had disappeared from sight, but Gemma caught a glimpse of the man in the flowing blue robe as he left the square. Acting on impulse, she followed, running when she could, and caught up with him. When she tapped him on the shoulder he spun round, hands raised defensively, his blue eyes blazing with mad intensity. Gemma drew back, slightly out of breath.

"May I . . . talk with you?" she asked.

The man relaxed slightly and nodded, his gaze fixed unnervingly on her face.

"Where *is* the blue wall?"

"Far to the west. Where few but my brothers dare to go."

"And beyond it?"

"Another world. The world that will destroy us!" His fanatic's tone was returning. "We must march on them. Attack!"

"How . . ." Gemma began, but he cut her off.

"The world is breaking apart. The gods have shown us, and now demand that we attack. The world is breaking apart!" he repeated dramatically.

"Like The De—like The Leveling?" Gemma offered.

"No! This will be final. The Earth has become mad."

"Is there magic?" she asked softly.

The man laughed. "Magic is dead. It cannot save us. Only the gods can do that." He paused, eyed Gemma narrowly. "Join our sect," he demanded. "Help us. Pray. We need intelligent young men like you. Join us!" He stretched out his hands as if to grab her wrists and Gemma drew back reflexively.

"No!" she exclaimed, then turned, and ran back to the square. She mingled with the crowd for a while, allowing the noise and color to wash over her as she tried to sort out her thoughts.

She came to her senses eventually, and hurried back to the tavern. Arden was waiting for her in their room and he jumped up as she came in, pent-up energy exploding into action.

"Wasn't it wonderful!" he exclaimed. "Those geese! I couldn't believe it. Where have you *been*?"

Gemma fell into his outstretched arms and they hugged each other fiercely.

"You *keep* asking me that," she replied. "I got caught up in the crowd."

chapter 20

As their embrace seemed destined to end, Arden drew Gemma
back toward him and kissed her firmly on the lips. She was
surprised by the intensity of his action and was breathless
when they finally moved apart.

"I won!" he said. "I can hardly believe it!"

Gemma smiled at the boyish delight in his face. Then she
laughed aloud.

"What's so funny?" he asked, though he laughed with her.

"You have boot polish all over your mouth," she replied.

Arden licked his lips, then wiped them on his sleeve.

"I thought you tasted peculiar," he commented.

They laughed again; then, as they looked at each other,
their expressions slowly became serious. They were both
aware of the attraction that was growing between them and
felt that something more was required of them. But neither
could find the words to express it and both were preoccupied
with other matters. So their eyes made promises for the
future, and eventually Gemma spoke, breaking the spell.

"What happens now?" she asked.

"We celebrate!" Arden exclaimed, flinging his arms in the
air.

"No. I meant about the trial."

"It's already been set," he replied gleefully. "For two days'
time. It's unbelievable! These things usually take anything up
to a month to come to court. The gods must be smiling on us,
Gemma."

"I thought you didn't believe in gods," she teased.

"If the gods can help me save the valley, I'll believe in
them," he replied unabashed. Looking at the ceiling, he
added, "You listening up there?"

Gemma laughed and said, "You're looking the wrong way."

For a moment, Arden looked puzzled, then realized what
she meant.

"Of course, the Earth-mind," he said and glanced down at

his feet. "You too," he instructed the floor, pointing at it sternly.

Gemma did not criticize his flippancy, but there *was* a matter she had to discuss with him.

"Arden," she began hesitantly. "About the geese . . ."

"That was incredible," he said eagerly. "Their timing couldn't have been better—the way they pointed straight to the valley! What a piece of luck!"

"It may not have been entirely due to luck," Gemma said quietly.

Arden frowned. "What do you mean?" he asked, then before she had the chance to reply, held up his hands defensively. "And don't tell me it was magic. You'll be seeing islands disappear next!" He smiled and Gemma's next words stuck in her throat.

"Well?" he asked.

"It was probably just their normal migration route," she said, after a pause. "The city must be a landmark they use to navigate by."

"Well, whatever it was," Arden replied, "I am enormously grateful." His excitement still shone within him. "I wish you hadn't got yourself into all that trouble, though. We could have gone out and celebrated properly."

"I can go out like this," Gemma replied. He had accepted her lame explanation about the geese, and she gave up all hope of a serious discussion. "Besides, you haven't won yet. There's still the full trial."

"I know that," he said, sweeping her words aside. "But I never really expected to get *this* far. Can't I enjoy my small successes?" He sounded so plaintive that Gemma could only smile.

"Have you any money left," she asked, "after keeping me all this time?"

"That's a point," he replied. "Perhaps I should sell you after all."

Gemma winced at his words but Arden was too elated to notice. Putting on a brave face, she said, "Someone else tried that. And look what happened to him!" Stricken, Arden took her in his arms again.

"I'm sorry, Gemma," he whispered. "I'm sorry."

After a few moments, she said, "It doesn't matter. Let's go and make merry."

As it turned out they didn't need to go far to celebrate. Nor did they need much money. News of Arden's performance and the manner of his victory had spread throughout the city, and when he went down to the bar, there were already several people waiting to congratulate him. Drink flowed freely and Arden was called upon to describe the wonders of the valley over and over again. When Gemma joined them, after repairing her disguise, the celebration was in full swing, and she joined in happily, though she drank little. Her mind was busy replaying the events of the morning and she wanted a clear head to sort out all the implications.

Had she really affected the movement of the geese? She had believed so at the time but now it seemed more and more improbable. And yet . . .

She tried to remember the exact sequence of events. In the terrible silence that had followed Arden's speech, she had looked up, alerted by the sound of the birds' call. Seeing the dramatic formation in the sky, she had been filled with an alien knowledge, understanding the purpose behind the flight. Then it occurred to her that if only they could change direction and fly toward the valley, then the superstitious citizens of Newport would perhaps take it as an omen. No sooner had this thought struck her than the phalanx had broken apart. Gemma had sensed confusion and conflict. Then, in a process beyond thought, beyond her conscious mind, she found herself *guiding* them, restoring their purpose. Except that now it was *Gemma's* purpose.

As the arrowhead re-formed, she felt the minds of the geese relax, and once more they pointed the way across the sky. As Gemma had predicted, the crowd took it as a sign. What had followed needed no further interference from her.

Did I really do all that? she wondered again. *Or is my memory playing tricks on me? Perhaps it was just coincidence compounded with wishful thinking. And yet . . .*

The contact with the birds had seemed so real, the very strangeness of their avian minds somehow proof that she had *not* imagined the whole affair. *It's as if they all think together.* That idea was familiar, but Gemma could not place it.

I wonder where the geese are now, she thought, and a shiver of guilt made her frown. *They might die crossing the desert.* Gemma fervently hoped that the birds' natural instincts would take over again before any harm befell them. Then it occurred to her that her guilt was proof of the fact that, deep down, she *did* believe that she had been responsi-

ble for their change of course. This realization prompted
another rush of memory. She was suddenly a seven-year-old
girl again, back on her island home, in the happy days before
The Destruction had changed everything.

———————— • ————————

Cai's bees had always fascinated Gemma. She knew that all
wizards had a familiar, an animal with whom they shared a
bond of love and the ability to communicate silently through
mind-talk. She did not know how this worked but took it for
granted, as did all those in close contact with wizards. Even
among such strange company, though, the swarm was considered unusual. It was the only familiar to consist of not one
but a group of animals; it was the complete entity of the
swarm that Cai communicated with, not any individual insect.

Cai was a great favorite with the young princess. He was
funny, and always willing to invent new games. Gemma was
not afraid of the bees, as some silly people were, and she
often observed them closely. She even imagined sometimes
that she knew what they were saying to Cai. When she told
her parents about this, they had laughed and commented on
her vivid imagination. This had annoyed her greatly. She had
proved them wrong in the end, of course.

Cai was visiting Heald's court in order to help Moroski, his
friend and fellow wizard, shed his magical power. Gemma
did not understand the reasons for this at the time, but all the
grown-ups were very serious about it. Then something went
wrong during the occult procedure and the bees had gone
mad, terrorizing the palace with their wild and raging flight.
Gemma had found this enormously exciting and was disappointed when her parents insisted that she stay safely in her
bedroom with them until the danger was over. However, by
means of a simple trick—adults were so easy to fool!—she
had escaped from her confinement and found the swarm.

Gemma would have known that the bees were angry and
confused even without the evidence of her eyes and ears.
They had tried to fly away from her but she was having none
of that.

"Naughty bees!" she shouted. "Come back." She ran after
them and stood, unafraid, in the midst of the swirling mass.
She talked calmly to the bees all the time, telling them how
silly they were and trying to persuade them to return to their
master. To the astonishment of all who witnessed the bizarre
event, the swarm responded, and Gemma led them back to

the tower where the two wizards were unconscious. In doing so, she had enabled them to complete their task successfully. At the time, she had not realized just how helpful she had been. Nor had she noticed the existence of the magical shield through which she had passed in order to reach Cai.

———•———

"Do you want another drink, G . . . Pazia?" Arden asked, his face flushed with alcohol and success.

Gemma flashed him a warning look; some of Mendle's associates might be in the noisy group about them.

"No thank you," she replied coolly. "Don't you think you've had enough yourself?"

Arden winked. "I'm all right. I'll be careful," he assured her, and turned away in answer to a call from one of his newfound friends.

Gemma suddenly felt lonely and out of place, and her thoughts returned to her earlier life. It had not been until she was much older that the significance of what she had done had sunk in. At the time she had just acted from instinct. She smiled as she remembered her conversation with Cai the following day.

———•———

"Gemma!" Cai shouted. "I need to talk to you."

The girl detached herself from her group of friends and joined the wizard. Together they walked to Cai's chambers.

"Your grandmother told me what you did yesterday," he began. "I wanted to thank you."

"That's all right," she said brightly. "It was fun."

"I've always known that you got on well with the swarm, but how did you get them to come back to the tower?"

"I just told them to," Gemma replied.

"How?"

The princess considered this question. "They weren't happy," she said at last, evidently in some confusion.

"Did you *make* them happy?"

She nodded slowly. "Then I brought them back to you. Wasn't that right?"

"Oh yes!" Cai replied emphatically. "If you hadn't . . ." He paused. "But how did you get through the shield?"

"What shield?"

Cai regarded her thoughtfully. "You know, Gemma, I wouldn't be at all surprised if you became a wizard yourself one day."

———————•———————

Gemma came back to the present with a jolt as one of the revelers jostled her as he walked past. There were tears in her eyes as she recalled her response to Cai's surprising statement.

"Would you marry me then?" she had asked at once. It was not the first time the child had asked this question of the wizard, but it was to be the last.

How things have changed since then, she thought wistfully. *In so many ways.*

The world had changed—literally reshaped by The Destruction. So many of her childhood family and friends were dead now. Cai had changed; he no longer believed in wizardry, denying his own talent, let alone any latent powers that Gemma might possess. It had been the only cause of friction between them as she grew to womanhood.

I have changed too, she mused, and wondered about the fate that had led her so far away, to this noisy tavern in a corrupt city of strangers, hundreds of leagues from the only place that she could call home.

"Had a bit too much to drink, have we?" one of the revelers said, observing Gemma's bleary eyes and melancholy expression. He smiled patronizingly.

"No," she replied defiantly. "Not enough!"

And held out her glass to be refilled.

chapter 21

Gemma lay in bed that night, listening to Arden's regular breathing and wishing that she could fall asleep as easily as he had. Even the large amount of ale she had finally imbibed could not stop the workings of her overactive mind. Memories, both old and new, competed for her attention.

She moved restlessly beneath the bedclothes, turning over for what seemed like the twentieth time, but still could not get comfortable. At least the return to their room had allowed her the relief of being able to remove her disguise. This had been put together using items borrowed from the chambermaids she had taken into her confidence, and had become hot and oppressive after a while, making her skin itch unbearably. She had felt that people were looking at her strangely, and knew that it was time to leave. She had slipped away alone and was Gemma again by the time Arden joined her.

"This place is not so bad," he had commented before falling on to his bed and laughing. "Hope nobody saw you comin' in here. Might get some funny ideas." He chuckled again, looking up at the ceiling. "They'd never believe you were a princess."

Gemma watched him indulgently, realizing that he was in no fit state to talk—which was a shame, as there were so many questions she wanted to ask—but unable to scold him for having celebrated so well. She had helped him undress, then tucked him into bed.

"You've got the job," had been his last remark before he fell soundly asleep.

Now, as the final sounds of the tavern's late-night trade died away, Gemma was still wide awake. Closing her eyes only made her memories more vivid, so she stared at the walls of the darkened room and tried to make sense of what was happening to her.

Try as she might, she could not escape the feeling that something was at last being born inside her, something that had lain hidden and repressed for so long. Something that she could only call magic.

You know, Gemma, I wouldn't be at all surprised if you became a wizard yourself one day.

She could hear Cai's voice as clearly as if he were standing beside her bed. But she could hear him say much more; so often in her memories he sounded angry or bitter.

———— • ————

"You're eighteen years old, Gemma. It's time you put aside these ludicrous ideas."

"You didn't think they were ludicrous once," she replied. "Why shouldn't we try to utilize *all* our potential?"

"You're not talking about potential. You're talking about magic."

"It's the same thing."

"No it isn't."

"Give me credit for *some* sense," Gemma said angrily. "I remember things from when I was a little girl. I can read. There is *so* much that we don't know about the workings of our own minds. Magic was there once. How can that have changed so completely?"

Cai looked at her sadly. "You know the answer to that as well as I do," he said calmly. "The Destruction was the end, the *consummation* of magic. When the world no longer has need of something, it discards it. Magic would have no purpose now. The potential, as you call it, isn't there anymore."

"How can you be so sure? Just because you choose to deny it . . ."

"I do not choose . . . it doesn't exist!" Cai was angry now. "And even if it did, I wouldn't want it. Magic *killed* millions!"

Gemma was shocked by Cai's twisting of the facts. The Destruction had indeed been responsible for a huge number of deaths, but their only alternative had been a living hell, ruled over by a vicious force of unimaginable evil. No one could have contemplated such a world and chosen otherwise.

"The Destruction was necessary," she pleaded. "You know that. We *saved* millions."

"From what?" Cai's bitterness shone in his green eyes, and Gemma did not answer. She could not. "From what?" he demanded again. "I'll tell you. From a corruption of *magic*."

Gemma looked away, unable to meet his stare. When he spoke again, his voice was quiet but still had an edge of steel.

"That age has ended, Gemma. Forever. The moonberries

have gone. Brogar's gone—with its master. It's *all* gone. All the wizards are dead."

"You're not," she whispered defiantly.

"I'm not a wizard," he replied, exasperated.

"Then why don't you age?" she asked, looking at him again.

"My body is still adjusting." There was a note of defensiveness in his tone, and Gemma knew that Cai's youthful appearance was a burden he carried with difficulty.

"After more than a decade?" she probed gently.

"I *will* age," he replied firmly. "It just takes time, that's all." He smiled weakly as he realized what he had said. "Besides, you wouldn't want to be seen in the company of an ugly old man, would you?"

Gemma smiled back, but refused to be put off her argument. "The swarm is still with you," she stated.

"We're used to each other," Cai replied easily. "They're like any other domestic animal."

"Don't you talk to them any more?"

"No."

"I think *I* hear them sometimes," Gemma said, almost to herself.

"You were always imagining that when you were little," Cai said, smiling at the memory.

"It was more than imagination. Honestly, the way I'm treated, anyone would think I was *still* a young child. I feel so trapped in this place sometimes."

Cai tried to think of something to say to her, glad that the conversation had shifted ground but unhappy with Gemma's new train of thought. He was beaten to it as Gemma returned to her original argument and tried once again.

"You still heal people," she accused.

Cai sighed. *How many more times?* he wondered. Aloud he said, "All I do is use my knowledge from when I was . . . from earlier days. There's nothing wrong with that."

"That's just my point," Gemma went on eagerly. "Why must the good disappear just because the evil had to be destroyed?"

"It's two sides of the same coin, Gemma," Cai explained impatiently. "Magic has ended. It's dead."

With those words he turned and strode away, unable to face any further discussion. He was not seen at court for the next few days, and it was assumed that he had gone to his remote sanctuary deep in the mountains.

In spite of their vehement disagreement and ill-tempered parting, Gemma was in low spirits until he returned, and it was some time before her willful mind forced the issue to the surface again. By then, she had begun to formulate other ideas of her own.

————•————

When Gemma awoke, she was alone in the room. Her head ached abominably and her throat was dry. With the unfamiliar taste of ale now stale on her tongue, she lay there cursing her own stupidity. Then she got up, poured some cold water from the ewer, washed, and rinsed her mouth. She lay down again, wishing that Arden would return.

He was back within the hour, a broad smile on his sun-darkened face.

"Still in bed?" he chided. "And on such a beautiful day?"

"I find your cheerfulness absolutely appalling," she replied. "After the amount you drank last night, you should be suffering as much as I am."

"No time to be hung over," Arden responded brightly. "I've bought you a present."

Gemma struggled to sit up, smiling in spite of her head's protests. Arden's mood was infectious and his eager expression was irresistible. He sat down beside her and handed over a small box.

Inside was a pair of beautifully crafted gold earrings, shaped like two flying geese, with wings down and necks outstretched.

"They're lovely!" she exclaimed, laughing at the memory of his earlier comment and at the aptness of the design. Her hands went up to remove the simple studs which pierced her lobes, but Arden stopped her.

"Not yet," he said. "I can understand you wanting to be rid of those, but the new ones might cause some comment here in the city." He grinned.

Gemma saw what he meant. "Not quite Pazia's style, are they," she said. "Thank you."

chapter 22

Gemma forced herself to put aside her own conjectures for the rest of that day, and instead set herself the task of ensuring that Arden was properly prepared for his appearance in court. She brought him food and drink, made sure that his clothes were as presentable as possible, and talked when he wanted to. They discussed the best ways of presenting his case, and he told her about the procedure that would be followed.

"You *will* be allowed to speak yourself, won't you?" she asked anxiously at one point. "You were so wonderful in the square."

"So wonderful that I reduced everyone to silence," he replied ruefully.

"That was no mean achievement," Gemma said indignantly. "They were silent because you had touched their hearts."

"It was all right emotionally," he conceded. "Legally, it was nearly a disaster."

"I won't have this!" she retorted. "You are going to be brilliant. That's an order!"

"Yes, ma'am." He gave her a theatrical salute.

"Then you *do* get to speak."

"Yes. The problem is, I'll probably get too much help." Arden's tone was resigned.

"What do you mean?"

He explained, and once again Gemma felt both confused and outraged by this city's alien system of justice. Arden did not seem unduly concerned, however, and they went on to discuss details of his final petition.

They ate in their room that evening, and decided to have an early night. They were in need of a good night's sleep.

"Will Lord Lunkett himself be presiding?" Gemma asked.

"I doubt it," Arden replied. "He'll probably leave it to one of his underlings. Though you never know. . . . Anyway, there is one thing you can be sure of."

"What's that?"

"If he does, it'll be for some devious reason of his own."

Something in Arden's tone made Gemma hope that they would be spared such subtlety.

———————•———————

The Central Guild Court of Great Newport was housed within one of the imposing buildings off Colosseum Square. Here at least was some of the solemnity that Gemma expected of legal proceedings and which, for the most part, had been missing from the preliminary hearing. The interior of the building was dark and quiet, with many solid wooden doors leading off the massive entrance hall. Banners and boards with lists of names hung on the smooth stone walls.

Gemma, in disguise once more but, thanks to certain improvements, rather more comfortable than before, followed a number of people, who obviously knew where they were going, to the public gallery. She suspected that some were runners for the gamblers outside, for whom it would be business as usual. She was pleased to be caught up with the crowd—it meant that she did not have to draw attention to herself by asking the way.

Uniformed guards eyed each person suspiciously as they went through the doors into the court. Some were stopped and searched, presumably for weapons, and Gemma began to worry about the possibility of her disguise being discovered. After all, there were some aspects of being female which could only be hidden so much. As it turned out, however, she was only subjected to close scrutiny, then allowed to pass. She found a place in the second of the long wooden pews which filled the balcony. Below was the scene Arden had described to her the night before.

At the far end of the hall, underneath colorful banners which displayed the Guild's emblem of balanced scales, was a bench similar to that in the square outside. This one was made of highly polished wood, as was the table in front of it. The scales that stood on the table were of brass.

To either side of the hall, running its entire length, were four rows of long wooden benches adorned with cushions. Between the two sides was an open area, at the center of which—the focal point of the room—was a raised area surrounded by wooden railings. *That's where Arden will stand*, Gemma thought, her heart fluttering a little.

The public balcony was now full of noise and chatter, but Gemma was too tense to take any notice of what was being said. Finally, a hush fell over the room as the members of the Guild filed in and took their assigned seats on the long benches. Those to Gemma's right were dressed in orange robes of startling brightness. *They'll argue for and with Arden*, Gemma thought, remembering what he had told her. Those to the left wore similar garments, this time of dark blue. *And those are against us*. She studied their faces, wondering which would be skilled in debate and which liabilities, but there was no way of knowing. All were of thirty summers or more; some looked positively ancient, and a few even had to be helped to their seats.

When all were settled, Arden appeared from beneath the balcony and strode confidently to center stage. He bowed to each side of the court and mounted the podium, but did not look at the balcony. This left Gemma with mixed emotions. While she did not want her presence to distract him from the task in hand, she wished she could have at least given him an encouraging smile and, at the same time, seen for herself that he was all right. It was as much as she could do to keep from calling out to him.

Unnoticed, three officials had taken their seats at tables below the judges' bench. They busied themselves with papers, presumably, Gemma thought, getting ready to record the details of the petition and the judgment. One then rose to his feet and declared the proceedings open. When he also announced the names of the five judges who would preside, there was a murmur of surprise from those around her. *So Lunkett has chosen to involve himself*. Gemma felt a shiver of apprehension.

The judges appeared and took their appointed seats. Gemma studied the one in the middle. Lunkett was a large man, his body draped in a green robe, as were the other adjudicators. Shrewd eyes looked out from a plain, square-jawed face. Like the other four, he had placed his stone marker on the table before him. This time Gemma was able to see that each was sculpted into the shape of an animal, bird, or heraldic object, presumably an emblem of the owner's rank or trade. Lunkett's was more difficult to identify but Gemma eventually realized that it was a representation of the city itself, from the outer walls to the major streets and buildings. It was also considerably larger and heavier than the others. *So it all depends on him*, Gemma thought.

The herald now read out a short summary of Arden's

account of the valley and of the arguments he had used to press home his appeal for its salvation. The statement was read in an apathetic manner, which rendered the words ineffective and unconvincing. It was also inaccurate in places and Gemma saw Arden struggle to keep from interrupting. The official finished by repeating Arden's formal petition.

"The plea is that the resources of Great Newport be used to bring water back to the valley." Now Lunkett spoke for the first time.

"The plea is heard," he said, his voice deep and commanding. "Now we must decide—is this to be done? And if so, in what manner?"

I've heard that voice before, Gemma thought. *Where?*

"Petitioner, do you wish to add anything to the statement before the court begins its deliberations?"

"I do, my lord." Gemma breathed a sigh of relief as Arden spoke clearly and with confidence.

"Then name yourself for the record and proceed." Lunkett sat back and folded his large hands in his lap.

Arden did as he was asked and described once more the wonders of the valley, laying a subtle stress on the points which had been misinterpreted earlier by the herald. Facing each side in turn as he spoke, the love and passion in his voice was obvious, and Gemma heard the people about her murmur in appreciation. The Guildmen, however, remained outwardly unmoved. There were even some frowns and whispered asides which Gemma could not interpret, but then one of the blue-robed men interrupted Arden.

"We have listened to this for too long," he said loudly, to nods of agreement from both sides of the chamber. "The case for treating this valley as a place worthy of preservation was presented at the outset in quite sufficient detail. It is the purpose of *this* court to determine whether such a course of action would indeed be desirable, and, more important, practical." He had addressed the judges' bench and Arden, who had been forced into silence, also turned to look that way.

Lunkett held a hasty consultation with his fellow judges, though Gemma doubted that it was for more than show.

"Agreed," he said. "Unless the petitioner wishes to put forward any pertinent facts as to how his plea may be undertaken, should the court decide in his favor . . ." He paused.

"I do, my lord," Arden said quickly.

"Then proceed," Lunkett responded, a faint smile touching his lips. "But remember to remain within what has been asked of you, and be as brief as possible. Rhetoric will gain you little reward here. When you have finished, the debate will begin."

The auction, Gemma realized suddenly. *This man nearly bought me!* She shuddered and tried to make herself smaller, huddling down behind the people in the front row. Arden was speaking again and she tried to concentrate on his words, to shut out all other thoughts.

"Great Newport has many skills," Arden began. "That it flourishes is proof of that. Water is scarce because the population is so large, and the river cannot supply more than a fraction of your needs. If Great Newport can achieve this great feat, it would certainly be in your power to supply the mere hundreds in the unique valley for which I speak. You already have the means at your disposal. The water convoys that travel the coast road, the water-farm which extracts the salt from seawater to make it drinkable, the engineering expertise to build canals—"

"Yes, yes," a blue-robe interrupted tetchily. "You need hardly advise the members of the Guild about the resources of its city. Our record speaks for itself," he added pompously. "That is not at issue here."

"With respect," an orange-robe intervened, "the petitioner is merely doing as instructed and proposing ways that his plea might be fulfilled. Courtesy—and the law—demand that we hear him out."

"*You* may have time to waste, Merrill," the first speaker replied. "Others are not so *fortunate*." His sarcastic tone brought forth a ripple of amusement.

"My lords," Arden said firmly, and Gemma breathed a sigh of relief at his intervention. "I have but one more idea to put forward before I pass the matter for adjudication. With your permission . . ." He looked at Lunkett, who nodded. Arden continued. "I have told how, since The Leveling, the valley's river flowed once every two years. No one knows the reason for this, but it is obvious that the answer must lie in the southern mountains. The people of the valley have neither the men nor the skills to equip an expedition to enter that hostile region. But this city does. I am sure that a simple work of engineering is all that would be necessary to divert the river's flow at its source and thus return water and life to the valley. Please consider it, my lords."

Gemma applauded mentally. Arden has been firm and convincing—he had deflected the first signs of bickering and offered a practical proposal. *Win or lose*, she thought, *no one could say he hasn't tried*.

A blue-robe got to his feet.

"As the petitioner has so rightly pointed out, our city is itself in need of water. Why then should we expend vast sums of money, energy, and time on a remote and unproductive area? We are not uncharitable, my lords, but surely there are better uses of our resources."

"That has already been answered," one of his adversaries replied smoothly. He adjusted his orange robe and rose to his feet. "Arden's valley is a unique place. Even if it were not our moral duty to preserve it as such, think of the benefits that closer ties would bring. If only a fraction of the petitioner's reports are true—and we have no reason to doubt him, as he has nothing to gain personally from his plea—then we can learn much from the people of the valley. Just imagine a city without disease, where a life span of over a hundred summers would be commonplace. Such a prospect is before us—are we to give it up just for the sake of a little effort?" He resumed his seat, looking sure of himself.

Does he really believe that? Gemma wondered. *Or is it just another game?*

"A *little* effort?" another blue exclaimed, not bothering to stand. "Even if you give credence to these . . . *stories* of health and long life—and I for one would require further evidence—how can it be said that only a *little* effort is involved? The journey to the valley is hundreds of leagues—over *desert*, mark you, and then mountain. How is a water convoy to make such a journey? It's impossible."

"And at best the convoy would provide only temporary relief, even if it could get through," one of his colleagues added.

"There is no sea there, so the water-farm would be of no use," another put in.

"It is clear," an orange said, "that such temporary measures are of little value. We can all agree on that. What is needed is a permanent solution. Arden's suggestions that a research party investigate and, if possible, alter the source of this curious river is surely the course we should adopt."

"Perhaps while we're about it we could move a mountain or two," a blue replied, to general laughter. "That ought to solve the problem."

How can you have the nerve to make a joke like that? Gemma thought angrily.

"Maybe we could train wizards to conjure a few rain clouds in the right places," another comedian suggested. "With all their magical talents, I'm surprised the valley people haven't already done that themselves!"

Gemma was taken aback. *Is it possible?* she wondered. *Could you have done it, Cai?*

The argument went back and forth, with Arden turning to face each speaker in turn until Gemma thought he must become dizzy. He was asked direct questions several times, and always replied in measured tones, giving his answers as succinctly as possible. This was in marked contrast to the frenzied verbiage which was becoming increasingly common on both sides of the court as the trial progressed. Gemma often saw Arden bite his tongue to stop himself interrupting. *How can he stand this? To have the fate of the valley in the hands of these pompous fools?* She was having difficulty keeping her own temper.

It was eventually established that if the plea *was* granted, the city's aid would take the form of an exploratory group of engineers and workers, going high into the mountains to investigate whether the river could be restored. All other methods of transporting water to the valley had been discussed and discarded as impractical. Whether any effort at all was desirable took much longer to determine.

The debate hinged upon two points. Did the valley deserve such special attention in its own right? And what were the possible benefits to Great Newport? The first caused some heated disagreement, which in the end came down to morality versus commerce. The orange-robes claimed that such a place was worth more than monetary consideration, while their opponents made much of the fact that the valley paid no taxes, exported no goods, and contributed no knowledge or skills to the general good because few of its inhabitants ever left their isolated home.

However, this was nothing to the furor which the second point aroused. Arden admitted reluctantly that the valley people were remarkably healthy while they stayed in the valley, but those few that *had* left had become prone to sickness and early death. The blues inevitably questioned whether this much-vaunted vitality was of any value since it could not travel. The other advantages—the beauty, the harmony, and well-being—were too nebulous to be taken into account. Nobody put a high value on philosophy. The most controversial subject was naturally the shared awareness of the valley people. Here the blues had ample opportunity to exercise their wit and, though their adversaries made much of the tremendous possibilities such an ability afforded, it was obvious that their hearts were not in it. Arden, because of his own exclusion from the mind-link, or telepathy, as one of the debaters named it, was unable to give a convincing explanation of the phenomenon. He grew agitated when he realized that this factor was harming his overall case.

Stay calm, Gemma urged him silently. *You've still got a chance.* Indeed, several of the orange robes had made a number of points in Arden's favor. Although they lacked his passion, they made logic their ally against the taunts and ridicule of the other side.

After more than an hour's exhaustive and continuous exchange, Gemma's attention was drawn to the judges' bench. Lunkett was completely ignoring the debate raging below him, and was conferring with his fellow adjudicators. *He's bored,* Gemma thought, her heart thumping. *It's time for a decision.*

She was proved right when, at the next opportunity for interruption, the Overlord spoke in unequivocal terms.

"The debate is concluded," he boomed. "Herald, the summary, please."

The uniformed official rose to his feet and gave an analysis of the discussion.

"In conclusion," he went on, "the oranges claim that compassion combined with the benefits that must accrue from contact with such a remarkable society make an expedition not only just, but wise and profitable. The blues have it that it would be a foolhardy venture, with little chance of success and no hope of any return, and thus the proposal should be abandoned. How say you, my lords?" He took his seat again, looking as bored as ever.

That should inspire them, Gemma thought bitterly, horrified at the way in which the fate of so many people had been reduced to a few, impersonal words.

Gemma was surprised when Lunkett rose to his feet; she

had expected him to pass his judgment last. Judging by the sudden stir about her, others in the balcony were similarly surprised.

"As Overlord of Great Newport, I exercise the right to place my stone first." His voice rolled over the quiet courtroom. "I am concerned for *all* my subjects, even those that are so far away." Gemma's hopes rose. "But compassion must be tempered with reason." And fell again. *Which way will he decide?* Lunkett went on, "That we may gain from the exchange is also an important consideration. But this is speculation. My duty to justice is thus."

In the breathless silence which followed, he leaned forward, picked up his stone image, and placed it on the orange side of the scales. Arden's side.

As the balance tipped decisively, Gemma's heart leapt and all about her were exclamations of surprise. Some people left in a hurry. *The odds must be changing dramatically,* Gemma thought in jubilation. She guessed that it would take all four remaining judges voting in unison against the plea—*against their Overlord*—to defeat Arden's purpose.

We've done it! Gemma exulted. *We've won!*

Conversations had broken out all over the court and it was difficult to hear what the second judge said. To Gemma's surprise, he voted against the plea, but her euphoria did not lessen. When the next judge also placed his weight in opposition to Arden, she began to harbor tiny doubts. *Surely . . .*

When the fourth green-robed man stood up, the court had calmed down a little, and it was possible to hear what he said. In any case, he confined his words to a formal statement.

"The judgment of Holda is thus."

His stone emblem was placed on the blue side of the scales, which now tilted only very slightly toward Arden's side.

Gemma couldn't believe it. *This can't be happening! After all this, it would be too cruel to lose.* Once again, the fate of the valley depended on the final judge. *He wouldn't comdemn them now. Surely not . . .*

The court was silent, the implications and possible reasons for this rebellion against the Guild's Overlord as much a matter for concern as the outcome of the trial itself. All eyes were on the last judge as he rose to his feet.

"Hard decisions need hard logic," he said slowly. "For that reason, the judgment of Parle is thus."

Gemma stared, open-mouthed, as the fourth tablet was placed in opposition to the plea. Slowly, smoothly, the scales tipped. For the first time the balance favored the blues.

The hall erupted. Amid the sudden agitation, the herald rose to announce that the blues had prevailed, and the petition was therefore denied. Then Lunkett rose slowly to face the court.

"This decision saddens me," he said, "but I must accept the justice of the court. Let it be seen that the Overlord of Great Newport does not stand in the way of justice. The plea is denied. This court is concluded."

No sooner had he finished speaking than another voice was heard.

"*No!*" Gemma screamed, jumping to her feet. "No!" Inside her, anger raged, building forces of strength and desperation. She wanted to reach out, smash those traitorous scales, destroy the complacent men who had denied the valley life. Her face contorted into a mask of fury. She could do it! The power was there if only she could reach it.

Her venomous gaze fell briefly on Arden, who like all the others below, was looking up at her, mouth agape. His expression was petrified, white with shock and helplessness, yet in his eyes was another fear, and his denial of her need for violence was clear. *Don't do it*, his eyes said. *Get out of here!*

Gemma came back to life. Finally aware of the danger she was in, she rushed to leave the court, scrambling over others in her haste. Once in the aisle she pelted toward the door, only vaguely aware of the shouts echoing all about her.

As she flew through the open doors, two guards tried to grab her, and though she was not halted, her hat and false hair were ripped away. She twisted away from her would-be captors, and fled onward, outdistancing her pursuers. As she broke into the sunlight of Colosseum Square, she paused for a moment, her hair a fiery beacon, then set off again. Plunging through the crowds, the terrified girl tried to ignore the cries of those who followed.

"The witch!" one of them was shouting. "Stop the witch!"

chapter 23

The guards' cries of "witch!" actually helped Gemma escape because most people shied away from her rather than risk the anger of the northern enchantress. They had all heard of her impressive destruction of Mendle's auction hall, and had no wish to suffer in like manner. Besides, few citizens of Newport would actually go out of their way to apprehend a fugitive, no matter who it was, preferring to leave this hazardous task to the guards. Many had reason enough of their own to steer clear of the Guild's law enforcers.

Thus it was that in the first stages of her wild flight, Gemma found a pathway miraculously open up before her as she ran full pelt across the square. All she had to do was avoid the stationary objects—stalls, trader's carts, a statue, disdainful felines—and keep going. For a while her pursuers were able to keep sight of her, but their progress was hampered by the crowds. When, after what seemed like an eternity, Gemma reached the far side of the square, she ducked into the nearest lane and continued to run blindly, turning corners at random, losing herself in the maze of back streets and alleys.

At last her aching legs and laboring breath forced her to slow down, and she began to take notice of her surroundings. Nothing was familiar. The conditions of the dwellings told her that she was in one of the city's poorer districts, but beyond that she had absolutely no idea where she was. Still she forced herself onward, half-walking, half-running, always listening for the sounds of pursuit.

She received several curious glances from the denizens of the district and only then thought of the need to conceal her hair so that she would be less noticeable. She dodged into a doorway and, thankful to catch her breath, hurriedly improvised a hood by ripping away the lower part of her shirt. Desperation lent her strength. Then, as she peered round the corner, she heard shouts which, whether they were anything to do with the search or not, spurred her into action again. She set off in the opposite direction from the voices, moving at a steady jogging pace and continuing to twist and turn at every opportunity.

Eventually, quite exhausted, she turned into an alley that was long and narrow but promised open spaces at the far end. However, it was not as she had imagined; the alley ended abruptly, as did the buildings on either side of it. Before her, the ground dropped away vertically and she found herself looking out over the gigantic field of rubbish that had so nauseated her just a few days ago. There was no wall or railing; had she still been running at her earlier pace she would have gone straight over the edge and been badly injured, if not killed. Gemma estimated that the fall would be more than twenty paces; then, as she peered over the edge, she noticed small metal rungs set into the side of the pit. Glancing back along the length of the alleyway, she tried to catch her breath and wondered whether her hunters were closing in. In spite of the absence of any noise, she dared not go back. Yet the alternative was appalling; the stench alone was nearly enough to drive her away.

Down! she ordered herself. *This is no time to be squeamish!*

She gingerly lowered herself over the rim, testing each rung with one foot. One or two were a little loose and in one place a couple were missing. This caused momentary consternation, but she made steady progress, eventually landing safely on the surface below. Gemma was thankful that at least part of her disguise gave her protection against the hazards of this alien landscape. She turned to survey the prospect before her.

And found herself looking into the aggressively curious eyes of two ragged boys and an equally unkempt girl.

"What d'you want?" the larger boy demanded. "This is *our* patch."

"Yeah!" the smaller added defiantly.

"I don't want anything," Gemma said. "I'm just trying . . . to get away from some people."

"They keys?" the leader asked.

"What?"

"The key-men. Guards," he explained condescendingly.

The girl spat on the ground. "Scum!"

Gemma could see no point in lying.

"Yes," she conceded. "Guards."

"Why didn't you say?" the bigger boy asked, as if her admission was an entrance ticket to this strange land.

"Well, I'm new here," she said lamely.

"That's obvious," he replied with derision.

The girl eyed her narrowly.

"You got any stuff?" she asked harshly.

"Stuff?"

"The guards ain't chasin' you for nothin'. What'd you get?"

"N . . . nothing," Gemma stammered. "I had to ditch the stuff to get away," she added, improvising quickly.

"Pity."

"You talk funny," the little boy chimed in. "Like a girl."

"Stupid! Girls don't wear stuff like that." The female urchin cuffed the young child, but Gemma saw no sense in disabusing them.

"Where d'you want to go?" the elder boy asked. "Carmen? The Stickles?"

Gemma's expression told its own story. "I don't know," she said, glancing up to whence she had come. The children looked up too.

"We'll take 'im to the tunnels," their boss decided. "He can decide from there." With that, he set off over the mounds of refuse, carefully picking his way along paths that Gemma could hardly see. She followed, with the other youngsters close behind her, and felt glad of the escorts. Pools of slimy liquid, tangles of barbed undergrowth, rotting vegetation, and treacherous hollow banks were all avoided by the narrowest of margins. Alone, she might have been claimed by any of them. The strange group passed several scavengers working alone amid the debris. One group of men was sitting around a bonfire, in spite of the summer heat, passing a bottle between them. They stared at Gemma and the children as they passed, but made no comment. Deeper and deeper into the strange world the convoy went, until even Gemma's nose became acclimatized and stopped protesting her surroundings so violently.

I must be safe from the guards here! she thought, then wondered what other dangers she faced amid the rubbish and its people.

Eventually they marched up to a man sitting atop a mound of broken stone and rubble. He was picking his teeth with a needle-sharp knife.

"This here needs the tunnels," the gang leader said, pointing at Gemma with a dirty finger. "He's on the run from the keys."

The man, who was dressed entirely in black, looked up slowly. His scarred face gave him a sinister air as he stared at Gemma.

"Take that scarf off your head," he ordered, his voice a low growl. Gemma reluctantly removed her makeshift hood, and the children gasped.

"See! I told you," the youngest exclaimed. "He's a girl."

"*She's* a girl, stupid," one of his companions retorted.

The man just stared, a grim smile creeping over his face.

"There's someone here wants to meet you," he said slowly, getting to his feet. "Clear off, you lot," he told the urchins. "And keep your mouths shut."

They ran off instantly, their faces glowing with secrets.

"Everyone will know soon," the man said resignedly. "So you'd better come inside quick."

Inside?

He shifted a few small boulders, then grasped an iron ring set in a slab of stone. As he pulled, a trapdoor opened and Gemma saw steps leading down into darkness.

"Welcome to the tunnels, home of sewer rats and others— like myself." He lowered himself inside and beckoned Gemma to follow. She hesitated.

"Afraid of the dark, are we?" He smiled again. "Would you prefer to try and find your way out of here alone?" He disappeared into the gloom, and after a moment Gemma gave in to the inevitable and went inside. The steps were narrow and steep; she moved cautiously downward, placing her hands and feet very carefully. "Shut the door behind you," the man's voice advised from below. "And try not to get your fingers caught in the gap." His deep chuckle echoed about her as she struggled to lower the stone. When she had succeeded, the darkness about her was total. "Keep coming down," he advised. "I'll catch you if you fall." Again he laughed.

Your sense of humor is getting on my nerves, Gemma thought, but said nothing. She kept going, and at last found herself on level ground.

"Stand still while I light a torch." There was a click, a spark, and then oily flames sprang into life. Gemma's eyes took a few moments to adjust, then she saw that they were standing in a tunnel, the roof of which was scarcely higher than her head. It was very cold, and water glistened on the walls and floor. In the distance, something scurried away from the light.

Her companion was looking at her appraisingly.

"You've got guts, I'll say that," he remarked, and walked off down the dank corridor. Gemma hurried after him, not wanting to lose the only source of light. The floor was even beneath her feet and the tunnel ran straight. They went past other passageways branching off to the side, but her guide continued straight ahead until Gemma saw another light in the distance. It soon became clear that this was an oil lamp hanging above a door.

The man knocked a complicated pattern on the door, and an eyehole appeared. Then the door was opened and they walked into a remarkably homely, lamplit room, which was furnished with tables, chairs, and even a shelf of books. A fire burned in the grate, and the floor was smooth and dry. All the room lacked was a window. As someone closed the door behind her, Gemma stared at the man who rose from his chair and came to look at her. It was Jordan.

The black man smiled at her.

"So this is what you really look like," he said. "Pazia, if I'm not mistaken. Though I suspect that's not your real name."

Gemma was speechless.

"I see you've already met Hewe," Jordan went on. "Our doorkeeper is Paule, and you already know my name. Won't you let us have yours?"

"Gemma."

"I've been wanting to meet you, Gemma. You've caused quite a stir in our fair city."

"Who *are* you?" Gemma whispered, utterly confused.

"Let's just say I am . . . someone who shares your dislike of the way this city is run. I take it that *is* the case after this morning?"

"You know about that already?" she said, astonished.

Jordan's smile widened.

"Now what happens?" Gemma asked. "What do you want with me?"

chapter 24

"I just want to talk," Jordan told her. "Exchange information."

"And then?"

"And then you do whatever you like. Were you expecting us to hold you against your will?"

"Your front door is hardly a normal one, is it," Gemma replied, beginning to recover her poise. "I didn't know *what* to expect."

The men laughed. "That doesn't mean we're not civilized," Jordan said. "Would you care for some wine?"

"I'd prefer water. I'm parched," she answered.

Her host moved to pour her a drink from a jug on one of the tables. Gemma took the glass and examined it warily, but the contents looked harmless. She drank the cool clear liquid and felt her throat give thanks.

"Please sit," Jordan offered, and Gemma relaxed into one of the chairs. He took the one beside her, but the other men remained standing, obviously intrigued by the situation.

"Now," Jordan began. "Tell me all about yourself, how you came to the city and how you managed to burn down half of it."

"No," Gemma said firmly. "First *you* tell me why you want to know."

"You *are* feeling better," he responded, laughing.

"And you can also tell me what's happened to Arden," Gemma went on. "You seem to know everything else that went on this morning," she added defiantly.

"I'll take that as a compliment," Jordan replied. "Arden is well. The authorities have no grudge against him, he is merely another unfortunate pawn, used and discarded in Newport's power game. He is of no real consequence to the Guild, and is therefore free to go. At the moment he's just a little confused by your behaviour and worried about where you are, but we can soon put that right. Paule, see to it, would you." The man left without a word.

"Just like that?" Gemma asked.

"Why not?"

"Because in this city no one does anything without *some* ulterior motive."

"You've noticed that, have you?" Hewe growled, laughter in his voice.

"You're right to be suspicious," Jordan said. "I'd like to have the time to persuade you that we are worthy of your trust, but if you'd prefer, you can go now. Hewe will escort you to any part of the city you choose."

Gemma, intrigued, looked back and forth between the two men. Even if Jordan was to be believed, the prospect of a return journey through the dark tunnels with the bearlike Hewe was not inviting. There were too many mysteries here for her just to walk out now. Besides, if they were going to let Arden know where she was, she had a better chance of being reunited with him by staying there.

"You have my permission to try to persuade me," she said, as boldly as she could.

"Well said!" Jordan responded delightedly. "You think we should tell her a bit about ourselves, Hewe?"

"I doubt if she'll go rushing off to the Guild with our secrets," the big man replied. "Not with their threats against her."

"What threats?" Gemma asked quickly.

"It seems that our friend Mendle was not the only one injured by your pyrotechnics," Jordan said. "There are others—members of the Guild no less—who have promised you a spectacularly unpleasant experience should they catch you. It was lucky that you escaped this morning."

"No good ever comes from arson," Hewe commented. "And I speak from personal experience." The two men laughed at a private joke.

"I'm glad you find it amusing!" Gemma snapped. She was annoyed by their flippant attitude—and they *still* had not told her anything about themselves.

"My apologies," Jordan said. "Living the way we do tends to encourage a rather grim sense of humor."

The implications of this began to register with Gemma.

"You live outside the law." It was a statement rather than a question.

"Better say below it," Hewe suggested mildly.

"We like to utilize all our talents," Jordan said. "Including some which our rulers consider illegal."

"You keep saying 'we,' " Gemma went on. "Are you part of an organization?"

"I suppose you could call it that. Though that word implies rather more structure than there actually is."

"Who *are* you?" Gemma asked, frustrated by their continued evasiveness. "What are you trying to achieve? What's the purpose of your organization? Structure or no structure."

There was a pause; then, "Time to get serious, Jordan," Hewe said.

The black man nodded, but it was a few moments before he spoke.

"You could call us the underground," he began. "That's appropriate, after all. We are a motley collection of people, united by our common dislike of the way this city and the province are run. You've seen enough in your few days here to know that Great Newport is hardly a haven of sweetness and light. Or of justice. Half its people can hardly feed themselves, while others indulge in the most outrageous gluttony. Some live in palaces, others in hovels—if they're lucky."

"Some live underground," Hewe put in. "Some on that rubbish tip over our heads." He jerked a thumb at the roof.

"As you've already seen, the judicial system is corrupt and open to all sorts of connivance," Jordan went on. "Commerce is controlled by a fortunate few.. And the gods help anyone who steps out of line—the Guild would sell their own children for a night's pleasure. They can't see that their world will soon come crashing about their ears. When it happens, it'll be too late for all of us.

"We must get rid of the Guild. That's only the first step, but we have to start somewhere."

"And then?" Gemma queried.

"We have our dreams," Jordan said solemnly. "This land can provide enough for *everyone* to live a good life. Not soft or indulgent, but worthwhile. Humanity deserves that at least."

"How do you plan to overthrow the Guild?" Gemma asked softly. "With violence and bloodshed?"

"Against them, we don't have any choice," Jordan answered. "The core is too rotten to heal. We have to cut it out."

"If our numbers are big enough," Hewe added, "there

need not be much fighting. Even the most degenerate of men can be made to see the obvious."

"That's why we've moved slowly," Jordan continued. "We don't want to kill, though we're prepared to do it. We won't get a second chance, so when we *do* move, it will have to be right." He paused. "It will be soon, though. I think you're beginning to realize that." He regarded her calmly.

How different he is from the manic chatterbox who monopolized Arden in the tavern, Gemma thought.

"You mean what's happening outside the city?" she asked. "The things you were telling Arden about?"

"Yes, though I'm afraid he found my tales rather tedious," Jordan replied with a smile.

"He had a lot on his mind."

"You, on the other hand . . ." Jordan was silenced by the expression on Gemma's face. She leaned forward abruptly, dipped her finger into the glass of water, and drew a pattern on the tabletop—a pair of scales, unbalanced by what looked like a fish. Hewe grunted derisively when he saw what it was.

"Is that your symbol?" Gemma asked.

"No!" Jordan replied with surprising vehemence. "Though many people share that misconception."

Gemma sat back again, feeling unaccountably disappointed.

"That sign has gotten us into a lot of trouble in the past," Hewe said.

"Why?"

"It crops up at the scenes of various crimes," Jordan explained. "I suppose we're an obvious place to lay the blame, and in the minds of many, that sign ties it to us."

"Who's behind it?" Gemma asked.

"I wish we knew. There are plenty of theories," he added jovially, "but none of them makes much sense."

"Such as?"

"The Guild itself, to discredit us. Rival business guilds from other cities, to discredit the Guild. The skyravens, for reasons of their own. The gray raiders, because they're crazy anyway. The people from beyond the southern mountains, because they're getting ready to invade Cleve. Men from another world, for the-gods-know-what reason." Jordan paused. "Enough?" he asked.

"Enough," Gemma agreed, more confused than ever. "I'm sorry I asked." She grinned, and Jordan returned her smile.

"Does that answer all your questions about us?" he asked.

If only you could *answer all of my questions*, Gemma thought ruefully. Aloud she said, "Not quite. Where are the other members of the underground?"

"You mean where do we get the support to give us any hope of overthrowing the established order?"

"Yes. I suppose so."

"There are few walks of life in this blessed metropolis in which some citizens have not come to see reason," the black man said carefully. "They usually make contact with us, rather than the other way round. Believe it or not, we even have a few friends in the Guild itself. You'll forgive me if I don't tell you who they are." Jordan paused. "Tradesmen, artisans, many of the poorer people inside and outside the city walls, a few guards. Zealots, idealists, travelers, and adventurers—a complete mixture really."

"And which category are you?"

"Me?" Jordan was taken aback, but recovered quickly. "I'm a professional idiot," he said with a grin. "Attempting the impossible for the sake of pride."

"Yours?"

"No. Humanity's."

Gemma stared at his smiling face. She was beginning to like him very much; beneath his airy exterior was a spirit she could respect and honor.

"You're risking your lives, aren't you," she said quietly.

"We laugh at death," Jordan announced theatrically.

"We have to," Hewe added. "His jokes are awful, but they're the only ones we have." The two men laughed happily.

"Aren't you ever serious for more than a few moments?" Gemma asked, astonished.

"I hope not," Jordan answered.

"I believe the lady has not concluded her examination of our motives," Hewe said with mock solemnity. "The next question, please."

They looked expectantly at Gemma, and she burst out laughing. Their expressions had become so obsequious that it was impossible for her to remain solemn.

"You two should be on the stage," she exclaimed. "What a double-act!"

Jordan and Hewe exchanged glances.

"I knew we'd win her over eventually," the big man said.

"It was our charm," the other replied. "Simple, really."

"Idiots!" Gemma laughed.

"*Professional* idiots," Jordan amended.

For a while no one said anything, then Gemma grew serious once more and tried again.

"Does the underground extend beyond the city?" she asked.

"Yes."

"All walks of life again?"

"Yes."

"Gray raiders?"

That struck a nerve, and Jordan's eyes grew cold. He looked at her thoughtfully.

"Some of the raiders were once our friends," he said. "At least they can see that something is wrong, but they blame the wrong people."

"Most of them are completely mad," Hewe added. "We couldn't use them even if we *wanted* their help."

There's more to it than that, Gemma decided, watching their uncharacteristically guarded expressions. *Don't push your luck,* she thought. There was a lot more she wanted to ask.

"Are you the leader of the underground?" she asked, looking at Jordan.

"No," he replied.

"Yes," Hewe contradicted.

Jordan shrugged. "As much as anyone is, I suppose," he conceded. "Is it important?"

"I'm just curious," she said.

"So we've noticed."

"What's wrong with that?"

"Nothing. On the contrary," Jordan replied. "It is a trait shared by all intelligent people. Including ourselves."

"The time has come . . ." Hewe began.

". . . for you to tell us about yourself," Jordan completed.

"*Are* you a witch?" Hewe asked.

chapter 25

"If I *am*, you'd better watch out," Gemma said. "You could be spending the rest of your days as a frog."

Hewe cowered in mock terror.

"So this is how you repay me for rescuing you," he complained.

"Do you want to hear my story or not?" Gemma demanded, smiling.

"Of course we do," Jordan replied.

So Gemma told her tale. She skimmed over her original impulse to travel south, the disastrous voyage, and her rescue by Arden, and concentrated on their arrival in Newport. Her audience already knew the reason for Arden's visit, having been present at the preliminary trial.

"I have an interest in such matters," Jordan said smoothly.

"Arden's a good speaker," Hewe commented, "but it so nearly went wrong. Those geese did him a big favor."

"I don't suppose you had anything to do with that?" Jordan asked, his eyes fixed on Gemma's face.

She hesitated.

"Why do you ask?" she replied eventually.

"Just an idea."

"I'm not sure," she said, answering his original question. "I think I did, but sometimes it seems absurd." She described her feelings from that occasion as best she could, and watched the two men exchange glances. "But this is getting ahead of the story," she added. "A lot happened before that."

Gemma described her boredom in the tavern, her explorations, and her subsequent capture by Mendle. Jordan and Hewe questioned her closely about the events leading up to the auction, wanting to know every detail, but Gemma explained that her memory of that time was rather confused. And she told them why.

"Dragonflowers!" Hewe exclaimed. "He wasn't taking any chances, was he."

"As it happens, he was," Gemma replied, and went on to

tell them of the auction and the dramatic events that led to its abandonment.

"Gods!" Hewe breathed. "And you think *we* should be on the stage!"

"You did all that?" Jordan queried. "By yourself?"

"I did *something*," Gemma replied. She could not bring herself to use the word "magic," remembering Arden's adverse reaction. "I'm still not sure what or how, but it *was* my doing. I'm positive of that."

"I wish I'd been there to see it," Jordan said.

"I'm glad you weren't," she responded. "You don't strike me as the slave-owning type."

"Thank you," he replied, bowing his head.

"After that," she continued, "it was obvious that I would have to assume a disguise."

"I can understand that," Hewe remarked wryly.

"And that's when I met you in the tavern bar." As Jordan nodded in acknowledgment, Gemma paused. "The things you talked about that evening, what do you suppose they mean?"

"We'll come to that later," he answered. "Carry on with your side of things for now."

"There isn't much more to tell," she said. "You know about the preliminary trials, and the geese."

"And the celebration that followed," Hewe said with a grin. "You were Pazia again then, I presume."

Gemma nodded. "Were you there?"

"The underground has eyes everywhere," Jordan said melodramatically. Gemma looked at him. "Well, almost everywhere," he amended.

"In most taverns at least," Hewe added.

"That doesn't surprise me," Gemma laughed. "Well, after that it was just a question of waiting for the full hearing. Today. After they gave the judgment, I sort of went mad. For a few moments I just didn't know what I was doing."

"I'm surprised you didn't burn the place down," Hewe remarked.

"I might have done! But I came to my senses in time, and got away—just. I kept on running, and ended up here," Gemma concluded.

"Spratt and the kids found her climbing down from Rattle Alley," Hewe told Jordan, "and brought her to me."

"Make sure they know we're pleased with them," the black man responded.

"Do those children really live on the tip?" Gemma asked.

"Here and there. Don't worry about them—they're survivors. Like you, it seems."

"That's what Arden said," Gemma replied awkwardly. "But each time I owe my survival to others."

"That's part of the technique," Jordan put in. "Knowing whom to use, and whom to trust."

"Me, for instance," Hewe added. Spreading his hands wide, his face a picture of innocence, he addressed an imaginary audience. "Would *you* follow this man into a hole in the ground?"

"I didn't have much choice," Gemma said, smiling.

"True, but why spoil my high opinion of myself?"

Footsteps were heard from the tunnel and Hewe froze, listening. When a knock sounded at the door, the same pattern as before, he went to the spyhole, then unbolted the door and opened it. Paule was there. Hewe spoke to him and he went away again, leaving Arden, who stepped inside. He looked about him suspiciously, and blinked in the lamplight. Gemma stood up, waiting for his embrace, but Arden just glanced at her and gave no greeting. Then he stared at Jordan.

"Who are you?" he asked harshly.

"They're friends," Gemma said quickly. "They hid me from the guards."

Arden looked at her again, but his expression did not soften.

"If you hadn't been so *stupid*, they wouldn't have had to," he snapped.

"You do your friend an injustice," Jordan interposed calmly.

"And what do *you* know about it?" Arden demanded, turning on him. Jordan faced his glare with equanimity.

"Gemma was outraged by what happened in court," he said, "and she reacted according to her nature. It was just bad luck that caused her to be unmasked—you can't blame her for that."

"Oh, quite the expert, aren't we," Arden said sarcastically. "Well let me tell you, *friend*, this woman is trouble!" He pointed at Gemma but continued to stare at Jordan. "Ever since she got here, my life has been chaos. That's her *nature*. Luck has nothing to do with it." He spat the words out as if they were poison, and to Gemma they were. She felt something shrivel up inside her. The rational part of her mind told her that he had taken the court decision hard and was now striking out, trying to heal his own pain by hurting others. Yet his words did hurt, whatever his subconscious motive, and hurt all the more because she knew they held at least a grain of truth.

"Take it easy," Hewe growled.

Arden spun round and for a moment Gemma thought he was going to hit the big man, but he wisely refrained from doing so. Instead, his shoulders sagged and Gemma saw some of the anger drain out of him. He turned back to face her.

"Why did you do it?" There was anguish in his quiet question.

"I couldn't help it," she replied. "I'm sorry."

Throughout the altercation, Jordan had remained in his seat; now he stood and offered his place to Arden. "Wine?" he asked. Arden nodded and four glasses were filled. When they were all seated again, Jordan said, "The trial was fixed."

"You think I don't know that?" Arden replied bitterly, his eyes downcast. "I think I can even see why."

"Political chicanery," the other went on. "Your cause had made quite an impression on the citizens, but the Guild had no intention of countenancing the expenditure to grant your plea. So the judgment was organized so that Lunkett appeared to be a compassionate man, who was nevertheless willing to bow to the law."

Arden nodded wearily, but Gemma exclaimed in disbelief, "All that ritual was just for *show*?" Her mind balked at such devious cruelty.

"When you've lived here as long as I have," Jordan answered, "such things are no longer surprising."

There was silence for a while.

"What will you do now?" Hewe asked eventually, and Arden looked up from his wine.

"If the city won't help, I must," he said, but with little conviction in his words. "I'll find the source of the river and find a way to divert it." He sounded as if he were merely reciting from memory.

"I wish you good fortune," Jordan said.

"I'll need it." Then a new thought occurred to him. "Can your people help me?"

"We have enough problems of our own, I'm afraid," Jordan replied sympathetically. "Diverting rivers is not something we've had much call for, and we've no one who would even know how to start."

Arden nodded, sinking further into depression.

After another pause, Jordan said, "There is an alternative, though."

"What?"

"You could join *us*, help to overthrow the Guild. Then—"

"That could take years," Arden interrupted. "By then the valley and everyone who lives there would be dead."

"What about you, Gemma?" Jordan asked. "We could certainly use your skills."

"Me?" Gemma was surprised and looked to Arden for guidance, but he just stared into space over the rim of his glass. "I think I'd be more of a liability."

"To begin with, perhaps," Jordan replied honestly. "But we must look beyond the time when we have put this city to rights." He grinned at Hewe. "You've seen it, I know you have. There are greater things wrong with the world, and to solve those problems we're going to need all the special talents we can get."

"If you've lived here such a long time," Gemma asked thoughtfully, "how can you know about all those things?"

"Because I'm a traveler—of sorts." Jordan smiled. "We have eyes everywhere."

"What does it mean?" she asked.

"That's the problem—we don't know. What do you think?"

Words and images sprang into Gemma's mind. The fisherman at the preliminary trial: *The gods be my witness but it was sorcery. What else can it be?* The blue-robed fanatic: *The world is breaking apart.* Jordan himself in the tavern: *The whole world is going insane.* Her head was spinning as more visions appeared: skyravens screaming overhead; the gray raider shouting, "Death to the demon-spawn!" a gray monolith flickering with blue flame; elementals swooping past; a stage exploding into flame; *something* calling her from the far south; islands disappearing; rivers drying up. *The magic is fading.*

"It's as though . . ." she began hesitantly, "as though they were all parts of something too big for us to comprehend." She paused. "None of it makes sense. How can we hope to put it right when we can't even see what's wrong?"

"We have to keep trying," Jordan said. "Gathering information. That's why people like Arden can be so valuable to us."

Arden looked up at the mention of his name.

"What are you talking about?" he asked.

"More of the nonsense that you were so eager to escape from the other night," Jordan answered.

Arden showed signs of waking up now. "*Please* don't start her off on all that again! Flame walls and other worlds, dying suns and madness. You'll be extolling the virtues of magic soon," he added sarcastically.

"You said yourself that the valley is a place of magic," Gemma interjected.

"That's different!"

"Why?"

They stared at each other in silence.

"I think the valley is important," Jordan said softly. "There may be lessons for us all there. I would dearly love to visit it." Gemma nodded vigorously in agreement.

"Well, you'd better be quick." Arden was bitter now.

"But, Arden, there are so many other mysteries in the world," Jordan continued.

"Not for me," the other replied obstinately.

"Go back to the valley, then. Do what you can for them," the black man went on. "But help *us* at the same time. You can send us information—about anything and everything. The strange sights that you witness. Eventually it will all become clear."

Arden thought for a while.

"All right," he said at last. "You deserve help if you're trying to get rid of the stinking bastards who run this place."

"Thank you. Will you want to leave quickly?"

"The sooner the better," the traveler replied.

"We can have your horses outside the eastern gate in an hour," Jordan explained. "Packed and ready to go."

"Good," Arden said. "That'll be fine." He sounded impressed.

Jordan turned to Gemma.

"What will *you* do?" he asked. "I still want you to stay and help us."

"What?" Arden looked from one to the other, surprise and dismay in his eyes.

"Gemma has certain . . . abilities," Jordan said evenly, "whether you choose to believe in them or not."

"Don't do this!" Arden sounded desperate now. "It'll hurt her."

"She can be of use to us." The black face was impassive. "I'm sure of that."

Arden turned to Gemma. "I suppose this is what you want," he said.

Is it? Gemma wondered. *These men take me seriously, at least. But I want to see the valley so much—and I still need to go south. But perhaps I should help here. . . .*

In the face of her continued silence, Arden stood and went to the door.

"Well, I'm going back to the valley," he said. "Are you coming or not?"

Gemma hesitated, then glanced apologetically at Jordan.

"I'm coming," she said.

chapter 26

As Jordan had promised, their horses were waiting for them just outside the city walls. Arden checked their harnesses and equipment quickly, and thanked the young lad who had taken care of them. The boy disappeared silently and the travelers left. They rode slowly through the tangle of make-shift buildings, but this time they were not greeted with suspicious or envious stares. To their amazement, they even received a few smiles; Jordan's help had obviously extended beyond the walls of Newport.

Avoiding the main routes away from the city, they came to the edge of the shantytown and rode over open scrubland, heading southeast. "Steer clear of the coast road for a league or so," Hewe had advised. "After that, there's little chance of your meeting up with a patrol—they don't like to stray too far from their lunch."

Once clear of the narrow thoroughfares, there was a great temptation for them to urge their horses to a gallop, to get as far away from the vile and threatening city as quickly as possible. They restrained themselves, however, knowing that it would be foolish and possibly dangerous to risk attracting attention to themselves now. They had already avoided too many pitfalls, and, in any case, Lark and Mischa would not appreciate working so hard at the beginning of a long and arduous journey. Nevertheless, each step that took them further from Newport brought with it a corresponding rise in their spirits. They were free!

They owed this, in great measure, to Jordan and his friends. Once the decision to leave had been made, Gemma and Arden had been led through part of the massive underground network that existed below the city, eventually emerging inside one of the shacks beyond the eastern gate. The exis-tence of several tunnels under the city walls was a closely guarded secret, and one which would play a major role should Jordan's plans ever come to fruition.

In making their exit in this fashion they had, of course,

avoided potential difficulties with the gate sentries. Explaining their unauthorized stay in the city and concealing Gemma's identity would have been a terrifyingly risky business. Jordan told them that it *could* have been arranged, but not at such short notice. "There are limits to my powers, after all!"

Now they rode in silence, intent on making good progress in what remained of the day. Both were occupied with their own thoughts, but after a while, having become accustomed to her horse's motion, Gemma turned back to look at the city.

"I wonder what will happen there?" she mused quietly. Arden also glanced back.

"I hope it burns to the ground," he said sourly. After a moment he realized what he had said and laughed, the sound bringing a smile of relief to Gemma's face. "Perhaps I should have left you there after all," he said. "You'd already made a good start."

"I nearly did stay," Gemma told him softly.

"I know." After a moment he added, "Do you regret coming away?"

"In some ways."

The rode on in silence once more, Arden concealing the hurt he felt at her words. As the sun went down, Gemma thought she saw a faint blue corona about its edge, but decided that she must be imagining things. She looked away, spots dancing before her eyes.

"It's not that I *want* to doubt you, Gemma," Arden said suddenly, a note of pleading in his voice. "It's just that there are too many *real* things for me to worry about in this world. I'm never going to be able to believe in this magic of yours until I see some *proof*. You can understand that, can't you?" He looked at her, green eyes appealing mutely.

Surprised by his outburst, Gemma did not answer for a few moments. Finally she replied, "I understand. But it doesn't make it any easier."

"Do you . . . do you want to go back?" he asked hesitantly.

"No. I want to see the valley. It *is* important—even Jordan recognized that," Gemma said. "And I still have to go south. The longing hasn't gone away." Silently she added, *And I want to go with you.*

"You're sure?"

"Yes. Don't you want me to come?" She laughed, sounding shrill and nervous to herself, but Arden grinned happily.

"Of course I do. I didn't mean all those things I said about you back there. I was just so angry over that ridiculous trial."

"It's all right, I don't blame you," she answered. "I *have* been nothing but trouble for you so far, and probably will be again. Are you prepared for that?"

"I'd be disappointed if it were any other way," he replied happily, and they smiled at each other.

The blossom in Gemma's heart, which had shriveled in the underground room, began to bloom again.

———•———

That night they camped beside a small pond.

"I wish I could pick it up and carry it with us," Arden said wistfully, eyeing the still water.

They reached the Abbey the next day, and although there were still several hours of daylight left, they decided to stop. Arden was confident now that they were not being followed and they decided to make the most of the brothers' hospitality before setting off across the arduous Diamond Desert.

The eerie silence of the ancient buildings left Gemma unnerved once more, but this time she sensed the peace behind it and, knowing what to expect, found the experience less of an ordeal. They left early the next morning but traveled slowly, resting often, especially during the hottest part of the day. Arden had acquired more of the brothers' fiery liquor, but did not drink any this time.

"We'll save it until we're on the other side of the desert," he explained. "It's not a good place to get drunk."

As if to emphasize his words, the desert produced a new surprise for Gemma that evening. They had camped while still on the edge of the barren plain, savoring the last vestiges of green, and were sitting quietly beside their fire when the horses began to snort and stamp nervously.

"What's gotten into them?" Gemma asked.

Arden shrugged and went to investigate. Gemma heard him talking softly, reassuring the horses, then jumped as he cursed loudly and yelled, "Gather everything up! Quick! We're moving."

"What's happening?" she shouted back as she began to shove items into their saddlebags. Arden came over, leading the horses, and helped her pack, hurriedly loading their wild-eyed mounts.

"What *is* it?" she asked again, frightened by his grim urgency.

For answer Arden picked up a branch from near the fire, and as he swept the burning embers away, dozens of tiny fires sprang across the soil.

The ground was moving.

By the flickering light of the quickly dying fires, Gemma saw that the earth was covered with a mass of creatures. They were about the size of her hand and looked like a cross between a spider and a crab. Their tails arched above their backs, ending in a venomous prong. They were hideous and Gemma shuddered helplessly.

"What *are* they?" she whispered, mesmerized by their rippling approach. Inarticulate squeaking noises sounded painfully in her head.

"Later," Arden said shortly. "Let's go!" He hoisted her up into the saddle and then mounted Lark. The horses needed no urging to move off and the horror was soon left far behind.

"We can circle back now," Arden said. "Get out of their path." They turned and went on at a more measured pace.

"What are they?" Gemma repeated.

"Scorpions. They usually move in groups of two or three, and are easy enough to deal with then. Just occasionally, though, they gather together and travel in their hundreds, like that. No one knows why. The only thing you can do then is to get out of their way."

"Are they poisonous?" Gemma asked.

"Yes," Arden replied, confirming her thoughts. "A sting is very painful, though it won't kill you. More than one . . . It's a good thing we weren't asleep."

"Do they always make noises like that?"

Arden was taken aback. "What noises?" he asked.

"The squeaking," Gemma replied. "Didn't you hear it?"

"No." He was puzzled, but just said, "We can turn again now. We'll soon be behind them and then we can relax."

Gemma leaned forward and ruffled Mischa's mane. "Thanks for the warning," she whispered. The mare neighed softly.

"That means 'You're welcome,'" Arden said, laughing. "They weren't too keen to hang around either."

———————•———————

They set up camp again, but it took them a while to get to sleep, in spite of Arden's assurances that they were perfectly safe now that the scorpions had passed by. They jumped each time the horses moved or snorted.

However, no harm befell them that night, and in the

morning they started across the desert. Arden spotted the standing stone late into the next day. Pointing it out to Gemma, he said, "That means we're halfway across, and we're exactly on course."

"How can you navigate so accurately?" she asked, gazing at the featureless landscape that surrounded them.

"By the sun; the stars too if they're still visible," he replied. "But mostly by natural talent."

"I see your usual modesty is reasserting itself," she remarked with a smile.

"I'm as much at home here as I am anywhere," Arden said, his tone serious. "Out here, I understand life. What's important and what isn't."

"Whereas in the city you're just a poor, befuddled country boy," Gemma completed for him.

"I wouldn't go *that* far," he retorted, grinning. "Shall we camp by the stone tonight—for old times' sake?"

"Yes," she answered eagerly, glad that he had suggested it first. Arden was too preoccupied with memories of their earlier encounter to notice her enthusiasm. Something of his mood touched Gemma and after a few moments' silence, she said, "It wasn't that long ago, was it?"

"No, I suppose not," he replied, then glanced at her. "It seems much longer, though."

Gemma chose to make light of his comment.

"Does time drag by *so* painfully when you're in my company?" she demanded petulantly.

"Actually, it seems just like yesterday," Arden said, matching her mock anger with equally unconvincing timidity.

"Have you forgotten *so much*?" she retorted.

"As much as possible!"

"Oh, the nerve of this man!" she exclaimed to Mischa.

"I give up," Arden said to Lark. "Women. You can never satisfy them."

Both horses neighed in apparent agreement and their riders burst out laughing. Behind their merriment and their war of words, however, Gemma and Arden recognized unspoken messages.

All this time, the steady pace of the horses had been bringing them nearer to the monolith, and as they approached, Gemma felt a thrill of anticipation, mixed with a little fear. This place had marked a new beginning for her last time—almost a new birth. What would it bring now?

They set up camp as the sun set, and once again Gemma saw a faint blue flickering at the edge of the golden disc. She pointed it out to Arden, asking if he saw it too, and he nodded, a puzzled expression on his face.

"What do you think it is?" she asked.

Arden shrugged. "Who knows?" he said, turning away. "Right now, I'm more interested in dinner."

That, Gemma thought, *is the end of* that *conversation*.

After their meal they sat beside the fire, feeding it with small pieces of thorn bush. Arden produced the Abbey liqueur and poured two generous measures into their cups.

"I thought the desert wasn't a good place to get drunk," Gemma said.

"Only if you're about to travel or are already lost," he replied. "Neither of which applies to us. And you have a whole night to sleep it off."

"Me? What about you? *You're* the navigator."

"Strong drink never affects me," he responded airily. "Sad, really. I'm sure I'm missing a great pleasure." His face wore a ridiculously mournful look, but his eyes were twinkling.

"That's not what I would have said," Gemma replied, laughing. "I remember putting you to bed one night back in Newport."

"What? I deny it!" he exclaimed.

Gemma didn't know whether he was still joking, or whether he really could not remember the end to the tavern celebrations, and decided to test him.

"It's true. Did you know you have a pear-shaped birthmark on your—"

"Enough!" Arden cut her off. "Drink," he ordered, raising his own cup. She obeyed, smiling over the rim as she sipped gently at the fiery liquid. They drank in companionable silence for a while, then Arden threw some more sticks on the fire. They spluttered and smoked for a few moments before catching alight.

"The job's still yours any time you want it," he said quietly.

"I'll bear that in mind," she replied, trying to keep her tone light, then found she could no longer trust her voice. *What are you waiting for?* she demanded of herself. *You can't deny how you feel, and it's obvious that he's in the same state. Say something!* But no words would come.

"Want some more?" Arden asked, offering the bottle.

Gemma nodded, hating herself for not speaking. For a time the only sounds came from the crackling fire.

"I . . . I'm not very good . . ." she began at last. "I don't know how to deal with situations like this." It sounded feeble, but Arden appeared to understand.

"It doesn't matter," he said, and Gemma could detect no hurt in his voice. "I'm not exactly an expert myself."

"But—"

"Don't mention the dancing girls!" he ordered. "For your information, I've never been in this situation before." He paused. "Has anyone ever told you how beautiful you are?"

Me? Gemma thought in amazement. When she did not reply, Arden went on, "Here we are, all alone under a desert sky, with enough stars up there to fill a dozen love songs, enough drink in this bottle to shed anybody's inhibitions, and neither of us knows what to do with any of it! Just relax, Gemma, and enjoy the moment. *I* am. I think I've died and gone to heaven."

"To where?"

Arden laughed. "Here I am being wonderfully romantic, and all you want are facts!" he said. "According to the brothers, heaven is where you go after you've died—providing you've lived a righteous life and not offended the gods."

"Oh."

"Don't look so worried," he went on. "I'm not planning on making the trip just yet."

"That's not what—"

"I know," he interrupted. "Don't worry anyway." He stood up, then crouched before her, putting gentle brown hands on her shoulders. "We have plenty of time." He kissed her lightly on the forehead, then stood up again. "I must check the horses before we go to sleep," he said, then turned and walked away. Gemma watched him go, her thoughts in turmoil. Tipping her head back, she gulped down the rest of her drink. Her throat and stomach burned, but she hardly noticed.

We have plenty of time.

She glanced at the deeper blackness of the standing stone. *Do we?* she wondered.

chapter 27

Gemma soon regretted drinking so much so quickly. She would need to stay clearheaded and alert tonight—and the last thing she wanted to do was fall asleep before Arden. *How do the brothers reconcile this stuff with a righteous life?* she wondered maliciously. As she lay wrapped in her bedroll, she tried to remember the frightening details of the scorpions' march in an effort to remain awake, but the alcohol-induced drowsiness fought her. At last, and much to her relief, she heard Arden's breathing change and knew that he was fast asleep. She roused herself, crept slowly from her bed, and slipped out of the tent. Arden did not stir.

The night air was chill, and Gemma shivered in her underclothes but did not consider returning for warmer garments. A crescent moon and a multitude of stars cast a pale light over the barren landscape; the last embers of the evening's fire glowed a deep red. The horses were quiet beneath their canopy, and there was no wind. All was quiet.

Gemma took several deep breaths to clear her head, then walked barefoot toward the stone. She moved carefully, avoiding the spikes of the desert bushes and walking only where the rock and sand underfoot appeared smooth.

She halted beside the great pillar, standing where she had the first time. Looking first up at the rock, then down at the black pit in which it stood, her resolve wavered. Doubts and fears assailed her, especially as she had not told Arden of her intention. He would have objected, and this was something she *had* to do.

Reaching up and placing a hand gently on the stone, she was shocked at how cold it felt. The rock was smooth and icy to the touch. Surely it should have retained *some* heat from the day's sun? *One more mystery.*

Planting her feet so that she would not be caught off balance this time, Gemma pushed firmly. The huge stone moved immediately, tipping away from her and sliding smoothly to a new position, where it came to rest with a faint click. Gemma could not help but take a step back as she watched intently. Beneath her feet she felt—and heard—rumblings which gradually died away until all was still once more. *What did the noises mean?* It was as though the rocking stone was connected in some way to subterranean rocks, which were adjusting *their* positions in response to the movement above ground.

Gemma was still watching the stone like a hawk. *What if I imagined the whole thing? And there's no blue fire?* Pilgrim's fire, Arden had called it. What did the phrase mean? She wondered if she was going to be standing here all night, and smiled in spite of her apprehension.

"*There is no singing ox,*" an unfamiliar voice said. Her heart thumping, Gemma spun round to look at the tent, but it was still, and there was no sign of Arden. Suddenly terrified, she looked all about her, straining to see into the dark night.

"*It is wrong. The clan cannot gather. Odd,*" another voice said. Again Gemma looked around desperately, but could see nothing. *Am I going mad?* she wondered, but then her attention was caught and held—the blue flames were returning.

Once her eyes caught the first flicker, she was mesmerized. The flames grew as she watched, spreading through the grooves and channels of the rock, flashing off the smoother planes. Patterns—always moving, evolving—formed and changed before her eyes. As they grew in strength the stone became a beacon in the desert, lighting up a circle of sand and thorn with its eerie blue glow. Awake now, the horses shuffled and snorted and a tiny part of Gemma's mind wondered how long it would be before Arden was disturbed. For the most part, however, she was concerned only with the spectacle in front of her and the feelings it inspired.

She had been delirious the last time she had seen the pilgrim's fire, suffering from dehydration and sunstroke, and close to death. This time she was healthy and determined to take everything in. She found that her memory of the flames themselves was remarkably accurate; she could almost forecast their progression, and even thought at one point that she saw the design of the unbalanced scales within the flickering patterns.

What she had not remembered was the feeling of dread that accompanied the fire's growth. It was something cold, which started deep inside her, a simultaneous recognition of power and rejection of it. Her own experiences of magic gave her an insight into what she was witnessing, yet the power at work here was different. It was immense, remote, implacable. Gemma recognized its nature but could not begin to understand its source.

Gemma also knew from the depths of her being that this power was also cruel, cold, and inhuman. Yet it *was* magic, and further proof that she was right. Magic might have changed—indeed she was certain that it had—but it still existed!

Why should this stone be guarded by such power?

The flames now covered the entire surface of the stone, so bright that it hurt Gemma's eyes to look at it. Yet she could not turn away. The chill repelled her, but the power could not be denied, and drew her to itself against her will. The air grew heavy with an arcane pressure, making it difficult for Gemma to breathe. She was spellbound, unable to move or shout for help.

What have I done? Arden, help me! she cried silently.

A strange voice answered her.

"Tall-one-sheds-skins sings in need. Ox."

"Unaware. Not to the clan. Ed," yet another stranger said.

Gemma's mind reeled. To be held captive by the awesome power of the stone was frightening enough. To have the terror multiplied by unseen observers who spoke in riddles was too much for her to bear, and she felt a familiar blackness swirl within her head. As she fell, strong hands caught her and steadied her fainting body.

A voice spoke close to her ear, a strong, familiar voice, now tinged with awe. She could not tell what he said, but Arden's presence sent a warm glow of security flooding through her and she leaned back gratefully into his embrace.

The stone moved. Slowly, remorselessly, it tipped back toward them until it rested in its original position once more. Arden dragged her away from it, but Gemma was no longer frightened. The power that had transfixed her was receding, its job done. The flames gradually died away, leaving only a few glow-worm specks.

Beneath their feet the earth trembled and boomed once more. Then all was silence.

Holding her tenderly but firmly, Arden turned her round so that he could look into her face. Gemma's eyes were glazed but she managed to smile weakly.

"Are you all right?" he asked, the concern obvious in his voice. She nodded slowly. "What were you doing out here? No, don't answer that now. Come back to the tent and we'll talk about this in the morning.

"There's no one else here," he repeated. "Come inside."

Gemma obeyed, too weary to do anything else. Sleep was an inviting prospect. But she knew that Arden was wrong, and they were not alone in the desert. She had seen them at last.

Several pairs of eyes, pinpoints of blue, as if reflecting their memories of the pilgrim's fire. But they had not been focused on the stone.

They had been looking at her.

chapter 28

"Don't ever do that again!" Arden said forcefully. "Whatever it was out there could have killed you. What were you trying to prove?"

Although Gemma had woken up early the next morning—much to her surprise—Arden had still been awake before her. When he saw her eyes open, he hastened to make sure that she was all right. Then, obviously satisfied, he gave her a stern lecture.

"I had to see if it would happen again," she replied, trying to justify her action. "And it did!"

"What?"

"The blue flames, after I pushed the stone over."

"After you did *what*?" he exclaimed.

Gemma told her astonished companion how the fire was apparently a response to the stone being moved, as if it were necessary to restore some inexplicable balance.

"You saw it move back, didn't you," she stated.

"A rocking stone," Arden said. "Who would have thought it?" Then his rapt surprise changed to anger.

"Why did you have to sneak off alone?" he demanded. "Why didn't you tell me what you were doing?"

"Because you don't like me fooling with magic," she replied, gently mocking.

"Who said anything about magic?" Arden exploded.

"I did!" she retorted. "What do you think caused those flames?"

He was shaken by the certainty in her voice, but said, "There could be any number of other explanations."

"Name one," she ordered.

"Well, you often see flickering lights on mountaintops during a storm," he replied.

"I'd hardly call this a mountain, and there wasn't a cloud in the sky!" Gemma was sarcastic now. "Stars, what will it take to convince you?"

Arden said nothing.

"Well, I can think of *something* that might," Gemma said, throwing off her bedclothes. "I'll push it over again, and this time you can watch the whole thing."

"No!" Arden's voice was firm. "You're not going anywhere near that stone."

"How are you going to stop me?"

"I'll manage."

"But Arden, *why*?"

"Stupid woman!" Arden said through gritted teeth. "What a question." He sighed. "Because last night was too much for you. You nearly fainted and if the horses hadn't woken me up . . ." He paused for breath. "*Then* you started talking nonsense, saying someone had spoken to you," He smiled. "And you'd not even had any sunbalm this time."

Gemma did not hear his feeble attempt at humor; the memories came flooding back, of strange voices—what had they said?—and the eyes. *Watching*.

"What's wrong?" Arden asked anxiously. Gemma was perfectly still, her face pale and her eyes unfocused. His words broke her reverie.

"Someone *did* speak to me," she said. "They were watching too. We have to find them!" With that, she scrambled up and dashed out of the tent. Arden followed, cursing her as a lunatic. Gemma looked all around, but even in broad daylight could see no other living thing save the horses.

Her gaze returned to the stone as Arden reached her.

"That's far enough," he said, but, deep in thought, Gemma did not respond. "Come and help me pack up the camp," Arden went on. "I want to be underway before it gets too hot."

"No." Gemma turned to face him. "I'm not leaving until we find out what all this means."

"Gods," Arden said wearily, rolling his eyes upward in exasperation. "Will you never learn?" He paused. "Let me put it another way. *I* am leaving, and so are the horses and all my equipment." He held up his hands to forestall her objections. "And I am not about to let you commit suicide by staying here alone. Have I made myself quite clear?" They stared at each other for a few moments, measuring their respective strengths.

"I don't understand you," Gemma said at last.

"*You* don't understand *me*?" Arden exclaimed.

"In the city, you asked me to prove the existence of magic

by breaking the lamp," she went on calmly. "I couldn't do it.
Now I have the chance to prove it to you conclusively, yet
you reject the idea out of hand. You don't *want* to see it, do
you."

"I *want* to get to the valley," he shot back. "My main
concern is to save that place and its people, not to go on a
wild goose chase after some mythical condition called magic."

"But it's the same thing!" Gemma yelled, her eagerness
almost lifting her off the ground.

"What are you talking about?" Arden was clearly mystified.

"You said it yourself," Gemma replied quickly. "*The magic
is fading.*"

"I didn't mean it like that."

"What you *meant* doesn't matter. You were right!" she
went on enthusiastically, her eyes begging him to listen. "It's
all connected—I know it is. The world has lost something
important, and unless we get it back, *everything* may be
destroyed, not just the valley!"

Her outburst over, Gemma took Arden's hands in her own,
pleading silently for understanding. He was quiet for a long
time.

"You are the strangest creature I've ever met," he said
eventually. Gemma let her breath out in a sigh of relief. "I
don't understand half of what you're saying, but . . ." he
went on, "even if you *are* right, what possible use can your
magic be if all it does is tip a stone over?"

"That wasn't *my* magic!" Gemma exclaimed, shocked at his
misapprehension.

"Then what . . . ?" Arden's frown showed his confusion.

"*That* magic came from somewhere else," Gemma said,
trying to explain what she had experienced. "And it was
much more powerful than anything I could aspire to."

"All that just to move a stone you can push over with one
hand." Arden's scepticism was obvious, but Gemma was thankful that he was at last prepared to discuss it. It was a step in
the right direction.

"I don't understand it either," she said. "That's why I have
to investigate further." She let the words hang in the air as
Arden looked over her shoulder at the stone. *He can't deny
he saw the fire last night*, she thought.

"Are you going to let me do it again?" Gemma asked softly.

Arden shook his head. "No." Then, before she could argue,
he added, "*I'm* going to do it. You stay well back."

With that he released his hands from her grasp and strode away, not giving her time to respond. Gemma could only turn and watch as Arden approached the monolith. She willed herself to concentrate, to learn everything she could in the sober light of morning, but found herself worried about Arden's safety. *Too late now*, she thought as he reached up and pushed the stone away from him. He stepped back, amazed at the ease with which it moved.

Once again the huge rock moved silently and steadily to its alternate position. A moment after it came to rest, they heard the subterranean rumbling, and Arden looked down at the ground in astonishment. Then he switched his attention back to the stone.

Gemma felt the difference from the instant the first blue sparks appeared, and tried to call out, but both she and Arden were held motionless by the uncanny power. As the flames grew and multiplied, so did her feeling of dread. By the time the blue fire was at its brightest, she was screaming silently at Arden, *Get away! Get away!* Still neither of them could move.

An instant later, Gemma realized what the crucial difference was. The power had been impersonal before, emotionless and icy cold. Now there was anger and vindictiveness within its strength.

An ugly purple color appeared in the midst of the blue, like an old bruise. Slowly it changed, a rough circle of pulsating color. It grew brighter and brighter, first purple, then red, and finally an angry orange.

An explosion rent the air, and jagged streaks of light arched from the orange glare toward Arden. He fell as if poleaxed and Gemma was forced to her knees by the noise, the sudden release of energy, and an uncontrollable surge of fear which turned her legs to jelly. At the same time, the monolith moved back to its original position and the flames disappeared, much more quickly than before. The ground trembled for a few moments, then all was still.

The sound of the horses' frantic neighing roused Gemma from her stupor. She stared at them as they strained at their tethers, seeing their wild eyes and foam-flecked mouths, but could do nothing for them now. Half-walking, half-crawling, she made her way to Arden's unmoving body.

His eyes were closed and she could not tell if he was breathing or not. She searched for a pulse beneath the cold skin of his neck, and found a weak, erratic fluttering. Knowing that she could not move him easily, Gemma glanced up at the stone which towered above them both. She decided it must be safe now—having already done its worst—and she stumbled off to collect blankets to cover her companion.

Arden regained consciousness three hours later. Gemma's head was not the only one which turned to look anxiously at him, and under the scrutiny of so many inquisitive eyes, he almost fainted again.

chapter 29

After making Arden as comfortable as possible, Gemma sat down beside him, with her back to the stone, and began chafing his cold hands, trying to rub some life back into them. She checked his pulse often, terrified by his shallow breathing. It was there each time, but remained very weak. Feeling quite helpless, she left his side after a while and went to check on the horses; she knew that Arden would have wanted her to do this, and besides, both their lives might depend on the services of Lark and Mischa. The animals were quieter now, though still wide-eyed, and Gemma fussed over them for a while, talking and stroking them gently. She glanced every few moments at Arden, and when she had calmed the horses, she returned to her companion, overjoyed to see a little more color in his face. He was still unconscious but—unless this was wishful thinking on her part—his pulse seemed a little stronger.

She spoke quietly to him, promising that if he got better she would never meddle with magic again.

"Well, not this sort anyway," she amended. "Why did the stone hurt you and not me? It's almost as if it was angry at being disturbed again." She smiled, then frowned. *Ridiculous thought!* "In any case, I don't think we'll try it again. We'll leave here just as soon as you're well enough and head straight for the valley." *Which is what you wanted to do in the first place.* "Oh, Arden, I'm so sorry. If only I could make you hear me." She stared at his unmoving face, tears welling up in her eyes.

I love you, Arden, she thought, unable to say it out loud even though she knew he could not hear.

"*Ard-en?*" a voice replied, sounding confused. "*Is that one name or two? Av.*"

Gemma started violently, looking about her but seeing no one. Then it gradually dawned on her that no sound had disturbed the desert air—the strange noise had been *inside her head.* She was frightened again, beginning to doubt her own sanity.

Another alien voice spoke in her mind.

Tall-one-sheds-skin is clanless. Ed. There was sorrow in its
tone.

"Who are you?" Gemma shouted, desperate now. *Who are
you?*

The response was a feeling of consternation, which only
served to reinforce her confusion. She shut her eyes.

Can she be nameless? Ox.

The nameless do not speak. Yet we hear. Ed.

Before she said Ard-en. Perhaps one of these. Od.

Gemma clasped her hands to her ears, though she knew it
would make no difference. *Stop it! Stop it!* she implored
silently.

The voices ceased.

Gemma put down her hands and cautiously opened her
eyes, afraid of what she might see. The horses stood patiently
beneath their canopy, and the stone remained a silent presence behind her, but there was nothing else except sand,
rock, and thornbush.

A sudden movement on the ground caught her eye and she
froze, a new and more immediate fear clutching at her. A
scorpion, its yellow body glistening in the sunlight, was heading straight toward Arden. Gemma looked about desperately
for a weapon, but could find none. In his weakened state
Arden would not survive a sting from the venomous creature,
and Gemma stepped between the two, kicking sand at the
advancing animal. It hesitated, then came on. Just as Gemma
was steeling herself to attack it, help came from an unexpected quarter.

One of the animals of her dream came bounding out of the
scrub, moving quickly on four straight legs, its tail erect and
curled at the tip like a walking stick. It darted straight at the
scorpion, and pounced on it, biting off the poisonous extrem-
ity with one swift movement. Having thus disarmed its prey,
the furry creature stuffed the scorpion into its mouth and
munched with evident enjoyment.

Gemma watched with a mixture of relief, fascination, and
disgust. *A meyrkat!*

Having finished its meal, the animal stood up on its hind
legs and looked at Gemma, as if to determine whether she
represented any danger. Looking into its eyes, Gemma realized who had been watching her the night before. The meyrkat
stood no higher than her knee, and was covered with dull

brown hair, shorter on its head than the rest of the body. Its eyes were black, a circle of dark fur around them making them appear larger than they actually were. A sharp nose sniffed inquisitively. Its forepaws, which ended in long claws, hung loosely down in front of its body.

As they faced each other only a few paces apart, Gemma saw how perfectly the meyrkat blended in with its surroundings. *No wonder no one ever sees them,* she thought.

The clan hears you, nameless one. Ox. The words came into Gemma's mind unbidden. There was a pause, as if awaiting a response, then the voice went on. *You disturb our burrow. The young do not understand namelessness. Are you Ard? Or En? Ox.*

Neither, Gemma thought. *I am Gemma. Ox.*

The meyrkat gave a small yelp. Gemma knew that she was communicating with the animal, but did not understand what they were talking about.

Ox is clan-name. I bear it. Ox. The voice now sounded indignant as well as confused.

Gemma began to understand. *You are called Ox? My name is Gemma,* she thought deliberately, full of wonder at what she was doing. Could this really be mind-talk—like that between a wizard and his familiar?

The meyrkat appeared to be considering her last statement.

Gemma, it said eventually. *That is two names. Ox.*

In my clan it is one. Gemma, she replied, remembering to add her own name to the end of her statement.

It implies lack of knowledge. Of self. Ox, the meyrkat responded.

Why? I don't understand. Gemma. She was beginning to get the hang of this, and had no more doubts about the genuine nature of the conversation or with whom she was speaking. Adding her own name to each statement was obviously expected, presumably to identify the speaker, and it was her failure to do this which had caused the earlier consternation. In addition, she was also beginning to realize that not all her thoughts could be heard by the meyrkat. It was possible to project some while keeping others "quiet," either because of the demands of privacy, or irrelevance. She found this immensely comforting.

Long names, little knowing. Ox. The meyrkat's voice was patient now, as though explaining something to a child. Gemma thought she saw what he meant.

It's the only name I have. Gemma.

Not Ard? Ox.

No. This is Arden. Gemma. She pointed to the still prostrate man, and saw the meyrkat's eyes follow her movement. *This could get confusing,* she thought to herself.

Ard-en. Is he without warmth? Ox.

No. He's still alive. Gemma, she replied, hoping that was what Ox meant. She knelt down and felt Arden's pulse. It was a little stronger.

God-sky-fire-stone angry. Bite him. Ox, the meyrkat commented.

Gemma nodded.

Can you help him, Ox? Gemma.

I will ask the clan. The clan stands tall in knowing. Ox.

———•———

With that he turned and ran off, soon disappearing in the tangle of thornbush. Gemma felt a wrench at the parting; there had been something close and uplifting about their intimate contact, something beyond mere communication. For the first time in her life she began to appreciate why wizards became so emotionally attached to their familiars. She hoped that Ox would return soon.

———•———

When Arden opened his eyes, the first thing he saw was the row of meyrkats, standing only three paces from where he lay. They were looking in all directions, so that he saw some in profile, the backs of some heads, small rounded ears protruding, and some sharp little noses pointing toward him. Within moments of his return to consciousness, however, they all turned toward him in unison, and he was faced with a dozen pairs of shiny black eyes. Their synchronized movement gave Arden such a strange feeling that he wondered whether he was still insensible—and the animals a dream-illusion.

Then Gemma's face came into his field of vision, her eyes full of hope and worry.

"Are you all right?" she asked anxiously. When he did not respond, she added, "Can you hear me?"

He tried to speak, but could barely move his tongue. All that emerged from his lips was a feeble hissing sound, but Gemma seemed to gather what he meant, and smiled.

"Can you move?" she asked.

Arden tried, but his body felt remote and numb, and his

limbs did not respond. He was frightened by this, and something of what he felt must have shown in his eyes, for Gemma's expression grew concerned.

"You'll be fine soon," she said reassuringly. "Don't try to rush."

Arden realized then that he had no idea what had happened. Why was he lying helpless on the ground? Had he been bitten by a snake or a scorpion? And why couldn't he remember?

"It makes a change for me to be nursing you," Gemma said brightly, but Arden recognized the false cheerfulness in her voice. She moved her head to look at the meyrkats, and Arden saw the standing stone behind her. Its gray presence filled him with a nameless dread. A tiny sliver of memory came back, and he tried to speak, but could not. Gemma noticed his effort.

"Do you want some water?"

"Sss."

She dipped a finger in a cup and moistened his lips, then dropped a little into his mouth. A painful tingling sensation began in the tips of his fingers and toes, and he embraced the sensation gratefully, willing it to spread, to prove there was life within his body. His wish was granted. He was soon in exquisite agony as every muscle, every fiber, and every nerve within him awoke, protesting. With Gemma's help he was able to sit up and exercise his limbs, accelerating the painful return to awareness. He drank some more water and was at last able to talk.

"What happened?" he whispered. "What are *they* doing here?"

"Don't you remember?" she asked. When he shook his head, Gemma told him about the ill-fated experiment with the rocking-stone. He recalled none of it but deep inside he knew it for the truth. Fear of the unknown grew within him.

"You've been unconscious all morning," Gemma finished.

"Feels more like several days," he replied hoarsely. "And them? The meyrkats?"

"The clan have been helping me," Gemma answered, an eager smile on her face. "Ox saved you from a scorpion, and they've all been singing for your recovery."

"Ox?" Arden said in bewilderment.

"The tallest one. In the center."

The meyrkat Gemma indicated ducked its head quickly

and made a soft peeping sound. Arden blinked, wondering if
he *was* still dreaming.

"I can talk to them, Arden. Isn't it wonderful!" Gemma
said excitedly. "I have so much to tell you."

Arden nearly gave up then. For reasons he did not understand he found himself wanting to cry, and an unbearable
weariness overcame him.

"Not now, Gemma. Please. I have to sleep."

Though obviously disappointed, Gemma acquiesced and
made his resting place more comfortable. The last thing
Arden saw before he surrendered to sleep was one of the
meyrkats climbing onto a thornbush. With incredible agility
and balance the little creature stood upright on a flimsy
branch, scanning the land all about as if she were on lookout
duty.

———————•———————

When Arden next awoke, feeling much better, it was nearly
dusk. He was both thirsty and ravenously hungry, and Gemma
catered to his needs immediately, delighted by his return to
normality. The meyrkats were nowhere to be seen but Arden
could tell that Gemma was restraining herself—with some
difficulty—from bursting out with her news.

At Gemma's suggestion, Arden allowed himself to be helped
over to the tent. A fire had been prepared, and he looked
forward to its comfort. He felt very weak; whatever the stone
had done to him had robbed him of more than part of his
memory.

Gemma lit the fire, although the day was still warm, and
Arden relaxed, appreciating its glow, though he still felt cold.
His nurse noticed this, and went to get a blanket.

When she returned, Arden asked her about the meyrkats,
and the relief on Gemma's face was almost comical. "But tell
me slowly!" he added as forcibly as he was able, and smiled
weakly as she marshaled her thoughts.

"You remember when I said someone was talking to me
last night?" she began. "But you couldn't hear anything?"

Arden nodded. *That* he could recall, but there were other,
inexplicable gaps in his memory. He put the puzzle aside as
Gemma continued.

"Well, I didn't imagine it. It was the meyrkats!" Her eyes
were bright with pleasure. "They communicate among their
clan by mind-talk, and for some reason I can hear them

too—and speak to them. All from inside here." She tapped the side of her head.

"You're not making this up are you?" he asked, knowing the answer already.

"No, of course I'm not—and what's more, this is something I can *prove* to you," she replied eagerly. "Come and see them. The clan-burrow isn't far."

"Not now, Gemma. I already believe you," he said wearily. "I'll see them later. Just tell me about them for now."

"I've found out such a lot," she said proudly. "Sometimes it's difficult to understand what they're saying, because their words and ideas are so different from ours . . ."

"That's understandable," he muttered wryly.

"But I'm getting better at it. While you were asleep, we talked almost all the time." She hesitated.

"And?" he prompted.

"You told me to go slowly," she retorted, grinning. "I'm *trying* to tell you everything in a logical order."

"I stand corrected," he said, eyes meekly downcast.

"Stop it!" Gemma laughed. "Right," she went on, becoming serious again. "First of all, they do everything as a team, and the clan is all-important. I didn't know animals could be like that. Some are very good at certain things, but they pool their talents for the benefit of the others. Whenever they go hunting for food, one or two will keep an eye out, watching for predators. Some of them can climb to higher spots, on bushes for instance. They have incredible balance."

"I saw one of them," Arden put in, amazed at his own calm acceptance of Gemma's strange tale.

"That was Av," Gemma said. "She'll always find the best vantage point. If the coast is clear, she'll make little peeping noises, but if she sees an eagle or something like that, she'll bark a warning and they can all be safe in the burrow in a few moments."

"Why don't they use mind-talk for that?"

"I'm not sure," Gemma replied thoughtfully. "I suppose it's used for conversation, whereas the audible calls act directly on their instincts."

"You *are* an expert already," Arden commented. "It's a pity they can't get to the top of the stone. They could see for leagues from up there."

"They wouldn't use it for that even if they could. They hold the rocking-stone in awe," she answered.

"We've got that in common then!" Arden said ruefully.

"They call it the 'god-sky-fire-stone,' " Gemma added, "which shows they don't understand it. That's interesting, considering they live so close by."

"Why does it show that?"

"Because the less they understand something, the longer the name they give to it," she said. "For instance, humans are obviously a bit of a mystery to them because we're called 'tall-ones-shed-skins.' I think that refers to the fact that we wear clothes. Whereas their own names are all very short—Ox, Av, Ul, and so on."

"It must be nice to understand yourself so well," Arden remarked. Gemma was not sure how seriously to take him.

"Gem-ma and Ard-en cause them a few problems," she said. "They think we have two names each, and can't understand why." She shifted slightly, making herself more comfortable, then went on. "As far as I can tell, they eat anything that moves. Between them, they'll take on anything. I know they eat scorpions. They call them 'stinger-food.' Ox ate one that was threatening you. Ugh." She scowled at the memory. "There's also curve-food, whatever that is."

"Snakes?"

"Probably." Gemma shuddered. "I asked them if they drank water from the thornbush roots, but they didn't understand the question. I don't think they know what water is."

Arden looked thoughtful for a moment, then shook his head and asked, "How many of them are there?"

"About thirty. They're enormously proud of their burrow, which they've dug themselves." Gemma paused. "Od said something about another giant burrow with singing air, but I don't know what he meant." It was her turn to look puzzled. "He seemed to connect it with the stone, though."

"Singing is important to them?" Arden asked, remembering an earlier conversation.

"Yes," Gemma replied, laughing. "Though goodness knows why. They make an awful noise."

"It's no wonder I woke up then," he said, smiling. "Do they have a leader?"

"Yes. That's Ox. He's the largest, strongest male," she answered. "They are *so* like humans in some ways."

Arden let that pass. It was dark now and he was very tired.

"We'd better get you into the tent," Gemma said solicitously. "You can see the burrow tomorrow." Arden did not move, but stared into the fire. "They have a saying," Gemma went on. " 'The clan stands tall in knowing.' We can learn so much from them! And the mind-talk—have you realized? It's like the people of the valley."

Arden looked up at her, his face blank.

"What valley?" he asked.

chapter 30

At first Gemma thought Arden was joking, but realized very quickly that this was not so. He could remember his journey to the city and some of the events which had occurred there, but the details of the trial and all knowledge of the valley itself had vanished entirely from his memory.

Gemma tried to explain, patiently repeating all he had told her of the valley. She kept expecting him to react to some of the things she said, but he only listened intently. It seemed incredible, but the object of his recent obsession was now an unknown quantity. Having exhausted her second-hand knowledge, Gemma asked, "Is nothing familiar?"

Arden shook his head.

"But you loved it so!"

"I don't even know where it is," he replied gravely. "I remember a lot about the mountains—after all, I grew up there—but the valley . . ." His voice trailed away.

"So now where do we go?" Gemma asked softly.

"It must be somewhere to the southeast," he said. "Otherwise we wouldn't have come this way."

"We'll find it," she said firmly, wishing she could be as confident as she sounded. "Then it'll all come back."

Arden's eyelids were drooping. "For now we'll sleep," she added.

———•———

The tent was full of dreams.

Gemma looked down at her shadow skimming the desert floor far below. She saw the stone, a gray finger pointing skyward, encircled by tiny figures. Their singing reached her, recognizable above the rush of wind and the steady rhythm of wing-beats.

Her shadow passed over the stone, a flicker of darkness, and on its surface blue flames sprang into life. Gemma flew on, the familiar presences beside her.

Then she felt her companions shift and change, until there was only one other at her side. The familiarity was now tinged with sadness and regret. The nature of her flight had also changed; there was no effort involved in the smooth glide, but there was also less control. Her shadow-shape was different too, a sharp triangle that slid ever closer over green fields and frightened sheep. There was no desert here.

They landed, rolling over in the grass, laughing with exhilaration and the release of nervous tension. Gemma looked up at the massive city walls from whence they had taken off, and judged the distance they had traveled.

"Half a league?" she asked her companion.

"Half a thousand," he replied. "You can never come back now." There was such sadness in his voice that Gemma turned to look at him, suddenly frightened. She saw only the swarm at the far side of the field, retreating quickly. In their midst was a remote and shadowy figure.

"I need you!" she called, but a scream drowned her words. "Help me, Cai!"

———•———

The tent was full of dreams.

Arden was lost in a maze of metal. He walked endlessly down long corridors, across iron bridges, over chasms of steel, up and down gleaming stairways. Noise and heat assaulted him from all sides. Water rushed through channels, inducing dread in his heart; steam spouted from hidden geysers.

He walked on and on, but made no progress. He was on a treadmill, doomed to repeat his journey forever and forget it every time he completed a circuit, an endless discovery of something he already knew.

The bridge was narrow and crossed a ravine. Far below, white water rushed past. Arden was already halfway across when he saw the group of men and women who waited silently at the far side, arms folded, impassive metal faces watching his progress.

They're wearing masks, he thought.

Then the group started to shout, pointing at him. Arden tried to smile at them, but could not. He put up a hand to touch his cheek and instead touched cold metal. He tore desperately at the mask but it would not budge—no matter how he tried, he could not remove the terrible thing that had been sealed to his face. He screamed, losing his balance and falling from the bridge. As he did so, he glimpsed Gemma amid the iron-faced group. She was shouting, but he only heard her final words.

"Help me, Cai!"

Arden plunged into the metal depths.

———————•———————

They found themselves sitting bolt upright, facing one another, as the first light of the new day filtered in through the open tent flap. Though their eyes were wide open, they both saw different worlds, and their faces were marked with shock. Slowly they came back into focus and they truly saw each other.

"You were dreaming," Gemma said, testing her voice. She looked at him closely, frowning. "What are those marks on your face?"

Arden gingerly touched his cheek. It felt reassuringly warm and soft, but there were sore patches where the skin was tender and almost broken.

"It was a nightmare," he said slowly. "I think." The details were already fading from his mind. "Why do you need Cai to help you?"

Gemma was taken aback.

"I don't know. I dream of him sometimes," she said eventually.

"You obviously thought a great deal of him." There was the faintest hint of resentment in Arden's tone.

"Yes, I did. He was the only one who ever came close to understanding me."

They were quiet for a long time then, neither of them keen to continue their conversation. The day became real about them and the dreams gradually lost their power.

"How are you feeling?" Gemma asked at last.

"Much better." He grinned suddenly. "Almost human in fact. And hungry."

"Good. Let's eat, then we'll go and see the meyrkats. I want to learn as much as I can from them while we're still here."

After breakfast, Gemma led the way to the site of the clan burrow, where there was already a good deal of activity. Finding enough food in this inhospitable land required almost constant effort by the small animals. Nevertheless, as soon as the lookout spotted the humans' approach. Gemma sensed the news being passed to the clan, and a number of meyrkats began to gather. She was already a great favorite, as strange and interesting to them as they were to her. However, as she led Arden into an open area next to one of the burrow entrances, she received a sharp word of warning.

Don't talk, an adult meyrkat ordered. *It will distract the little one. Od.*

Gemma obeyed, and motioned Arden to stand still, putting a finger to her lips. In front of them, watched over by Od and an ever-increasing number of interested spectators, a very young meyrkat was circling a scorpion. For one so young, the sting would probably be fatal and Gemma felt the tension of the onlookers. *Why don't they help him?* she wondered privately.

The tiny animal was patting at the scorpion, darting in to try and bite off the venomous tail. His prey eluded him for some time, but eventually he succeeded, and happily ate his prize.

Well done, Em. You are learning. Od. The elder's congratulations echoed the mood of the entire group.

Thank you, mentor. Em, the youngster replied; his mouth full of scorpion and his tone full of pride.

"What was all that about?" Arden asked quietly.

"Each of the children is taught how to find food by one of the adults. The scorpion is one of their most important lessons," she replied.

Then Gemma was approached and bombarded with questions from all the meyrkats. Her head was soon spinning and she had to ask Ox to impose some sort of order to their queries. He complied and Gemma was then able to convince Arden of her ability to communicate with the clan. Not that he needed much proof—the fact that the elusive animals allowed them so close at all was evidence of a special relationship. Even so, he insisted on a demonstration, telling Arden in advance what she was asking the meyrkats to do. The animals then obeyed her instructions, amid much amusement. It was a game to them, and when Gemma finally announced that they had done enough, there was a chorus of protests. As a consequence the game continued and soon both humans had joined in the laughter. Gemma had originally asked for simple actions—a particular animal to move forward, another to give a lookout call, and so on. Now her requests brought forth somersaults, meyrkats burying each other up to the neck in sand, and three young ones jumping over Arden's outstretched leg.

The lighthearted atmosphere induced by all this spilled

over into the proceedings that followed. Gemma had several
questions she wanted to ask and a group of five meyrkat
elders, who agreed to answer as best they could. A number of
the others stayed to listen, but did not interrupt. Arden
excused himself after a while as he wanted to tend the horses;
he was also frustrated at not being able to join in the communication and did not feel that he should interrupt Gemma to
ask for explanations.

"They wish you well," she called out to him as he walked
away.

She was obviously trying to keep from laughing—what Ox
had actually said was *May your territory always be strong,
and your matings produce fine children.*

"Tell them thank you," Arden replied, smiling. "I wish
them well too. They're entertaining little bastards."

Gemma returned his greeting to the meyrkats, amending it
slightly in translation. Then she eagerly began her interroga-
tion. She was already familiar with the subtle differences of
coloring and stature, and had even begun to differentiate
between their "voices." After a while the statement of their
names at the end of each contribution became almost unnecessary, and she was able to face each speaker in turn.

How long have you lived here? Gemma.

Before knowing. Od.

The clan renews itself. Av.

New burrow after the Shaking. But same territory. Ox.

The Shaking was evidently the meyrkats' term for The
Leveling. Gemma knew from her earlier conversations that
the clan attached great importance to their territory, defend-
ing it against all comers, but found it hard to believe that
they could not have found a more hospitable home than the
exact center of the Diamond Desert. She asked if they ever
thought of traveling; the first answer came from a female who
had not spoken before.

There were wanderers once. Long ago. Ul. Her tone was
wistful.

Our ways of knowing are better now. Av, the older female
said gently, but Od interrupted firmly.

*We cannot leave. The god demanded our singing, and the
clan will not risk his anger. Od.*

What singing? Gemma.

To the god. When the wind turns. Od.

Gemma was not sure what to make of this but decided to make a guess.

Is the stone the god? Gemma.

Her question provoked agitation among the meyrkats, and their heads turned quickly this way and that, as if studying each other's reactions. It was the third male who eventually answered.

The god-sky-fire-stone is the god's gift to us. He stood here once and turned the air to stone. Ed.

We guard it still. Ul.

Some tales say he is within the rock. Ed.

Then you sing to the stone? Gemma, she ventured.

When the wind turns. Od.

When is that? Gemma.

The meyrkats did not understand that question, and Gemma had to wait for an answer.

When it does. Ox. The clan leader had been silent for some time, and now his voice contained an odd mixture of authority and confusion. Gemma gave up that line of inquiry and asked them instead what happened when they sang to the stone.

Our singing turns to fire and the ground moves. Ul. Her words were communicated in the romantic way that Gemma had learned to expect with Ul, but this time it was as though she were reciting an important and well-remembered lesson.

Blue fire? Like last night? Gemma, she asked eagerly.

No. There was no singing. The wind does not turn yet. Od.

But the flames are blue. Av.

They are not the same. Od. He sounded dogmatic, even angry, and there was an awkward mental silence. Then Ox re-entered the conversation.

We sing. That is right. Ard-en push. That is wrong. God-sky-fire-stone angry. Ox.

There were murmurs of approval from the others. Gemma could not fault his logic and the manner in which his words were imparted dissuaded her from pursuing the subject. She asked instead about the giant singing burrow that had been mentioned the day before. From their answers, she gathered that they were referring to the cave systems below the desert, but could not grasp why the meyrkats held them in such awe.

The roaring turns aside. Ed.

A solid wind, white with cold. Ul.

The singing sands are caused by the wind? Gemma.
For some reason this question caused them much amusement.
Gem-ma, you speak strange. Ox.
She laughed herself at this. The meyrkats were delighted
by the sound and some of the young ones who were listening
rolled about on the ground, chirruping happily.

After that, Gemma confined her questions to practical matters, and was rewarded with information about the clan's
organization and habits. She was shown their lookout points,
the special areas they used for lying in the sun, and several of
the burrow entrances.

Eventually, hunger ended the conversation, and Gemma
returned to Arden. Over lunch she told him what she had
learned; he was especially interested in the meyrkats' de-
scriptions of the caves.

"I can't help feeling that it's all connected with this valley
I'm supposed to be trying to save," he commented. "Perhaps
the cave systems reach right under the mountains."

"It's *all* connected somehow," Gemma replied. She was
learning to trust her own feelings—whatever had caused her
to come to this land had instilled in her a firm belief in
irrational truth.

"Their tales about the stone are interesting," Arden said.

"Some *tales*!" she replied. "It nearly killed you."

"It'll take more than that to get rid of me. I'm tougher than
I look!" He grinned.

"If only I could make proper sense of what they're telling
me," Gemma mused, pretending to ignore his last comment.

"Well, you don't have much time," Arden replied, serious
again. "Our supplies are running low. If we don't leave first
thing in the morning, we may never get out of this desert.
We can't eat scorpions."

Gemma spent the rest of that day making further attempts
to unravel some of the enigmas of her strange new friends.
She met with little success, however, because the animals
were now intent on foraging, having lost much of the morning in conversation. Food was scarce at this time of the year,
and filling thirty bellies was a full-time job. She did learn a
few more details of the clan's life—fascinating in themselves,
but of little practical value.

Gemma and Arden both slept well that night, and in the
morning they broke camp and prepared to leave. The clan
was there to see them go. After a number of farewells, which

indicated the meyrkats' sadness at their departure, Gemma and Arden were treated to some singing. The noise was excruciating and their expressions could not help but reflect this. The song of parting came to an abrupt end when one of the meyrkats announced, *That's enough singing. Ed.*

The humans then mounted their horses and with a further chorus of goodbyes and a final wave, Gemma and Arden left. Gemma found it painful to leave her new friends behind; the inside of her head seemed very quiet all of a sudden.

"I wish they could have come with us," she said longingly.

"So do I," Arden replied. "*They* might have had some idea where they were going!"

chapter 31

Eight days after leaving the desert, Gemma and Arden had found several small vales and their village communities in the mountains, but none had been in any way out of the ordinary, or had elicited any response from Arden. He remembered some of the places from his earlier wanderings, but could not relate them to the lost valley, and he gradually began to doubt the existence of their goal. Gemma, certain that it was there—*somewhere*—tried to console him.

"You told me that you had never heard of the valley before you arrived there," she said. "So it's not surprising that nobody else has heard of it."

"We could be in the wrong region altogether," he replied dejectedly. "Unless I remember *something*, we could wander around for months. And apparently we don't have that much time left."

Arden still had a little money and had used this to replenish their supplies from the villages as they passed through, but he and Gemma both knew that the time was soon coming when they would have to become self-sufficient. This would inevitably delay their search.

"I've kept a careful note of where we've been so far," Gemma told him, "so at least we won't be retracing our steps. Eventually we *have* to find it."

Her prediction came true at noon on the eighth day, though only she realized it at first. As they crested a pass between two vales, with rugged mountain peaks on either side, they looked down on a predominantly brown landscape of farm and forest. The air was still and quiet. Gemma felt a tremor of hope and glanced at Arden, but his face was blank, unreadable. He stared at the valley as he had done at each new vista.

"Recognize anything?" she asked quietly.

"No."

They rode on, descending now. The scene below fitted Arden's description; the dried-up riverbed, empty reservoirs, houses scattered widely, a village in the distance to the south. But still he gave no sign of recognition. The feeling that they had arrived at their destination continued to grow within Gemma, in spite of the fact that there was nothing substantial to back up this intuition. It was a force in the air, an energy, something she had never felt before. It drew her on; although this was not the beautiful and luxuriant valley that Arden had first seen, there was something special here.

Gemma's hope turned to certainty when, a little further down the mountainside, a rabbit bounded into the open just in front of the horses. The small creature stopped and calmly watched their approach; there was no fear in its posture, and when it eventually moved away it was at a leisurely pace. Arden watched it incuriously.

"I should have got him," he said. "We could do with some fresh meat."

Not here, Gemma thought, but said nothing.

A little while later she saw a fox which was similarly unafraid, watching them pass from beneath a withered tree.

The dryness of the valley soon became more obvious—dust rose from the horses' hooves, and the grass was brown. When they reached a plateau just above the farmland, they stopped to survey the scene before them. Everywhere was the same; withered and dying crops with only a few patches of pale green visible, trees whose leaves had fallen unseasonably early. Some were completely bare. There were very few animals in evidence.

Gemma was about to speak, to ask the inevitable question when they were hailed by a woman's voice. She emerged from a thicket of brambles to their left, waved, and called again. She ran toward them, lifting the skirts of her long dress as she did so. Arden dismounted and stood facing the newcomer who came to a halt when she was a few paces away. Her face was pretty but lined with care, and her arms were thin.

"Arden, it's really you!" she gasped. "We thought you'd never come."

Gemma saw Arden flinch at her words. The hope on the woman's face died as she watched him, to be replaced by pain, and then compassion. She took a step closer.

"Arden?" Her tone was soft, consoling.

"I failed you." His words were harsh but there was a catch in his voice. "I'm sorry."

"Don't . . ." she began, then glanced up at Gemma as if seeing her for the first time.

When Arden turned around Gemma saw that his memory had returned, and with it the pain of his failure.

"This is Mallory," he said.

———————•———————

By the time Mallory led them to her home, her husband and two sons were already there, summoned by the mysterious shared knowledge which still flourished—within their family at least. After noisy greetings had been exchanged and cut short by their parents' evident worries, the boys took charge of the horses, leaving the newcomers with Mallory and Kragen.

Arden introduced Gemma to them, and they went through into the kitchen. Arden sat down, stony-faced, then took a deep breath and said, "I failed you, Kragen. I failed all of you."

"You did what you could," Mallory put in. She had heard a brief account of the trip to Newport on the way down to the farm.

"Well, it wasn't enough!" Arden snapped viciously, and Mallory winced.

"It was a long-shot," Kragen said calmly. "We all knew that. If you couldn't succeed, no one could. You mustn't blame yourself."

"Well I do," Arden replied grimly. "I wouldn't have got as far as I *did* without Gemma's help."

Gemma was so surprised by his admission that she forgot what she had been going to say, and could only shrug as the farmer and his wife looked at her.

"You obviously have your own story to tell," Mallory said.

"It's not important," Gemma replied. "What matters is the valley. Arden's told me so much about you all . . ."

"Do you feel at home here?" Mallory asked suddenly.

"Yes," Gemma responded without hesitating, not knowing that the question had a deeper meaning. Kragen and his wife exchanged glances.

"Most outsiders don't," the farmer said. "You and Arden have a lot in common."

Gemma and Arden turned to look at each other. For a few moments they just stared, then burst out laughing while their hosts regarded them with bemused smiles.

"We've managed to disagree about almost *everything* since we met!" Arden said.

"Then perhaps the valley will bring you to your senses," Mallory replied.

"You always did have an odd way of looking at things," he responded, looking at her curiously. He turned to Kragen, his face serious once more. "How are things here?"

"Pretty bad. There hasn't been much progress on the wells since Caley was killed in the last collapse. The deeper we go the more difficult it gets, and they all turned out to be dry anyway."

"What about the stream to the east?"

"No good. We got a bit of use out of it but it just wasn't enough." Kragen sounded weary. "And it dried up a few days ago."

"Has anyone else left?"

"Three or four families," Mallory answered. "We've heard nothing of their progress. And more of the old ones have died." She paused. "Alida's baby was stillborn a few days ago."

Arden looked stricken; such an event had previously been unheard of in the valley.

"Some of the young children are sick," Mallory went on. "They just aren't getting enough food to grow strong, and have no defense against illness."

"We're all vulnerable now," Kragen added soberly.

Into the silence that followed, Gemma posed a question of her own, one that had been preying on her mind.

"Do you still share the knowing?" she asked quietly.

"We do, but it's slower now," Kragen replied. "And less reliable. We have to send messages outsider-fashion to be sure."

"The boys are on their way now," Mallory added. "We've called a council tomorrow in Lower. Now that you're back."

"I wish I had better news," Arden said unhappily.

"Will Kris be there?" Gemma asked.

"No. He's been unconscious for several days," Mallory explained sadly.

———•———

There was indeed very little good news at the following day's council meeting. Arden's memory of such events was of joyous social occasions, but this time the mood was understandably grim. Arden was nonetheless made welcome, and

Gemma greeted courteously for his sake, but the news they brought deprived the people of what seemed the last hope. Dissension and bad temper were openly displayed, and it was obvious that most people considered the remaining choice to be between two forms of slow and painful extinction.

They tried to be fair to Arden, listening to his story patiently, but while most understood and appreciated his difficulties in dealing with a corrupt and alien city, some could not hold back their bitterness and grief. They said that they should never have entrusted an outsider with such an essential task. This was doubly unjust because none of them could even have attempted such a journey, and a number of people came to Arden's support.

Nevertheless, the acrimony was painful for the visitors, and Gemma had difficulty in not responding to some of Arden's detractors.

No one could have done more! she raged silently. *You don't know what it cost him.* However, she wisely held her peace.

At the end of the discussion, it was concluded that they could only carry on doing what little they could, in the hope that the river would eventually return. More wells would be sunk, more streams diverted where possible, and so on. The idea of planting desert thornbushes in the remoter areas of the valley was rejected on the grounds that their roots could only save water, not produce it. Calls for more emigration were also dismissed, although it was clear that some would go anyway. Trading for food with neighboring valleys would still be attempted by the hardier among them.

Only Arden had anything new to suggest, and his ideas brought little response from those who heard him speak.

"The city people will not send engineers, but the idea of looking for the source of the river is still a good one. There are others living in the mountains who may help us, and I am going into the high region. I do not ask any of you to come with me, for I know that your health will suffer as mine will not, but if we could only succeed in finding the source and diverting it once more, would the risk not be worth the effort?" He paused, looking at the solemn faces around him. "What choice do you have? I leave the day after tomorrow with any that dare to join me. Alone if necessary. Think on it."

The council broke up swiftly after that, and Gemma was introduced to Elway and those of his family who had come from their farm at the southern end of the valley. She felt as if she knew them already.

Arden, who had not had a chance to speak to them before the meeting, was greeted warmly by the burly farmer, his wife Teri, who hugged him fiercely, and by Horan, his boyhood friend. Mallory and Kragen completed the group.

When the introductions were over, Gemma looked at their solemn faces, wishing she had known them in happier times.

"Will you really go into the high ranges alone?" Mallory asked Arden.

"Of course not," Teri answered for him. "It's perfectly obvious that Gemma is going with him."

"You mustn't assume . . ." Elway began.

"Teri's right," Gemma interrupted. "I can't stop now." *I'm too involved—in more ways than one,* she added to herself.

Arden was grinning at her, looking happier than he had for days.

"I'm coming too," Horan said unexpectedly. They all turned to him and the variety of their expressions made him laugh. "Don't look so surprised," he said. "It makes sense. I'm not married, and I'm still relatively strong. Father can easily take care of the little work we can still do on the farm. Who better to go?"

Mallory was the first to speak, voicing a thought in several minds.

"But you got sick when you went over to the western valley last year," she said unhappily.

"The mountains might be different," he replied.

"But . . ." Teri began, a mother's concern in her eyes.

"The boy's mind is made up," Elway stated. "If Arden wants him, he should go."

The "boy," who was nearly forty years old, looked gratefully at his father, then hopefully at Arden.

"I don't really have to answer that, do I? I can't think of anyone I'd rather have join us."

The decision was made and Gemma knew that everyone would now cooperate wholeheartedly with the venture.

"Is there anyone else who might come?" Arden inquired.

"There aren't many without wives and children who would be of much use to you," Horan replied thoughtfully. "But I'll ask around."

Their conversation veered from future plans to present conditions, and those on Elway's farm in particular. It did not make pleasant listening. All the family were still alive—apart from Fletcher—but there was concern for the health of the small children.

"And then of course there's Kris," Teri said. "No one can understand what's happened to him."

"Where is he?" Arden asked.

"At Dugan and Clare's place," Elway answered. "Just south of here."

"Clare has better healing skills than any of us," Teri added, "but even *she's* baffled."

"How long has he been like this?"

Elway did a quick mental calculation. "Twelve or thirteen days," he said. "He just went to sleep one night and didn't wake up."

"Can we see him?" Gemma asked.

"I don't see why not."

They clambered onto Elway's cart—all except Arden and Horan who walked behind, deep in conversation—and the farmer drove them along the dusty track. There was little talk, but Gemma felt no awkwardness at the silence. *The magic may be fading, but it hasn't gone yet,* she thought.

Clare met them at the door, and ushered them all inside. After a brief conversation, she led Arden and Gemma upstairs to the bedroom where Kris lay. He was covered with a white sheet but Gemma could see the outline of the tiny, misshapen body beneath. Only his head and one crooked arm were exposed; his eyes were closed.

He was very still and it was only when Gemma knelt down beside the bed that she saw the slight rise and fall of his chest. *What secrets are trapped inside your head?* she wondered, taking Kris's hand in her own and holding it tight.

She heard Arden gasp, and for an instant thought that there was an answering pressure from the hand she held.

Then the room disappeared.

I've been waiting for you, a voice said. *What took you so long?*

chapter 32

Gemma slumped forward, her eyes closed. Arden moved quickly to go to her aid, but Clare's hand on his arm stopped him.

"Leave her," the healer said quietly. "She's not in any danger."

Arden looked at her. "How do you know?"

"The warmth is still there—I've felt it often. Kris will not harm her." She sounded certain. "Who knows? Perhaps some good may come of it."

Arden was unsure, and turned back to Gemma. She appeared perfectly relaxed, leaning on the bed, Kris's hand still clasped in hers.

Where are you now? he asked silently.

————— • —————

Gemma was still in the valley—but not the dry and dusty place she had entered the previous day. Her wish to see it as it once was, in all its beauty and happiness, was being fulfilled. Her spectral presence allowed her to watch and no more—she could not take part in the scene before her—and yet she *was* there. It was as real as anything she had ever experienced, and she instantly accepted both the miracle and her spectator's role.

"I've been waiting for you," Horan said. "What took you so long?"

"I got held up," Arden replied sheepishly.

The two young men stood on the edge of a small pond. They were surrounded by trees, and green and yellow light dappled the water's surface. Mallory emerged from the wood and both men turned to look at her.

"So I see," Horan commented as Arden blushed. "I hope Kragen doesn't catch the two of you together!"

"Kragen hasn't asked me to marry him yet," Mallory retorted, as Arden tried to keep the flames in his face from growing worse.

"Besides," she went on, "when you're as pretty as I am it's only to be expected that I will have more than one suitor."

"I . . ." Arden began.

"What *have* we done to deserve such a girl in our innocent family?" Horan asked teasingly, hands outspread. His eyes were laughing. "Arden, my friend, beware the temptress."

"You can talk!" Mallory exclaimed. "Thirty years old and you *still* haven't got any manners."

"Never mind her," Horan advised Arden. "We have work to do."

"Cheek! Whose idea was this in the first place?" she demanded.

"I forget," he replied, his grin telling a different story.

"Oh, you're impossible," she said, threatening to push him into the water. "You know perfectly well it was me—it's a good thing someone in this family has brains to go with all the brawn!"

She lunged at him but Horan evaded her easily and she nearly fell into the pond. Only Arden's quick reactions saved her.

"I'm glad there is at least one gentleman here," she remarked haughtily. "Thank you, kind sir."

"Beware the temptress," Horan whispered from behind his hand.

"I'll get you! One day," she promised, extricating herself from Arden's grasp and pointing an accusing finger at her brother.

"That'll be the day," he replied, laughing.

Hunley's voice sounded from the trees.

"If you three have quite finished!" he shouted. "Lang and I have been up to our knees in mud for long enough. We want to see if this thing works!"

"Of course it will!" Mallory yelled back. "*If* you've made it properly."

"I'll open the sluice," Horan said.

"Come on, Arden. We'll go downstream." With that, Mallory led the way past the bank which formed one side of the pond. As they moved, Gemma's perspective moved too and she could see Hunley—Elway's eldest son—and Lang, bending over a wooden contraption. It spanned the bed of the stream, along which ran only a trickle of water.

"By turning that handle on the right," Mallory explained,

pointing, "we can adjust the quantity of water that flows down each of the two branches of the stream."

"How will it work?"

"See that plank of wood in the middle?" Mallory went on. "It moves to one side or the other."

"Like a ship's rudder?" Arden suggested.

"If you say so," she replied, sounding slightly put out. "I've never actually seen a ship."

"Water's coming!" Horan called from above.

"Watch," Mallory instructed.

A surge of water boiled down the stream-bed. When it hit the barrier, a wave of spray shot up, soaking Hunley to the skin. Mallory burst out laughing and her brother shook his fist at her in mock anger. Lang, on the other side, fared better, and when the flow of water grew steady, he began turning the handle slowly. The stream, which until then had been going into the right-hand channel, was neatly divided into two.

"It moves as smooth as anything," Lang commented, sounding pleased. "A child could turn it."

"What, even Mallory?" Horan had come up unnoticed behind his sister and Arden.

"I shall ignore that comment," she said loftily. They watched Lang and Hunley make further adjustments, varying the proportions flowing into each channel.

"Not bad," was Hunley's verdict.

"Now we can put in a series of these, and make sure the water is spread evenly over all the land," Mallory explained to Arden, "however far from the feeder it is. As things are now, we have very little control over irrigation streams when they have to be divided."

Arden was impressed, and said so.

"Did you hear that?" Mallory demanded of the others. "At least *somebody* here appreciates talent."

"Don't encourage her, Arden," Horan said. "You're the only one who hasn't been around her long enough to know how insufferable she really is."

"I'll suffer her gladly," Arden replied gallantly.

"I'm in love!" Mallory declared, throwing her arms around his neck. Arden's startled expression brought roars of laughter from the watching men.

"She's not quite the little girl you first met, is she?" Hunley commented.

"Please, take me away from all this," Mallory implored, gazing adoringly into Arden's eyes.

For a moment he wondered if she was serious. "I can't . . . you know . . ." he stammered, then saw the glint in her eye and the slowly spreading grin, and decided upon a measure of revenge. Pulling her toward him he kissed her passionately and at length, while their audience whistled and clapped. When they finally separated, they were both laughing.

"Is our sister safe with this man?" Hunley asked with false gravity.

"Well, brother," Horan replied. "I believe I would still put the question the other way round."

"But he's a madman!"

"True. No sane man would *want* to kiss her like that."

"Ignore these oafs," Mallory put in. "Show me more of your animal passion."

Arden entered further into the spirit of things by growling ferociously, but his rather feeble attempt brought forth howls of derision from the others. Mallory threw up her hands in mock terror, screamed, and ran away. After a few paces she stopped, turned round to face the still stationary Arden, and commanded, "Well, come on then. Chase me!" Then she turned on her heels and stalked away. After a moment's hesitation, Arden followed, enduring the taunts of his friends—which took the form of yelping animal calls.

He caught up with her and they walked on together, following the path out of the wood. The view that opened up before them was serene and beautiful; fields, green and gold, spread a patchwork over the valley floor. Houses dotted the landscape, and far down the valley to the north they could see the cluster of buildings which was Lower. The mountains, girded with trees, rose up on either side of the valley, and higher up, bare rock was framed by a clear blue sky.

"Will you be staying much longer?" Mallory asked eventually.

"No. I'd better go soon." His tone was apologetic.

"You don't . . . you mustn't worry about me," Mallory said carefully. "I know you have to go."

"It takes all my courage to come back at all," Arden admitted.

"Why?"

"Because I want to so badly."

"That doesn't make any sense."

Arden smiled ruefully. "This isn't my home. I don't really

belong here, and every time I come back I'm forced into that realization. And it hurts to leave."

"It *is* beautiful," she said, her eyes sweeping the verdant prospect before them.

"That's only one of the reasons it hurts," he replied.

———•———

The images faded abruptly from Gemma's mind, and she found herself back in Kris's room. His hand had slipped from her grasp. For a moment she considered taking it again, but decided that she had been shown enough. She tried to stand and found that her legs had gone to sleep beneath her. Arden was quickly at her side, older again but just as handsome, and helped her to rise.

"What happened?" he asked. "Are you all right?"

Gemma nodded, ignoring the clamor of her tingling legs.

"Kris showed me the valley," she said. "Before . . ."

"It was so lovely," he said, a sad and faraway look in his eyes.

"It will be again," she replied, gripping his hands tightly.

chapter 33

"Don't you see?" Gemma cried. "Kris gave us the answer."
She had wondered several times why he had shown her that
particular vision, and now she knew. She looked at the faces
around her; their expressions varied from dawning hope to
outright scepticism. The kitchen at Elway's farm had been
turned into an impromptu meeting place—as well as the
family, there were four young men present that Horan had
persuaded to come in the hope that they would join the
expedition. Gemma's vision had given them all food for thought.

"Why should Kris have given *you* this sign?" one of them
asked. *An outsider*, his tone implied.

"Who knows?" Gemma replied. "Maybe it's because I'm an
outsider."

"We've all tried to contact Kris," Elway said. "But we've
failed. Perhaps as one channel closes, another opens."

"That's not really the point," Gemma put in. "I saw what I
saw. I didn't make it up."

"But we only have your word for that," another of the
visitors remarked.

"That comment does you little credit, Bowen," Teri responded briskly, but Gemma had not taken offense.

"You're right," she said, looking at Bowen. "I know that
those images came from Kris, but it's your choice whether to
believe me or not."

"Why should she lie?" Arden demanded angrily. "What
would we gain from that?"

"Company," Bowen answered flatly.

There was an uncomfortable silence. Eventually Horan
entered the debate.

"I believe Gemma," he said quietly, "but, wherever you
think that scene came from, it *is* relevant to our problem. It's
just too much of a coincidence. We desperately need to
divert at least part of the river, and the water gates are a
miniature version of what we need to do now. If anything can

save this valley, it's something like that, but up in the mountains this time. That's why I'm going with Arden."

"Even if you discount Gemma's story completely," Mallory put in, "finding the source of the river is the only hope we've got."

"Why aren't you going then?" one of Bowen's companions asked.

Mallory bridled. "Maybe I will!" she retorted, and was met with open disbelief.

"No one goes unless they are willing and able," Arden put in quickly.

Bowen then acted as spokesman; his words held none of the earlier cynicism but the gist remained negative.

"Leaving visions aside," he said, "the very scale of this project makes it a nonstarter. You'd need a large number of people to be able to build something big enough to divert a whole river, assuming you can find it in the first place. The mountains are unknown territory to everybody except Arden, and the high ground will soon start to get cold. And we know that all of us suffer ill health as soon as we leave the valley." He paused. "I'm sorry, Horan. I can be more use to the valley and to my parents by remaining. If you're set on going, I wish you well, but I'm not coming." He looked about at his companions, receiving nods of agreement, then he and two of the others left. The youngest, Ashlin, remained, embarrassed to find himself the center of attention.

"I'll come, if you want me," he said nervously.

"And welcome," Arden declared.

"I'm going too," Mallory said firmly, her decision made. There was a moment's silence, then a chorus of protests from her family. She waited until they were quiet again, then said, "Gemma is going. Why can't I?"

"Gemma is used to traveling," Teri said kindly. "You've never been out of the valley."

"We'll *all* have to leave soon enough," Mallory replied. "Or stay here and die. Besides, I've got skills which might be useful. You've all said I'm good at inventing practical things. We haven't got large numbers, so we must use ingenuity instead."

"But what about your children, your home?" Teri asked, then turned to her son-in-law. "Kragen, can't you talk some sense into her?"

The farmer thought for some time, and at length said,

"Desperate times call for desperate measures. The boys will be well enough here, if you'll have them, and our farm is as near to ruin as makes no difference. We *need* that water. Mallory's got more spirit than most in this valley, man or woman." He looked at his wife and they exchanged knowing grins. "Besides, I'll be there to keep an eye on her. Will you take us both, Arden?"

For some moments Arden could not speak, but only looked back and forth between Mallory and Kragen.

"Of course he will!" Gemma exclaimed, breaking the tension. She was delighted at the prospect; the little that she had seen of Mallory—past and present—had already convinced her that she would be an asset to their small party, and Kragen's strength and calm, sure temperament would be just as valuable. "Arden?" she prompted.

He nodded. "If you're both sure." He was wondering to himself what he had done to warrant such loyalty, and was even more determined to repay his old debt to the valley and its people.

The discussion then turned to practical matters and the party split up soon afterward. Mallory, Kragen, and Ashlin returned to their homes to set their affairs in order, arrange supplies, and prepare for the morning, while Gemma and Arden stayed with Horan at Elway's house, this being the most logical setting-off point.

They spent the evening planning their route as far south as their knowledge permitted.

"Why don't we just follow the riverbed?" Gemma asked logically.

"Because there are places where the river flows over sheer escarpments," Arden replied. "Even if *we* could climb them, the horses couldn't."

"And its passage is underground in places," Horan added. "At least, that's what everybody says."

"We just have to pick it up where we can," Arden concluded. "And where we can't, we guess!"

"Any river will do," Horan said, grinning. "As long as we can persuade it to come here."

"Preferably one that runs all year, every year," Arden said.

"With clear water and fish by the shoal," Horan added dreamily, gazing at the ceiling.

"Why not throw in a few nuggets of washed gold while you're about it," Teri's voice added from the next room.

"Let's not be greedy," Horan replied. "I'll settle for the fish."

"You can't drink fish, or water your crops with them," Gemma put in, both gladdened and appalled by their ability to joke about the grim subject.

"I'm glad that at least one of you has her priorities right," Teri called, then appeared in the doorway. "Gemma, I am expecting you and Mallory to keep these men in order."

"I'll try," Gemma promised, smiling.

"Your room's ready whenever you are," their hostess went on. "Make the most of your last night in a proper bed."

Teri had naturally assumed that Arden and Gemma would wish to sleep in the same room and now they said nothing to make her think otherwise. Anticipating an early start to the next day, the household retired early. Gemma followed Arden up to their chamber with a mixture of fear and hope in her heart, her speculation fueled by Teri's assumption. She felt confused and happy, unable to think coherently. Memories of the last two days became mixed with recollections of earlier times, and she was further confused by the prospect of the hazardous journey ahead—and of the night to come. *What's he thinking?* she wondered. *What does he expect from me? What do I expect from me?*

As they went inside the room, Gemma saw two single beds standing primly apart, not the double bed she had anticipated, and did not know whether to laugh or cry. She glanced at Arden who was also staring at the beds, his face as uncertain as hers. He looked up, and as their eyes met they started laughing.

Gemma felt the tension within her melt away. Whatever happened now would happen because they wanted it to. They could be friends or lovers—it did not matter which. Arden took her in his arms and they hugged each other tightly, then he drew away a little.

"It's a conspiracy," he said. Their faces were only a handspan apart and Gemma watched his eyes watching her. "The whole world is pushing us together." He smiled.

"Don't you want it to?" She smiled in return.

"You're . . . you're too important, Gemma. There's never been anyone like you before."

"I should hope not!"

"I'm serious," he objected, though his eyes still danced mischievously.

"So am I," she returned, grinning from sheer happiness.

"When all this is settled . . ." he began, then ran out of words. Gemma watched his face as the thoughts struggled to turn themselves into words, and loved him all the more for this unexpected show of vulnerability.

"You don't have to say anything," she said softly. *I understand.*

"We'll need all our strength for tomorrow's journey," he said, sheepish now.

"It wouldn't look too good if we fell asleep on horseback, would it," she agreed. "Not when they're looking to you for leadership."

"No." Arden was relieved now that their understanding was complete. They separated and undressed on opposite sides of the room. *False modesty?* Gemma thought, amused by the memory, then climbed into bed and looked over at Arden. He was already tucked in, hands beneath his head, and was staring at the ceiling.

"Six of us," he said quietly. "Not exactly an army, is it."

"It's quality, not quantity, that counts," she replied.

"Mmm."

"Are you happy about Mallory coming?"

There was no answer for a while.

"Why shouldn't I be?" he said at last, sounding slightly defensive.

"You seemed taken aback when she said she wanted to come."

"So was everyone! I'm *glad* she's coming. She's got a practical nature, and that will be useful."

They chatted idly about other aspects of the expedition for an hour or so, then settled down to sleep, Arden turning out the lamp which hung between their beds.

Where will we be tomorrow night? Gemma thought. *And the night after that? Not that it matters. As long as you're still there.*

"Arden," she whispered.

There was no reply.

"You know I love you, don't you?"

In her mind the conversation continued, Arden replying, "That's only natural." "I'm serious," she responded, at which point their eyes met and he said, "I love you, too."

The reality was rather different. Arden's only response was a gentle snoring. He was fast asleep. Smiling to herself, Gemma soon followed his example.

chapter 34

The six members of Arden's expedition left the valley early the next morning, riding the strongest mounts their respective households could provide. Their saddlebags were laden with as much food and water as could be spared. They were a strange group; Arden had been virtually silent throughout their preparations, whereas Horan and Mallory chatted and joked constantly, obviously intent on raising everyone's spirits. Kragen was his usual unflappable self, though he did laugh at some of his wife's more ridiculous comments. Ashlin was visibly nervous, fumbling over his horse's harness and rarely reacting when spoken to.

"What's the matter, Ashlin?" Mallory asked. "You look as though you've been drinking wine that turned out to be corn oil."

"What?" He looked up, startled, and Mallory repeated her question.

"Bowen's been talking to my parents. They didn't want me to come," he said quietly.

"Oh."

Now that he had started, Ashlin's words came in a rush.

"I've never been anywhere but here," he went on. "I don't even know the paths at the southern end *inside* the valley."

"Don't worry," Horan advised, overhearing the young man's worries. "We do. And after a few days we'll *all* be lost, so you'll be in the same state as everyone." He smiled encouragingly.

"I'm a bit scared," Ashlin admitted almost defiantly.

"Who isn't?" Horan said. "You'd be stupid if you weren't."

"You've already been braver than any of us," Mallory put in, "by standing up to Bowen and your family. We haven't had to fight to go. You know what's right and you stick to it. Conviction and courage like yours will stand us all in good stead."

The youngster looked much happier.

Gemma observed this exchange, and felt lucky in her companions. She was feeling distinctly vulnerable, not because leaving the valley held any terrors for her, but because so much depended on the outcome of the trip. She pushed aside the nagging doubts about whether they could actually achieve anything, and remembered instead the glimpse of the valley that Kris had shown her. Those few moments had instilled in her an iron determination to save both the place and its people—whatever the personal cost. When the time for departure came she waved her farewell to Elway, Teri, and the others as vigorously as if she had known them all her life.

As the group rode away, Mallory and Kragen held back a little. Saying goodbye to their children had been hard, and they took comfort in each other's silent presence, and in the knowledge that the boys were excited by the prospect of staying at their grandparents' home.

The navigation was easy at first, as they followed the dry riverbed over relatively gentle slopes. For a time everything went well, and after three days of slow but steady riding, they were well beyond the boundaries of the valley. Looking back, the valley floor was no longer visible; it was sometimes difficult to tell where it ended and neighboring vales began.

They were excited by the sight of a couple of small streams, but they turned out to be too meager to be of any real use. However, they were able to replenish their own supplies.

On their fourth night in the open, they decided to light a campfire. Even though autumn was only just giving way to winter, they had already climbed enough into the mountains to make the night air chill. A fire would be a comforting sight, surrounded as they were by uninhabited wilderness. The three tents were erected, then the group gathered around Kragen, who was setting the fire. He tried to light it, but his flint failed to ignite the tinder.

"Come on," Horan urged. "Call yourself a countryman?"

"Gemma could do that for you," Arden remarked. "She's good at starting fires." Gemma reacted in kind to the faintly malicious humor.

"Oh, so you believe me now, do you?" she demanded.

Kragen eventually lit the wood, but curiosity had inevitably been aroused, and Gemma was called upon to explain what had happened in Newport. Her audience listened raptly, apparently taking her seriously, but Gemma could not help glancing at Arden. He was sprawled on the ground, a small smile on his face.

"Except, of course, that Arden doesn't believe a word of

it," she concluded. "As you can tell by that odious smirk on his face."

He sat up at this, his eyes shining in the firelight. "Come off it, Gemma. You have to admit that you couldn't be considered the most *reliable* of witnesses in the state you were in," he argued. "But I've seen you do a few interesting things *since* then. I don't know what magic is, or how it works, but if you have some strange talent you might be able to use it to help our cause, and I won't deny anything that might do that."

"I thought magic and wizards were just mythical stories," Ashlin said.

"They are here," Arden replied. "But where Gemma comes from, they apparently existed just a few years ago."

"Until The Leveling," Gemma said. "Something happened then."

"That's quite true," Arden said flippantly.

"Don't mock me!" she replied. "You know what I mean."

"Tell them about your friend Cai," he said.

Gemma looked at him, trying to fathom his attitude toward Cai. *What exactly does he want to know?* she wondered.

"He was a wizard," she began, "but after The Leveling he hated that title, and denied the very existence of magic. Yet he could still use it to heal people, and the bees . . ." A thought struck her. *The bees.* Of all the wizards, only Cai had an immortal familiar. Because the swarm was a renewable entity, the death of any individual within it only meant a change of character, not the extinction of life. *Perhaps magic . . .*

She gradually became aware of the five pairs of eyes looking at her curiously.

"I hope you're going to tell us what you're thinking," Horan said, "because judging by your expression it was pretty amazing."

"It's only an idea," she said, smiling self-consciously, but in her heart she knew she was right. "Perhaps the old magic *has* died, but it's been replaced by something else, something more complicated . . ."

"Don't!" Arden pleaded, holding up his hands.

"Be quiet!" Mallory said sharply, and they looked at her in surprise. "Go on, Gemma."

"It no longer depends on, or can be controlled by, one mind. There must be several, linked together somehow."

Now the facts were slotting into place. "In a way, Cai was right. There *are* no more wizards. *He's* special because of the bees, not the other way around—it's the swarm that has perpetuated his talent." *Oh, Cai, if only you knew!*

"Bees?" Horan asked, incredulously.

Gemma explained about Cai's unique familiar, and then went on to relate further aspects of her theory to her willing and captive audience.

"The meyrkat clan is a unit," she said, "and they share telepathic communication. You told me yourself that they always act as a team," she added, glancing at Arden. "And I could talk to all of them." The valley people had not known about this further facet of Gemma's character, and she was forced to tell them all about the desert creatures.

"And the geese, of course!" she continued. "I was only able to influence them because they were a group, flying with a united purpose." She looked at Arden, daring him to contradict her, but he said nothing. "Remember the scorpions?" she asked him. "Alone they're nasty but insignificant, but when they get together in a large group their character changes. Why, I even heard them talking!"

"I'll wager that wasn't a pretty sound," Kragen commented wryly, but Gemma did not hear him. She was intent on making the most important point of all.

"The valley is an enclosed society," she said, "separate and complete. *That's* why you share the knowledge, and why Kris was able to predict events and do all those wonderful things. He was harnessing the magic of you all—as a *group*."

Her rush of words came to an abrupt halt, and for a few moments the only sound was the crackling of the fire, as they all thought about what she had said. Surprisingly, it was Ashlin, normally the most reticent of them all, who pinpointed the most obvious flaw in Gemma's argument.

"Where does that leave you then, Gemma?" he asked quietly. "What group are you a part of?"

The silence which followed lasted a long time.

"I don't know," she admitted eventually.

"Perhaps you don't need to be," Mallory said. "Perhaps your talent is to recognize and channel the talents of other groups."

"That would certainly explain your being able to talk to Kris and the meyrkats," Ashlin put in, eager to atone for his awkward question.

"But where does all this leave us?" Kragen asked, bringing their speculations down to earth with a bump. "Do you suppose the six of *us* could become a magical group?"

Although his question was a serious one, they all burst out laughing. The images his innocent question had summoned were too ludicrous to contemplate.

The fire was dying down now, and the cold of the night was beginning to seep into their limbs. Horan yawned and got to his feet.

"I'm off to my burrow," he said. "Coming, Ashlin?"

"Looks more like a hive to me," Arden decided. "At least we stay above ground."

"Just don't compare me to scorpions," Horan returned, grinning. "Goodnight." He and Ashlin went off to the tent they shared. Arden and Kragen retired soon afterward, leaving the two women sitting over the last embers of the campfire.

"It's more than just the valley, isn't it?" Mallory asked after a few moments' companionable silence. "What's happening to the rest of the world?"

Gemma's forebodings, recently suppressed in the need for action over the parched valley, awoke again at these words.

"I wish I knew," she said with feeling. "But something is dreadfully wrong, and unless we do something about it, it's just going to get worse."

"Then why help *us*?" Mallory asked.

"Because the valley is a symbol for all that's good," Gemma replied. "If we can't save that, what hope is there for the world?" She paused, considering. "It's as if some dreadful force is at work, trying to destroy everything we hold dear— love, happiness, magic. We can't let it win."

"So magic is important?"

"I *know* it is." She heard again the words of the fanatic in Newport. *This will be final. The earth has become mad.* "But just now, anything recognizably magical seems to be either insane or destructive—or both. The travelers' tales I've heard are horrible."

They talked for a little while longer, and Gemma told the stories she had heard in Newport of the blue flame walls, elementals, disappearing islands, and the like.

Eventually Mallory said, "It's too big!" and Gemma nodded, knowing exactly what she meant. It *was* too big for any one person to comprehend. How could they find out exactly what it all meant?

They went to their respective tents with ill-defined feelings of impending doom.

The next day their troubles began in earnest.

chapter 35

Horan awoke coughing. Although he insisted that it was nothing serious and that their journey should continue, everyone was worried. By mid-morning it was obvious that he was unsteady in his saddle, and Arden called a halt. They rested for a while, and Horan recovered some of his usual good humor as his coughing abated. However, his breathing became labored after even a small amount of exercise.

"We'd better find that river soon," he said to Mallory, who was tending him. "My lungs feel as if they're full of dust."

She saw the pain beneath his grin and said nothing.

Arden had ridden a little way ahead to scout out the land and he now returned with the news that he thought he recognized a pass over to the west.

"If I'm right, there's a village there, and with luck we'll find a welcome."

"But it means turning away from the river," Horan objected.

"Only temporarily," Arden replied. "Shelter and fresh food will make the small delay worthwhile."

"Can you ride?" Mallory asked her brother.

"Of course," Horan answered, but had to be helped into the saddle. His sudden weakness left him angry, and increased the others' anxiety.

Kragen began to cough as they set off.

———————•———————

They reached the village of Braith shortly after noon. It was a relatively poor settlement, existing on the proceeds of upland hunting and the produce of poor soil. Nevertheless, it maintained the mountain tradition of a guest house; this was a functional wooden hut containing simple furniture—bunk beds, a trestle table, and benches. As the travelers arrived they were greeted first by a group of noisy children who ran alongside their horses. Visitors were obviously a rare event in this part of the world, and as they drew nearer, the older residents appeared, watching the newcomers with suspicion.

During their two and a half days' stay in Braith, Arden

learned the reason for this initial hostility. The vale had seen few visitors in recent months, but one party had abused the villagers' hospitality, stealing food and weapons before leaving in the middle of the night. The village elders described the thieves as mad. On another occasion, more of these madmen had been seen fighting gray-clad warriors in the upper end of the vale. Although the villagers had not been directly involved, and the survivors had vanished without trace, the mutilated bodies left behind had been more than enough reason to treat any group of travelers with extreme caution. The number of skyravens flying overhead had also increased recently, and though they had not suffered from anything but noise, the villagers regarded the metal birds with fear and awe. Arden told his companions what he had learned.

"Gray raiders! Here!" Gemma exclaimed.

Arden nodded. "We're going to have to be careful," he said. "We don't want our purpose to be mistaken." He watched Gemma as she struggled with unpleasant memories.

While Arden was the obvious contact with the village elders, being far more knowledgeable about mountain ways than his companions, Gemma and Mallory made their own friends among the children. They enlisted their help in looking after the horses and in preparing food. The latter was of particular interest to the youngsters when they learned that the visitors ate no meat—this idea was quite alien to them. The villagers provided as much food as they could spare and as the unwritten laws of hospitality demanded, but Arden insisted that they accept payment. The few coins they had brought with them were accepted gratefully, Braith having reasonably regular contact with the outside world.

None of the villagers was able to help with the location of the river. They were barely aware of its existence at the end of their vale and knew nothing about its upper course.

Of more immediate concern, however, was the state of Horan and Kragen. Both were now feverish and very weak, and none of the remedies tried by their companions or the village wisewoman had any effect. Bad dreams wracked their sleep, and pain their waking hours; after two days in Braith it was obvious that neither could continue. The valley was punishing them for their desertion. Even Ashlin, who until then had remained relatively fit, now complained about chest

pains and admitted to an almost uncontrollable longing to
return home.

This left the other three in a quandary. Arden insisted that
he was going on, alone if necessary, although he hated to see
the suffering of his friends and wished he could spare the
time to see them safely home. Gemma was also torn, but
knew in her heart that she would go with Arden. Mallory had
the hardest choice of all. She hated the thought of giving up,
yet her husband and brother were ill and needed her. She
accepted that they would have to return to the valley but was
loath to entrust their care to Ashlin. himself in poor health.
She spent several hours at their bedsides, deep in thought,
but her decision, when it came, was prompted by forces
beyond her understanding.

It began at dusk. Gemma heard the skyravens first, but
soon they were all aware of the sound as the monstrous metal
birds passed over the village. As the noise faded away, the
listeners relaxed.

"They're gone," Arden said quietly.

But now Gemma heard a different sound, one that awoke
in her feelings long suppressed and recently forgotten. The
South was calling to her again, with a siren song beyond the
hearing of most men. She stood up, moving as though in a
trance.

"Where are you going?" Arden asked, not looking up.

"Outside."

Gemma left the guest house and glanced up at the darken-
ing sky. The skyravens were long gone, but the song remained, drawing her on, and making rational thought impossible.
Why am I wasting time here? she asked herself in torment. *I
should be going south. To my destiny.* She turned to face the
looming mountains that barred her path but knew that she
could surmount any obstacles; the source of the song would
surely answer all her longings, and would be worth any
amount of effort.

The word "source" echoed in her head. *Perhaps the source
of the song is the source of the river too—they're both in the
south—and everything is connected.* In her mesmerized state,
this was too good a theory to discard. Then she heard someone coming up beside her, and glanced around to see Mallory,
her eyes shining, gazing at the southern mountains.

"Do you hear it too?" Gemma breathed in astonishment.

"Yes," Mallory replied. "We must go there."

Gemma was delighted to have found a kindred spirit, but said nothing more. Words were unnecessary while the song washed over them. Only their subconscious will to survive prevented them leaving there and then. Then the song stopped abruptly.

"No!" Mallory cried, the loss plain in her voice.

Gemma shivered. Arden's voice seemed an unwelcome intrusion as he shouted from the hut door.

"What are you two doing out there?"

The women looked at each other almost guiltily.

"Just talking," Gemma called back.

"Don't stay out too long, then," Arden replied. "It'll get cold soon." He went back inside, leaving them to gaze once more at the now quiet South.

"Have you heard it before?" Mallory asked softly.

"Many times," Gemma replied. "It takes different forms, but the call was the reason for leaving my old home in the first place. It's stronger than ever here,"

"You heard it from so far away?" Mallory was incredulous. "What can it mean?"

"I wish I knew."

"How have you been able to stand it all this time?" Mallory turned back to look at her companion. "I wanted to march into the mountains that very moment."

"But you didn't," Gemma replied. "It *can* be overcome."

"But in the end it won't be denied." Mallory's statement was confident, but had an underlying fearfulness.

"Have you never felt it before?" Gemma asked, and Mallory shook her head.

"Never. I'd have remembered something like that! How often does it happen?"

"I don't think there's any pattern to it," Gemma replied.

"Does Arden hear it?"

"No." But then Gemma thought about it. *Does he?* she wondered, and remembered an earlier experience. "It's a *trick*, Gemma," Arden had said. "If you follow that sound you'll die." *Did that mean he* had *heard it, but believed it to be something else? How could anyone hear it and not heed the call? To deny it completely was surely beyond human strength.*

"What are you thinking?" Mallory asked.

"When I first mentioned it, he told me I was crazy," Gemma replied. "But perhaps—"

She was interrupted by Arden's voice, louder this time and sounding rather angry.

"Are you coming inside or do I have to fetch you?" he called.

"We'd better go," Gemma whispered, and they walked back to the hut. Arden waited for them, regarding them both suspiciously, then followed them inside. Mallory went straight to Kragen's bedside to explain her decision to stay with Arden and Gemma.

chapter 36

They left Braith the next morning, parting company when they rejoined their original route. Ashlin, who was the fittest of those returning to the valley, held ropes attached to the reins of the other two mounts. The very thought of going home had already improved the condition of Horan and Kragen. Their spirits were higher now, but they had no thought of changing their minds, and Mallory's decision had been accepted with surprising equanimity. Kragen could see that she was both healthy and determined; he bade her a fond farewell, then was content to turn north.

The others rode south, following the course of the elusive river, and although Mallory cast many a backward glance while her husband remained in sight, there was no doubting her resolve.

The terrain grew progressively more rugged, but here at least there was water and hence greenery, even large tracts of woodland. There were a few clouds overhead, and many more to the south. Far in the distance were huge mountains capped with snow, something Mallory had never seen before.

"It's so beautiful," she whispered to Gemma. The same thoughts were in both minds: *Is it from there that the song comes?*

For the first time since she had arrived in the southern continent, Gemma felt the pinch of cold during the daylight hours. At night they shared a single tent, huddling together for warmth while they slept.

Their progress was further hampered by the route they were forced to follow. It was no longer possible to track the riverbed; at times it would have meant passing over broken rock—certain disaster to the horses. They were occasionally forced to make long detours in order to avoid a precipitous climb, and had to retrace their steps sometimes when they made a miscalculation in their route. They lost the river for hours at a time, but always managed to locate it again, continuing their laborious journey toward its source.

It was a frustrating process and was made worse by the fact that they eventually had to hunt to replenish their food supply. Water was no longer a problem. Mallory could not bring herself to eat any of the game that Arden had killed, and as a consequence she existed on a meager diet of roots, berries, and leaves. Her face became gaunt, and she shivered often. At night she lay between Gemma and Arden, taking comfort in their warmth. Yet in spite of her weakness, she did not fall ill as the others had done.

Twelve days after leaving Braith, they came upon the sight they had dreaded. The river course ran out of a short narrow valley, which they entered from the lower end. In the distance the land rose in a steep, scree-covered slope to become a mountain peak; there was no sign of where the river entered the vale. Riding on, they knew with dreadful certainty what they would find.

For some leagues now the riverbed had contained a trickling stream at its bottom, and as the riders reached the foot of the scree slope, their worst fears were realized. The water bubbled out of the broken rock as if from a spring at the base of the mountain. Beyond that, the river flowed underground, where they could never follow.

Investigation revealed several small caves, into which Arden crawled for a few paces, but there was no point in his attempting to go further. Disheartened, they made camp even though it was barely past midday, and Gemma lit a fire while Arden and Mallory replenished their food supplies as best they could.

Sitting round the campfire later that afternoon they were all reluctant to begin the necessary discussion, but eventually Arden said, "We knew this had to happen sometime, and it'll probably happen again. We haven't seen another human being since we left Braith—so it's up to us."

"There's no point in going back. We'd only have to try the other side of these ridges," Mallory said, indicating the hills to east and west.

"And we can't go up there." Gemma nodded at the mountain that barred their path. "Even if there was any point. The river is *inside* the mountain."

"So it's down to guesswork," Arden concluded. "Which side shall we take?"

"Neither way will be easy for the horses," Gemma commented, looking at the steep valley sides.

"And if we go the wrong way," Arden went on, "it could be days before we find out. Then we'd have to come back." His voice was harsh with anger and frustration.

"Do we have any choice?" Gemma asked.

"We could split up," Mallory suggested. "We'd be able to see each other for leagues, and we could arrange a signal for whoever finds the river first."

Arden shook his head. "It's too risky," he said. "Besides, we may have to go halfway round *that* thing"—he gestured toward the mountain as though it had been put there simply to annoy him—"before we get to the river, and we'd never be able to see each other then."

"We stick together," Gemma said firmly.

"Which then?" Mallory asked. "East or west?"

"West," Gemma decided. "That way we'll get the benefit of the sun earlier in the morning."

The decision made, they tended their horses, gathered more wood for the fire, and tried to spy out the best route.

That night Mallory began coughing in her sleep and shifting restlessly. Gemma stretched out a hand and touched her friend's cheek gently. Mallory's spasms subsided, but Gemma's newborn worries did not.

They left early the next morning. It was cold and they were soon glad of their western route. They were able to ride at first, zigzagging up the grass-covered slope between boulders and rock outcrops, but later were forced to dismount and lead the horses. The ground grew progressively rougher and they had to head directly upward more often in order to avoid larger areas of scree. As the day wore on, Mallory had to stop frequently and her breathing was labored. She would occasionally start coughing again, and each time this happened Gemma hastened to sit beside her and hold her hands while they rested. The contact seemed to give Mallory comfort.

Arden watched them anxiously. To turn back now would mean an intolerable delay, but in spite of her infirmity, Mallory remained steadfast. It was not the out-of-valley disease, she said, but a perfectly ordinary cold.

"I'll survive," she said, smiling weakly. "I'm just not used to the mountain air."

"She needs warmth and rest, and proper food," Gemma told Arden. "Can we find another village?"

"I don't think it's likely—not around here," he replied.

"But as soon as we find a good spot, we'll set up camp for a few days until she's better. We could all do with the rest."

Their laborious climb continued, the mountain on their left seeming to mock their puny efforts. They finally crested the ridge in the late afternoon and found, to their great surprise, that it did not fall away into another vale. Instead, they stood on the edge of a vast, flat plateau which lay to the west of the mountain and extended far to the south. Even in the fading light it was obvious that no river crossed this plain. Arden swore loudly, but Gemma's keen eyes had spotted something hopeful.

"Is that smoke?" she asked, pointing.

Arden squinted. "I think so," he said, "but it's leagues away. We'll never make it that far tonight."

"Then let's make camp now and go on at first light," Gemma responded. "Do you think it's a village?"

"Let's hope so," Arden replied, sounding thoroughly dejected.

"Come on, it's not so bad," Mallory said. "We may not have found the river, but at least this plateau should make traveling easier. We can be round to the south of the mountain in a day."

Arden's expression brightened a little but Gemma said firmly, "If that *is* a village, we're staying there. At least for a while."

"Well, Arden could always scout ahead for us," Mallory went on. "I'd hate to see him doing nothing."

"He never did have any patience, did he," Gemma added.

Arden looked at the two women, who were standing side by side and grinning at him.

"If you two have quite finished . . ." he said, then smiled back. "How did I get myself into this?" he asked the heavens. "Stranded alone in the wilderness with two nagging women!"

"Most men would think themselves lucky to be alone with such beauties," Mallory replied.

Arden took on the expression of an imbecile and his accent became exaggerated.

"Oi'm just a simple country boy, ma'am. Moi equipment only accounts for one at a time." As they burst out laughing, he added in his own voice, "Besides, you're a married woman."

"Does that mean you don't love me any more?" Mallory pleaded in a ridiculous whine, then laughed again. An instant later their mood changed as Mallory's amusement turned into

an uncontrollable coughing fit which left her on her knees,
gasping for breath. Gemma stayed with her, wrapping her in
blankets, while Arden got a fire going and set up the tent.
Throughout the night they lay close together, and Gemma
felt Mallory's body shudder as the fever-dreams ruled her
sleep.

With dawn came renewed hope. Mallory was quiet again,
though weak, and a thin plume of smoke was clearly visible
across the plain to the southwest. They set off as soon as
possible threading their way between the boulders that lit-
tered the plateau.

The village, when they reached it, consisted of only twelve
huts. After an initial wary inspection, the inhabitants decided
that the travelers presented no threat, and welcomed them
warmly, leading them to the guest house. It was a smaller
building than the one in Braith, but it was clean and dry and
one of the stone walls contained a fireplace. As soon as
Mallory's condition became known, the head-man, who was
called Ehren, sent two youngsters to fetch kindling and logs.

"I will bring Mousel," he said. "She is our wisewoman."

Mousel turned out to be a small, dark woman whose bright
eyes belied her slow movements and even slower tongue.
She took charge of Mallory, shooing everybody except Gemma
from the hut. A short while later, Mallory lay beneath several
blankets and, with the fire blazing merrily in the grate, she
felt warmer and more at ease than she had done for days.
Mousel had examined her tongue and throat, deft fingers had
probed her neck, and she had listened to her breathing.
Apparently satisfied, the wisewoman produced a stone flask
and gave her patient two sips of the contents.

"You like?" she asked.

Mallory smiled. "If that's medicine, I don't mind being ill!"
she said.

"Is good," Mousel agreed. "You have more later." Mallory
nodded drowsily. "She drinks three, four times, just a little,
before night," the wisewoman told Gemma. "You too if you
need strength."

"What is it?"

"Special. Very special. I make myself."

Mousel took one of Mallory's hands in her own, and Gemma,
who was sitting on the opposite side of the bed, reacted by
taking the other. Immediately she was aware of a new sensation, a mixture of warmth and wrongness. She instinctively

shied away from the wrong, trying to push it away and embrace only the warmth. As Mallory murmured sleepily, Gemma found Mousel's bright eyes fixed upon her own.

"You have healing hands," the wisewoman said. "Is good."

Me? Gemma thought, trying to analyze what was happening. *But surely this is coming from you.* She was confused.

"Relax," Mousel advised. "Help her."

"I don't understand."

"You will." Mousel's tone implied that she would not be drawn into further explanations, and Gemma retreated into her own thoughts, still holding Mallory's hand. They stayed like that until Mallory drifted off to sleep.

Meanwhile, Arden was learning all he could from Ehren and his fellow elders. Their village was named Keld, and the plain upon which it stood was known as Maiden Moor. The plateau extended south for many leagues and curved round to the east, so that it half-encircled the mountain, Blencathra. This was good news for Arden as it meant that their onward journey would be that much quicker and safer. Unfortunately, the villagers did not know of the existence of a river beyond the plateau. To the west, Maiden Moor ended in a huge vertical cliff, which plunged hundreds of paces to a forest-filled valley far below.

"Not a place to recommend for an evening stroll," Arden commented.

"Aye. You'd be yelling a good while before you hit the bottom," Ehren replied with a grim smile.

When Arden returned to the guest house, Mousel had left.

"How's Mallory?" he asked.

"Much better," Gemma replied and told him how his valley friend had been fed with the mysterious liquid and had then drifted in and out of sleep.

"It's warm in here," he said. "I could do with a drink myself."

Gemma handed him the bottle and he uncorked it, sniffed, then raised his eyebrows.

"I didn't think anyone made this any more," he remarked, and took a swig.

"What is it?"

"Mountain mead. Don't ask me what's in it, apart from wild honey, alcohol and—unless I'm very much mistaken—a touch of dragonflower."

"I'm not touching it then!" Gemma exclaimed.

"Don't worry," Arden said. "It's not like the stuff those bastards gave you in Newport. The amount is minute and if it's used properly can be wholly beneficial." He grinned and took another mouthful. "And it tastes wonderful."

"Leave some for Mallory," Gemma ordered. "It's really for her."

"We could all use some extra energy," Arden replied, unabashed, but stoppered the bottle. "You can try some later. They'll be bringing us some food soon."

"We've been lucky to find such friendly people."

Arden nodded his agreement.

"*You* seem to have made quite an impression," he said.

"Me?"

"The women have all been in council since Mousel came out," Arden went on, "and I believe you were the topic of conversation."

"She said I had healing hands," Gemma told him thoughtfully. "Whatever that means."

"I know no more than you do," he replied. "I wasn't privy to their discussion. But I *did* find out something of our location." He went on to tell Gemma what he had learned. "Tomorrow I'll take Lark round to the south of Blencathra," he said enthusiastically. "See what's there."

A knock sounded at the door and Arden stood up to let the food-bearers in. Eda, Ehren's wife, entered with her husband. They were both carrying large wooden bowls, wreathed in steam, from which enticing aromas spread. Mousel came in behind them with small bowls, wooden spoons, and another bottle of mead. All this was set down on the table beside Mallory's bed. She woke up on cue, and sniffed appreciatively.

"I'm ravenous," she whispered.

"Eat," Eda said happily. "There's no animal stuff in it."

"Drink too," Mousel said. "All of you." She looked particularly at Gemma, who said. "Thank you. You're very kind."

"And welcome," Eda replied.

"We come back later," Mousel went on. "With the demons."

The villagers filed out as Gemma and Arden looked at each other in bewilderment.

"What did *that* mean?" she asked.

"I haven't a clue," he replied.

"We'll find out soon enough," Mallory put in. "Feed me!"

An hour or so later, all the bowls were empty and so was

the first bottle of mead. Mallory was almost asleep again, a contented smile on her face, while Gemma, having been persuaded to sample the drink, felt light-headed and very warm. The fire cast a red glow over cheeks which were already pink. Arden was also in high spirits, full of plans for the morrow and confident of their eventual success. Gemma knew it was the alcohol talking, but was so glad to see him positive again that she said nothing. He was just about to open the second bottle when the villagers returned. This time Mousel led the way, followed by two women they had not seen before. Each carried a small child, and Gemma saw at once that something was wrong with the infants, who lay quietly in their mothers' arms. Pity welled up within her.

"The children are sick," Mousel stated. "Demons have them. My strength is not enough to bring them back." There was a pause, then she said to Gemma, "You have the healing hands. You must save them."

chapter 37

Gemma turned from Mousel to the mothers, and saw their newborn hope; then she looked at the listless, unseeing eyes of the children.

Oh Stars! she thought desperately. *What am I supposed to do?* Facing the expectant women she stood up slowly, feeling dizzy from the mead.

Mousel beckoned to one of the mothers.

"Lay him on the bed," she instructed. "Come, Gemma. I guide you."

They knelt together beside the child's bed.

"The demons are in here," Mousel said, tapping the boy's naked chest. "See. Feel." She took Gemma's hand and placed it on the clammy skin. "You feel?"

No! Gemma was frightened. *I don't feel anything. Help me!*

A channel of light opened in the swirling dark mists that were her thoughts, and suddenly is was Cai who knelt beside her, not Mousel.

"You know what to do," he said calmly. "I won't always be here to show you these things." His voice opened other channels and awareness flooded in.

"Stay with me," Gemma said quickly, afraid that he would abandon her.

"Of course."

She relaxed, and her consciousness spread beyond her own body, into that of the child who lay so quietly before her. She followed tendrils of health in blood, bone, and sinew until . . .

The wrongness of it struck her like a blow, and she recoiled, sickened, wanting only to withdraw and hide.

"There!" Cai said. "You see it now."

"It's horrible."

"Then heal it!" Cai demanded. "Why else do you think I'm teaching you?"

"*You* do it," she cried fearfully.

"I cannot. It is your task."

The room had ceased to exist. Gemma's awareness was limited to the dreadful thing in the infant's chest. She "saw" the diseased valve and the consequent buildup of liquid in the boy's lungs, and knew that it would soon drown him. She "saw" the ways in which she could drain the water and set that in motion, then turned her attention to the valve itself. It was a cold, hard abnormality and she raged at it, feeding it with the heat of her anger until it grew warm and soft. Quickly she moulded it, letting the strands of health fill it anew, and stepped back mentally to assess her work.

"Good," Cai said. "You're learning."

Gemma lifted her hand and the room gradually came back into focus. The boy's chest heaved and pale green water spewed from his mouth and nose.

"The demons!" Mousel exclaimed, as the boy's mother screamed in terror.

The infant coughed and spluttered, his eyes no longer dull but alive and frightened. He began to cry, and his mother quickly gathered him up in her arms, tears in her own eyes, and held him tightly.

"Thank you," she said in a broken voice. "Thank you."

Gemma looked up at her in disbelief. *What have I done? Have I succeeded?*

"You succeeded," Cai answered, but it was Mousel's lips that moved. Gemma suddenly grew weak and slumped toward the floor. She felt arms tighten around her and she relaxed into Arden's warm embrace.

"Are you all right?" he asked, his voice awestruck. She nodded, unable to speak.

"Take him home. Keep him warm," Mousel was telling the boy's mother. "The demons are gone. He will be well now." She turned back to Gemma. "Are you strong enough for the other?"

"No, she's—" Arden began, but Gemma had seen the look in the remaining mother's eyes, and she interrupted him. "Yes. Give me a drink. I'll be ready in a few moments."

Arden helped her up and she sat on the edge of Mallory's bed while Mousel cleaned away the mess on the other. He brought the second bottle over, and she drank gratefully, feeling its strength flowing through her tired body.

Mallory stretched out and held Gemma's free hand, squeezing it tight.

"I thought you were asleep," Gemma said.

"I wouldn't have missed this for anything," Mallory answered. "There's more to you than I realized."

"There's more to me than *I* realized," was the quiet reply.

"You argue with those demons all right," Mousel declared.

The only demons are in my head, Gemma thought, and took another mouthful. *This stuff certainly does something to me.*

The soiled bedclothes had been replaced now, and the second infant, a girl of perhaps four years of age, lay on the bed. Her eyes were blank and she did not move.

"Are you sure about this?" Arden asked.

Gemma nodded and resumed her place, kneeling at the bedside. She was struck as she did so by the similarity between this and the time by Kris's side. *If only I had known enough then—I could have helped him,* she mused, then put away the distressing thought and concentrated on the sick child and on her link with Cai.

"Are you still there?" she asked in a moment of panic.

"I'm here," he replied. "Though you don't need me now."

"I do. Please stay."

There was no answer but Gemma felt his comforting presence beside her still, and became absorbed in her task. At Mousel's request she placed her hand on the girl's forehead, and was immediately engulfed by a searing pain that almost overwhelmed her. *This is her whole world,* she thought, aghast at the idea of anyone, especially one so young and innocent, having to live with such torment. *No wonder she has withdrawn from the world.*

The source of the girl's illness needed little finding. It drew Gemma's attention irresistibly, angrily defying her to oppose it. The growth was inside the skull, behind the child's right eye; it's final victory was close at hand. Gemma saw it as an appallingly cold knot of malice, intent only on its domination of the being that harbored its evil presence.

This time there were no easy solutions. It was a battle of wills, and Gemma threw herself headlong into the fight. Before long she was struggling against exhaustion, wondering if this was beyond her powers. *Help me, Cai.*

"Keep trying," he urged. "Nothing is beyond you, so long as you believe in yourself."

Somewhere in another world a cup was held to her lips. She gulped reflexively and felt new reserves of strength growing within her.

"Go!" she shouted at the ghastly tumor. "I will tolerate your presence no longer!"

She felt the internal structure of the growth give way a little and, sensing victory, pressed home her advantage. The knot began to unravel, slowly returning to its original form, but she pursued each strand relentlessly, hunting them down and utterly destroying their malevolence. She knew instinctively that to do otherwise would be to invite a repetition of the illness.

At last she was satisfied and withdrew, lifting her hand. Cai was no longer beside her, and the last thing she remembered before collapsing was wondering where he had gone.

———•———

"I thought you'd never wake up," Arden said. The words were spoken lightly, but the relief showing on his face was plain to see.

"What time is it?" Gemma asked.

"Just before noon. You've been asleep for fifteen hours."

It took a while for this to sink in.

"The girl," she said. "Is she all right?"

"She's been running around outside since sunrise, playing and making as much noise as the other kids," Arden replied, smiling. "In Keld you are a fully accredited miracle worker."

Gemma smiled. "I feel as weak as a baby," she said.

"I'm not surprised. You were three hours healing that child, and it didn't look like easy work."

"Three hours?" Gemma was astonished. Where had the time gone?

"I nearly stopped you several times," Arden went on.

"I'm glad you didn't."

"So am I."

He leaned over and kissed her gently.

"Favoritism," Mallory remarked from her own bed. "This invalid wants a kiss too."

"You're looking better," Arden said, obliging her with a kiss on her forehead.

"I'm *feeling* better. Who wouldn't, with a famous healer in attendance. Gemma, that was amazing. How did you do it?"

"I can't even begin to explain. I wasn't alone, though."

"You were talking to *someone*, that's for sure. And you said some very strange things." Arden grinned. "Mind you, I suppose that's normal with you."

"I don't seem to be able to remember much of it," Gemma said.

"Are you hungry?"

Gemma was famished, and said so in no uncertain terms.

"Right, I'll go and organize a feast," Arden said, striding to the door. "From now on, the people of Keld will be treating us like royalty." He went out.

"What *are* you laughing at?" Mallory asked.

————•————

The entire population of Keld gathered that evening for an outdoor celebration to honor the travelers and the children's return to health. They danced and sang around a huge bonfire just outside the village, consuming more food and liquor than was good for them. Indeed, it would probably leave their stores short in the coming months, but the festivities would not be denied. It was a long time since Keld had known such a day.

Naturally, Ehren and his villagers had wanted the visitors to join in the celebration, but Arden refused point blank to allow either of his charges to leave their beds, let alone venture out in the chill night air. The people of Keld therefore had to content themselves with frequent visits to the guest house, bringing offerings of the choicest food and drink. Gemma and Mallory delighted in these attentions and the general air of gaiety, but as the night drew on they both grew weary. Arden began to shield them from the rowdier visitors, and eventually, using a blend of tact and charm which Gemma could not help but admire, he refused entry to everybody.

It was accepted that the women needed to rest, but Arden was invited to join in the festivities. He declined, but the villagers persisted good-naturedly, and he finally gave in. Assuring Gemma and Mallory that he would return soon, he gave them a what-can-I-do? shrug and went out, closing the door behind him.

The two tired women were left in relative calm, sitting up in bed, each with a cup of mead in her hands. Mousel had assured them that there was nothing like it for restoring both spirit and strength, and they felt no inclination to argue—especially as she had also said that nothing else in Keld tasted half as good. Their stomachs pleasantly full, they sipped slowly, and savored the peace.

"I hope Arden enjoys himself," Mallory said. "He deserves

happiness, and he's been so grim recently. He was never like this before."

Gemma remembered the scene that Kris had shown her.

"You loved him, didn't you."

"I still do," Mallory replied. "Like a brother," she added quickly as she saw Gemma stiffen.

"He's told me a lot about the valley, especially about his first visit," Gemma said. "It's no wonder he's so determined to save the place."

"I don't think his life was very happy before he came to us," Mallory said quietly.

"Has he ever talked about it?"

"No. Never. But I've often wondered . . ." Mallory lapsed into silence and took another sip. "Can I ask you something?" she asked after a while.

"Of course." Gemma was expecting another inquiry about her relationship with Arden, but Mallory surprised her by changing the subject completely.

"Has it occurred to you that the occasions when you've made the most spectacular use of magic have been after you've taken dragonflower essence?" Gemma looked at her in surprise, and Mallory went on. "Especially as those were the times when you were acting alone, and not with one of the groups you were talking about the other night." She waited expectantly for Gemma's answer, but there was such a long silence that Mallory wondered if she had offended her. "You don't have to talk about it if you'd rather not," she added.

"It's all right," Gemma answered, reacting to Mallory's concerned tone. "It *has* occurred to me, but I was rather hoping that it was just coincidence. I hate the idea that something like that is needed to make magic possible."

"Is it so bad?" Mallory asked.

"Magic should be a natural part of the world," Gemma replied, gazing at the liquid in her cup, "and all that *should* be necessary is the knowledge to use it wisely and well."

"And you could find no one to teach you?"

"No."

All Gemma's self-doubts and confusion rose to the surface, as it dawned on her once more that she was playing with forces she did not understand. *What right have I to meddle with children's health? I could have killed them!* She broke out in a cold sweat at the thought of the possible consequences of her ignorant interference. *But Cai would never have helped me if it wasn't right.* Then she thought back. Cai had not actively helped her in Newport. She had only *used* his knowledge. Yet the wizard had come willingly to her aid in Keld. *Healing,* she decided. *He permitted the use of his power because it was for healing purposes. That must be it.*

Mallory was speaking again.

"What?" Gemma asked, her train of thought broken.

"Perhaps the dragon flower essence enables you to seek that knowledge," Mallory repeated. "To find a teacher—Cai, perhaps."

Gemma looked at her, astonished.

"How do you know about Cai?"

"I'm not as stupid as I look," Mallory replied, smiling.

You're not stupid at all, Gemma thought.

"Besides, you mentioned his name a few times last night while you were healing the girl," Mallory continued. "And Arden's told me about him."

"My ears are burning," Arden said as he came in. "You must be talking about me." His face was flushed from dancing or drink, but probably from both. "Only natural, of course," he added, grinning.

"Actually, we were talking about Cai," Mallory told him.

"Oh, him!" Arden said dismissively. "The wonderful wizard of the north." He waved his arms around and half-stumbled. "Why bother about him? He is leagues away, while *I* . . ." He sat down suddenly on the foot of Gemma's bed and placed a hand over his heart. "I am here. In person."

"In-toxicated," Mallory added.

Arden switched his gaze from Gemma and glared at his accuser.

"Would you deny a man the simple pleasures in life?" he inquired.

"Oh, Arden, nothing about you is ever simple," Gemma said.

"How perspicacious of you," he said, half mocking. "I blame it all on my mother, really. Ever since I was a child—"

He stopped abruptly, his whole demeanor changing, and the color drained from his cheeks. In the silence that followed, the faint sounds of the revelry outside went unnoticed. Arden stared into space but eventually became aware of the two women watching him intently. Then Gemma spoke.

"Arden, why don't you tell us about it? It may help."

He gazed at her unseeingly for a few moments, then began speaking quietly.

"I could never understand why I was their only child, and by the time I found out, it was too late to help her." He paused, his eyes seeing a different scene. Gemma and Mallory waited in silence for him to continue.

"She was *so* beautiful," he said. "She could have had any man she chose, yet she stayed with him . . . my *father*." He spat the word in disgust. "He was a brutal man, but I only found out what he was *really* like when my mother was called."

Gemma and Mallory exchanged glances, but Arden did not notice.

"She went crazy then, and just walked out. He caught up with her soon enough, and beat her senseless. I hated him so much for that . . ." Arden's hands clenched. "It didn't do any good. The next time it happened she went off again, without even thinking about what he might do to her. She'd have walked over the edge of a cliff if that had been the most direct route. There was no sense to it at all—she didn't even take a horse, or any provisions." His expression had become disbelieving, like that of a lost child.

"He caught her again, of course, and dragged her home. This time he was so angry he went mad—and he killed her. Then he got blind drunk and started talking to her, swearing and shouting, then crying and saying he was sorry. I saw her lying there, not moving, broken but still beautiful." He swallowed hard, but his eyes remained dry. "I realized she wasn't ever going to get up. Then he lay on his bed in a stupor, unable to move."

Arden's eyes came back into focus, and he looked at Gemma and Mallory in turn, noting their stricken expressions.

"I burned the house down," he said. "With them both inside."

The two women could think of nothing to say. His confession was evidently over, but they knew that no words from them could take away his pain.

"My mother got the call from the South," Arden told them suddenly. "And look what happened to her. Now you two want to go! Oh yes," he added, seeing their expressions, "don't think I don't know what was happening that night. I heard something too, but I've got more sense than to listen to it."

When he next spoke, Arden's voice was drained of all anger.

"I don't want you to go. But I'm terrified of becoming like *him*," he pleaded.

"You could *never* be like that," Gemma said firmly, surprised that she had found her voice at last.

"Couldn't I?" There was a touch of madness in the eyes that stared back at her, and for a moment Gemma wavered. Then she gathered herself to meet his gaze.

"Never," she repeated.

He looked at her for a moment longer, then his shoulders sagged.

"So now you know my dark secret," he said, making a brave effort to sound flippant, but failing miserably. "Just like Kris did all those years ago. I'm surprised he didn't tell you."

"Kris could see what was important in you," Mallory said. "He showed us that, and we've not been disappointed."

"I'll believe that when we get the river back," he whispered ruefully, looking at the floor.

"How old were you when it happened?" Gemma asked softly.

"Fourteen." He glanced up, smiling bitterly. "We grow up fast in the mountains."

"Let it go, Arden," Mallory said. "You can't change anything, and it *was* a long time ago."

"A long time ago," he repeated slowly, emphasizing each word. "I need a drink," he added a moment later.

"So do I," Gemma and Mallory said in unison.

A little life came back into Arden's eyes then and Gemma watched as he marshaled his resources, forcing himself out of his melancholy mood. *You're braver than you'll ever know*, she thought. *To have lived with that alone for so long*.

"Your wish is my command," he said, getting up and fetching the bottle of mead. He refilled their cups and found one for himself. Although he swayed a little on his feet, his hand was steady as he poured.

"You've done that before." Gemma remarked.

"True," he replied. "I missed my real vocation. I should have been a professional drunk. I have the perfect qualifications." Suddenly, his face screwed up in fury. "Goddamn!" he yelled. "Why did I have to bring all that up?" He flung the bottle at the cabin door. It did not shatter, but bounced on to the floor, where it came to rest, the last few dregs dripping out onto the wooden boards. Arden stared at it in disbelief, while Gemma and Mallory held their breath.

"Gods," he said eventually. "Doesn't *anything* do what I want it to?" He continued to gaze at the bottle as if he could shatter it by the force of his will.

"That was the last of our mead," Mallory said timidly. "Us girls need to keep up our strength, you know."

They waited to see how Arden would react to this gentle cajolery.

"Right!" he exclaimed dramatically. "I'll get another bottle. No! A barrel. We'll need it before the night's out." With that, he left, staggering slightly, and kicking the offending bottle as he passed. He closed the door behind him with exaggerated care.

Gemma and Mallory looked at each other and let out a sigh of relief.

chapter 38

They stayed in Keld for another three days, by which time Gemma and Mallory had recovered their health, and Arden had shed the last remnants of a mammoth hangover. Despite his self-imposed suffering, he had made several reconnaissance trips and was now eager to be away, believing that he knew where to pick up the river's course once more.

So, on a bright, cold morning, they took their leave of the village and, as the last of the farewells faded away, they rode southeast, intending to skirt round the scree-slopes of Blencathra's southern rim. It was easy traveling for most of the morning, but then, as the ground began to rise, they found themselves having to pick their way along a precarious trail, sometimes needing to dismount. They were on such high ground now that breathing was a little difficult, and the horses had to travel slowly.

At the top of the main ridge, due south of the mountain's peak, Arden stopped and pointed eastward.

"See that little closed vale, the third one along from here, with the line of trees on the far side?" His companions nodded. "That's where I think the river disappears underground," he went on. "We should be able to get there by dusk."

Gemma squinted into the distance, shielding her eyes from the bright mountain sun.

"I think I can see the riverbed higher up," she said.

"I'm glad you spotted that too," Arden replied.

"It makes sense," Mallory put in as she studied the surrounding terrain. "There's a direct route from that pass between the two big peaks. If a river flowed from there, it would end up in that vale."

"All agreed then," Arden concluded, sounding pleased. "Let's go."

He led them down the twisting path from the ridge, and through the first valley. Navigation became a matter of judgment and memory now, as they could not see their goal, and it was a relief when they topped the brow of a bracken-covered hill and looked down into the vale they sought.

The dry bed of the river was clearly visible in its upper reaches, but further down, below where they stood now, there was no sign of it at all. They rode on in the fading light of late afternoon, and inspected the place where the earth swallowed the river. Fissures and sink-holes lined the center of the valley floor, making riding impossible and walking dangerous. Why the rock here should be so broken and porous was a mystery, but one Arden did not stop to worry about.

"This is definitely the place," he said triumphantly. "To-morrow we'll head on upstream. We must be getting close by now."

The others did not want to dampen his enthusiasm by asking, "Close to what?" Instead, they collected wood and helped him set up camp on a level piece of grass. They were soon sitting round a cheerful blaze as Mallory brewed tea from some herbs that she had chanced upon. The horses grazed contentedly nearby, blankets draped over their backs. Gemma glanced at them and smiled as Lark nuzzled Mischa's neck. Apple, Mallory's mare, bent down to pull up another mouthful of grass.

The pot of water came to the boil, and Arden reached out to take it from the fire. But in an instant, the pot, the fire, and everything about them disappeared and they were lost in a dense cold fog which isolated each of them in a world of their own. Blue flamelike beings slipped with incredible speed in and out of their sight.

All three tried to cry out, but their words were swallowed by the all-enveloping mist. And then, suddenly, it was gone. And so was everything else.

The travelers found themselves sitting on the floor in the middle of a large, dimly lit room.

"What . . . ?" Arden began, glancing about open-mouthed.

"Where *are* we?" Mallory whispered.

"Looks like someone's library," Gemma replied, fighting the urge to laugh hysterically.

They got slowly to their feet, and inspected their surroundings. The room was rectangular, perhaps thirty paces long by ten paces wide, but it contained no furniture. Three walls were entirely covered by shelves of books of all shapes and sizes, stretching up to the rafters far above. The fourth wall was bare save for a wooden door under a pointed archway. The air was warm but musty, as if no one had disturbed it for centuries, but there was no dust on the floor or shelves. From the ceiling, several globes illuminated the scene with a soft, constant light.

"Definitely a library," Arden agreed. "The question is— whose?" He took one last look around and strode toward the door. Halfway there he stopped, looking back at Gemma and Mallory, who were still in the center of the room. "Well, we're not going to find out by standing here," he remonstrated, then turned back to the door.

Grasping the handle, he turned it, pushed, then pulled, but the door did not budge. Arden tested it with his shoulder, shoving hard, but to no avail.

"We're locked in," he said indignantly, as if this were more of an affront to him than their inexplicable transportation. He kicked the door, which boomed dully, but only succeeded in hurting his foot. The others came up beside him, and Mallory laid a palm on the solid, iron-studded panels of the door.

"I think we'll have to wait to be let out," she said. "Whoever built this knew what they were doing."

"But this is crazy!" Arden exclaimed, his bewilderment fast turning to anger.

"You can say that again!" Mallory commented.

Arden hammered on the door a few times. "If we make enough noise, perhaps someone will come and let us out," he said.

"Are you sure you *want* someone to come?" Gemma asked. "Whoever lives here may not welcome intruders."

"We're not intruders!" Arden retorted. "We've been kidnapped."

"By a library?" Gemma said, beginning to laugh.

"What do you suggest we do then?" he snapped, refusing to see anything funny in their situation. "Just sit here?"

"Well, we won't be bored," she replied. "At least there's plenty to read."

Arden grunted dismissively.

"Perhaps the books will tell us where we are," Mallory suggested.

"And how we got here, I suppose," Arden said sarcastically. "Don't be absurd, Mallory."

"Have *you* got any better ideas?" Gemma asked him.

"We could try burning the door down."

"I think making a lot of noise is a better plan," she replied.

"We'd probably suffocate in the smoke before that thing gave way," Mallory said.

"I haven't even got a knife," Arden said mournfully. "They're all back at the camp." He shook his head. "This is beyond me," he admitted, and began thumping on the door again.

"Come and help us explore!" Mallory shouted over the noise. "You can come back and bang on the door every so often. If you go on like that, you'll only hurt yourself."

Arden's fists stopped, and he rested his forehead quietly on the door for a moment before he turned round.

"All right," he said, admitting temporary defeat. "Which of these several thousand volumes would you ladies care to read first?"

An hour or so later, there were books all over the floor. Arden had worked out how to use the three movable ladders which were situated along the shelves. They rested on metal wheels and were attached to runners on the top shelf, thus enabling even the highest books to be reached with relative ease. He had studied their construction in the hope of being able to use them to force the door, but their sturdiness showed the futility of his trying to take them apart. He climbed all three of them, but could discover no means of escape. Above the endless rows of books, the walls were bare stone.

As well as making the higher shelves accessible, the ladders also enabled Arden to get a closer look at the globes of light. They were unlike anything he had ever seen, and he was intrigued. Their steady, even glow was almost white, and each sphere hung from the rafters by a thin wire or string. That none was in reach was frustrating, but while standing on the topmost rung and inspecting them, Arden made out something else hidden in the wooden rafters—long thin tubes made of a dull, white material which were attached to the roof. They too were out of reach.

Meanwhile, Gemma and Mallory were gleaning what they could from a random selection of the multitude of books. Some volumes had titles on the spine—none of which was recognized by either woman—but most were unmarked. They came to the conclusion that the owner of the library either had a phenomenal memory, or had a wonderfully mysterious cataloguing system. Or else he had decided that he never wanted to read the books again anyway.

Most of those they picked out appeared to be obscure histories of places they had never heard of, and they could find no connection at all between adjacent volumes.

"Listen to this," Mallory said, holding one of her discoveries close in order to quote from the tiny print. " 'In the next five years, seventy-six peace treaties were signed between Olcondoria and Sled. None but the last held for more than two months; the shortest was broken after less than one hour. On each occasion, both sides claimed that the other had been the aggressor, and demanded the right of retaliation. The result of this was that warfare became essential to both economies. When peace was finally established, the ensuing social chaos led to both states experiencing a huge increase in crimes of violence, suicide, and epidemic disease.' " Mallory looked up at Gemma. "Can they really have been so stupid?" she asked in disbelief.

"That's nothing," Gemma replied. "Listen to this." She began to read from her own book. " 'The fervor instilled by this religious belief led to the torture and killing of innocent people, on the grounds of heresy. Many of these were illiterate peasants who were not even capable of reading the supposedly perverted works. It was ironic that the most ardent and ruthless investigator of these heretical crimes, who had taken a sacred vow of chastity, was found to have kept a secret harem of over twenty women and girls, all of whom he slaughtered shortly before his death from venereal disease.' "

"What *is* this?" Mallory asked. "A library of human madness?"

Their musings were interrupted by a tremendous flash of lightning. Mallory gave a little scream, and they both instinctively covered their heads. The bright flashing continued for a few moments but was not followed by any thunder. The only sound was the thump as Arden landed on the wooden floor, having been taken by surprise from his relatively lofty position. The lightning stopped, but the whole room was now bathed in a harsh white light which emanated from the white tubes. Each now shone with a bright, steady radiance which made the globes seem dull by comparison.

Then the door swung open, and the three "intruders" stared at the extraordinary figure which shuffled into view.

He was dressed in a shapeless robe of dark brown material, and stood no more than half Arden's height. Completely covering his head and drooping down over his shoulders was a voluminous leather hat of the same dull color. In the gloom beneath its brim, two small eyes glowed brightly above a long, pointed nose. The lower half of his face was covered with an unruly, off-white beard and moustache, dispelling any notion that this might be a child.

The newcomer treated them all to a brief but intense stare before muttering darkly, "Damned thaumaturgical maps are never accurate. These ranges are supposed to be uninhabited." With that, he turned on his heels and went out again. The travelers were galvanized into action by his imminent departure.

"Wait!" Arden yelled, scrambling to his feet.

"Don't go, please!" Mallory added as she and Gemma also rose.

The tiny stranger paid them no attention. Moving with surprising agility, he shuffled out of the room and closed the door behind him. Swearing viciously, Arden ran to the door. He wrenched at the handle and almost fell over as the door swung open quite easily. The others hurried to join him, and they stepped through, finding themselves in a large, tiled hallway. They were faced with a large number of other doors and a curving staircase which led up to another floor.

The bearded stranger was nowhere to be seen.

chapter 39

"This gets worse," Arden remarked. "Insane libraries and now disappearing dwarves!"

"Oh, stop complaining," Mallory responded. "He let us out, didn't he? At least now we can explore."

She sounded almost enthusiastic, and Arden looked at her in disbelief, then shook his head.

"Let's go outside," he said. "We can find the horses and—"

"*Arden,*" Mallory said, sounding like a long-suffering schoolteacher. "Don't be stupid."

"Wherever the horses are," Gemma added, "we're not going to be able to reach them just by stepping outside."

"All right, all right," Arden conceded, holding up his hands to forestall any further lectures. "But I still want to get outside. This house makes me nervous."

A slight draft blew across the hallway, apparently coming from a large doorway across from the stairs; daylight shone through the cracks around the double doors.

"This looks like our exit," Arden said purposefully, and marched off without waiting to consult the others. Gemma and Mallory exchanged a resigned glance. They would both have preferred to try and uncover the secrets of the house and its eccentric inhabitant, but postponed their plans in the face of Arden's intransigence.

"We'd better stick together," Mallory said.

Gemma agreed. "We can always come back later," she said as they followed Arden. As they were leaving, they noticed that some of the doors on the ground floor had a symbol carved deeply into the wood. None was instantly recognizable, but they reminded Gemma of the judges' sculpted markers in Newport. Arden had reached the large doors by now, and opened them without difficulty. Bright sunlight flooded in, and emphasized their displacement from their campsite, which by now would have been almost dark. Here the sun was at its zenith. Blinking and shading their eyes, the travelers stepped into a city street. As Arden shut the door

behind them, the door to the library closed of its own accord
with a quiet click.

The street was deserted and silent; nothing moved except
the wind, and even that seemed torpid. They had never seen
buildings like these before—rectangular structures with very
few features, whose plain surfaces were uniform in color and
whose sharp corners dominated the architecture. The only
exception was the house from which they had just emerged;
this was built of gray stone, with arched windows of leaded
glass, and a slate roof. An iron railing separated it from the
street, and it looked totally out of place amid the smooth,
gleaming structures that surrounded it. The road beneath
their feet was made of a hard, black substance that they did
not recognize.

"It's like another world," Gemma breathed.

"Not many people about for the time of day," Arden
commented.

"I don't think there can be *any* people," Mallory said. "It's
too clean. There's not a speck of dirt anywhere."

As the others looked about them, the silence grew more
eerie.

"Well, let's try to find someone," Arden eventually suggested.

"All right," Gemma answered. "We shouldn't have any
difficulty finding *this* place again. It sticks out like a sore
thumb."

To her astonishment, both Arden and Mallory laughed at
her words.

"It does *what*?" Arden spluttered.

"What's so funny?" she demanded.

"Let's just say," Mallory explained when she could get her
breath, "that that expression is—how shall I put it?—not
used in polite conversation." She dissolved into giggles again.

Though still baffled, Gemma was finally forced to join in.
The incident brought home to her the fact that Cleve was still
an alien land to her, in spite of the fact that she had been
there for almost three months.

"Are you going to stand there all day?" she asked, feigning
anger. "Or are we going to explore?"

"Onward!" Arden replied.

They walked down the street. It ended in a T-junction, from
which both branches of the road ran straight. After a hundred
paces or so, however, they also ended in right-angle turns to
left and right. The buildings were all alike, anonymous and

inhuman. All normal features—doors, windows, chimneys— were conspicuous by their absence. The only variations in the faceless rectangles were of size and color.

"Which way now?" Mallory asked.

Arden shrugged. "Doesn't matter. One way's as good as the other."

They walked to the next corner, and the new road ended as before.

"It's like a maze," Mallory said.

"Made from a child's building blocks," Gemma added.

"A giant's child," Arden amended. "Let's hope daddy doesn't turn up."

They all pictured a gigantic pair of boots descending on them from the sky and found the idea so ridiculous that they started laughing again.

"Well, its no sillier than our being here in the first place," Arden commented.

"We have enough problems as it is, without imagining new ones," Gemma said. "For a start, if we carry on like this we'll just get hopelessly lost."

"We'd better mark our way," Arden decided.

"What with?"

"Have you got anything sharp?" he asked, but both women shook their heads.

"Then it'll have to be this," Arden said, removing his belt and testing the point of the buckle. "I trust you will avert your eyes should my breeches fall down."

He tried to scratch an arrow on the surface of the corner building, but could make no impression.

"What *is* this stuff?" he said, running a hand over the silver-gray surface.

"Try the road," Mallory suggested.

Arden did as she advised, and grunted with satisfaction when he found that he was able to make a mark quite easily. He drew two arrows, one showing the way they had come, and the other the direction in which they would turn. That done, they set off again, repeating the procedure at each corner.

Gemma gradually became convinced that this freakish city would reveal no secrets; they saw no people, heard no sounds, and found no signs of life. Each of the short, straight roads was as featureless as the rest, but Arden seemed intent on continuing, always turning left, then right, so that they traveled a zigzag route. It was Mallory who eventually voiced Gemma's thought.

"We should go back to the house," she said. "At least there's somebody there."

"No," Arden replied. "I want to get out of here." He glanced up at the sun. "We've been going alternately east and south all the time, so we *must* get to the edge of this place sooner or later."

"But it'll be dark before long," Gemma objected. "We've no food and no shelter, and there doesn't appear to be any way to get into one of these things." She indicated the buildings about them. "We should go back."

"No!"

Neither of his companions could understand Arden's vehement aversion to the house.

"But I'm getting hungry!" Mallory objected.

"Me too," Gemma added.

"So am I, and that's all the more reason for getting out of here," Arden replied irritably. "We could be near the edge now." With that, he marched away and, reaching the next corner ahead of the others, bent to mark the customary arrow. As he rounded the corner, he came to an abrupt halt, staring at something in the new street. Gemma and Mallory hurried to his side.

The front of one of the buildings stood open to the street. Inside was a brightly-lit room, containing a table and three chairs. As they drew closer, they were surrounded by enticing aromas, and could see that there was a meal set out on the table. Plates of steaming hot meat, fish, and vegetables lay beside bowls of crisp salads, fruit, and nuts. A jug of water and two bottles of amber-colored liquid stood in the center, with glasses and cutlery set at each place.

They stared at the feast, not able to believe their eyes, yet equally at a loss to discount the evidence of their noses and salivating mouths. Once more they experienced a joint vision, one conjured up this time by an old children's tale.

"The enchanted cottage," Mallory said, quoting the valley's version of the story.

"Food that's not real," Arden added, though this looked real enough.

"Or poison," Gemma concluded, and the other two looked at her warily.

"Why would anyone—" Mallory began.

"Want to poison us? Or lay a feast out for us?" Gemma interrupted. "I don't think we should accept this at face value. Doesn't it strike you as very strange how one moment we're all saying we're hungry, and the next some food pops up just like that?"

They considered this for a while.

"All right," Arden said. "I'll test it first, then if I don't suffer any ill effects, you can eat it too."

"Why don't I do it?" Mallory volunteered.

"No, let me," Gemma put in. "You've been ill, and besides, you can't test the meat."

"We'll need you to do any healing that's necessary," Arden said. "*I'll* try it."

With that, he sat down and sampled each dish in turn. At first he took only tiny morsels, but as his confidence grew, he ate and drank larger portions. The women watched him closely.

"Well?" Mallory queried.

"It's real enough," Arden stated. "It tastes a bit bland, but that's the only thing wrong with it as far as I can tell." He took another helping.

"Hey, leave some for us!" Mallory said, smiling, but Gemma still wasn't convinced.

"I'll wait a bit," she said, ignoring the cries of distress from her stomach. "Just in case." She contented herself with inspecting the remarkably fine craftsmanship of the glass and pottery. *We couldn't make anything like this,* she mused.

An hour later, when Arden and Mallory still showed no ill-effects, Gemma relented, and ate. The food was cold now but still tasted wonderful. Soon everything except the last of the amber wine was gone.

It was growing dark outside and, their hunger appeased, their thoughts turned to shelter. Returning to the house was not a realistic possibility that night.

"We could stay here," Arden suggested. "It's open to the air, but at least there's a roof over our heads."

"What I'd *really* like," Mallory said dreamily, "is a bed like the one I have at home. After a meal like that, I could sleep for hours."

Arden snapped his fingers. "Waiter! Beds for everybody!" he shouted over his shoulder.

"Idiot," Gemma laughed.

"Well, why not?" he replied. "If the city can provide us with a meal . . ."

Mallory, who sat facing the street, stiffened suddenly, then rose and walked quickly toward the road.

"I saw something move," she said, and the others turned to watch her, sudden hopes and fears rising within them. She stopped at the edge of the room then beckoned to them urgently.

"Over there," she said, pointing. "You're not going to believe this." She crossed the street and they hurried to join her. The front of one of the buildings opposite had become transparent, like an impossibly large sheet of glass. Light shone from within, illuminating the three beds which stood inside.

They were beyond astonishment now. Drawing closer, they saw that a glass door was set in the wall; Arden opened it and they stepped inside. The beds proved to be as real as the food had been. A small table stood between two of them and above each bedhead was a single switch. Arden pushed one of them experimentally, and one of the three lights above went out. He pushed it again and, with a familiar flickering, the white tube glowed brightly once more.

Gemma then discovered another door leading to an adjoining room, opened it, and went inside. She emerged a few moments later, her face a picture of wonderment.

"It's a bathroom!" she exclaimed. "Water comes out of pipes in the walls and there's even a sort of chamber pot . . ."

"Thank goodness for that," Arden said. "I'm dying for . . ." He disappeared, shutting the door behind him.

After a few moments Mallory hammered on the door.

"Come on!" she yelled. "You're not the only one in need."

Arden emerged, smiling.

"Amazing," he commented as Mallory gratefully took his place.

They were soon taking the miraculous plumbing for granted and preparing for bed.

"Don't sleep too long," Arden warned. "We want to be up at first light if we're ever going to get out of here."

"That makes sense," Gemma agreed.

"All right, you sadists," Mallory conceded. "Rise and shine at the crack of dawn."

"Make sure you carry on believing in these beds," Arden said. "I don't want them to disappear in the middle of the night."

———————•———————

They were woken at first light by a soft intermittent warbling that sounded like a insistent dove. As they awoke, Arden realized that the noise was coming from a curious contraption on the table beside him. He was sure it had not been there the previous evening. He studied the object as the warbling continued; there were several buttons on the front, but pressing these had no effect. On top was an oddly shaped handle with a curly cord running from one end. He picked it up and the sound stopped; in its place a tiny, remote voice could be heard saying, "Thank you, sir. Your early morning call."

Arden dropped the handle, and it dangled from its cord while the three of them regarded it with fear and suspicion. Gemma reached out and gingerly picked it up, holding it in front of her face.

"Thank you, sir. Your early morning call," the unknown woman repeated.

"It's coming from one end of this," Gemma said.

"Talk back!" Mallory said. "Maybe she'll hear you."

"What!" Gemma was completely out of her depth.

Then the handle began emitting a dull buzzing noise.

"Don't go!" Mallory cried, grabbing it and shouting, "Hello?" But the buzzing continued, and no amount of urging or investigation of the device could produce any other sound. The travelers were left shaken and more confused than ever.

"Well, at least it got us out of bed," Arden said. "Let's get going."

The women wanted to head straight back to the house, but he persuaded them to continue their explorations, at least for a while.

"We must be near the edge now." The experiences of the night had increased his eagerness to return to a world he understood.

And so, albeit unwillingly, they went on as before, turning left then right, and marking each corner.

"I should have kept one of the knives from the meal," Arden said, ruefully inspecting the damage to his buckle as he scored another arrow in the road's surface.

"Look at this!" Gemma called urgently. She was standing on the other corner of the junction, looking down at the ground, and the others went to join her. They gazed in disbelief at the two arrows which were marked there.

"That's impossible!" Arden exploded. "We *can't* have been here before."

"We're going round in circles," Mallory whispered. "No wonder these streets all look so familiar."

"No, no, no," Arden insisted. "We haven't taken any wrong turnings. I *know* we haven't."

Yet the evidence was there before his eyes. They believed that they had followed his intended route, but the lack of real progress was obvious.

At Arden's insistence, they continued as before for a while, now inspecting both corners each time. On several occasions they discovered arrows already there, and Arden grew angry and despondent.

"This is a maze to end all mazes," Gemma said. "It changes as you walk through it!"

Arden no longer had the will to argue—another precious day was almost gone and they had got literally nowhere. Although he still desperately wanted to escape, he agreed reluctantly to try to retrace their steps to the house he dreaded. Something about the place made his blood run cold, and for reasons he could not fathom, he hated the idea of Gemma being there. And yet it was the only place they had seen another living being.

As the second day drew to a close they discovered another meal, identical to the last, and a similar bedroom. They could not tell if they were the same places as before but were glad of them nonetheless.

They were woken next morning by natural daylight. The speaking contraption had not reappeared. Though still reluctant, Arden went along with the plan of following their trail of arrows in the opposite direction, but this idea foundered when they arrived at a corner which had two sets of arrows pointing in opposite directions. After a short and panicky discussion, Arden finally made up his mind.

"Just pick one," he said. "Either way, we'll find it soon enough." He was heartily sick of the city and now wanted to return to the house as much as his companions did. He rationalized that, as it was where they had entered this accursed place, perhaps they could also leave from there. In any case he would prefer anything to this monotonous landscape of meaningless blocks and endless corners.

"All right," Gemma said firmly. "This way."

She led them to the next junction and peered around the corner.

"There is is!" she exclaimed joyfully.

Even Arden was relieved.

chapter 40

"What's this?" Mallory asked, pointing to a small metal plaque attached to the railings.

" 'Protected Building. Preservation Order RN42,' " Gemma read.

"Protected by what?" Arden asked suspiciously, scrutinizing the outside of the house for concealed weapons. "I can't see anything."

"Never mind," Gemma answered. "He showed no sign of wishing to harm us when we were here before. I don't think it means that sort of protection. Come on." And she led the way up the three steps to the large doors.

"Should we knock? Or just go in?"

"See if the door's open first," Mallory advised.

When Gemma tried the handle, she was dragged inside by the door itself which, once unfastened, swung inward of its own accord. The others caught up with her and the three kept close together as they saw two strange-looking figures cross the hall. One was the dwarf they had met earlier, the other was almost his exact replica. However, this man stood a head taller than Arden and towered over his diminutive companion. Otherwise they were identical—and but for the discrepancy in size, could have been twins.

At the abrupt entrance of the "intruders," they both turned sharply, and stared at them with eyes that sparkled from beneath their huge, absurd hats. The taller of the two reacted first, taking a step back and slamming shut the large book he held in his long, bony fingers. The other seemed unperturbed.

"I thought you'd be back sooner or later," he said offhandedly. "Do try not to get in the way."

"Skape ni odec!" the tall man snapped.

"Why should I? They're no danger to us. They're not even adepts." The dwarf sounded resigned.

"Oyu kwon hwy. Oru krow sumt ont eb despi noup yb troudessi."

"Oh rubbish! Anyway, we'll be gone soon." The small one

turned to face the travelers. "I am Wynut," he said, and the taller grunted with disfavor.

"I'm—" Gemma began, thankful at last for an opportunity to speak, but she was interrupted.

"Your identities are of no consequence to us," Wynut said. "I am sorry you have been troubled by our travels, but you will be returned to your own place. In the meantime, have patience and— *please*—do not seek us out. At all cost keep away from Shanti." He jerked a thumb at his large companion.

"Og yawa. M'i grynti ot krow!" the other said.

"Idiot! They can't understand you if you talk like that," Wynut said disgustedly.

"Lal het rome orsane hent. Yeth'er ont fo oru knid."

"Of course they're not. They're not *supposed* to be."

Gemma had been watching this exchange in bewilderment. Although Shanti's words sounded like gibberish, she felt that they would make sense if only she could discover their secrets. She was about to try to speak to Wynut again when, with no warning, both characters disappeared. One moment they were there, the next the travelers were alone in the hall.

Alone, that is, apart from the tortoiseshell cat which walked lazily down the staircase, eyeing them curiously. It was the largest, fattest cat Gemma had ever seen, yet it still moved with feline grace. When it reached the lowest step, it sat down, tail curled neatly around its legs, and locked stares with Gemma, as if trying to prize forth her secrets.

"Where did they go?" Arden whispered, sounding close to panic.

"Let's just do what he suggested," Mallory said quietly, also unnerved, "and keep out of their way."

The cat meowed loudly as if in agreement. Then, to their amazement, the sound did not die away but echoed and reverberated around the hall, gaining in complexity and modulation. And as it did so, the sound took form, becoming not an animal cry but speech, strange in tone but perfectly coherent. When the dizzying transformation was complete, they heard the cat say, "A wise choice. And then again, a foolish one."

This latest shock to their senses was almost too much, and they stood, gazing at the animal, their eyes wide and their mouths open. It returned their stares complacently, and meowed again. This time they were prepared, and recognized the words before they reached their final clarity and volume.

"You must not tempt them to anger. And then again, you *do* need their help."

Arden shut his eyes and groaned.

"I can't take much more of this," he complained.

Mallory and Gemma were still mesmerized by the cat's echoing words. As if sensing their helplessness, the animal gave one last long cry, then turned on its heels and scampered with surprising speed up the stairs. It was out of sight by the time its words were intelligible, but there was no mistaking the amusement in its voice.

"I suggest the acorn room for food. And then again, hunger is only relative."

"Let's get out of here," Arden said urgently, turning back to the door.

"No," Gemma responded quickly.

"Anyway, my legs won't move," Mallory added, abruptly sitting down on the floor and holding her head in her hands.

Gemma put a hand on the back of her friend's neck for comfort, then turned to Arden.

"You heard what they said, didn't you?" she asked.

"All too well," he replied.

"If we stay here, we will be returned. Isn't that what you want?"

"But how can we go back if we're not moving?" Arden's logical mind found this aspect hard to understand.

"Wynut said, '*We'll* be gone soon.' Not '*They'll* be gone soon.' Don't you see? This whole city must be moving—and when it leaves our campsite, we'll find ourselves back there." She felt confident that she had interpreted Wynut's words correctly, but to Arden it seemed too incredible to believe, and he threw up his hands in defeat.

"I give up," he said. "Just tell me what to do."

"First, let's find the acorn room," she replied. "Then at least we'll know if we can trust the cat." She grinned at her own words. "Come on, Mallory. Feeling better now?"

Her friend nodded, accepted a helping hand, and got slowly to her feet. They looked around the hall.

"That's the library. Where we came in," Gemma said, pointing.

"What's the sign on the door?" Mallory asked.

"A clover leaf?" Arden suggested.

"Whatever it is, it's definitely not an acorn," Gemma said.

"There it is." Mallory indicated one of the doors on the opposite side.

"Are you hungry?" Gemma inquired, but the others just looked at her.

"Well, let's go and see if it's there anyway," she went on, and crossed the hall. They all looked about nervously, as if expecting new apparitions at any moment.

Gemma confirmed that the carving was indeed that of an acorn, and tried the handle. The door opened easily enough, but the hinges creaked noisily, setting all their teeth on edge.

"It's another library!" Mallory exclaimed as they stepped inside.

Books covered the two main walls; at the far end of the room stood a bare table and several chairs.

"There's no food in here," Arden pointed out.

"Possibly because we don't want any yet," Gemma replied.

"What do you mean?"

"This city caters to your needs," she said slowly. "When you want something, it's there."

"In that case," Arden responded, "I want three horses and a map to show us how to get out of here."

"Within reason," Gemma went on.

"What I don't need are all these *books*," Arden added, looking around at the packed shelves. "What's reasonable about that? It would take centuries to read all this lot."

"We've got nothing better to do," Gemma replied.

"Where shall we start?" Mallory asked.

Arden slumped into one of the chairs.

"How did I get stuck with you two?" he asked despairingly. "We're lost in an impossible maze of a city, inhabited only by bearded madmen who vanish into thin air and a cat who seems to delight in tormenting us with riddles—and all you can think of is *reading*."

The women ignored him and inspected the lower shelves.

"Some of these look familiar," Mallory said thoughtfully.

"I was just thinking the very same thing."

"Are they the same as the ones in the clover room?"

"Let's find out."

They set to work, enlisting Arden's help to reach the higher shelves with the movable ladders, and soon had the floor covered with piles of books. Occasionally they read passages to each other for amusement, or in wonder, but it was not until much later in the day that they actually found what they were looking for.

"Here it is!" Mallory exclaimed, then began to read aloud. " 'In the next five years sixty-four peace treaties were signed between Olcondoria and Sled. None but the last held for more than two months—' "

"How many treaties?" Gemma interrupted.

"Sixty-four."

"That's not right. It was more than that."

"I don't remember," Mallory said. "Shall we carry on?"

Gemma nodded.

' "The shortest was broken after less than one hour. On each occasion, both sides claimed that the other had been the aggressor and demanded the right of retaliation. The result of this was that warfare became essential to both economies. When peace was finally established, the ensuing social chaos led to both states experiencing a huge increase in crimes of violence, suicide, and, in the case of Sled, epidemic diseases which left the entire province an unpopulated wasteland.' "

"That last bit's different too," Gemma said slowly.

"You're right," Mallory admitted, remembering now. "But the rest sounded just the same."

"Word for word," Gemma agreed.

"Two different versions of the same story?"

"I'll go and get the other book," Gemma said. "And we'll compare the two."

"This is intriguing," Mallory remarked, relishing the mystery.

"Not as interesting as the thought of food," Arden said, from the other end of the room. "I'm hungry, but nothing's appeared. Just shows—you can't trust cats."

" 'Hunger is only relative,' " Gemma quoted.

"Very funny," he replied. "Tell that to my stomach."

"I'm hungry too," Mallory said.

"We all are," Gemma agreed. "But let's check this book first." She got up. "What was the book called?"

The Wars of Olcondoria by Brother Incantasius Septimus."

Gemma opened the door to the hall, about to go back to the clover room.

"Thank you," a very large lady said, marching into the room with a tray held before her. She put it on the table, then looked around at the piles of books on the floor and sighed.

"*Another* mess to clear up," she commented resignedly,

then indicated the tray. "I hope the food's to your liking." she said to her speechless guests. "Don't let that cat near it."

With that she turned and walked over to one of the bookshelves. She pulled a hidden lever, and a section of the wall, complete with shelves, opened like a door and she left, with the parting advice, "Eat well, my dears. My cooking's not for wasting."

"Wait!" Mallory called.

"Don't go," Gemma pleaded.

But the section closed again, and the library was complete once more. Mallory ran over and tried to find the lever.

"There's nothing here," she said, as Gemma came up beside her.

"This pie is excellent," Arden mumbled, his mouth full. "Try some."

They turned to look at him, and he grinned apologetically.

"I've had enough mysteries. At least the food is real."

It also proved to be quite delicious, much tastier than the meals in the silent city—even Gemma was persuaded to eat before continuing her research. Then she went in search of the clover room edition of *The Wars of Olcondoria*, crossing the hall on tiptoe, much to her own amusement and that of Arden and Mallory, who were watching from the doorway. The clover-leaf door opened easily, and she slipped inside. All the books had been put back on their shelves, but it only took her a short time to find what she was looking for.

Tucking it under her arm, she made her way back across the hall, but as she crossed the threshold, something affected her eyesight; everything blurred for an instant and she found herself walking back into the clover room. At the same time she heard Mallory screaming from the other side of the hall.

Stunned, she shook her head and went back into the hallway, still carrying the book. Mallory and Arden were pale with shock.

"Are you all right?" Arden asked, as he and Mallory hurried across to her.

"Yes. What happened?"

"You disappeared," Mallory answered. "Just like Wynut and Shanti. There was a slippery, popping sort of noise . . ."

"And then I was back in the clover room," Gemma said thoughtfully.

They stood together in the middle of the hall, looking back and forth between the two libraries.

"Let me try that again," Gemma said. "You stay here."

She walked up to the acorn doorway, hesitated, then stepped forward. Again there was that strange moment of disorientation, and she found herself walking back into the clover room once more. She turned quickly and saw the others twist round to find her new location, their eyes wide in astonishment. She rejoined them.

"Are you thinking what I'm thinking?" Arden asked.

Gemma nodded. "Hold this for me," she said, and gave him the book. Then she walked to the acorn door and stepped inside with no difficulty at all. She turned to face her friends.

"They don't like you misfiling their books, do they," Arden remarked.

chapter 41

They carried out a series of experiments, and established that no book from one library could be taken into the other. Arden and Mallory both tried it, at Gemma's insistence, and survived the experience shaken but unharmed.

"So we can only compare volumes here in the hall," Mallory concluded. "I wonder why."

It was dark again outside, but a gently breeze still blew through the large open doors, and very soon they were sitting side by side on the tiled floor, comparing the books.

Arden sat nearby, keeping a watch on the many doors about them, and on the stairs. He wasn't quite sure what he was watching *for,* but he felt better for doing it.

"This is the page," Gemma said. "Right. Seventy-six treaties."

"Sixty-four," Mallory replied.

". . . epidemic disease in both states."

". . . in the case of Sled . . . the entire province an unpopulated wasteland," Mallory completed.

"But all the rest is exactly the same?"

"Yes."

"The same title, the same author, most of the contents identical . . . but with certain details changed. It doesn't make any sense." Gemma was mystified.

They carried on leafing through the two volumes, discovering several other minor but significant discrepancies. Throughout, the style remained consistent, and there were very few major disagreements.

"I wonder if any of the other books are duplicated." Mallory said.

"Let's go and check."

As they stood up, Arden spoke for the first time in an hour.

"I hate to mention this," he said, "but we have company." He nodded toward the stairs.

Wynut stood at the top, peering at them through the banisters.

"Put those books back at once!" he ordered sternly. "You're

246

upsetting all my calculations, and I wouldn't like to be in your shoes if Shanti finds out." With that he turned and shuffled out of sight. Gemma and Mallory looked at each other, eyebrows raised.

"Better do as he says," Gemma decided, and they hurried off in opposite directions. Arden stayed where he was, looking up at the now vacant balcony.

"Calculations?" he muttered darkly. "What are they up to?"

His life had seemed fairly straightforward, until recently, but now he was surrounded by even more examples of the inexplicable— he still balked at calling it "magic"—than he could cope with. For a while he had had difficulty in recalling the central purpose behind his recent exploits; the valley had seemed a world away, and he did not enjoy being stuck in a situation he could not influence, let alone control. Three days had already been wasted, and he began to feel a measure of despair.

They slept that night in the acorn room, preferring to stay in familiar territory despite the hard floors. They had no wish to explore further, especially as the hallway and stairs were now cloaked in darkness.

Morning came, and with it another encounter with Wynut. Urgent need had driven them from the library, and just outside the room they were hailed by the large, matronly woman, who popped her head round the door.

"It's in there, dears," she said, smiling, and pointed to another small, unmarked door beneath the stairs. "Breakfast's on its way." She was gone before they had a chance to ask her anything; Arden tried to follow her but the door would not open, and by the time they returned to the acorn room, fruit and bread were already laid out on the table.

"Do you get the feeling they don't want to tell us very much?" Arden remarked.

There was a pause, then Mallory said, "And yet we have free access to the two libraries."

"Perhaps they don't consider these books to be of any importance," Gemma commented.

"Or they think we're harmless," Arden put in. "We're not even adepts after all," he added sarcastically. "Whatever *that* means."

After their meal Gemma and Mallory decided to carry on sampling the volumes about them, in the hope of learning something of relevance to their own world. The didn't want to risk the ire of their unwilling hosts by exploring further, but Arden insisted that he wanted to go outside.

"The air may not be country-fresh, but at least it's better than in here," he explained. "And I'd like to be able to see the sun."

"Don't go far," Gemma warned. "I don't know when we'll be leaving, but we should all be together when we do."

"I'll sit on the doorstep," he assured her, then left them to it. The women watched him go.

"If we don't get out of here soon, he'll go mad," Mallory said, "This delay is really hurting him."

"But what can we do?" Gemma replied helplessly.

An hour later, as she was leafing through another ancient tome, Gemma's eye was caught by two names in a footnote. The words were "Cleve" and "Jordan." Quickly, she read the note, her heart beating fast, then skimmed the chapter that preceded it. This described the overseas trade of a province called Quaid, and was a mass of boring detail. The footnote was anything but dull, however, and she read it aloud to Mallory.

" 'Note: In the seventeenth year of King Tul's reign, trade with Cleve was disrupted by internal strife within that remote province. However, by the year nineteen, the new regime, led by the former renegade Jordan, had established a stable government and contact was resumed.' "

"That's the man you met in Newport!" Mallory exclaimed but Gemma hardly heard her. *This book is incredibly old,* she thought, amazed, *yet the events it describes haven't happened yet!* She skimmed through the other chapters in the book, but could find no other reference to these events. A new idea was forming in her mind, and she handed the book to Mallory, who had been watching her closely, concern written clearly on her face.

"Read through this," Gemma said quickly. "And see if Jordan or Cleve are mentioned anywhere." She got up and ran to the door.

"Where are you going?"

"To the clover room." With that she was gone, leaving her friend none the wiser.

In her haste, Gemma did not notice the cat watching her as she rushed over to the other library and flung open the door.

It watched her impassively, then sauntered across the hall, following her into the clover room.

Gemma recognized the dark green binding of the history of Quaid almost immediately, and turned to the last page of the chapter on overseas trade. She groaned. There was no footnote in this version of the book. *It's as if nothing had happened,* she thought. *Did the underground succeed or not? Or rather: Are they going to succeed?*

"If these are alternative futures," she whispered, "which one is real?"

She was answered by a drawn-out meow which made her spin round in fright just in time to see the cat's tail disappear into the hallway. The sound echoed all about her, then coalesced, so that she heard the words with horrible clarity.

"They are *all* real," the cat informed her. "And then again, reality is a measure of perception. Choose your reality before it chooses you."

"What does *that* mean?" Gemma cried, but knew she would receive no answer.

From the hallway, she heard the murmur of voices. The whole house seemed to creak and moan, but she stood rooted to the spot.

"Gemma! Mallory!" Arden's shout was urgent, tinged with fear. "Come quickly!"

———— • ————

True to his word, Arden had not gone far. He had sat on the doorstep, watching the unchanging scene before him; only the creeping progress of the shadows provided any movement at all. After an hour or so he grew bored, climbed slowly to his feet, and went back into the relative gloom of the hallway. The draft that always seemed to blow through the door assisted his passage.

Wynut and Shanti, a large book open in his hands, stood at the rear of the hall, and looked up from beneath their hats at his approach. Shanti shouted angrily.

"Og yawa, M'i grynti ot krow!"

Wynut just looked puzzled and shrugged his shoulders.

"Haven't we gone yet?" he muttered. "There must be a thaumaturgical logjam. What's caused that?" He gazed curiously at Arden as if he would glean the answer from his face. Then sounds came from the clover room.

"M'i ont gastiyn rhee!" Shanti snapped and turned abruptly to go into another room, pushing Wynut in front of him. He slammed the door shut, but not before Arden had seen a little of the room beyond. This excited him so much that he did not notice the cat come out of the clover library and scamper away on its own mission.

"Gemma! Mallory! Come quickly!"

They were at his side in an instant, driven by the urgency in his tone.

"In there!" he said, pointing. "They've just gone in there, and I saw through the window at the far end. I saw the mountain! Blencathra!"

The women looked at the door, but said nothing.

"What are we waiting for?" he asked impatiently.

"They told us to stay away from them," Gemma replied.

"And they're not the sort of people to annoy," Mallory added.

"But that's *our* world out there!" Arden exclaimed. "The real world—of mountains and living cities—the place where your home is—where the valley is *dying*." He threw up his hands in exasperation. "Well, I'm going in," he stated with determination.

"Wait!" Gemma said quickly, putting a restraining hand on his arm. "We'll stay together. Let's go cautiously."

They walked quietly across the hall. When Gemma saw the device carved into the door, she had to stifle a gasp. It was the unbalanced scales, with the fish sign above the lower tray.

"Why didn't we see this before?" she whispered.

"Because we weren't looking," Arden replied.

She put her ear to the door, straining to hear the muffled conversation within.

"It's failed, then," Wynut said.

"Of course it's failed," Shanti retorted. "Any idiot could see that. The question is why? That spell should have been good for at least half a century." He sounded very annoyed, but when he next spoke his voice was sad. "And I can't even return to reestablish it now. What *have* we come to?"

"To a mess," Wynut said bluntly. "Both of them lost."

"It's such a waste," the other went on.

"What can you hear?" Arden whispered to Gemma.

"Shhh!"

There was no sound now from within the room.

"Perhaps they're not there any more," Gemma said softly.

"Then let's go!"

She carefully turned the handle, but both sides of the door swung open immediately, and they found themselves face to face with two irate residents.

"Who opened that door?" Shanti demanded, shock making him speak intelligibly. "It was sealed."

"I did," Gemma admitted, as boldly as she could.

"Hist si teggint ryve degrauson," Shanti said to his companion, who nodded.

"Maybe we underestimated them," Wynut mused.

"Teg dir fo meth."

"No, they have to stay here. *That's* what's been delaying us." Wynut was delighted by his discovery, but Shanti was not at all happy.

"Oto degrauson!" he snapped.

"Do we have any choice?" the small man replied.

"We need help!" Gemma blurted out. "We . . ."

"It is forbidden!" Shanti yelled and, grabbing Wynut, they both disappeared again.

"What was all that about?" Mallory asked as Arden ran to the window at the far end of the room. Gemma shrugged.

"It's gone!" Arden exclaimed disgustedly, then swore viciously. Outside were the plain, square boxes of the silent city; nothing else was visible.

The doors slammed shut behind them and when Mallory tried to open them again they would not budge.

"Wynut was right," she said wryly. "We have to stay here."

"Trapped." Arden was thoroughly miserable now.

"No more than we've been ever since we got here" Gemma replied calmly, and looked around the room. Shelves covered the two main walls, but this time there were few books on them. The upper shelves were completely bare. "Not much history here," she said to herself, wondering at the implications.

An imposing desk stood beneath the window, with writing implements and books scattered on its top. Gemma sat in its accompanying chair as Arden sank to the ground, curling up into a ball of dejection, and Mallory knelt beside him to try and console him. Mallory knelt beside him to try and console him. Gemma seemed unaware of them—she knew that there was a purpose to their apparent imprisonment in this room, and it was up to her to find it.

Examining the desk, she pulled open one of the drawers and took out a plain, leather-bound journal. This intrigued

her, and, opening it at random, she saw at once that it was
handwritten. The letters varied from precise, spiderlike symbols to illegible scrawls. There were even a few tiny pictures
and diagrams; the writing was divided into short passages,
divided by meaningless numerals. Most of it made no sense
at all.

It's a diary, Gemma realized. *Shanti's diary!*

She turned back to the beginning, intending to read as
much as she could, but the first words in the book almost
made her wish she had never found it.

> *I feel the city breaking free. If I am to be a wanderer,
> this is not the mode of travel I should choose, yet I will do
> what I can before darkness falls upon us all. It is little
> enough compared to the events that The Leveling set in
> motion, but though I cannot leave my friends without
> some effort, I fear that in the end nothing can save them.*

There followed several passages which made as much sense
as Shanti's speech, and some of which were made up of
symbols and signs that Gemma did not recognize. Then another section caught her eye, and as soon as she began to
read it, the letters seemed to glow with an inner life. She
found herself able to read fluently, and her spirits soared as
the import of the words struck home.

> *It is almost time now. I must decide. And yet perhaps
> there is a way. Hurry. Hurry!*

There followed a strange series of squiggles and arrows,
and then:

> *I have done it! My smallest friends are now the guard-
> ians of two clans they will never know. When the wind
> changes, on the shortest day, they will sing my praise to
> the stone. As it shifts, so will the other, and so the water's
> course. Both the Valley of Knowing and the Lightless
> Kingdom will receive their share every other year, and
> will thus survive. A heavy weight has been lifted from my
> heart, and I can leave with a little happiness in my song.*

Could it really be as simple as that? Gemma wondered.
His description of the biannual river was too exact to be

coincidence, and the "Valley of Knowing" could only be one place. The "Lightless Kingdom" was a mystery, but the "smallest friends" were surely the meyrkats. Shanti must be the god who had placed the rocking stone and left them to guard it, singing "when the wind changes" in order to act in some way as a trigger to control the source of the river. Gemma was sure it must be true—it all fitted so exactly.

So what's gone wrong? She recalled the conversation she had heard a little earlier. Shanti had said, "I can't even return to reestablish it now."

Well, maybe he can't, Gemma thought excitedly. *But I can!*

She was about to share her discovery with the others when her eye was caught by the first line of the next entry.

> *We are lost now. Farewell, my friends. I will not give up the hope that we will meet again one day, for what is the use of immortality if you are beyond all that you hold dear. I refuse to give up hope. Yet the darkness closes in—I will see it before all of you. Farewell.*

Gemma turned the page, tears running down her cheeks, but the next few sheets were blank. She felt quite differently about Shanti now. Looking up, she saw the others watching her, their faces clouded with worry. She got up and carried the book over to them.

Squatting down on the floor, she said, "I've found the answer to the river. Here, read this." She leaned forward, handing the diary to Arden.

He reached out to take it, then drew back quickly as the steam from the pan of boiling water scalded his fingers.

chapter 42

The water bubbled merrily over the campfire before their astonished eyes. They were back in their own world. The horses grazed placidly nearby, Lark still nuzzling Mischa's neck, and Apple looked up at them, munching a mouthful of grass. The sudden reappearance of their riders obviously caused them no concern.

Although it was dusk, Gemma was still able to see a bank of fog blowing away from them on the far side of the vale.

"There," she said, pointing. "The city's leaving."

They watched the mist recede into the darkness.

"Thank the gods!" Arden said. "Now we can carry on." He paused, and looked at Gemma with a sudden intensity in his eyes.

"What do you mean, you've found the answer?"

The book was gone, of course, along with every other part of Shanti's city, and Gemma tried desperately to recall the exact words she had read. At the time they had seemed straightforward enough, and their message obvious, but the conclusions they had led her to sounded farfetched now, even to her. Arden would think them ludicrous.

"That book I was reading," she began hesitantly, "was Shanti's diary." She explained what she had learned about the meyrkats and the rocking stone, using as many of the phrases as she could remember.

" 'When the wind changes, on the shortest day, they will sing my praise to the stone.' That fits exactly with what the meyrkats told me!" she said excitedly. " 'As it shifts, so will the other, and so the water's course.' But the spell has gone wrong somehow, and that's why the river has failed. All we have to do is go back to the stone and reestablish it," she ended triumphantly.

"All?" Arden exclaimed. He had been openly sceptical of Gemma's words at first, but her confidence and enthusiasm had nonetheless given him a little hope. Now he began to doubt again, as he was struck by the size of the task still

confronting them. After a few moments' reckoning his spirits
sank completely.

"What's the matter?" Gemma asked, on seeing his downcast expression.

"It's hopeless," he replied. "The shortest day is only three
days away—there's no way in the world we can get back
there in time."

"Three days? Is that all?" Gemma felt absolutely crushed.
To have come so far and found what she was certain was the
solution to their problem, only to have it dashed away by a
simple lack of time was the ultimate cruelty.

"With fresh horses and a good road it would still take us at
least ten days to get back to the valley," Arden went on.
"And it's at least another four days hard riding from there.
There's no point trying. Even if we hadn't wasted four days in
that accursed city . . ."

"But we didn't!" Mallory interrupted, and the other two
looked at her. "We weren't there for any time at all."

"Don't be ridiculous," Arden said disgustedly.

"It's true," she insisted. "Look about you—everything is
just as we left it when we were taken into the city. The
horses haven't wandered, or become fretful. If we'd been
gone all that time the fire would have burned out long ago
and the water would have boiled dry. And these herbs are
still fresh." She pinched some of the leaves between her
fingers. "Here, smell."

"Mallory's right," Gemma added, remembering the horses'
movements just before the city arrived. "Four days may have
passed in the city, but in our world it was only an instant."
New ideas stirred in her mind; ideas that both elated and
frightened her.

"All right!" Arden retorted angrily. "Have it your own way.
That still leaves us only seven days, and it's *still hopeless*."

"Maybe not," Gemma said quietly.

"And just how do you propose to get there in seven days?"
he asked sarcastically.

"I can fly," she replied in a matter-of-fact tone.

"Spare me!" Arden exclaimed. "Not more magic."

"No, not magic," she said calmly. "Craft." She paused,
remembering. "I've often flown in a kite big enough to hold
two people, and I'm sure we can build one for me alone."

"You're crazy," he stated flatly. "Absolutely, stark raving
mad."

"At least let me explain," she pleaded. "I know how to make them—Cai showed me how."

"I'm getting sick of the sound of that name," Arden said quietly, but Gemma ignored the interruption.

"With wood and cloth and rope, it's possible to build a structure that will glide and can be steered. We're so high up here that given the right start I could go on forever."

"The right start," Arden snorted. "I suppose . . . No!" His eyes widened in horror. "Oh, no."

"Those cliffs are massive," Gemma said, "and there'll be powerful updrafts there as well."

"You *are* crazy," Arden said.

"Have you got any better ideas?" she asked.

"Yes. We carry on to the source of the river. If we don't succeed, at least we won't get killed!" He almost shouted the last word, and in the uncomfortable silence which followed neither would look at the other. Mallory was also quiet, helplessly caught between the needs of her two friends.

"I've got to try," Gemma said at last. "Will you help me?"

Arden did not answer, but got up and walked away from the fire. Soon he was invisible in the dark.

"Are you really going to fly?" Mallory asked in a whisper.

"Of course," Gemma replied with grim humor. "How far I get before I stop flying is another matter."

"From the cliffs at Maiden Moor?"

"Yes, that's the obvious place. Besides, I'm sure the villagers at Keld will help—we'll need plenty of materials and willing hands. She glanced into the darkness that had swallowed Arden.

"You're braver than I am," Mallory said. "Just the thought of it makes me feel sick."

"I'll probably be paralyzed with fear myself," Gemma replied, shrugging. "But it's the only hope we've got."

"Why are you doing this?" Mallory asked softly.

"I've told you all that," she said wearily. "The valley is important. So are you, *all* of you." *I will do what I can before darkness falls upon us all. It is little enough compared to the events The Leveling set in motion.* "Besides, I feel responsible."

"Why?"

"I can't explain now." Shanti's words continued to haunt her. *I cannot leave my friends without some effort.*

They sat in silence, and eventually Arden returned. Gemma looked up at his face. In the firelight it was grim but calm, and when he spoke, in spite of his dismissive words, she knew that he was reconciled to her course of action.

"How far did you fly in this kite of yours then?" he asked. "Half a league?"

"No," she replied. "Half a thousand."

chapter 43

They arrived back at Keld the next afternoon. At first, the villagers were worried by their unexpectedly early return, but Gemma explained the reason, and confirmed that the time spent in the floating city had not passed here; as far as the inhabitants of Keld were concerned, the travelers had left only a day ago.

"So we've got six days," Gemma said.

"Five," Mallory corrected. "Even flying, it'll take you a day to get there."

"Will you help us?" Gemma asked Ehren, and he replied for the whole village.

"If it can be done, we will do it," he stated firmly. "We owe you far more."

All that evening and late into the night the three travelers discussed the construction of the kite with Ehren, Eda, and a man called Bullin. Gemma told them as much as she could recall from her earlier experiences and, with the help of diagrams scratched on wood or drawn on cloth, she explained her ideas. Ehren was bemused by the whole thing, but felt that, as head-man, he should be involved in the project. However, his wife quickly saw the way that the triangular sail would act like a bird's wings, and began considering the best material to use.

"It has to be light, but also strong and windproof," she said thoughtfully. "We've a little that would suit, but for something this size . . ." Then her face lit up. "Don't worry," she went on eagerly. "I've got just the thing. We can start work in the morning when the sizes are all set." She left them then, to carry out an investigation of her own and, later, to bring them food. In the meantime, the others worked on the design for the kite's frame and Gemma's harness. Bullin, who was the father of the little boy whose "demons" Gemma had exorcised, and who was reputed to be Keld's finest woodsmith, listened eagerly and was soon making suggestions of his own.

"Green wood will be best," he declared. "Something with

a bit of sap left in it. If it's too dry it could break under all the stresses you'll be putting on it."

"I'd prefer that not to happen," Gemma responded with a wry grin. The villager regarded her closely, as if measuring her true nature.

"You've got more guts than most," he said admiringly. "But why is it *you* that has to go?"

Gemma had never considered any alternative, and was almost surprised by the question. The reasons were obvious to her.

"I've flown a kite before. I'm quite light. And I'm the only one who can talk to the meyrkats . . ." She paused. "Besides, it's my idea. I'm *meant* to do it."

"Arguing with her is a waste of time," Arden put in. "I discovered that long ago. But on this occasion, she's right, though I hate to admit it. The risk she's taking terrifies me, but if anyone's going to try this, it has to be her." There was a lot he left unsaid, but Bullin was not aware of that.

"Fair enough," he said. "Back to the wood—I'll take a few of the lads up to Beckman's Copse first thing in the morning. We'll be able to cut plenty there. Now, about this harness . . ."

The conversation became increasingly technical then, with Arden and Mallory adding their own practical suggestions to the discussion. Finally, when weariness at last drove them to their beds, they all knew that there was much work to be done, and many problems to be solved, but they were also agreed that their purpose could be achieved.

———— • ————

"We have more visitors," Bullin told Ehren the following morning, pointing to the northeast. The head-man and Arden turned, and saw a group of about eight horsemen approaching, moving at a steady pace across Maiden Moor. They were all dressed in the familiar gray, and Arden's stomach began churning at the sight of them. He turned and ran to Ehren's hut where Gemma was busy with Eda. As he burst in, the two women looked up from the yellow cloth they were examining.

"Gray raiders!" Arden exclaimed breathlessly. "You've got to hide."

"But surely—" Gemma began, startled and uncertain.

"They'll only have to look at you!" he snapped, panic making him angry. "The color of your hair will be enough to condemn you."

She still did not move, and Arden's exasperation increased.

"Do as I say! *Please*, Eda, can you find her somewhere safe to hide?"

The woman nodded.

"Go and tell Ehren to get word around," she said. "I'll take care of her."

"Thank you." Arden turned on his heels then, and raced back to the head-man. Soon everyone in Keld knew that Gemma had ceased to exist. Mallory joined Arden and the village men as they watched the gray-clad warriors arrive. The soldiers each carried longbows on their backs and had swords hanging from their belts. The coarse gray material of their uniforms matched the leaden color of winter clouds, and the expressions in their eyes gave a further impression of cold. They came to a halt, and Ehren stepped forward.

"Welcome to our village," he said. "I am the head-man here. How can we assist you?"

The newcomers' leader regarded him disdainfully.

"We need no help," he replied. "Just information." His cool blue eyes surveyed the men with saws and axes. "Your village is certainly industrious," he commented.

"We are about to collect wood," Ehren replied.

"There's building to be done," Bullin explained.

"Would you care for something to eat?" the head-man asked, but the gray raider ignored his offer.

"Have you any travelers staying here?" he asked, glancing toward the guest house.

"Yes," Ehren replied. "So I'm afraid there won't be room for all of you—"

"You mistake me. We will not be staying, but I wish to talk to your visitors." His voice was suddenly eager.

"Then talk," Arden said, stepping forward with Mallory at his side. The horseman glanced at them appraisingly, and nodded to his men, who dismounted.

"I would like my men to take a look around," he told Ehren, his manner thawing a little.

"Go ahead, we have nothing to hide," the head-man replied. "Come to my house. We can talk there."

"Thank you." They headed toward Ehren's hut, and the other gray-clad raiders spread out and began their search of the village, each followed by curious locals.

Eda was sewing as they entered. She rose and made them

welcome, then bustled off to brew tea. The others sat down, the warrior leaning his bow against the wall.

"May we know your name?" Ehren asked.

"Starak, And yours?" He looked at the travelers.

"Arden."

"And Mallory."

"Where are you from?"

"I'm from Manesty," Arden replied, "though I haven't been back there for some time. My companion is from a valley to the north, two days' journey from the Diamond Desert."

"You are both far from home then. What brings you here?"

Mallory and Arden saw no reason to conceal their true purpose, and gave Starak a lengthy explanation of their search for the source of the river. He listened intently, showing no surprise and making no comment. He weighed the truth of their words.

"You do not have far to go, then," he said eventually. "The Cascade is only three days' ride away."

"The Cascade?" Arden queried.

"I've not seen it myself, mind," Starak replied. "We don't often come this far south. It's supposed to be quite spectacular."

Arden groaned inwardly at the thought of how close they had been to their goal, only to turn back on this crack-brained scheme of Gemma's. He wondered where she was.

"You do not intend to travel any further south than the Cascade?" Starak asked.

"No," Arden replied. "If what you tell me is correct, then there'll be no reason to. Besides, winter is coming on, and the high mountains will soon be too cold."

"A wise decision," the soldier commented. "Make sure you stick to it." The threat beneath his words was barely veiled. "I wish you luck with your project, though from what I've heard, the scale of the Cascade is such that it will take much to divert it."

As Eda handed round bowls of tea, Starak was called outside. After a brief conference with one of his men, he returned and accepted his drink.

"We will be riding on soon," he told them, "though we may return in a few days." Turning to Ehren, he added, "I would appreciate it if you could keep a note of any other travelers coming this way."

"Are you looking for anyone in particular?" the head-man asked.

"No. Merely those with an unnatural desire to travel south." Starak smiled, but there was no warmth in his expression. He glanced at Mallory and his next question almost caught her off-balance. "Why did you bring three horses?"

"We swap mounts to even their load." she answered, recovering quickly. "Traveling over such rough ground, there is always the chance that one of them might go lame. In these mountains it is better to be safe than sorry."

"I admire your foresight," Starak returned, then he stood up and took one last look around the hut. "That's remarkably fine material," he said to Eda, nodding toward the skein of yellow cloth which curtained off a small alcove at the back of the room.

"It was part of my dowry," she replied. "I'd hoped to pass it on to my daughters, but we've only had sons."

"May I touch it?"

Eda hesitated and Arden grew alarmed.

"Will you need to feed or water your horses before you go?" he asked Starak, trying to divert his attention.

"No. We are well supplied. May I?" He addressed Eda again.

"Of course," she replied, and Starak stepped forward. Arden tensed, prepared to fight if necessary, as the gray raider fingered the cloth appreciatively.

"Our gray is practical," he remarked, almost wistfully, "but sometimes I miss a little luxury."

Then he threw the curtain aside. The space behind was empty, and Arden felt his heart start beating again.

"We must go," Starak said. If he was disappointed his expression did not show it. He thanked them for their hospitality, then strode out, calling to his men. Soon they were all gone.

The villagers watched them ride south in silence, no one daring to speak until they were well out of earshot. Then Arden turned to Eda.

"Where is she?" he demanded.

"You were sitting on her," she replied, and laughed. She took him back to the hut and lifted the top of the settle on which he and Mallory had been sitting. Gemma was curled up inside. They told her that the gray raiders had gone, and she got out of the box, stretching her cramped limbs in relief.

"Wasn't that taking a risk?" Arden asked.

"Not really, I knew Ehren would bring them here," Eda replied confidently. "And what better place to allay suspicion?"

"Did you hear what was said?" Mallory asked Gemma, who shook her head. They explained what had happened.

"So we're closer than we thought," Arden said. "Do you still want to try this crazy idea?"

"Of course," Gemma said firmly, and Arden turned away, unable to hide his disappointment.

The villagers set a watch to spy out any further visitors, and the preparation for the kite's construction was resumed. The next four days passed in a flurry of activity, made even more pressing by their approaching deadline, and by the gray raiders' promise to return "in a few days." Wood was cut and shaped, joints carved and tested. They used a mixture of mature wood for strength and young for flexibility, and the design of the frame was constantly modified. Eda's bridal cloth was cut and sewn, and with the judicious addition of other lengths of material, the wing of the kite took form. The leather harness and straps which would hold its passenger secure were adapted from saddles and reins, and a rope device to enable Gemma to open and shut flaps in either side of the wing was built and tested. If all she remembered from Cai's designs was correct she would be able to control the kite's direction and, to some extent, its height.

The component parts were ready by the end of the fourth day, and all that remained was to put them together. If that could be achieved early the next morning, Gemma decided she would make the attempt then. She already knew which direction she must take, and had studied the land she must cross from the top of the cliffs. The view from there had been awe-inspiring, and she tried not to dwell upon the moment when she would have to throw herself out into that terrifying void. Instead, she concentrated on watching the birds who lived on the cliff, noting where the winds helped them to soar effortlessly. She decided that she would leave from a flat slab of rock which jutted out over the edge. The wind was funneled upward there and would give her the maximum help.

I'll need all the help I can get! she thought, wondering for the first time if she was really capable of carrying out such a dangerous task. *I wish Cai was here to help me.*

chapter 44

She told Arden of her decision that evening.

"I thought as much," he said. They were alone in the guest house, Mallory having sensed what was coming and found an excuse to be absent. Arden had been fretting ever since their return to Keld, partly because he still wanted to get to the river's source, but mostly because he had been dreading this moment. He had done as much as he could to help with the kite, reckoning that if Gemma insisted on her insane course of action, he must try to ensure that she had a chance of survival. Now that the time had arrived, he could not hide his doubts and fears.

"Is there no chance that you'll change your mind and come with me instead?"

"No." She looked at him sadly. "I *have* to do this. You know that."

"All because of an old book which may not really exist?"

"Of course it exists. The floating city may not be in our world but it *is* real. You were there." They had had this argument before. "And it was no accident that brought us there. I was *meant* to find that book. As soon as I had, the city was able to leave."

"Destiny, of course," he scoffed. "What an absolute load of nonsense."

"Not everyone believes that," Gemma replied. "Think of the way we met."

"I am."

They sat quietly for a few moments, facing each other across the space between their two beds.

"When you get there," Arden said eventually, "how do you know that you'll be able to reestablish the spell? You're not a wizard."

"Perhaps I am," she answered, smiling. "Strange things do seem to happen to me. It can't *all* be coincidence."

"That's true enough," he replied, his face still serious. "But this is different. Shanti's book didn't tell you what was involved, did it?"

"No. But the meyrkats will do that," Gemma said, hoping that she was right. "Their legends must hold the clues."

"You're risking your life on such flimsy evidence," Arden said, shaking his head in confusion.

"I'm risking it for the valley," she replied, adding silently, *And for you.* "Just as you would if the situation was reversed."

"You haven't even had a chance to test that contraption," Arden objected.

"You know there isn't time for that," she replied patiently. "Besides, what would happen if it flew perfectly but I smashed it up on landing? If that's going to happen, then I want it to be at the stone, where it won't matter. We won't have the time to make repairs."

"And that's another thing," he went on. "If you *do* get to the stone and succeed, what will you do then? You'll be alone in the middle of the desert, with no horse and no supplies."

Gemma burst out laughing, much to his surprise.

"I've got to fly many leagues over mountain and desert, and somehow renew a failed magic," she said. "*Then* I'll worry about being in the middle of nowhere."

"Don't joke about it!" he snapped, his face a crumpled mixture of anger and misery.

"Oh, Arden." She moved across and knelt in front of him. Taking his hands in her own, she looked up into his downcast face. "Don't worry so. The kite is as good as anyone can make it. The worst that can happen is that I'll mess up the navigation and end up too far from the stone to be able to get there in time."

"The worst?" he retorted incredulously. "The thought that the cloth might tear, or the frame fall apart in midair doesn't bother you?"

"They won't. I've got every faith in the people who helped make it. Including you."

Arden went on as if he hadn't heard. "Or a storm? Rain would make the kite too heavy. And you could get caught by strong winds and blown completely off course."

"There's no point worrying about what we can't control," she replied. "Arden, I'm not stupid. I've thought of *all* those things, and I've still got to try."

"I know," he conceded at last. "But I won't . . . I can't bear to stay and watch you." Gemma saw the pain locked away beneath his eyes. "I'm sorry," he said, begging silently for her forgiveness and understanding.

Gemma felt a lump in her throat, and could not speak. She had underestimated the depth of Arden's feelings for her, and now it was too late.

"I'll go at first light," he said quietly. "I want to try and reach the Cascade by the shortest day."

"What about Mallory?"

"She can wait here until I get back. Anyway, she wouldn't want to leave before you do."

It was a long time before either of them spoke again. Gemma rested her head upon his knee, his hands still clasped in hers.

"Will you come back to me?" he whispered at last.

"Do you want me to?" she asked, looking up.

"Gods, woman, what a stupid question!" he said. "I want it more than anything." He slid down from the bed so that they were both kneeling, took her in his arms and kissed her with a roughness that surprised her.

"Me too," she whispered when they parted.

"It can't end like this," he said. "After all we've been through, it would be too ridiculous."

She smiled and replied, "We're obviously destined to be together."

"That kind of destiny I won't argue with," he added, and kissed her again, more gently this time.

There was a knock at the door.

"Can I come in?" Mallory called.

"Yes," Gemma shouted back, remaining in Arden's embrace.

"I'm not interrupting anything, am I?" Mallory asked, looking at them from the doorway. "I can sleep at Eda's if—"

"Come in," Arden said. "Don't look so worried." He turned to Gemma.

"We need our strength for the journey tomorrow," they said in unison, then burst out laughing.

———————•———————

It was still dark when Arden left Keld the next morning. Gemma had slept surprisingly well, fortified by a nightcap of mead, and had been only vaguely aware of his movements until he bent over and kissed her softly on the cheek.

"Good luck," he whispered. "Remember our destiny."

"I will," she mumbled. "You too."

Gemma heard the door open and close. She found it hard

to believe that he had really gone. By the time she got up, Arden and Lark were already well on their way, and she soon had other things on her mind.

The morning proved to be an exercise in frustration. Everything seemed to go well for a time, only for a last-moment snag to disrupt the final construction. On several occasions she thought all was finally ready, but minor adjustments caused a series of problems and it was not until noon that the kite was at last assembled. The large triangular sail, mostly bright yellow but with strips of white and gray woven in, was supported by a crosshatched frame of supple wood which rested on the lower casing that held the harness and control ropes.

"You won't have many hours of daylight left once we've carried it to the cliff," Bullin pointed out. "Do you still want to go today?"

Gemma was torn. Flying at night would multiply the risks and uncertainties of navigation, but the next day was the shortest of the year, and unless she reached the stone before dusk, she would be too late.

"Let's get the kite out to the cliff," Mallory suggested. "Then you can decide."

They acted upon that advice, and the whole village followed in procession behind the kite-bearers. They made slow progress because nobody wanted to risk damaging the kite. Overhead, gray clouds were massing and more than one villager glanced up at them anxiously. The frame was protected by resins that had been carefully rubbed into the wood, but no one knew how the material of the sail would react to heavy rain.

By the time the kite reached the launch site, too much of the day had gone, and it was clear that Gemma's flight would have to be postponed until the following morning. The kite was turned over so that the sail rested on the ground, thus minimizing the risk of it blowing away. The villagers also took the precaution of tying it to pegs hammered into the ground. That left the problem of protecting it from rain. Short of dismantling the sail—a course of action nobody favored—there was little they could do. They covered it with as much protective material as could be found, and a temporary shelter was built around it. The construction was hardly waterproof, but it was the best they could manage.

Watches of two men at a time were arranged to guard the

kite throughout the night, and everyone else returned to the village. It began to rain during the evening; listening to it drum on the guest house roof, Mallory wondered aloud if it would stop by morning.

"I'm going at first light," Gemma replied. "Whatever the weather."

As it turned out, the next day dawned cold but clear. Gemma was up to see the shortest day of the year begin, as were all the inhabitants of Keld. Everybody trudged across the wet grass and bracken to the launch site, and the guards reported that although no rain had fallen for the previous three hours, some water had seeped through onto the sail. After the kite was carefully set upright, there were indeed several damp patches in evidence, but it would have taken much more than that to deflect Gemma from her purpose.

Her sleep had once again been aided by mead, and Mousel had brought another bottle along this morning.

"Here. Drink all," the wisewoman said. "For strength."

"I don't want to be drunk!" Gemma joked, but was happy to comply. "Dragonflowers?" she asked.

Mousel shrugged. "A little."

Gemma took a deep breath. "Well, here goes," she said, and began strapping herself into the harness. When she and her assistants were satisfied that she was quite secure, she tested the control ropes. They worked, so with the help of several people she carried the kite to the edge of the cliff. She could just lift it on her own, taking the weight on her shoulders, but walking any distance would have proved difficult.

Once in position, she waited, breathing deeply to try and steady her nerves and racing heartbeat, and trying not to look at the forest hundreds of paces below her. The wind tugged gently at the sail, but Mallory and Bullin held it steady at the rear corners.

Now or never, Gemma thought. *If I am to be a wanderer, this is not the mode of travel I should choose.* She laughed aloud at the memory of Shanti's words.

"Wish me luck!" she called.

"Good luck," Mallory replied, glad that Gemma could not see the tears in her eyes. "Come to the valley when you're done. We'll see you there." It took all her willpower to sound so positive.

"It's a date," Gemma said, then raised her voice so that the villagers could hear. "Thank you all. I hope I am worthy of your efforts."

There was a chorus of good wishes.

"We've no fear on that score," Bullin said. "Good luck, and farewell."

"Goodbye!" Gemma shouted, then stepped forward and plunged into the shuddering embrace of the windswept void.

———————•———————

Arden had ridden out of Keld with a mass of conflicting emotions roiling within him. Although he was undeniably glad to be on his way again, and getting ever closer to his goal, he felt the loss of his two companions keenly. He could not rid himself of his desperate fears about the risk Gemma was taking. He hated himself for being unable to stay and watch her flight, but knew that he could not alter her course or help her now. If he had to watch her die, it would break him in half; his love made him weak, and while he despised the weakness, he could not deny its hold on him.

He rode slowly that morning, frequently looking back to see whether there was any sign of movement from the village. Shortly after noon, he saw the kite being carried out and watched as it crawled across Maiden Moor like a monstrous yellow moth. After a while, he went on his way, unconsciously making for higher ground to the south of the mountain in order to get a better view.

Dusk found him on a hilltop due south of Blencathra. It was an unsuitable site for a camp and he knew it, but it had a view over all the southern end of the plain and so he stayed there anyway. It had long since been obvious that Gemma would not attempt her flight that day and Arden assumed, correctly, that she would try again the next morning. In spite of his terrible misgivings, he knew now that he could not go on until he had seen the attempt.

He slept little that night, listening to the rain on his tent and cursing it, half-hoping that it would prevent the kite from flying at all but knowing in his heart that she would go anyway. He rose at first light, cold and cramped, and looked out over Maiden Moor, the sun at his back. He could already see the people making their way from the village to the launching site, and before long he saw the kite being turned over.

He prayed then, to all the gods he'd ever heard of, imploring them to keep her safe. The kite seemed to stand still for an eternity, perched gracefully on the edge of the world. Arden's heart was thumping so hard that he could hear the blood pulsing through his veins. His gaze was transfixed by the distant yellow wings.

"Fly, you bastard," he muttered under his breath. "Fly!"

Suddenly, the kite was gone.

Arden held his breath. For a few agonizing moments he could see nothing more, and he felt sick as his worst fears rose up to claim him. But then, as suddenly as it had disappeared, the kite came back into view, soaring out beyond the cliff, high above the void.

"Fly, you bastard!" Arden yelled, punching the air in jubilation and relief, unaware of the tears streaming down his face.

"Make sure you come back, you crazy bitch!" he roared into the empty space that was Gemma. "I love you!"

chapter 45

Gemma had remembered the gut-wrenching sensation of the first moments of flight, but had never before been so absolutely terrified. The drop from the city walls from whence she and Cai had first taken to the air had been formidable, but that was nothing compared to the depths which faced her now.

The kite felt impossibly heavy, and it seemed ridiculous that they had ever expected it to fly. For a sickening instant, she thought that it would not, and her heart was in her mouth as she plummeted like a stone. She shut her eyes and swore repeatedly to herself. Then, as the kite picked up speed, she felt the wings start to bring their own power into force, and the nose lifted. She opened her eyes, and was filled with an enormous surge of elation as the kite came under her control, leaping up into the sky on the updraft from the cliffs. Far away, beyond the roaring of the wind, she heard the sound of cheering from Mallory and the villagers, and felt linked to them by a bond of gratitude; it made her all the more determined to succeed.

For some time she played the air currents, gaining height and getting the feel of the control ropes. She was delighted with the way the kite responded, and despite the biting cold and thin air she felt absolutely wonderful.

Arden, she thought, willing him to hear. *I'm all right!* Then she grinned. *If only Cai could see me now.*

But I can, her absent friend and mentor replied. *And you're scaring the living daylights out of me.*

Gemma laughed aloud for joy and for the unexpected companionship, adrenaline and mead singing in her veins.

You're not in any danger, she retorted. *Help me fly this thing!*

You're doing just fine, he responded. *But don't go much higher. You might not be able to breathe.*

Gemma looked down. Apart from the dizzying drop to the forest, she could see almost all of Maiden Moor spread out below her, and could just make out the village and the people at the edge of the cliff. *I've gained more height that I thought. Time to turn north.*

Don't forget you also need to go a little to the west, Cai responded.

How do you know that? Gemma asked, but did not hear his answer; at that moment the siren song began again in all its terrifying beauty, and she found herself torn in two. She circled once more, uncertain and confused. The South was calling her again, and now, with the kite, she had the means to travel far in that direction. The temptation was staggering, but all her instincts implored her to turn north, and fulfill the purpose for which she and Arden had labored for so long.

Cai's voice—or was it Arden's?—sounded in her head once more. *If you follow that sound, you'll die.*

Gritting her teeth, Gemma turned the kite onto a northward course and began her long journey, her mind reeling in agony at the refusal of the seductive invitation.

Help me! she appealed to Cai, and was rewarded by a sense of approval and fellowship. He did not—indeed, he *could* not—steer the kite for her, but his incorporeal presence kept the conflict in her mind from driving her insane. She was suddenly filled with the loneliness of her aerial voyage, hating the numbing cold which had long since made her warm clothes seem paper-thin. The kite soared on, weaving between the highest peaks that marked her route, but always going north—and a little to the west.

The siren song ended abruptly shortly before noon, and the relief almost made Gemma faint. She breathed a huge sigh of thanks, and studied the terrain below her with renewed vigor. None of it looked familiar, but she could see far to the north where the mountains were smaller, and she even fancied she could see the beginnings of the coastal plain. The increasingly barren nature of the land below was visible evidence that the desert beckoned and she began to wonder for the first time about the task ahead should she manage to reach the rocking stone. Until now, all her energies had been directed solely toward getting there; now her confidence was growing and had reached such a pitch that she knew herself ready for the next stage.

Will I get there in time? she wondered. *Does the spell-song have to be sung before dusk, sunset, or midnight?*

Sunset, Cai replied unexpectedly.

How do you know?

I'm a wizard, he said, and his bitter, ironic laughter sounded in her head.

What must I do? Gemma asked quickly, too eager to notice Cai's sudden change of mood. Increasingly manic laughter was the only answer, and a new fear clutched at Gemma's heart. *Cai!* she cried. *What's the matter?*

For several heartbeats there was no reply, and when he eventually spoke it was so quietly that she could hardly hear his weary words.

Why can't you leave me in peace?

Feeling dreadful now, she pleaded with his remote presence. *Don't leave me, Cai. I need your help.*

No, you're beyond that now, he told her dejectedly. *I've tried, but my power is giving out. You're more than a match for me, Gemma—you'll succeed on your own.*

Hearing the hurt and self-reproach in his voice, Gemma wanted to reach out and comfort him, but found herself doubly helpless. She could not even speak.

Make them all proud of you, Cai went on. *As I am. I always loved you, Gemma. Don't remember me too badly.*

He was gone, and Gemma rode the skies alone. She cried frozen tears for his loss, and also for another reason. *How could he believe that I think badly of him?* It was almost too much for her to bear.

Then, as if it too were reacting to Cai's departure, the kite lurched and dipped in sudden turbulence. Gemma forced herself to concentrate and tried to smooth her passage, remembering not to fight the wind's changes but to use them as best she could—direct opposition to the forces of nature could rip her fragile craft apart. Although she lost height, she kept up her forward progress so that all her efforts were now spent upon steering and seeking out ways to gain height.

By the middle of the afternoon she was nearly exhausted, her whole body numb, and her mind operating without conscious thought. Below her, the mountains had been replaced by the rolling foothills, parched and brown, that she knew preceded the desert. Gemma could see it in the distance, stretching out before her, apparently limitless, and despaired of ever being able to locate the stone at its center.

How long have I got? she wondered, but the question held little real meaning. Judging by the position of her shadow on the ground below, the sun was still high enough to mean at least two hours before sunset. But that also seemed irrelevant now.

The landscape soon became the all-too familiar mixture of sand, rock, and thornbush, and she scanned the scene ahead, searching for her marker stone. But the desert remained flat and featureless, mocking her with its immensity.

Further to the west.

The instruction came into her mind unbidden.

Cai? she thought automatically, but instantly realized that it was Arden's voice that she had heard. *Arden, can you hear me?* she asked, filled with wonder. Although there was no reply, no sense of companionship as there had been earlier with Cai, yet the words *had* been real, and she acted upon them, turning the kite gradually by adjusting the flaps. Her numbed fingers moved clumsily, and the sail shuddered as one of the ropes slipped. There was a horrible tearing noise from above, and the whole feel of the kite changed. Gemma could not turn around far enough to see how bad the damage was, but had to use the last vestiges of her remaining energy in fighting to keep a straight course. Left to itself the kite would now keep turning to the right; it was also losing height.

Movement in the distance caught her eye, and peering ahead, she saw a giant swirl of brown whirling across the desert. She watched, mesmerized, as the sandstorm drew ever closer, and became more frightening with each moment. She knew that her damaged craft would never survive its passage, and also knew that there was no way for her to avoid it.

The edge of the maelstrom caught the sail and the kite bucked, sliding sideways. Gemma gave up any pretense of control and abandoned herself to her fate. The tearing sounds above her multiplied as the sail was slowly ripped to shreds, and she closed her eyes against the sand as the world about her became a terrifying roar of darkness.

Gemma never knew how long she remained airborne within the storm; it seemed like a lifetime to her, and yet could have lasted only moments. Her eventual crash landing was surprisingly gentle, cushioned as it was by several thornbushes. She lay still for some time, unable to believe that she was back on solid ground once more, her arms and legs frozen in position. The smashed wreckage of the kite lay all about her. Feeling returned, gradually and painfully, to her limbs, and with it the sting of several cuts and grazes made by the ground and the cruel thorns.

It remained dark, the clouds of sand whirling in dizzying surges over her head.

When the wind changes, she thought, and wept with frustration as she struggled to release herself from the harness. Having done so, she lay face down in the sand, protecting her battered face as best she could.

As the last hour of the shortest day slipped away, the sandstorm gradually abated. Then, through her misery, Gemma heard another noise. At first, she thought her ears were playing tricks upon her, but in one relatively quiet lull, the new sound was unmistakable.

Meyrkats singing.

chapter 46

As Gemma was flying north, Arden rode first east, then south. He had watched the kite spiral up into the sky, but when it finally swooped away, dwindling rapidly from his sight, he set out immediately. He urged Lark to a fast pace when the ground permitted, and it was thus still early morning when he reached the spot where their camp had been swallowed by Shanti's floating city. He rode on, keeping a lookout for moving banks of fog, and staying well clear of the broken rock where the river went underground.

For the next two leagues, the riverbed was easy to follow. In happier times, great quantities of water had evidently raced down this steep vale, scouring out a deep channel of bare rock, but now it was completely dry. Not even a trickle flowed over the dusty bed.

On either side of the valley, the twin peaks that Mallory had noted earlier grew ever more imposing, the black rock near their summits glistening with ice-crystals. Beyond them to the south, even greater mountains came into view as Lark toiled on.

At a point midway between the two mountains, all signs of the river vanished, and within a few paces the channel changed from a boulder-strewn ravine to nothing. The floor of the pass became relatively smooth, made up as it now was of great slabs of rock and areas of soil, with rough grass growing through in places.

Arden groaned in dismay and got off his horse. This was the last place he had expected to lose the river's trail. There was absolutely no reason why it should emerge from the ground here. He clambered down into the channel to investigate, and grew even more puzzled. The riverbed just stopped. There were no bubbling springs, no caves or cracks where water could have emerged—only a blank, seemingly impenetrable wall of rock.

He climbed back up to his patiently waiting horse, and rode on slowly, constantly studying the ground underfoot. It was obvious that no river had ever flowed over this terrain, and it made no sense. Arden knew that rivers do not spring into being from nowhere, but all the evidence implied that this one did just that. There were no springs, no tributaries, nothing.

Arden was deep in thought, and so did not hear the sound that made Lark whinny softly. He had been so intent on studying the ground that he had not looked ahead for some time, and now, as his mount brought his attention back to their route, he gasped at the unexpected beauty of the scene before him.

Beyond the twin peaks the land rose again, but what immediately caught his attention was the perfect miniature rainbow which hung suspended over the pass. It looked as though it was a spectral bridge between the two mountains, lying in the mist of the ever-changing swirl of mist and spray that filled the air at the far end of the vale. At the same time, Arden became aware of a roaring sound, distant still, but filled with awesome power. He urged Lark forward, completely unaware of the horse's nervousness, the mystery of the river forgotten in the radiance of this new wonder.

As he got closer, Arden was able to catch a glimpse of what lay beyond the rainbow mist, and the sheer size of the waterfall took his breath away.

"The Cascade," he whispered. He felt utterly insignificant in its presence, and rode on as though in a trance.

The roaring grew louder, filling his mind and drowning out all other sounds. Lark became even more fretful and Arden, noticing now, dismounted. Leaving the horse to retreat a little, he went on alone. The flat slope of rock over which he walked ended abruptly in a sheer drop, and he stood on the edge, looking down into the boiling cauldron of white water which churned thirty paces below him. The rock bowl was filled with spray and mist from the cataract on the far side. This plunged fully a hundred paces down the black shining cliff that formed its upper side; the raging torrent mesmerized Arden, and he paid no attention to the droplets of water which now festooned his clothes and hair.

He walked on along the rim, treading carefully on the damp surface of the rock. As he did so, the view to his left opened up, and looking back, he saw how the water left the cauldron. It surged, a continuous mass of white, into a giant, vertical-sided crevasse to the far side of the mountain. Then

Arden blinked and stared—a hundred paces or so along this crevasse, something strange happened to the water.

At first he thought his eyes were deceiving him, but then, after several more glimpses, he became sure of what he was seeing. The river's course was blocked by a wall which traversed the ravine. The wall appeared to be made of metal, its sharp straight outline obviously artificial. Flickers of blue light shimmered over its surface, and Arden shivered with fear. Beyond the dam, the crevasse was empty—dark, bare rock.

Where does the water go? he wondered. *What is that thing?*

Then over the constant roar of the water he sensed rather than heard another sound, and his feeling of dread intensified. Far beneath his feet there was a dull, repetitive reverberation, as if the very foundations of the earth itself were under siege.

———— • ————

Amid the storm, the meyrkats sang, raising their high-pitched voices in a complicated, dissonant web of sound. Each animal knew its part, but there was an odd note of uncertainty about their singing, as though they were beginning to doubt their own ability. Some voices remained strong, daring the others to falter, but too many were growing weak or tremulous.

Gemma heard them more clearly now and realized that the sandstorm was blowing itself out. Though it was still dark, she was able to open her eyes without being blinded by flying grit. Raising herself up on her knees, she tried to pinpoint where the song was coming from. Her bruised and battered body protested at the movement, but she was now recovering some measure of her purpose, and forced herself to ignore the pain.

She moved slowly, crawling across the sand on all fours. *Has the sun set yet?* she wondered, shielding her eyes with her hands and looking around as best she could. She had no idea which direction was west, and the sky was still hidden by flying sand.

The meyrkat song grew louder. As Gemma gritted her teeth, forcing herself to move faster, she became aware of mind-talk as well as singing.

It is failing again. Ir.

The god does not hear us. Ül.

We must keep trying! Remember our promise. Od.

We sing. Ox.

Od's urging had the desired effect, and, though some still trembled, the voices of the clan were raised with renewed vigor.

A moment later, the last of the airborne sand departed, and Gemma saw the stone. It was no more than a hundred paces away—fate or luck had brought her closer to her target than she could ever have dared hope. Blinking in the sunlight, she got wearily to her feet.

Sunlight! Gemma's numbed mind struggled with the implication of this. Though the sun was low over the western horizon, it still shone. *There was time!*

A surge of mental confusion washed over her, at the same moment as the meyrkat's song faltered and died.

Gem-ma. You have returned! Ul.

The animals were standing in a circle about the stone, and they all turned to look at her, dozens of shiny black eyes, all with one focus. Then in an instant they were calling out their greetings, bounding toward her on all fours.

Gemma summoned up her last reserves of strength and, as they gathered round her, she asked for quiet and told them why she had come.

"Your singing is very important. You must start again. But first there are some things I must ask you. Gemma. She paused, marshaling her scattered thoughts, while the meyrkats waited in respectful silence. *I have come to help the god to hear you again,* she went on. *You must teach me the song. But quickly, for the sun is almost gone. Gemma.*

As she had expected, Od replied for the clan. He was apparently their expert on matters relating to the stone.

The song is simple. It is a claw-cycle. We each repeat the god-words in turn. Od.

Five times? Gemma asked, holding up one hand, her fingers spread out in lieu of claws.

Yes. The god-words are thus. Od. The song erupted inside Gemma's head, several "voices" blending and coalescing. She would never know how she managed to discern the individual words, but after a few moments they became clear to her.

Ask my brother to move,
For the year is past.

I will add my voice to yours, Gemma, she said, glancing up at the sun whose lower rim now touched the horizon. Privately, she wondered about the meaning of the words. What was it Shanti's diary had said? *As it shifts so will the other*. She pondered the oddly similar words. *My brother. The other*. And gained a little hope.

When the god gave the stone to you, what did he do? Gemma, she asked hurriedly.

He went within the stone. Ox.

Gemma looked at the silent monolith. *How did he lock the secrets within you?* she wondered to herself.

Join our circle. Od.

She walked forward, moving painfully and feeling suddenly helpless. *What am I supposed to do?* The meyrkats capered about her, making concerned peeping noises when they saw her cuts. The effects of the mead had long since worn off, and in spite of the animals' company, Gemma felt very lonely. Cai had abandoned her, Arden was leagues away, and neither Mallory nor Mousel was there to help her through this ordeal. She was on her own.

The meryrkats were standing in a circle facing the stone, each on their hind legs, and Gemma joined them. As soon as the song began again, she felt out of place. Her voice refused to form the enigmatic syllables, but it seemed that the clan had been given new hope by her arrival, and they sang louder than ever, a never-ending round of overlapping, recurring phrases.

Without her prior knowledge, Gemma would never have recognized the words. The animals' vocal capabilities limited their pronunciation, producing strange accents and stresses. No human voice could be anything other than a disruption of the pattern. *My place is within the song.*

Acting on instinct, Gemma stepped forward and walked slowly toward the stone. Without faltering in their song, the meyrkats shuffled round behind her to mend the broken circle, and the flow of sound became part of Gemma as she moved.

He went within the stone.

Black clouds were looming inside her mind. At first she thought they were the effects of exhaustion, but soon realized that they were in fact the hidden places of knowledge that she could only seek out in times of utmost need. So she welcomed the swirling darkness, finding the flashes of gold and silver light within.

Unthinking, she stretched out a hand to touch the surface

of the monolith. She had no intention of trying to push it over
but she could feel the meyrkats' nervous reaction, and swiftly
reassured them. As her fingers and palm came to rest on the
hard, cold surface, Gemma was unafraid. Tendrils of awareness grew from her fingertips, reaching out into the rock as
she had been able to reach inside the bodies of the sick
children.

He went within the stone.

Gemma's awareness of the world around her faded. She
was alone within a totally alien world—a world of hard permanence and crystalline obstinacy, a world of ancient growth
and unimaginably slow movement—a world of stone. At first,
she thought it was cold and lifeless but as her consciousness
spread even further, beyond the confines of her warm, fragile
body, she found that it was not so. Within the rock, *something* stirred.

She fought toward understanding, and although she fell
woefully short, her efforts produced their own reward. Her
experience could not be described by human words, but
here, at the very heart of the monolith, she found the embod-
iment of time and magic—the mirror which reflected all
forms of life—the dreams of stone.

Denial was beyond her now; she could not withdraw. The
dream enveloped her and pulled her to its core. A fire
burned within, scorching out letters that burned into her
mind. She sensed Shanti's presence, and another's; and shied
away from the opposing powers of each, but in the end she
could not ignore the message which formed the very essence
of the dream.

My brother shall not move,
For the year is never past.

She screamed, appalled by the overwhelming sense of
sickness, far more vile than any human ill. The secret of the
monolith had been corrupted, so simply that it was almost too
obvious, yet its whole existence was now an evil sham, mocking its creator.

It's wrong! Gemma screamed again.

Demons have them, she heard Mousel say. *You must save
them.*

No! she protested, feeling incapable of the task ahead. *It's
not the same.*

Why else do you think I'm teaching you? Cai asked.

I can't.

Then she was answered by her own voice.

Magic still exists. And I know where to find it!

The meyrkats' song was still running through her being, and she grasped it as the stable base on which to build her challenge. Slowly she used its unrelenting power to feed the dream, adding her own voice now, manipulating power from the remote, unknown sections of her mind. The cold sickness began to disintegrate and she pressed the advantage, feeling the genuine dream reassert itself, growing in health and strength until her feeble aid was no longer needed. The healing process was unstoppable now.

Ask my brother to move,

For the year is past.

The extra words had gone, and with them, the evil intent. Gemma took her hand from the rock's surface, and immediately stumbled and fell to the ground. Her legs had given way completely, and she sat on the sand, looking up at the monolith in a daze. The song went on all about her, vigorous and tinged with joy now, for the meyrkats had seen what she had not. The rocking stone was beginning to move.

The last rays of the setting sun turned the upper part of the stone to a red-gold beacon as it tipped gently to its alternative position. There was a gentle click, and then the familiar subterranean rumbling.

Gemma tensed, half expecting the blue flames and the angry movement back. She did not know how long she sat there watching the stone, but nothing happened, and she gradually became aware of the silence. The song was over, its purpose fulfilled. The meyrkats gathered timidly around her, their small bright eyes staring intently at their savior as the sun faded at the end of the shortest day of the year.

chapter 47

Arden stared at the flying water of the Cascade, hypnotized by the the constant motion, and by the riddle of the water's disappearance. When he finally came to his senses the rainbow was long gone and his clothes were soaking wet. Shivering, he glanced to his left where—beyond the western mountain—the sun was setting. He had found the river's source, but was no closer to solving the valley's problem, and was now faced with another mystery.

He looked again at the ravine and the dam—now almost invisible in the fading light—then back down at the vale he had just climbed. Lark stood patiently in the distance and Arden was about to return to his horse and set up camp for the night when a new burst of light caught his eye. The intensity and frequency of the blue flashes on the dam had increased dramatically, and Arden stared at them, wondering what this presaged. The metal seemed to burn, flame and sparks lighting up the darkness in an impressive display that reminded him of his confrontation with the monolith. He wondered how Gemma had fared in her reckless flight. *Where are you now?* he asked her across countless leagues. But he had no time for further speculation—the sight before him claimed his full attention.

As the blue fire reached a crescendo, the top of the dam bowed upward, bending into an impossible arch which shuddered under an unimaginable force. Then, with a crack that sounded as though the sky were being split apart, the dam exploded, and huge chunks of metal were thrown into the air in all directions. Some crashed against the nearby rock, others disappeared into the all-engulfing white water, and a few went straight up, turning lazy cartwheels in the air before plunging back to earth. A few smaller pieces fell near Arden, but he sought no shelter, and stayed rooted to the spot.

The river reclaimed the crevasse, surging down in a wild celebration of its new freedom, carrying away the last remnants of the metal that had once hemmed it in so cruelly. Far below the surface of the earth, the insistent, mechanical throbbing faltered, then stopped, only to be replaced by another, even more ominous noise. The rock beneath Arden's feet started to shake, and he had the presence of mind to move quickly away from the edge of the cliff.

The vibrations grew more violent and he had to struggle to keep his feet. And yet when the impossible happened, he was left in no doubt.

The mountain in front of him was moving.

The entire eastern peak was slowly, inexorably tipping over, and as it did so, the ravine through which the river now surged was narrowed so that the water roared through under even greater pressure. At the same time, another channel was opening, an ever-widening crack on the other side of the mountain. This ravine was soon as wide as the other, and the water coursed down both, the cleft of rock that was the mountain's base acting like the bow of a ship, cutting the flow in half. With a thunderous grinding, the mountain carried on moving, until it finally came to rest with a resounding crash that shook the earth for leagues around.

The original ravine was gone, and the river now flowed to the west of the mountain, between the two peaks. The ground still shook but Arden's worries about his personal safety in no way affected the overwhelming emotion of joy that filled him now. His dazed mind grasped the essential truth of what he had just witnessed. The river was flowing down the vale through which he had just ridden, the vale that contained the riverbed. The water was even now on its way to the valley; he had been present at an event that was beyond imagination, beyond his wildest hopes. He could only look on in wonder, triumphant happiness filling his heart.

A rocking stone the size of a mountain.

It defied belief, yet such it was. And Arden also knew what—and who—had triggered its movement.

"Gemma!" he yelled to the open sky. "You did it!"

———•———

When Gemma awoke, she looked up into a sky full of stars; they provided the only light and she judged the time to be close to midnight. She still lay near the imposing black bulk of the monolith, but it held no more terrors for her. She shifted position slightly to try and ease her aching limbs, and realized that she was covered with several layers of fine

material. Her mind was surprisingly alert; even her wounds
felt less painful.

Propping herself up on her elbows, she looked around, and
a voice immediately sounded in her head.

*We have given you bush-skins, but we can find you more if
you wish. Av.* The female meyrkat's tone was gentle and
solicitous. Gemma saw her as she moved, a darker shadow in
the dark night.

I am warm enough, she replied, *but something underneath
me would be welcome. Gemma.*

Av backed closer, dragging another skein of cloth behind
her, and two other meyrkats did likewise. Gemma was soon
able to soften her bed.

We brought them from the rootless-bush. Eda.

Gemma decided against trying to explain to them that the
"rootless-bush" was in fact a kite, and once more thanked
Eda silently for the gift of her dowry.

*We have licked your cuts to stop the blood and clean them.
Av.* She sounded timid, and for a moment Gemma wondered
about the possible effects of this treatment, but her wounds
did seem much improved, so she decided to trust the animals' instincts.

Thank you. I feel much better now. Gemma.

The meyrkats made contented sounds at this, and then the
last of the trio spoke.

*We wish you could come inside our burrow to rest, Gem-ma,
but you are a too-tall-one. Ox.*

Gemma took the invitation as the compliment it was meant
to be, and was honored. She told them this, and the clan-
leader nodded in an almost human gesture of acknowledge-
ment, giving a quiet peep of pleasure.

Are you hungry? Ed.

Although she had been fortified by nothing more than
mead in the last day, Gemma found that she did not want
anything to eat.

*Soon it will be green-time. Then you will have plenty of
food. Ox.*

Gemma felt too weary to ask what he meant, and lay down
again. Closing her eyes, she let an unexpected feeling of
well-being and comfort lull her back to sleep.

*We will speak again when the sun rises, but I must rest
now. Gemma.*

We will keep watch. Av.

Rest well, clan-friend. Ox.

———— • ————

When Arden realized he was trapped, he refused to be disheartened—he had not come this far just to lose faith at the last moment.

The mountain had not been the only part of the earth to move; another channel had been opened through the rock near to the Cascade, and Arden now stood upon a small island of stone, entirely surrounded by foaming white water.

He spent the night huddled on his lonely perch. Although he was cold and wet, he was fired from within by his joy for the valley, and by an unquenchable optimism. Now that the river had been won back, it seemed inconceivable that he would not be able to return to see his friends. While waiting for the sun's return, he planned his bid for freedom.

When daylight came, he picked his spot, then dived into the foam with an almost reckless abandon. The thunder of the waterfall, which had been an unchanging part of his world throughout the night, was instantly silenced, and a different sound now filled his ears. He fought his way to the surface, clawing through the churning water, and gulped down a lungful of air. Then he was swept along once more, unable to control his movements. He fought for his life, perilously close to deadly boulders, unable to see where he was. Just for a moment he found himself in calmer water, and was able to catch his breath. In the instant before he was dragged onward, he saw a cave, just above the waterline, and a little way downstream. Making a desperate bid to reach it, he managed to grab the rim of the dark cavern and hold on. His limbs and side took a fearful pounding as slowly, painfully, he dragged himself over the threshold. He lay there, gasping for breath.

Just as he was about to stand up and explore his new surroundings, a large surge of water caught him side on, and he started to slide inward. The floor of the cave was remarkably smooth and sloped downward at an increasing angle; before he knew what was happening, Arden was slipping ever deeper into the cavern. His frantic attempts to grab hold of something met only smooth surfaces, and the cave entrance grew smaller and smaller. Then the light disappeared altogether and he fell into the darkness of the earth.

The last thing he saw was a vision of his love, terrified, calling his name.

———— • ————

When Gemma awoke at dawn, she felt refreshed but very thirsty. A different set of meyrkats were there to greet her.

We have brought you food. Ir.

A dead snake lay on the ground between them, and Gemma regarded it doubtfully. She had no means of making a fire, and would have to be a lot hungrier than she was at present to be able to bring herself to eat raw snakemeat. The meyrkats sensed her disquiet.

Curve-food not good? Ul.

I need water. Gemma. The meyrkats did not appear to understand this, so she asked them to dig up one of the thornbush roots. As soon as they understood her, this was accomplished with alacrity, and they watched with great interest as Gemma chewed at the vile-tasting fibrous bulb in order to extract some water. It was not much, but it allayed her thirst a little.

She stood up then, and stretched. As she did so, her right hand brushed against the monolith, and she felt an odd tingling sensation. Puzzled, she placed both palms on the stone. Then her blood ran cold as she saw Arden's face as though within the rock, encased in black, and falling into darkness.

"Arden!" she cried in horror. "Arden!"

My brother has taken him.

The message came to her by unknown means, from a far-distant source that was not even vaguely human—and yet she heard it as clearly as she heard the meyrkats. And she accepted it. She took her hands from the stone, knowing that she would receive no further enlightenment.

"My brother has taken him." What could that mean?

Several possibilities occurred to her, all of them unpleasant, and she rejected them, unable to believe the worst. "We are destined to be together," she had told him.

"And that's still true!" she told the rocking stone firmly, trying to keep the tears from her voice.

Turning round, she saw the meyrkats. They had been waiting in polite silence, but were obviously agitated by her distress.

Will you help me? Gemma.

Of course. Od.

Gemma smiled and looked up into the sky. Clouds had built up to the west, and were moving toward them.

It's going to rain, she thought. *The green-time.*

In her mind, pictures formed of the desert bursting into short-lived bloom, and suddenly her situation seemed less hopeless.

She knew that somehow she would make it back to the valley. If Arden was still alive—and she was sure that he was—he would get there too. Sooner or later.

I have more wandering to do. Gemma.

Some of us will come with you. Ul.

As Gemma leaned over, making a gesture of thanks toward the meyrkat, she felt the first drops of rain fall on her outstretched hand.

chapter 48

Kragen recognized Mallory as she rode down the path to the valley, and thought his heart would burst with happiness. Even the realization that her companions were not those he had hoped to see did not dampen his spirits. He spurred his horse on, and galloped to meet his wife.

The river had returned to the valley nineteen days ago. This had been the cause of much celebration, but Kragen's thoughts were still in the mountains, and for the last few days it had become his habit to ride up the trail from the valley in the hope of meeting the returning travelers. On a couple of occasions he had gone even further, camping out for a night, but this had only made him feel ill. He fretted against the injustice of his frailty, wishing he could have gone deeper into the hills in search of his love. Sober reflection and wise counsel prevented him from doing so, but nothing could stop his daily forays to the south.

And now his persistence was rewarded. Waving and calling his wife's name, he sped toward the slowly moving group. Bringing his mount to a halt, he jumped from his saddle and went quickly to help Mallory dismount from Apple. Though she was smiling, her face was pale and gaunt, and as he lifted her down, Kragen was frightened by how light she had become. She seemed so fragile that he was almost afraid to embrace her, but she returned his hug with all the fierceness of old and Kragen knew that she was going to be all right.

They stared at each other, tears of relief brimming in their eyes, then kissed. They didn't need to speak to express the emotion that welled up inside them; to be together was enough.

Bullin and Hurst had accompanied Mallory from Keld, and now sat quietly on their own horses. They were moved and gladdened by the reunion they were witnessing. Theirs had been a long and arduous journey into the unknown, but was now doubly worthwhile. Eventually Kragen and Mallory pulled apart slightly, and she introduced her companions.

"I could never have made it home without them," she told him. "They've been the best of friends."

"I count them as such already," Kragen replied. "You are welcome, gentlemen. I owe you a debt I cannot repay."

"Good food and a bed for the night will be reward enough," Bullin answered, smiling.

"Well, you are no more than half a day's ride from them," Kragen said, then turned back to his wife. "But where are Gemma and Arden? Why aren't they with you?"

Mallory looked downcast.

"I hoped Gemma would have gotten back before me," she replied sadly. "And . . . oh, Kragen," she went on, trying not to cry. "I think Arden might be dead."

"Those are sad words. But you succeeded anyway," he said, and was unable to keep a measure of pride from his voice, in spite of his wife's unhappiness. "The river's back!"

"*They* succeeded. Not me."

He decided to postpone any further discussion when he saw the utter weariness in her face.

"You have a long story to tell," he said, "but it can wait until you're safely home." He kissed her again, then helped her up onto his own horse. He mounted behind her, and she leaned gratefully back against him. They talked little on the way down to the valley; the travelers were tired and Kragen too preoccupied with the state of his wife's health. By the time they got to Elway's house it was dark, and they were all glad to see the welcoming lamplight as they approached the farm.

The noise of the horses alerted Mallory's family to their arrival, and two small boys erupted from the kitchen door. Mallory's sons flew to their mother's side, and as she dismounted she was engulfed in their joyful embrace. Laughing happily, she allowed herself to be pulled inside. Elway, Teri, and Horan came out after a few moments to greet the newcomers and tend to the horses.

Soon they were all ensconced in the kitchen, eating a hastily prepared dinner. Her family was shocked by Mallory's appearance and obviously weak condition, but did not press her for information. For her own part, she already felt much better than she had for days. She told them the barest minimum, saying that it was too lengthy and complicated a tale to be told while she was so weary, and no one objected when she chose to go to bed soon after the meal. Even the boys were persuaded to curb their boisterious behavior and allow their mother the rest she so obviously needed.

Consequently it was from Bullin and Hurst that the valley people learned of Gemma's healing and of her amazing flight.

"What was she trying to do?" Horan asked.

"I never completely understood that," Bullin replied. "Something about moving a stone in the desert. All we knew was that it was important to Gemma, so we helped her. You'll have to wait for Mallory to answer the rest."

"Whatever it was, it obviously worked." Teri put in.

"But at a cost," Horan said, his face grim.

"Arden?" Kragen asked.

"Aye," Hurst nodded. "Looks like he walked into an earthquake."

"We'd better tell you what we know from the beginning," Bullin said. "It was hard enough for me to take in, and I was *there*."

———— • ————

After the exhilaration of watching the successful start of Gemma's flight, and when the yellow kite had become just a tiny speck in the distance, Mallory had trudged back to the village, feeling deflated and without purpose.

"What will you do now?" Ehren asked her.

"I don't know. I haven't really thought about it," she replied. Her preoccupation with Gemma's frightening task had left her little time to consider her own position. "I want to go after Arden," she decided.

"That's rough country to travel on your own," Bullin said. "Why don't we come with you?"

"A good idea," Ehren agreed. "I'm not so old that I can't sit in the saddle again." The head-man turned and called to another man. "Hurst, come over here!"

When Hurst reached them, Ehren asked him, "You know the high country better than most. Will you come with us after Arden?"

The newcomer shrugged. "Why not?"

"Hurst it our wanderer," Ehren explained jovially. "He can never stay in one place very long."

They left later that morning. Bullin rode Mischa, while the other two had their own mounts—mountain-bred ponies with stocky builds and shaggy hair. Mallory followed the route she had taken with Arden and Gemma, and led them to the hill overlooking the valley where the river disappeared into the earth. It was growing dark by then, and there was no sign of Arden.

"Shall we camp here?" Ehren asked hopefully; for all his earlier bravado, the unaccustomed day in the saddle had left him tired and sore.

But no one answered him; at that moment the ground beneath them shuddered, and they dismounted quickly, trying to calm their fretful mounts. But the shaking got worse, and was now accompanied by a roar of terrifying volume.

"Sounds like an avalanche!" Bullin shouted above the din.

"Too big!" Hurst yelled back.

"The whole valley is moving," Ehren said, his voice quivering. "It's an earthquake!"

Gradually, the noise and the vibrating earth quietened, and they waited anxiously to see if stability had been permanently restored.

"Look!" Mallory cried, pointing to the upper end of the vale.

A white wall was advancing down the slope beneath the twin peaks. Although at this distance it was eerily silent, the impression of power was unmistakable.

"An avalanche?" Bullin suggested again.

"No," Hurst replied. "There's not been enough snow yet for that."

"Water!" Mallory yelled suddenly, her eyes glowing. "It's happening! The river's coming back!"

All four watched, mesmerized by the advancing wall. Soon they could hear it too, a booming, rushing sound that grew in volume as boulders were picked up in the surge and hurled along the riverbed. The first rush of water reached the sink holes but sped past too quickly to be swallowed up. The lower end of the valley became a tidal whirlpool as the water crashed up against the confining slopes then swept back in waves, sending plumes of spray high into the air.

The water eventually became calmer as the flow from above steadied. Huge bubbles of air burst within the foam as the river found its underground course, and eddies swirled in dizzying patterns.

"I'm glad we weren't down there," Hurst remarked. "We'd never have survived that."

"I wonder where Arden is," Bullin said, voicing the thought that was already worrying Mallory.

"If he was on high ground, he'll be all right," Hurst said. "Unless the earthquake was worse up there."

"In any case, we can't find him in the dark," Bullin added. "We'll camp here now, then look for him first thing in the morning."

Although the water level dropped during the night, they rode on the valley's upper slopes, keeping well above the strongly flowing river. It wasn't long before they discovered Lark, alone but still bearing his master's saddlebags. The stallion was wild-eyed and nervous, but Mallory managed to coax him with food and soothing words and he eventually joined their group willingly enough, obviously taking comfort in the company of Mischa and the other horses.

"His tent's here," Mallory said, having checked Arden's saddlebags. "And all his supplies."

"Wherever he is, we'd better find him soon," Hurst said. "The nights are cold in the open now, and he won't last long without food or shelter."

After a brief discussion, Hurst decided that they needed more help for their search, and Ehren agreed to ride back to Keld while the others went on ahead. Mallory was haunted by visions of Arden lying hurt and alone.

Three days of searching failed to produce any sign of him, and during that time Mallory began to feel ill. When the pains in her chest began and she started coughing, she knew that she could not go much further. Distraught, she was forced to return to Keld, and the search for Arden was abandoned. Most people believed he had been killed either by the earthquake or the onrush of water. In her distress, Mallory realized that this would have been the supreme irony.

——————•——————

"And the next day she insisted on leaving to come straight back here," Hurst said. "Mousel didn't like it but Mallory wouldn't wait to rest."

"She kept saying that their protection had flown away with Gemma, and that only the valley could cure her now," Bullin went on. "We weren't rightly sure what she meant, but felt that the least we could do was bring her home. She'd not have made it on her own."

"The whole valley thanks you," Elway said. "There's not many people would go so far out of their way for a stranger."

"Well, not *all* upland folk are completely uncivilized," Hurst replied with a grin.

"In any case, we had a debt of our own to repay," Bullin said. "Keld is a happier place now."

"Long may it remain so," Teri said.

The news of Mallory's return spread quickly through the valley. The river's reappearance had revived more than one aspect of the community's life—and the knowing was one of them. Many people came to Elway's farm the next day, eager to see Mallory and hear her story at first hand.

She rose late, and the extent of her recovery—in both body and spirit—was so marked that even the valley people, used to the strange powers of their home, were amazed. For her part, Mallory was taken aback by the fact that when she arrived in the kitchen, a beaming Kragen at her side, she was greeted not only by her family and the men from Keld, but also by Ashlin and four other neighbors.

The waited politely for her to eat breakfast, but it was obvious that her story was expected soon. This was confirmed when Mallory's eldest son, who had been looking out of the window, cried, "Kris is coming! Kris is coming!"

The crippled man soon made his entrance, and brought his own special warmth to the room. He greeted Mallory with enormous affection.

"You're better!" she exclaimed in delight.

Kris's fingers flickered. *The river has returned health to many things. I felt it better to rejoin the world.* His crooked face creased in a smile and his unearthly eyes shone with happiness. Bullin and Hurst looked amazed, and a little fearful of the strange newcomer, but realized very quickly that there was no harm in him.

As if Kris's arrival had been a signal, Mallory began her tale, recounting the details of their long and frustrating search for the river, their welcome in Keld and Gemma's healing of the children, and of their subsequent abduction by the floating city. This part of the story caused the most amazement until Mallory reached Gemma's discovery of the secret of the rocking stone. Bullin joined her in the account of the building of the kite, and of the beginning of Gemma's flight.

"She must have reached the stone in time," Mallory said, "because the river was reborn that night."

"She flew all the way to the Diamond Desert?" Horan gave voice to the awe felt by everyone present.

"Yes. And now she's all alone in the middle of the desert, with no food and no water!" Mallory said. "We've got to find a way of helping her."

There was an uncomfortable silence.

"It's too late, Mallory," Elway said. "Even if we were able to leave the valley, it would take us days to get to her. Sweetheart, Gemma's fate has already been decided."

"It's more than twenty days since she flew from Keld," Horan added. "If she's survived this long, she can manage without our help. If not . . ."

"But we can't just sit here and do nothing!" Mallory exclaimed. "She saved us, saved the valley!"

"You must know how grateful we are for that," Elway said, "but there's nothing we can do. I wish with all my heart that it were otherwise."

Mallory wanted to argue, but realized that it would be futile. *I can't have lost them both,* she thought miserably.

"We'll send messages to the western valleys," Teri said. "And ask for news. At least that would be something."

"I'll go," Ashlin volunteered, and Mallory smiled at him gratefully. The young man's face was nervous but eager, and he glanced at Elway and then Kris as if to gauge their reactions. Elway nodded approvingly, but Kris remained quite still, his slitted eyes betraying no opinion.

"I'll go too," Horan said, to Ashlin's relief. "We'll do better together."

"I can't bear to think of Gemma all alone in that dreadful place," Mallory said.

Kris blinked and shifted in his seat; it felt to their others as though he had rejoined them after a few moments' absence. His birdlike hands fluttered—*Gemma is not alone.*

"Then she's alive!" Mallory exclaimed delightedly, but Kris would not elucidate. Even so, his message gave them renewed hope. No one thought to question how he knew of Gemma's situation.

The talk went on, Mallory answering an endless stream of questions, then asking several in return. Arrangements were begun for the trip westward, and supplies prepared for Bullin and Hurst, who wanted to return home soon. Mallory accepted her position as the hub about which the wheel of activity revolved, but although she enjoyed her reunion with family and friends, there was a feeling inside her like a leaden stone. Her contentment could not be complete without Gemma and Arden.

The following day saw a great deal of bustle within the valley. The men from Keld left on their southward journey, Ashlin and Horan went west, and Kragen, Mallory, and their sons made the shorter journey home to their sadly neglected farm.

Looking out at the valley from her place in the back of Elway's cart, Mallory was astonished at the difference that just a few days' supply of water had made to the landscape. New growth was everywhere; even the animals seemed to share the valley's happiness. Here and there she saw the forlorn sight of an abandoned home, but for the most part the signs all around her were positive.

They did this for us, she thought. *And they probably won't ever see it again.*

When they arrived home, she deliberately put aside her melancholy, and there was so much work to do to put things to right that at first she had no time to brood. However, their neighbors lent a great deal of support, and the farm and the house were both soon back in operation. This left Mallory with time to think, and she dwelt more and more on the dramatic events she had witnessed and on the two people responsible for them. She believed in her heart of hearts that Arden was dead, and as the days passed, it became difficult to hope that Gemma was still alive. This was made worse by the fact that she could do nothing to help her friend. Ashlin and Horan had returned to the valley with nothing to report, but Mallory watched every day, hoping for a message from the west.

In spite of Kris's assurance that Gemma was not alone, Mallory still secretly longed to go in search of her former companion, and found the enforced inactivity frustrating.

She had never had a friend like Gemma before, and she spent a lot of time remembering their arduous journey and all its discomforts. She daydreamed about the laughter they had shared, and was amazed at what they had eventually achieved. She had also come to believe that Gemma had somehow protected her from illness while they were outside the valley— although she had been unable to achieve this for the others— and this extra link made their friendship even more special.

Kragen recognized his wife's mood for what it was, and left her in peace to gather herself together, knowing that, given time, she would find her own contentment. The boys were so delighted to have their mother home again that they did not notice her distraction.

Mallory was searching for herbs on the edge of the farm one cool afternoon nearly a month after her return to the valley, when, looking up, she recognized the spot where she had first seen Arden and Gemma on their arrival from Newport. She sat down on a boulder and gazed unseeingly and unhappily in front of her for a long time. *Where are my friends now?*

Eventually, growing chill, she gave herself a mental shake and stood up, ready to continue her chore. Glancing around one last time, her attention was caught by the sight of a lone figure, still some way off, but recognizable by the cap of fiery hair.

"Gemma?" she whispered, not daring to believe the evidence of her own eyes. Then, "Gemma! Gemma!" she yelled at the top of her voice, and the two women ran toward each other, one staggering slightly, the other dropping her basket in her desperate hurry to embrace the friend she had thought she would never see again.